THE
MIDNIGHT
CROISSANT

A Pearly Gates Novel

BONNIE SOLOMON

Published by Bonsol Press

This is a work of fiction.
Names, characters, places, and incidents are
either the product of the author's imagination or
used fictitiously. Any resemblance to actual persons,
living or dead, or actual events is purely coincidental.

ISBN: 979-8-9926133-5-3
Cover design by Lana Shybinska
Printed in the United States of America
First Edition

For the Sixers

ONE

P early Gates is late—as in dead—but also late for a meeting. And not just a wee bit tardy. She is horrendously, spectacularly, ludicrously late. Pulling on her White Robe while trying not to ruin her still-wet manicure, she barges through frosted glass doors into the afterlife's Department of Human Relations. She considers the following excuses:

1) "I got stuck in one of those interdimensional potholes on the astral highway!"

2) "I realized I left my past-life altar candles burning and didn't want to start another reincarnation fire!"

3) "I had to handle an emergency involving a charge who got drunk and tried to astral project to Vegas!"

What she does not consider telling is the truth—she got caught up in conversation with her manicurist. But only because her department's new supervisor doesn't understand the important spiritual guidance a manicurist has to offer. Who better to ask about reaching out to her ex-soulmate, Thunder, now that they're both back in the spirit world after their most recent incarnations?

As she barrels down a labyrinthine corridor lined in silver shag carpet, she passes floating orbs illuminating holo-portraits of each graduating class of guides. Pearly's not in any of them, of course. It would be easier if she was. Her situation is a bit more... unique. Instead of getting proper schooling, she convinced Malcolm—a burnt-out senior guide—to let her sub for him while he went on vacation. She broke a lot of rules along the way, but in the end, she managed to win over the Higher-Ups. Was it worth it? Absolutely. But the job has been, well... a little more challenging than she'd expected.

Pearly careens to a halt in front of Conference Room B, adjusting the blinking rainbow halo atop her cotton candy beehive before flinging open the door. Twenty-seven heads swivel to stare at her. None of them look thrilled to see her, and especially not the one belonging to her new boss, Mildreth Snaggs.

Fuckety Fuckerton.

Mildreth Snaggs is not your typical soul—at least not in this corner of the afterlife. While most guides take on astral versions of their former human forms, Mildreth's incarnations played out on a fungal hivemind planet. And she still favors that aesthetic. She reminds Pearly of the Swamp Thing on magic mushrooms—a humanoid mass with moss-covered arms protruding from her White Robe, a portobello face, electric-blue eyes glowing like bioluminescent spores under a pair of black cat-eye glasses, and an unruly mop of lichen springing from the top of her head in all directions. A faint cloud of mildew lingers in her wake.

"Sorry, folks!" gulps Pearly, edging into the room. If only she could manage a low-key entrance! "Please do, uh, carry on."

"Well, if it isn't Pearly Gates." Mildreth quirks something that might be an eyebrow. "How kind of you to grace us with your presence. We trust the concept of time remains optional in your personal ethos?"

Pearly's tempted to bite back. Time doesn't *really* exist in the spirit world—at least, not in the way it does on Earth. But she doubts bringing that up is going to win her any points. So she just offers a vague set of prayer hands and heads for the empty seat at the far end of the conference table.

"Excuse me—*pardonnez-moi*—no, don't get up..." She squeezes past the other guides, clutching her scroll and a half-spilled latte. Her bejeweled chain belt snags on someone's robe, forcing an awkward dance of disentangling. Finally, she drops into her chair with flushed cheeks and a dramatic sigh of relief. Mildreth materializes a thick info-packet in front of her. Pearly tries not to groan at the title: *Karmic Rollover Period Compliance Manual (Version 7.3d)*.

"What page are we on?" she whispers to the guide next to her. Marty? Mitzvah? She should really make more of an attempt to befriend her colleagues. It's just... most of them are about as fun as an eye exam. And they seem to think she's more spectacle than substance. Maybe it's her past life as a drag queen. Or the fact that she skipped the line to become a White Robe. *Whatever.* She has Malcolm and her manicurist and her roommate. She doesn't need a posse of sticks-in-the-mud.

The guide holds up his manual, and Pearly flips to page 322. Mildreth could've just sent the info to everyone's scrolls, but she loves to brag about being old school. Pearly suspects she just likes to use mountains of paperwork as a scare tactic.

"As we all know," says Mildreth, "the rollover period exists to ensure the proper soul-cycle closure before vibrational reallocation can occur, thereby reducing the risk of karmic residue contaminating the next incarnation's energetic template..."

Pearly's eyes glaze. Her thoughts drift back to Thunder. They were partners and soulmates for so many lives, playing out every possible combination of gender, sexuality, and culture the Earth had to offer. Nobody knows Pearly like Thunder. But she hasn't seen him since their breakup.

Well, not this version of him.

She spent time with his last incarnation. In that life, he was the owner of the café where she guided her first set of charges. But he never knew it was her—a rare feat of discretion on Pearly's part. Now that they're both back in the afterlife, she keeps meaning to message him. Or spontaneously "bump into him," how weird! She's just been dragging her heels. It makes sense—she *is* the dump-ee. And she doesn't know what his situation is these days. Partnered? Single? Not that it matters. She totally wouldn't care one way or the other.

Besides, she's been busy. Could "busy" be a way of avoiding her feelings? Maybe. Probably. Almost certainly. But she's not hurt anymore. She's proud she learned to be more independent, to source love within herself. If anything, she's just... curious.

"Failure to properly neutralize past life triggers," Mildreth drones on, "may result in erratic soulmate entanglement, which—as you know—is no longer covered by cosmic liability..."

Pearly considers sending Thunder a telepathic message. Maybe...

Pearly: *Thunder! Hi! Long time, no see*

Long time no see? Ugh, delete. Maybe...

Pearly: *Would you believe I had the craziest dream*
And you were in it???

No way. Too desperate. How about something simple?

Pearly: *sup bro*

No. Absolutely not.

Pearly sighs. If she can't think of the perfect thing to say, it's better to hold her tongue—er, thoughts. Instead, she opens a line to Malcolm.

Pearly: *I don't think my new supervisor likes me*

Three dots shimmer in the corner of her vision. A moment later:

Malcolm: *Mildreth Snaggs?*

Pearly: *Yeah*

Malcolm: *She's... tricky*

And I speak from experience

We went to soul school together, you know

Pearly: *Really? What was she like?*

Malcolm: *Exactly what you'd expect*

Mostly kept to herself

Maybe it was the hive-mind thing but

I don't think she ever learned how to socialize

Not the way humans do, anyway

The dots appear again, then vanish, as if he thought something then deleted it.

Pearly: *Huh*

Maybe I should invite her out for a pint

Give her a little Pearly Gates pizazz

Malcolm: *uhhhh yeahhhh*

I wouldn't

Pearly: *Why not? It worked with you*

Malcolm: *She's less gullible than me*

Remember, you can't charm a fungus

Pearly: *Maybe YOU can't. I can charm anyone*

Malcolm: *OK. Let me know how that goes*

"Pearly Gates, are you *telepathing* in the middle of a meeting?"

Pearly snaps back to the conference room to find Mildreth staring daggers at her. "What? No!" She sits up tall in her chair, flashes her best bullshitter's smile. "I was just reflecting on the importance of following protocols. I mean, where would we be without them? Flying blind in the throes of cosmic chaos, that's where." She gestures grandly to her packet. "I'm *thrilled* to know someone went to the trouble of creating a seven-hundred-page guide for karmic rollover. I, for one, feel much safer knowing that unresolved grudges must be logged with a nine-step verification process and a laminated form." She leans in, all conspiratorial. "Do you know what they used to call me in soul school? *The Laminator.* Yup. Never met a sign I didn't... lacquer."

Silence. Mildreth is still staring. It's creepy how she never blinks, though that might be due to the whole "no eyelids" thing. Pearly shifts in her seat, suddenly hyper-aware of the other guides. One watches her like a zoo animal while sipping from a mug that says *Live. Laugh. Levitate.* Another types notes on her scroll while sneaking glances at Pearly. She can feel the attention closing in—twenty-seven guides pretending not to listen, all thanking the cosmos that they're not the ones under Mildreth's scrutiny. Pearly's aura flickers. If someone doesn't say something soon, she might actually combust from secondhand judgment.

A mushroom cap unfurls from Mildreth's shoulder with a papery *pop*, like some weird fungal cuckoo clock. "Aura realignment break." She nods at the timer. "You may adjourn for ten minutes."

The guides begin collecting their scrolls and standing up. Pearly practically bolts out of her chair. She can't wait to get out.

Mildreth clears her throat. "Pearly Gates. A word please..."

Fuckingham McFuckerton the Fourth.

Pearly watches the room clear out with a rising sense of nausea. It's like that time she ate an astral gnat tartine. Even without a digestive system, the idea was enough to make her dry-heave. With a sigh of resignation, she squares her shoulders and approaches Mildreth. In five-inch platform boots, Pearly still only reaches her boss's shoulder. But what she lacks in height, she'll make up for in confidence. Cool. Calm. Collected. Easy-peasy—

"These are your first official charges, are they not?" says Mildreth, manifesting a manila file with Pearly's name on it.

Pearly freezes. It's thick. That could be good. But it's not very likely. She brushes a wispy pink bang off her face. "They are."

"You've had them long enough to know better."

Probably. Charges are assigned to guides at birth for the duration of that lifetime. Technically, she'd been back from her last incarnation for ages—though it felt like a year, tops, given "astral time." But her old charges were under the radar and temporary. These new ones are official. And apparently, under review.

Pearly clears her throat. "Long enough to generate a file, it seems."

"Yes, well..." Mildreth rifles through the papers, muttering indecipherable sounds. "We all have a learning curve—but at some point, one must ask whether the curve ever levels out."

Pearly's smile fades. "The Higher-Ups seemed to think I was cut out for this when they gave me my robe."

Mildreth's lips twitch upward. "And what do you imagine they'd think now if I showed them your file?" She flips a page. "I see multiple incidents of administrative negligence. Your case notes are perpetually late and chronically underwritten. '*Mission served cunty realness. 10s across the board,*' is not a report. Nor is '*vibes were restored.*' And colorful as it might have been, a quarterly evaluation delivered via vision board does not meet departmental standards." She peers down at Pearly through her glasses. "What exactly were you thinking?"

Pearly was thinking that she'd rather get tossed into cosmic furnace for recycling than fill out one more goddamn spreadsheet—and honestly, what kind of spiritual potato sack doesn't appreciate an eye-catching vision board? Does no one appreciate rainbow glitter anymore? Or strategic use of decoupage? "Sorry," she says, swallowing her pride. "Guess I wasn't thinking."

"Clearly not." Mildreth nods. "Not only that, you've missed more department meetings than the rest of the department combined. You once took an emergency sick day due to—and I quote—'a bad hair day.' And you used your scroll to livestream a reality show recap during risk management training."

Pearly's throat constricts.

"And that's not even counting your protocol violations. Need I remind you that you may not place a karaoke machine in the break room without express permission from management? But worst of all is your questionable guidance."

"Questionable guidance?" She's starting to spiral like a rhinestone in a blender. "Now hold up, I have to object to that one."

"On what grounds? Did you or did you not permit a charge to bypass a soul lesson by faking emotional growth on social media? Did you not give a struggling charge a 'gentle nudge' to pursue interpretive dance... during her grad school interview? Did you not 'help' a bitter divorcee by subtly reinforcing the idea that relationships are nothing but a trap for codependency and better off avoided altogether? Did you not suggest that a charge having a spiritual crisis binge a full season of *The Great British Baking Show* and wait for divine inspiration?"

"Hey, that one actually worked," says Pearly.

Mildreth shakes her head. "Even if I were to overlook these indulgences in poor judgment, it's clear you don't take your job here seriously, and that's of great concern to me as your supervisor. I have reports to file too, and the Higher-Ups hold me responsible for your success—or failure."

"But I love being a guide," says Pearly. And she means it. She's never felt more suited to anything, in life or the afterlife. And she cares about her charges. She really does. "I've just been a little overwhelmed. This is all—it's a lot of responsibility. And paperwork. I mean, come on, there's a form to request a form! But I promise, I do take it seriously."

"Do you now?" Mildreth eyes Pearly, who shifts her weight uncomfortably. One platform boot squeaks against the floor. "May I see your scroll?"

Pearly's jaw tightens. She considers shoving the scroll into her cleavage or tossing it out the window. Except there is no window. So, she reluctantly hands it over. Mildreth pauses on the lock screen, where Pearly has replaced the Department of Human Relations logo with a big, glittery middle finger.

Pearly gulps. She wants to say it was a joke, but she'd just be playing into Mildreth's hands. Or her appendages, or whatever.

Mildreth tosses the scroll back on the table like it's contagious. "Allow me to spell it out for you. You are not here to express yourself. You are here to serve the department. I don't care how you managed to slip by. I have no interest in flair, or drama, or 'turning it out.' Do I make myself clear?"

Pearly grits her teeth. "Crystal."

"Excellent. I'd hate to see you back in waste management," she says, sounding like she'd love nothing more. "If there's even an opening. But I'm sure something will work out. I hear they're looking for recruits in the Null Region." She nods to the door. "Now—go realign that aura. It looks a little... flickery."

Pearly summons what's left of her dignity and sashays away. She wants to cry, but she refuses to let her new boss get the best of her. She was chosen for a reason, after all, and it sure as hell wasn't to blend in. She may not do things by the book, but she gets the job done. And if Mildreth Snaggs thinks Pearly's fashion choices disqualify her from guiding souls?

Well, buckle up, fungus.

She's just getting started.

Two

Pearly's still grumbling about the Mildreth Incident as she stomps across the parking lot. Her shape-shifting emotional support vehicle, Seraphina, senses the rising storm and pulls up to the curb. Originally a pink dump truck from Pearly's stint in cosmic waste management, Seraphina has adopted other looks, but there's no beating the classics. She gives a cheerful honk and opens the driver's side door.

"Hey girl," sighs Pearly, collapsing into the seat. "I feel like I just got run over."

Seraphina responds by squeezing the headrest around Pearly's neck like one of those airplane pillows, then turns on her radio. Elton John's "I'm Still Standing" kicks in.

"Alright, I hear you." Pearly's a survivor, and she's not gonna let some mid-level bureaucrat with an allergy to joy bring her down. Mildreth's indigo-violet aura may be impressive on paper, but it doesn't mean she's the kind of soul people want to party with—the kind of soul who'll pick you up from the airport, or let you cry on their shoulder at 2 am. Pearly is that kind of soul. That's her superpower. Whether the universe recognizes it or not, she knows it's what makes her a damn good guide.

"Enough moping. Let's blow this joint."

Seraphina peels out of the parking lot with a screech of tires and a trail of glitter. Sometimes Pearly isn't sure who's driving who, but it doesn't really matter. They get where they want to go. As they merge onto the astral highway, Pearly glances at the antique fountain pen hanging from the dashboard mirror—a memento from her most recent life. That incarnation came after she earned her White Robe, but before she took on her first official charges. She'd asked for the chance to live a life on her own, to prove she didn't need Thunder beside her to grow. It was a "successful" incarnation, by Pearly's metrics. She did what she set out to do. Though it's always hard to know what the Higher-Ups have in mind.

She remembers going to the Screening Room in the Cosmic Rebirth Center. A faceless projectionist in a black trench coat showed her three previews—no spoilers, of course, just glimpses. Like movie trailers for lives she could step into.

The projectionist pressed a button, and Pearly was transported to 1950s Philadelphia, or at least the afterlife's hyper-realistic simulation. She became the wife of one of those ad guys, spending her days vacuuming pastel living rooms and chain-smoking cigarettes while a toddler fussed in the background. It wasn't very "Pearly." But then she heard her own voice, late at night, speaking into a basement microphone while everyone else was asleep, hosting a pirate radio show on topics no one dared say out loud. It wasn't a guarantee that she would follow this path —people have free will, after all—but it was a strong possibility.

The second option was even farther from her norm. This time Pearly found herself teaching drama to a small class of eager high school students—on Mars. In 2104, the settlement was a bit like the Wild West: rough and tumble and likely to kill you if you weren't careful. The sweeping red vistas were undeniably gorgeous, but you could only view them from inside the domes or while suited up in full EVAC gear. And while the idea of pioneering a new frontier had its appeal, Pearly had been relatively pampered in her last few incarnations. The thought of incarnating somewhere without a nail salon? *Eww.*

Another press of a button, and the scene shifted to 1870s France. *Oooh, Paris!* Pearly saw herself emigrating there from London as a young woman and establishing a lucrative, if not exactly prestigious, career as tragic romance novelist Evelyn Ashcroft. The preview teased scenes of candlelit literary salons with Pearly as hostess, hobnobbing with the Parisian elite and American ex-pats, the shining center of her social circle at a charming estate in Montmartre. What she didn't see in that life was a romantic partner. Dalliances? Absolutely. Dramatic letters from scorned suitors? Dozens. But nothing that resembled love.

You'd think that'd be a dealbreaker for Pearly. But at that point, it was just what the doctor ordered. Even though she'd accepted it, she was still a little heartbroken after Thunder. No romance meant the perfect chance to explore who she really was, without any complications. Was it the "right" choice? She knows there's no such thing—the universe will keep offering the same lessons in different forms until you're ready to learn them. Pearly's still processing that lifetime, but she concedes she may have overcorrected. She didn't just keep romantic love from distracting her, she shut it out completely. As Evelyn Ashcroft, she didn't let *anyone* in—not intimately. She died with a large cast of mourners at her funeral, but she's pretty sure they only came for the spectacle.

By the time she and Seraphina coast down Lightbody Lane and pull into their driveway, Pearly's washed Mildreth out of her hair. Glancing at the home she once shared with Thunder—the home he built for her all those lifetimes ago—she feels a familiar pang. Could things have turned out differently? Maybe. The universe holds infinite possibilities, and she probably didn't fuck things up in some of them. But even with the heartache, she wouldn't trade her memories for anything.

As she steps into the house, her jaw drops. *We've been burgled.* Now, that's not a very rational thought—souls have manifesting capabilities and don't need to steal. Besides, this is a high-vibe neighborhood. Malicious intentions are against the bylaws. But how else do you explain the upturned sofa with exploded cushions, like someone was searching for cash stuffed in the lining? Or the smashed picture frames and swinging light fixture dangling precariously from a single chain? Or the scorch marks on the wall?

"Dumb Pearly? Is that you?"

She tiptoes past the living room into the kitchen, holding up her scroll like a baseball bat. The coffee pot overflows with glitter and the fridge stands wide open, shelves all ransacked, a large bite mark in the butter. Pearly wouldn't put this past her roommate. But something tells her this isn't entirely Dumb Pearly's doing.

A shrill whistle cuts through the air, snapping her gaze to the backyard. Pearly catches a flutter of movement, then a **FLASH**, followed by a **BANG!** Then... nothing.

Holding her breath, she steps outside.

So much for the picnic table. And the lawn. Every piece of outdoor furniture has been dragged into a makeshift fort draped in Pearly's favorite silk sheets. She peers through smoky haze into the opening. Inside, she finds her roommate, Dumb Pearly, sitting cross-legged on the ground, rocking a swaddled something as she hums a lullaby of Cyndi Lauper's "True Colors."

"Hey hunty!" whispers her roommate. "Look what the cat dragged in."

Pearly blinks. She knows Dumb Pearly isn't technically her responsibility anymore. After Pearly secretly created a body double at the Department of Design—hoping to fool her boss while she took over Malcolm's job—the Higher-Ups shocked everyone by granting the duplicate a soul of her own, along with Pearly's old position in cosmic waste management.

Even so, Pearly still feels a twinge of guilt. Dumb Pearly may be officially independent, but she was born from a five-percent donation of Pearly's consciousness—and some habits die hard. She forces herself to breathe.

"Dumb Pearly," she says, trying to channel her most enlightened self. Dumb Pearly had been offered the chance to choose a new name, of course. But after reviewing all available options, she decided she liked Dumb Pearly best. Said it had brand recognition. "Could you please explain what's going on here?"

"Shhh!" Dumb Pearly brings a finger to her lips. "Snatch is sleeping." She gestures to the swaddled creature.

Pearly can just make out a tuft of marmalade fur and a still-smoking tail. "Oh no no no, you are not adopting a pet."

"Oh Pearly, pretty please? Flaubert was gonna Recycle her."

Damn it, Flaubert! He was the one who Frankensteined Dumb Pearly into existence in the first place. She must've visited him and taken pity on another one of his experiments.

"Come on," Pearly sighs. "I can't take care of a pet for you. Work is hard enough with the Mean Mushroom breathing down my neck—I can't afford any more distractions. I'm already *this close* to getting fired." What she doesn't say is that keeping an eye on her roommate is basically another full-time job. It's not that Dumb Pearly can't function in the spirit world. She's just... innocent. And without the life experience of other souls, sometimes things get lost in translation. Like the time she tried to compost "emotional residue" and accidentally created a black hole.

"No cheese, girl! I'll take care of her. Pinky-swear."

Yeah, right. Pearly leans in. The creature exhales tiny puffs of smoke with every snore, its tail giving a lazy, ember-tipped swish. "Is that a... cat?"

"Umm..." Dumb Pearly considers. "Cat adjacent. Wanna hold her?"

Pearly really doesn't. She finds herself holding out her arms anyway.

She likes cats—she's had more than a few over her various lives—but there's something off about this one. As Dumb Pearly passes her the bundle, the creature blinks open its blue-green eyes. For a moment, Pearly is envenomed by the cuteness. The creature coos, scrunches its tiny face like it's concentrating on something. Then—

FLASH! BANG!

When the sparks clear and the ringing in her ears subsides, Pearly turns to assess the damage. One of Thunder's old garden lanterns is now a smoldering crater. A nearby lawn gnome is missing its head. A section of silk sheet flutters down from the roof in slow motion, singed around the edges.

"Dumb Pearly," she says, blinking. "Does this thing—"

"Snatch."

Pearly squares her jaw. "Does Snatch *poop lightning*?"

Dumb Pearly beams, snaps her fingers. "Yes! Isn't she sickening?"

Before Pearly can argue, Snatch wriggles out of the swaddle and hop-flies out of the fort. She's about the size of a cat, with that orange fur and kitten face, but she has an ostrich's long, skinny neck and the leather wings and claws of a bat. Whatever she is, she's too top-heavy for proper flight, so she just sputters around the yard chasing her tail.

As soon as Pearly manages to shepherd Snatch back indoors, the little monster starts terrorizing the enchanted wallpaper birds. Normally, they flutter about during the day, chirping melodies and perching on Pearly's shoulder while she slugs lattes and attempts case notes.

Not today.

Snatch spots one, yowls like a pterodactyl, and launches herself off the counter. The birds scatter in a panicked cloud as Snatch claws at the wall, paper feathers snowing down in her wake.

Pearly frowns at her double. "Didn't Flaubert at least give you a leash or something?"

Dumb Pearly shakes her head. "We could make one?"

But Pearly's too busy watching Snatch trot out of the kitchen, only to re-emerge a moment later with a sparkly lavender stiletto clamped in her jaws. The heel has been almost entirely gnawed off.

Pearly's fists clench. That was her favorite fucking shoe. From the time she and Thunder danced all night at that back-alley astral club with the singing alligators and the zero-gravity tango. She bends down to pick it up and—

WHUMP.

Snatch lands squarely on her head. Pearly freezes as claws tangle into her beehive and a warm mass burrows in like it's setting up camp. "Absolutely not," she spits through gritted teeth. "This is not a hat. I am not a nest."

"Sorry!" says Dumb Pearly.

Snatch fights a tug-of-war with Pearly's hair until Dumb Pearly finally plucks Snatch away.

"No way," Pearly shakes her head, readjusting what's left of her bangs. "We cannot keep this menace in our house. You have to bring it back to Flaubert."

Snatch's eyes widen. Her little body begins to tremble, and she clings to Dumb Pearly, claws digging in.

Pearly feels a lump in her throat, but she refuses to give in. "Home is supposed to be a safe space. A place to come back to after a hard day's work. Where I can relax and unwind and take a bath without worrying that I might get electrocuted by an unlicensed, unpotty-trained pyrotechnic pet."

Dumb Pearly looks down at the floor. "I thought home was for bed-rotting. For power breakfasts. For family."

Pearly opens her mouth, then closes it. "Look, I—"

"Please, Pearly. I'm—she's... like me. There's..." Dumb Pearly looks up, eyes glistening. "No one else. Like me."

The realization slaps Pearly in the face—her counterpart is lonely. Of course she is. All the souls around her have incarnated, lived big lives, returned with depth and memories and a sense of who they are. But Dumb Pearly? She's a misfit. An anomaly. She's not a mistake, but maybe that's how she thinks of herself. Pearly knows what that feels like.

"Okay," Pearly exhales. "Fine." She gestures to the bundle of fur and fire. "Snatch can stay. But you're feeding her, and walking her, and taking her to obedience school."

Dumb Pearly's face lights up like a disco ball. "Werk!"

Snatch looks up, gives Pearly a honk-purr. Then she poops another ball of lightning.

BANG!

Three

Alright, sure, fine, maybe there was the teeniest, tiniest kernel of truth in Mildreth's scolding. Pearly's been known to guide by the seat of her pants, and her case notes aren't exactly exemplary. But she won't let it get under her skin. In fact, she's ready to crack her astral knuckles and get down to business.

Time to check in on her charges.

And listen, this isn't snooping. It's not even bending the rules. Spirit guides are *meant* to peek in—discreetly, from the sidelines. A gentle presence. A whisper of intuition. A dream that lingers. That's the job.

But Pearly's always been more hands-on than most. She prefers to check in where the action's happening. Not from some cushy cloud in the afterlife, but right there on Earth, up close and personal. Invisibly, of course. She calls it "immersive guidance." Mildreth calls it "unregulated boundary issues."

To-may-to, to-mah-to.

First up: Lillian West. Pearly's been with Lillian, now 65, since birth. She's supposed to feel connected by now. Invested. But Lillian's a tough nut to crack. Pearly tries to recall the highlights. And the lowlights.

There was that fifth-grade report on Susan B. Anthony—her homemade poster curling at the corners, her too-big, hand-me-down shoes flapping as she stepped up to the mic. Her teacher gave her a B-. Both Lillian and Pearly still hold a grudge. That was A+ material! Even then, Lillian had a soft spot for women who refused to stay put.

There was the scholarship to UC Davis—first in her Bakersfield family to go to college. Then law school at UCLA. The firm. A life of crisp suits, perfect diction, and no room for error. She carved out a space in family law where no one could touch her, but she didn't seem to enjoy it much.

There was the messy marriage. The bitter divorce. No kids, just a deep distrust of intimacy and a fancy set of French cookware she never used.

Then came the fire. The house in Santa Rosa—her reward, her fortress—gone. The condo in Palm Springs had always been an investment. Suddenly, it became her exile. The one-year anniversary of her life burning down was coming up, and she was still numb. And angry.

When Pearly materializes in the grocery store parking lot, it takes her a moment to spot Lillian. Her charge blends into the desert with that godawful beige ensemble. Pearly *detests* the color beige. It's an affront to her spiritual essence—and yes, she's being judgy but hey, nobody's perfect.

Anyway. There's Lillian, climbing out of her Lexus—also beige—in her linen pantsuit and imported leather sandals. Thin gold hoop earrings dangle under her ash-grey bob, setting off her fair skin and the pink flush that announces her irritation before she does. She's frowning like someone gave her a ticket to the wrong movie and now she's just waiting for the goddamn thing to end.

Pearly trails behind her in invisible mode as Lillian wrestles a cart and heads into the store. As they approach the entrance, Pearly sends a little nudge—a hint of memory, the spicy-sweet scent of gardenias.

Lillian pauses at the flower display. Pearly leans in, hopeful.

But Lillian shakes her head. *What a waste,* she's thinking. *At least bleach removes stains. Flowers just attract fruit flies and die.*

Well, so much for that.

Lillian squints through her reading glasses in the produce section, scrutinizing tomatoes with such intensity that Pearly's afraid the poor heirlooms might cry.

The thing is, Lillian doesn't actually care about the quality of her food. That's obvious from the pre-cut fruit, frozen dinners, and generic yogurt cups she tosses in her cart. She just likes to find faults. It served her well in her career—she could spot a lie or a weakness before most people finished their sentence. But it's definitely not helping her now.

"Chocolate-filled croissant bite?"

Pearly and Lillian turn to face a gangly, sweet-faced teen in an apron holding out a tray. Lillian sniffs. Pearly holds her breath. Maybe this is it—the moment where Lillian finally comes alive. Hard to tell from her face, which is doing a slightly scrunchy thing. Her eyes flash, and a bead of sweat appears on the teen's brow. His smile wavers. Finally, Lillian looks up and cuts him down. "That is not a croissant," she says. "That is a travesty."

The poor kid flushes, pulls back the tray.

"And what if I have diabetes?" she adds. "Don't you think it's a bit reckless to offer chocolate to a stranger?"

She does not have diabetes.

"Sorry, I...my boss said..." the kid stammers, setting down the tray. "...I think we have some muffins made with Stevia in aisle twelve?"

"How lucky for us all." She pushes her cart away.

Pearly wants to apologize, to tell the kid Lillian wasn't always this much of an asshole. She used to be kind, before her house burnt down. But if Pearly's being honest, she's been getting less kind for longer than that. She hadn't been happy in years. Decades, maybe.

After Lillian pays for her groceries—by check, how quaint—Pearly follows her home to Vista del Sol, a gated condo complex so sterile you could operate on it. It's a nice enough place, if you're into Bosch appliances, skylights, cacti, and oh, look! Even more beige. Two bedrooms, one in use, one full of still-packed boxes. Art lighting installed but no art on the walls. As usual, the drapes are drawn.

Pearly settles at the breakfast bar and watches Lillian put away her groceries. She's quick. Methodical. Focused. The irony is that she has nowhere to go, nothing to do. So when she finishes folding her bags and bringing them out to recycling, she returns to the kitchen and just stands there, listening to the hum of the Sub-Zero fridge and wondering how in the hell to fill her time until her eight o'clock date with another re-run of *Murder, She Wrote*.

Her eyes drift to the microwave. She notices a few fingerprint smudges around the "start" button and retrieves a bottle of all-purpose cleaner from a cabinet, knees cracking as she bends down. After wiping away the smudges, she catches a glimpse of her reflection in the glass. *Useless*, she thinks, then gets angry at herself for thinking it. She's a powerful woman—or was once. She doesn't want to buy into the idea that her only benefit to society is supporting the economy by buying anti-aging creams.

She doesn't even want to be young. She just... doesn't want anything. That scares her. She suspects it probably isn't true, but it's less scary than wanting and being disappointed—again. She's too old. Too fragile. She doesn't think she could survive another heartbreak. Watching everything she owned turn to ash was enough drama for one decade, thank you very much.

Not good, thinks Pearly. *Not good at all.* She'd love to use her influence—make a photo fall off a shelf, nudge a memory, spark a call to a niece or an old friend. But there are no photos. No mementos. Nothing to knock over but ugly furniture and a wall of regrets.

This might be harder than she thought.

***

Next up: George Whitaker. He was born 70 years ago in Milford, Tennessee, and that's where he's been ever since. He's as much a staple of the community as the statue of the town's founder, most famous for losing an eye to a rogue cow. A mail-man for almost fifty years, George lives off a modest pension and spends his days whittling ducks and listening to jazz records on his dusty old Zenith. That, and church—which is where Pearly finds him on this Sunday morning in early April.

Looking up at the white clapboard A-frame with its modest steeple, Pearly can't help but shiver. It's not that she doesn't see the benefits of organized religion—community, structure, tra-dition, hope—but she's lived enough lives to have experienced hypocrisy and persecution in a variety of interesting flavors. Like everything, it's complicated.

George appears uncomplicated. At least, that's the vibe he's serving in his pressed pants, polished oxfords, and faded sport coat with an actual handkerchief sticking out. What's left of his once-red hair has long gone white, but the freckles of his youth remain. He smiles warmly, shakes hands, greeting friends and neighbors with the casual ease of a man who knows his place in the world.

Pearly shadows him, unseen, as he finally heads inside, past the vestibule and down the aisle to join his family. They're already sitting stiffly in the second pew, struggling to reconcile the blood ties that bind them. There's his daughter, Marla, in her floral blouse and shellacked hair, his son-in-law, Rick, all upright and righteous, jaw clenched tighter than his Bible cover. And then there's Beckett, their fourteen-year-old son, wearing a pained expression and a vest made from what might be old curtains—an outfit he stitched himself. Pearly feels the flicker in George's chest, a pang of nostalgia. It was his late wife who taught Beckett to sew despite his parents' objections.

"Morning, y'all," he says, sliding into the pew beside his grandson. "You're looking snazzy today." Pearly agrees—the kid's got style.

Beckett offers only a nod.

"Daddy," Marla hisses. "Don't encourage him."

Pearly rolls her eyes. She'd love to slap some sense into that girl. Maybe conjure a falling hymnbook or oxidize her foundation mid-sermon. But she can only influence her own charges, and Marla isn't one of them.

She shifts her attention to George. He sings the songs he's sung his whole life, nodding along to the preacher's platitudes about grace and family. But when the sermon edges into thornier territory about "walking the righteous path," George's smile fades. Pearly notices his shoulders tense and his gaze drift to Beckett.

"...the world may call confusion freedom," declares the preacher, "but the Lord calls it a test of faith."

Pearly watches Beckett retreat inward. He looks down, picks a piece of lint off his vest. She wants to tell him to pay no attention to that insidious bullshit, to not let others write his truth. But he's not her charge either.

It only gets worse on the ride home. Rick drives, with George sitting shotgun and Marla in the backseat with Beckett (and Pearly).

"So," George turns to Beckett, "big milestone coming up. You excited for the ceremony?"

Beckett hesitates, choosing his words carefully. "I'm excited to be done with middle school." He turns to the window, probably reliving a memory he'd rather forget. A shaft of sunlight falls onto his face, setting his red hair aglow and sharpening his delicate features. "And, you know, who can resist a polyester robe and a sea of Fortnite haircuts?" He glances at his grandfather's blank expression. "That's a video game, Gramps."

George chuckles. "Gotcha. How are we celebrating?"

Marla unzips her purse, starts rifling through it. "Dinner at Golden Corral after the ceremony." She pauses, suddenly aware of how lame this sounds. "We told him he could invite his Bible Study group, but he said he didn't want to make a fuss about it."

Pearly watches George's forehead crease. He's thinking they *should* make a fuss, gosh darn it. But he's an old man, not the boy's parents. He can't intervene. At least, that's what he tells himself.

Rick mutters something about bad drivers as they pass a slow-moving sedan. Silence settles in, sticky as fly paper.

"Hey Becks," says Marla, "I can't find my gum. Can I have a piece of yours?" Without waiting, she reaches for the backpack at his feet. He doesn't stop her, but he stiffens. A moment later, she pulls out a glossy, oversized copy of *Vogue France*—the spring/summer runway collection. The cover features a dozen scowling models in the latest couture looks.

Beckett flushes.

"What the..." Marla narrows her eyes. "What the heck is this?"

He sighs. "It's a fashion magazine, Mom. It's not contagious."

"Beckett," warns Rick. "We've talked about this."

George tightens his grip on the door handle, but he stays silent, looks straight ahead.

Pearly leans in, channeling her best bedazzled Jiminy Cricket as she slips a thought into his mind. *Come on, George—do something.*

But he doesn't. His thumb rubs the edge of his wedding ring. His thoughts drift to his late wife. She'd know what to do. Or rather, she'd be brave enough to do what needed to be done. George was never good with conflict, especially when dealing with angry people. It continues to surprise him how much his daughter reminds him of his father. George knows he must've had a hand in that. It keeps him up at night. He feels like he's supposed to surrender it to God, but deep down, he suspects God is asking him to step up. He's just not ready to do it. Not yet.

Free will, she reminds herself. *It's a blessing, and a bitch.*

***

Pearly's final check-in is with Reyna Cruz, 25—a product manager at a Seattle startup. Guiding Reyna has been especially challenging these past few years. Those tumultuous teens and twenties usually are. It can be hard to know when to step in and when to let the person fuck up and learn from it. Usually, the latter is advised. And anyway, "mistakes" are relative—just steps on the ladder of spiritual evolution.

Still, it was hard for Pearly to watch her charge struggle with sex and dating. Reyna didn't go "boy-crazy" (or girl-crazy) like her friends in sixth grade, and the few make-outs she had in high school were about as hot as licking a stamp. Her mother said she was just a late-bloomer, but Reyna wasn't sure. She distracted herself by focusing on academics, wanting to make her immigrant family proud by going to a good college. But they were more interested in her love life, especially as she got older. She forced herself to experiment in college—it never went well. Now she's drifting in a kind of existential limbo, making excuses for her singledom and working herself to exhaustion. Better that than facing whatever truth she's afraid might be waiting for her. Maybe there's something *wrong* with her. But how do you fix something you can't even name?

The thing is, there's nothing wrong with Reyna. Pearly knows it's normal not to feel attracted to other people. She even lived it once herself, in a lifetime with far fewer options than Reyna has now. Reyna's journey is one of clarity, acceptance, and identity—and she'll have to define it in her own time.

When Pearly materializes at the Cruz household—a cozy split-level with a stack of shoes at the door—she takes in the scent of garlic and vinegar, the plastic-wrapped furniture, the folding chairs, the crying baby, and loud chatter from the two dozen guests in mourning attire. That's right. Reyna's beloved grandmother—on the verge of death last time Pearly peeked—must have crossed over.

Pearly finds Reyna stepping into the living room with a platter of lumpia. She's wearing a black midi dress with a floral pattern that's a little off-kilter against the formality around her. On her feet: black Doc Martens with dull scuffs and untied laces. The boots land with a satisfying thud on the hardwood as she weaves between guests, like she's trying to stay grounded by sheer force of tread. Her thick, wavy hair hangs loose and slightly frizzy from the perpetual Seattle rain, a few strands sticking to her olive-brown skin. Her eyeliner's smudging at the edges, and her forehead shines from the heat of the kitchen.

"Ay, iha," says an auntie. "Use both hands—this isn't a circus act."

"Thanks for the tip, Tita Liza."

As she circles the room, relatives bombard her with cheerful critiques and barbed curiosities that leave her increasingly drained.

"You've lost weight. Are you eating?"

"That dress is so cute! I could never pull off floral at a funeral."

"Any new 'friends' we should know about?"

Reyna just smiles and shakes her head, but Pearly feels the irritation behind it.

She passes her older sister, showing off her baby bump to a group of cousins, and veers away from the knot of relatives swooning over her younger brother's proposal story—the one she's now heard at least fourteen times. Stopping in the corner to wipe her brow, she nods to her teenage cousin, Marisol, who briefly looks up from her phone.

"Did you move out?" asks Marisol.

"Yup," says Reyna. "I'm in Capitol Hill now. Two roommates. Less drama. No one to cook for me though."

"Ha. I'd take that trade-off any day."

"Get back to me on that after a few months living on reheated UberEats and cold brew for dinner."

Reyna loves her family, exasperating as they can be. They're proud of her big tech job and don't complain much when work pulls her away. But she still feels like she's disappointing them, even if they don't say it out loud. Like maybe she just needs to try harder. Pearly's tried a few indirect nudges—prompting Reyna's roommate to leave her that article about relationship anarchy, slipping her a dream about a cactus that blooms best alone, and once, in a moment of desperation, orchestrating a pigeon to poop on her head during a Tinder date gone wrong. But the message hasn't quite landed.

"Reyna, there you are!"

Pearly watches Reyna back into the wall as her mother and aunt approach like mafiosos on a mission. Her mother's holding a velvet box, which Reyna eyes with suspicion.

"Tita Mela and I were just going through your Lola's safety deposit box. We found this, and, well—your sister already has one and you saw that monstrosity Jason and Amber got at Tiffany's, so..."

She opens the box to reveal an antique wedding ring in worn rose gold, with a single, modest diamond set in a cluster of seed pearls and tiny sapphires. It's beautiful. Elegant. Personal. But to Reyna, it's more like a guillotine than a gift. She can't even exactly say why. She just has a hard time imagining someone she'd actually want to marry.

She sighs. "Mama—"

"Now before you start protesting," says the auntie, "just keep an open mind. You know I had to go through that disaster of a marriage before I met Fred, and now I'm the happiest I've ever been. There's no reason you can't have a Happily Ever After. When the timing's right, it just happens. You're a beautiful woman, Reyna. Smart. Accomplished. Kind. There's someone out there for you."

Reyna bites her lip. Frustration flares in her chest, before it's extinguished by resignation. Maybe her auntie's right. Maybe she is just a late bloomer.

Pearly's heart sinks as she watches Reyna take the box. She's not sure what her charge needs, but her aura is not a good sign. It's getting a little duller every day. Clearly, Pearly's going to have to step up her game—not just with Reyna, but with all three of her charges.

Before Mildreth benches her for good.

Four

Mildreth Snaggs does not do recreation. She's never understood the appeal. While most of her soul-school cohort opted for Earth-based lifetimes—humans with their snack rituals and seasonal sports leagues—Mildreth took a different path. Her incarnations played out on Mycotia-7, where there was no recreation, no free time. They focused on spore-pattern alignment drills, fungal memory loops, and competitive photosynthetic stillness. Participation was mandatory. Enjoyment was alien, unheard of.

A faint chant rises through the corridor walls, growing louder as it echoes down the hallway:

"Chakras blazing, strike with grace!
Third Eyez storm the sacred space!
We don't die—we ascend!
Elysium fights until the end!"

Mildreth grimaces. She recognizes the lyrics—Elysium U's fight song. Her own unfortunate alma mater, though she prefers to think of it as a strategic detour in her otherwise fungal-focused academic trajectory.

So no, she has no interest in attending tonight's astralball game—some interdimensional farce involving sticks and orbs and "multiversal slurpees," punctuated by truly questionable chanting. And yet, she can't quite shake the irritation that no one invited her. She's a supervisor now. Inclusion may not be required. But the lack of it is... *noted.*

Mildreth watches her colleagues file out of the office, laughing and congregating in emotionally entangled social units, and retreats into her spore chamber. There is work to be done. Reports to file. Numbers to crunch. And no one crunches numbers like Mildreth Snaggs. Maybe it's all those mycelial synapses. She sees patterns others miss. Probabilities. Projections. What others call "intuition" Mildreth calls "statistical inevitability with delusions of grandeur."

The chamber hisses closed, enveloping Mildreth in a fine mildewy mist. Her shoulders relax. The lichen sprouting from her head softens into gentle waves. Her spores can finally breathe.

Ahhhhhhhhhhhhhhhhhhhh...

She opens her console, begins sorting through files. Most of the guides under her supervision are performing in the adequate-to-above-average range.

Hylonome: Induced a dream so uplifting it triggered a full-spectrum aura recalibration. The charge woke up, quit her job, started a community garden, and forgave her sister. *Excessive but stable.*

Alathranax: Created a searchable database for cataloging failed soul lessons and their karmic rebound patterns. *Overambitious, but shows administrative potential.*

Six-in-Two: Pitched a television pilot to one of their incarnated charges—a prestige drama about spiritual growth through home renovation. Ratings were poor. Enlightenment metrics spiked. *Recommend monitoring.*

Harry: Finally got his charge to take a bath. *It's a start.*

She tabs to the next file and seethes.

Pearly. Gates.

In management training, they try to prepare you for all personality types. But they must have forgotten to include the chronically noncompliant, emotionally effusive, over-glittered chaos-monger. If it were up to her, Gates would've been terminated, or at least reassigned to some low-frequency outpost far from sentient interaction. Sector 7012, maybe—where guides log aura fluctuations in mineral-based lifeforms. Or the Null Region, where even glitter decays.

But no. Gates must have some pull with the Higher-Ups, and protocol violations aren't enough to move the needle, no matter how creative.

Malcolm has to be behind it. Gates was his protégé, after all. And she's just like he was back in soul school. This spore doesn't sprout far from the mycelium.

There is some hope. Gates's charges have not been progressing much lately. They're not in crisis—just stalling out. The retiree in Palm Springs is the most unpromising candidate. Her aura has dulled significantly since the fire. If her vibration dips into the negative again, Mildreth could initiate a formal reassignment review. The widower in Tennessee isn't much better. His empathy metrics have flatlined for three consecutive cycles. And the youngling, Reyna, is stuck in a recursive spiral of doubt and dissonance.

She composes a brief message to Gates—some routine inquiry about overdue check-in logs. She sends it with great restraint. The autoreply comes immediately:

Pearly Gates: *Out of Office – Astralball Game. Go Third Eyez!*

Mildreth stares at the message, then closes the console. The mist cools around her. Outside her chamber, the corridor is unnervingly still. Desks abandoned. Lights dimmed. Even the air feels nauseatingly festive, like the cosmos called in sick to go tailgate.

Mildreth exhales. She straightens her filaments and flips through her notes on Pearly Gates. It's not enough for escalation.

Not yet.

But all she needs is one big slip.

FiVE

Seraphina glides into the Elysium University parking lot like she owns the astral runway, in Party Bus form. Styled in pastel pink with oversized fenders and sparkling gold trim, she bounces to the beat of Prince's "Kiss" as Pearly eases her into a prime tailgate spot between a gang of cloud-cycles and a face-painting station.

As she settles in, Seraphina earns a flirtatious engine purr from a nearby dune buggy draped in school flags. She toots back—because yeah, she looks fly. And she knows it.

Pearly cuts the engine and glances at Dumb Pearly, whose eyes are wide as saucers. "Legendary," she breathes, breaking out into a grin. She insisted on embodying the "Third Eyez" with a full-body catsuit covered in bedazzled eyeballs, structured shoulder armor with crystalline tears dripping down her arms. Her full-length cape is lined in mirrored fabric and embroidered with the quote: "*You've already been here, bitch.*" She looks like what happens when the team mascot has a spiritual awakening in the midst of a lip-sync smackdown.

She turns to Pearly, brow furrowing. "You think Snatch is okay?" They left the pet at home, napping in a containment field with a cloud blanket and twelve chew toys.

"I hope so," Pearly shrugs. "I'm more worried about the house." She's still trying to shake off Mildreth—and the nagging feeling that she's failing her charges. A little breather seemed like a good idea. Dumb Pearly's been begging to go to a game for ages. Pearly's no sports aficionado, but the spectacle is fun.

"Let's do this," she says, smoothing her glittery tracksuit and stepping out of the Party Bus. "Have fun and be careful," she tells Seraphina. "If you do too many keg stands, I'm taking you off autopilot on the ride home."

They head through the tailgate toward the stadium, a glowing sphere ringed with halos of sound and light, pulsing in sync with the crowd's collective vibration. The parking lot is packed with truck beds, floating grills, aether-generators, lawn games, flags, merch, and fans sporting the school colors of ultraviolet and teal. Dumb Pearly insists on stopping to acquire face paint and a giant foam finger—or rather, a set of foam hands shaped like a triangle, indicating where the third eye should be. Pearly knows this is likely to block the view of the souls around them and generate a few dirty looks, but she can't bring herself to ruin the magic of her counterpart's first Game Day.

"Pearly fuckin' Gates!"

Pearly and Dumb Pearly turn to find a soul in a team jersey topped by one of those beer helmets with a can on either side. He's standing by a grill, waving a spatula in their direction. Pearly vaguely remembers him, but his name escapes her.

"Hey there," she says. "Good to see you…"

"B-rad! Remember, from Dimensional Travel 101?"

"Right. B-rad."

"Oh man, I will never forget the time you and Thunder got us stranded in the tomato bisque dimension. Classic." She remembers Thunder's laugh echoing through the steam, the thick pink-orange haze around them.

"This is my housemate, Dumb Pearly. It's her first astralball game."

B-rad grabs onto Dumb Pearly's arm for a vigorous, two-handed handshake. Beer sloshes out of his helmet. "A pleasure, mi hermana! You're in for a real treat."

Dumb Pearly bounces on her tip-toes. "O-M-G! I'm so gagged."

"First game, huh?" B-rad gives her a curious glance. "Where'd you go to soul school?"

Dumb Pearly blinks, her face flushing. She shifts back on her feet and turns to Pearly, a little lost and maybe—embarrassed? Pearly's never seen her double with that expression. It's like watching a child shrink into themselves the first time the world tells them they're not okay just the way they are. The joy drains out of her, and Pearly feels a dull squeeze in her chest.

"She bypassed all the academic mumbo-jumbo," Pearly says, a little too brightly, "went straight into full-time employment." She puts an arm around Dumb Pearly. "And she's killin' it in waste management. Gets better evaluations than I ever did, let me tell you."

"Dang, well, that's awesome," B-rad scratches the back of his head, unsure if he said something wrong. "Waste management's crucial. My ascension bro did a stint in reprocessing. Messy biz. Respect."

He sends them off with two astral burgers—double everything. As they weave through the crowd, mouths dripping with spicy mayo, Dumb Pearly perks back up. She high-fives a bunch of students, stops for a game of hacky-sack, and eats her glow stick. Pearly considers pressing the issue, but it seems like her counterpart is okay. Or surprisingly good at pretending. Either way, Pearly lets it go—for now. Sometimes, people don't want you poking at their wounds. And anyway, she's got enough to deal with.

Even to a seasoned alum like Pearly, the stadium is a sight to behold. Inside the sphere, concentric rings of seating float weightlessly around a glowing, multidimensional track laced with loops, gravity ramps, sudden portals, and the occasional glitch that sends a player into a short-term liminal dimension.

On the sidelines, sexy cherubs in ultraviolet crop tops and thigh-highs shake pom-poms made of pure light, flanking a marching band composed entirely of sentient wind instruments. At the center of it all hovers the school's infamous mascot: a disembodied, glowing third eye blinking in sync with the crowd's vibrations.

Dumb Pearly's jaw drops. "Holy girdle, Pearly! This is even more spaghetti than I thought!"

Pearly smiles, leading her double up the stadium stairs. The game's only just begun, and she spends most of the first half attempting to explain it. But Dumb Pearly insists on cheering at *everything*, including penalty whistles ("YAAAAS, BLOW THAT HORN, DADDY") and the astral snack cannon ("GIVE IT TO ME, SNACK-ZILLA"). Pearly enjoys the enthusiasm, but she does gently pull back the foam hand when Dumb Pearly tries to use it to slap the ass of the "hottie" in front of them.

Astralball is, to be fair, ridiculous. It's like roller derby meets multiversal capture-the-flag, with extra points for style, velocity, and emotional resonance. The only reason Pearly knows the rules is that she used to date a star player.

By halftime, Pearly's getting restless. Maybe it's the game, or maybe it's the nostalgia creeping in like wisteria—pretty, until it strangles everything else in the garden. Dumb Pearly is glued to the halftime show, screaming her head off as the two school mascots battle it out in a dance-off. Pearly leaves her to it and slips away for a breather. And a cosmic slushie.

At first, she thinks it's just the brain freeze messing with her senses. She can't really be hearing that deep baritone chuckle. But when she glances toward the concession stand, her heart expands and contracts, stuttering like a broken accordion.

Thunder.

She blinks, taking him in.

He's leaning against the railing, all casual, next to their old college suite-mate, Flaubert—still deep in their cephalopod era, apparently, glossy tentacles emerging every which way from cutouts in their oversized ultraviolet poncho.

Thunder looks the same and yet... not. He's still rocking the motorcycle jacket she had custom-made by that shadow person in the Celestial Tannery. Still in those sexy studded boots. Still carrying those broad, reassuring shoulders like they're built to hold everyone else's weight.

But they weren't. Not Pearly's dead weight, anyway.

The last time she saw him in his astral form, he kissed her goodbye and left. Like, permanently. Cut the soulmate cord that functions like a wedding ring in the afterlife— it only binds souls as long as both parties are still in it. And Thunder had enough. She doesn't blame him. He was right to do it. Look how much she's grown since then.

So why is she hesitating?

Just as she decides that Dumb Pearly probably needs her and she begins to slink away, Thunder spots her. Smiles. Stops her in her tracks. She can feel her damn aura brightening under his gaze. So much for "cool as a cucumber."

"Pearly." The word from his lips is so soft and inviting. She could curl up in it and binge-watch shows for days.

"Thunder, hi."

Flaubert turns to see her. "Well, ink me twice!" A tentacle slaps her on the back. "The old gang reunited." They gesture to the stadium. "I'm surprised to see you here, Pearly. Have you turned a new leaf since your last incarnation? Don't tell me you were some big corn belt football stud? Actually, that'd be fascinating."

"No, sorry to disappoint. I'm here with my housemate. She's never been to a game."

Flaubert beams, popping a fry in their mouth with the smug satisfaction of a plan well executed. "I'm so glad the two of you are getting along. Honestly, when you asked for a body double, I thought you were a few cosmic marbles short of the bag."

"Yeah, well, now I've got one of your reject pets who chews through walls like termites, so thanks for that."

Flaubert laughs. "Payback's a bitch, eh?" But neither Pearly nor Thunder is paying attention to Flaubert. Their eyes have now locked on each other.

Flaubert clears their throat. "Welp. I'm going to catch the rest of the game. Looks like you two could use some catch-up time—minus the third wheel."

"Sure, 'Bert," mumbles Pearly. "Good to see you."

But Flaubert is already oozing away.

Pearly swallows. It's harder to hide your feelings in the spirit world than it is on Earth. Everything's more permeable, and lying just seems dumb.

So what *is* she feeling?

Happy to see him, sure. And fine, maybe a little lit up inside—like someone flipped the "on" switch to her soul and then dipped it in glitter.

But also... protective. Cautious. More aware of her codependent tendencies than she used to be. She's unwilling to give up her newfound independence. Not that he's clamoring to get back together or anything.

Geez, Pearly—stop with the drama, mama.

Silence. She shifts her weight. Somewhere behind them, the crowd erupts in cheers. Either someone scored, or a mascot set something on fire again.

"So," she tries, "you back at the Nursery?"

"Yeah." Before his last incarnation, Thunder had just been promoted to Head Nurse for newborn souls. "Busy as ever. Maybe more so."

She nods. "I guess the universe is still feeling frisky." She wonders too late if a sex metaphor maybe wasn't the best call. But he just laughs.

"I guess so." He tilts his head, like he's seeing her again for the first time. "And I hear you became a guide for real. Congrats, Pearly. Seriously. I know how much you've wanted that—how hard you've worked. You deserve good things in your afterlife."

"Thanks." Pearly exhales, looks down at her feet. "How's, um... how's Hannah?" She forces herself to lift her head, hoping she's managed to put her face in neutral.

"She's good! Great." Thunder hesitates, setting his snacks on the counter. "Well, I mean she was great the last time I saw her. She and Theo decided to incarnate together. Han China, I think." Theo was Hannah's husband in her last life. He died before she and Thunder linked up.

"Oh. Cool. Coolio." She sucks down a big gulp of cosmic slushie—and now she really does have brain freeze. She winces. "So, like... are you two... I mean, not that it's any of my business. You don't have to answer that. Sorry! See my mouth? Zipping it!" She mimes the gesture with exaggerated flair, waving around her slushie.

Thunder smiles. "It's okay. No secrets between us." He shrugs. "Hannah and I decided to redefine the terms of our soulmate contract. The old customs are pretty archaic. We still care about each other, but we want to be open to all the experiences, and souls, that help us evolve. Eternity is a pretty long time, and neither of us felt like closing ourselves off to..." He lifts both hands, then spreads them open, palms up. "To whatever wants to emerge."

"Right," she says, feeling her cheeks flush. "That's, uh, smart. From an evolutionary perspective. I bet the Higher-Ups ate that up." She grimaces. "Wait, that came out wrong. I'm not saying you did it to win points or anything."

"I didn't think you thought that."

"Okay. Great." Except now she's second-guessing herself. Her jaw tightens. Time to cut this off before she really sticks her foot in it. "Anyway, I should get back. Dumb Pearly's probably trying to crowd-surf by now."

"Sure," he says. "No problem. It was... it was nice to run into you."

"Yeah. Likewise."

She tosses her empty slushie cup in the trash, then turns toward the stadium entrance.

"Hey, Pearly?"

She stops, glances back. "Yeah?"

He shifts, runs a hand along the railing. "You maybe want to grab coffee sometime? I just—I feel like there's more to catch up on. Maybe somewhere less..." He gestures vaguely at the chaotic crowd, the mascots, the chakra t-shirt cannons. "Cis-boom-bah."

Pearly's chest does that annoying expanding thing again. "I'd like that."

Six

Pearly's had a lot of gigs in her afterlife, but this is the first time she's had an office. Well, cubicle. Only management and senior guides like Malcolm get four walls and door. Still, it does have a plaque with her name on it. Bedazzled with rhinestones, of course. It doesn't quite make up for the bland corporate furniture or the weird smell, a blend of astral toner and someone microwaving ecto-lasagna. The only things on the walls are a few Impressionist lilies and the Inspiration Board, which highlights guides' successes. Pearly has never been featured. Most days, she just shrugs it off and tunes it out, especially since she only has to come into the office twice a week.

But not today.

Today, she marches past the breakroom and into her row of cubicles, carrying a honey lavender latte and a long roll of red velvet beneath one arm. She nods to a couple of colleagues in passing—one offers a strained smile, the other stares at her outfit with a raised eyebrow and a wrinkled nose. She's wearing an iridescent tweed blazer with exaggerated boxy shoulders and a cropped waist, matching cigarette pants embroidered with blinking gold fleur-de-lis, a blouse with a cascading satin bow and an enormous brooch at the neck, and a sequined beret tilted just so. She looks like a full-figured Coco Chanel... if Chanel got electrocuted... in a Sephora.

White Robes were required for meetings, fieldwork, and public appearances. The rest of the time, the dress code simply stated: *Maintain a stable vibrational aesthetic.* Which Pearly took to mean: *Sequins were fair game.*

At her cubicle, she unfurls the velvet banner, climbs onto her desk chair in velvet kitten heels, and pins it to the ceiling.

KEEP CALM AND CARRY LIPSTICK.

She sits down with a satisfied sigh.

The ceiling hisses. Not, like, metaphorically—an actual, static-charged, *we-don't-like-this* hiss. The surface ripples, flexes, then spits the banner onto the floor like it just tasted something tacky. And to be fair, it did.

Pearly sighs. She picks it up and tries again, only to get a petty little zap on her fingertips.

"Rude," she mutters, rolling the banner back into its tube. "You really need to enlighten-up."

She sinks into her chair, rolls up her sleeves, and takes a long sip from her latte. Her case notes are overdue—again—and while she'd rather stick needles in her chakras and call it shadow work, she knows she has to turn them in. It's tedious, joyless labor. But slightly more tolerable with noise-canceling headphones and the *Moulin Rouge!* soundtrack blasting at an obscene volume. By the time "Sparkling Diamonds" kicks in, she's almost in a flow state.

Then a notification flashes across her scroll:

UPDATED POLICY NOTICE: Effective immediately—to preserve vibrational coherence, personal enhancements to assigned workspaces (including banners, altars, and

glitter) are now prohibited. Compliance ensures full spiritual alignment. Thank you.

Pearly blinks at the screen. Then blinks again, just in case this is some kind of stress-induced interface glitch.

It isn't.

"You've got to be kidding." She pushes her chair back, nearly spills her latte, and glares at the hovering notification. No altar. No sparkle banner. No disco ball trash can. Her cubicle's going to look like a celestial DMV. Her aura starts flickering.

She composes a telepathic message to Malcolm:

Pearly: *Did you see this shit? I can't even...*

Malcolm: *Meet me in the breakroom.*

Pearly slams down her scroll and stomps out of the cubicle. She gets a few dirty looks from her colleagues but could not give fewer fucks. She already accommodated them with the damn headphones. If they didn't want to deal with noise—or other souls—they should've applied to the Department of Records.

Malcolm's already in the breakroom when Pearly arrives, sipping what can only be some kind of fancy herbal tea. He looks, as usual, like an angel from a Baroque chapel: flowing blond locks, sparkling blue eyes, pristine White Robe, and gently glowing halo. Most White Robes wear the uniform even when they don't have to. Malcolm once told her, "The robe makes the soul." Pearly rolled her eyes so hard she almost astral-projected. Obviously, for most White Robes, it's the prestige factor. Though Pearly has a theory they were just too comfy and complacent to think about fashion.

He perks up when he sees her. "Hey, Pearly." Steam rises off his mug in delicate spirals. "I put a pot on for you." He gestures to the department's shimmering approximation of Mr. Coffee.

"Thanks," she grumbles, plopping down next to him on a clear plastic chair. She's not sure what the designers had in mind—maybe you're supposed to look like you're levitating? Why bother when you can already do that anyway? She drums her long gold nails on the table, scanning the room. There's only one other guide here, eating a sad sack lunch at a table across the way—but of course it's Gangalilt, the department's biggest gossip.

Pearly leans in, lowering her voice. "Did you know about this?" she whispers to Malcolm. "It's like they're *trying* to kill me."

He smiles. "Good thing you're already dead. About a hundred times over."

She groans and drops her forehead on the table. "I'm serious, Malcolm. I've had it up to here with their bureaucratic bulldozing." She lifts her head, gesturing wildly with her latte and spilling the remainder onto the table. "They want to remove all personal touches in this spirit-sucking lightbox? I'd rather reincarnate as a leech."

He shrugs. "You get used to it after a few centuries."

She stares at him like he just suggested she start using a planner. "Maybe *you* did. But I'm not like you. You're agreeable. Everyone wants to work with you. You're pretty much the model guide. I'm a freight train in heels."

He raises an eyebrow, setting his tea down. "You might be surprised."

Pearly narrows her eyes. "What does that mean?"

Malcolm gives a sheepish grin. "Let's just say I was a little more rebellious in my youth. Protested the Mandatory Incarnation Rotation back in the Fifth Cycle. I was actually president of the Temporal Nonconformity League back in soul school. We didn't believe in timelines. Or midterms."

Pearly chuckles. "Now that is slick. We definitely would've been friends." She sighs. "I'm just—I'm trying so hard to make this work. Fit in. Play by the rules. But it's like the system's allergic to me."

"I wouldn't be so sure." Malcolm studies her over the rim of his mug. "The Higher-Ups saw something in you, and it certainly wasn't your ability to follow rules. Maybe you should trust in that."

The coffee pot chimes. Pearly gets up to fill her mug, returning with a latte and a frown. "Even if upper management is on my side—and that's a big if," she says, settling back into her seat. "Mildreth Snaggs is definitely not. I mean, sure, I'm a pain in the ass. But this feels personal. I honestly don't get it."

Malcolm sips his tea. It's a very long sip. Is he... nervous? Pearly brushes it off. It's Malcolm. He's always nervous.

"I just wish I could see what she's saying about me," Pearly sighs. "She files reports, right? To the Higher-Ups?"

"Yeeeeahhh," Malcolm winces. He can already see where she's going with this. "But they're not accessible to junior guides. You'd need a vibrational clearance level well beyond your current development tier."

Her eyes narrow. "But you could access them."

"I mean... theoretically..." He runs a hand through his golden hair. "But that would be, you know. A flagrant misuse of departmental permissions."

They stare at each other. Across the room, Gangalilt tosses their lunch and begins the slowest exit known to the afterlife—fumbling with their tray, then with the door sensor, then pretending to tie a sandal that doesn't have laces. They pause to admire the vending cloud. Linger by the floating bonsai. Finally, with one last theatrical sigh, they shuffle out.

"No," Malcolm says at last. "I'm still recovering from the last time you asked me to break the rules."

"Bend, Malcolm, bend. And anyway, didn't you just tell me the Higher-Ups like my rebellious spark? They'd probably want you to do this."

He shakes his head. "I'm not sure that's how it works, Pearly."

She could push. She's known for that. But she's not the same soul she was when they first met, and she's trying not to bully anyone the way Mildreth bullies her. "Okay, fair enough." Pearly drains the rest of her latte. "Maybe just, I don't know—think about it."

He nods, already checking his scroll. "I gotta get back," he says. "One of my charges is about to DM her disaster of an ex."

"Yeah. Of course." She rises, tosses her empty cup in the trash. "Thanks for letting me vent."

He gives her shoulder a friendly pat. "Anytime."

They both return to work. Pearly doesn't expect anything to come of it.

Which is probably why she has to replay the telepathic message three times before it sinks in:

Malcolm: *I gave you shared access to a folder named "Dog Chow." DO NOT DOWNLOAD. DO NOT TELL ANYONE.*

Pearly grins, rubbing her hands together. "Now we're cookin'."

She locates the file on her scroll. It's her most recent performance review. Most of it is predictable: notes on tardiness, unauthorized dreams and déjà vus, and a laundry list of procedural deviations—several of which she's pretty sure were creatively interpreted by Mildreth. But then she sees it. A single note near the bottom: "Subject flagged for potential reassignment to Waste Management, pending behavioral escalation."

Her grin fades. She stares at the line, heart thudding like a misplaced bass drop.

They want to send her back to the celestial garbage chute.

Or worse—send her away.

Far, far away.

Seven

P early watches Lillian get up for a midnight snack, monitoring the action from her scroll. The prickly retiree went to bed at 8:30, but she had the dream again—the one where everything she touches turns to ash. She tossed and turned for two hours before calling it quits.

Lillian shuffles to the closet and throws on a bathrobe that looks and feels like old peas. Then she wanders into the kitchen and stares blankly at the contents of the fridge. It's not exactly prime-time entertainment.

Pearly usually prefers to check in on her charges the old-fashioned way—invisible, in person, with front-row access to the drama. But tonight, she just had too much paperwork to deal with. The scroll would have to do.

Lillian closes the fridge, opens the freezer. She looks past a couple of pizzas, a frozen dinner, a box of popsicles, and—what's that in the back? She reaches in and emerges with something wrapped in a white paper bag. Her brow furrows. No idea. But as she unwraps it, it all comes rushing back.

Inside the bag: a single croissant. Slightly flattened. Freezer-burned on one end.

Oh right. *This* croissant. The one she picked up at a local bakery out of spite after rejecting that horrendous chocolate-filled excuse of a pastry at the grocery store. At least this one's classic butter. For a moment, she considers popping it in the oven so it can get nice and crispy. But she gets that horrible twinge in her stomach, and she can't bring herself to do it. She hasn't touched an oven since the fire.

She tosses it in the microwave instead, which deflates it even further, then moves the remains to the toaster. It looks like one of those aliens who dehydrated to death in that stupid sci-fi show she binged when she couldn't sleep for a week.

Ding!

She pulls out the steaming carcass. Lets it cool. Takes a bite. And...

Meh.

Pearly's just about ready to give up and switch feeds when the wish hits. It's so fleeting she almost misses it. But it's real—the first thing Lillian has wanted, even a little, in ages. It flares in Pearly's chest too. As Lillian chews the not-even-mediocre excuse for a pastry, her mind travels to a cloth-covered table at Le Meurice in Paris. Gold chandeliers hang from the ceiling. 18th-century art lines the walls. She sips strong coffee from a tiny porcelain cup and tears into a devastatingly good croissant—flaky, buttery, still steaming from the oven. Pearly could swear she smells it through the scroll.

And then it's gone.

Back to her kitchen. Back to beige walls and freezer crust. She stares into space, wondering if it's time to reinstall *Golf Battle* on her phone.

Pearly's not sure what to do with this flaky crumb of hope, but she tucks it away, just in case. In the meantime, she turns her attention to Reyna.

It's late, and Reyna's beat. She turns the key in the lock to her apartment, yawning from a late night at work. Her brain's still swimming in bug tickets and sprint deadlines. Or maybe drowning. Rest feels like a foreign language she never learned.

The quiet apartment is a refreshing change from the chaos of her parents' house, especially with all the relatives in town for her grandmother's funeral. But she was hoping to find one of her roommates at the kitchen table, maybe scrolling or half-watching a show. Someone to make tea with and talk about the Ai Weiwei exhibit or those stupid new parking restrictions or the fact that the indie bookstore down the street is being turned into an IHOP. Instead, one door is dark and the other shut, with muffled sex sounds coming out of it. She sighs. *It's fine, Reyna,* she tells herself. *This is what people do.*

Still, it's hard not to be a little resentful. She hasn't seen her roommates much lately now that they're both partnered. They don't make time for her like they used to. Maybe she'd act the same if she had a partner. It sounds nice, as a concept anyway—to have someone to do life with. The alternative just feels lonely.

Reyna makes a cup of chamomile and takes it to her room, a "hit-by-a-tornado" situation as always. Pearly notes the towering pile of clothes on the unmade bed and the stack of papers erupting from the mid-century desk. She upgrades the tornado category from "weak" to "strong." Well... at least it isn't "violent." Yet.

Still, she's made some effort to make the space her own. Vintage indie rock posters advertise bygone tours, and a photo of Reyna with her grandmother sits on the windowsill next to a collection of mugs. The one in the center features a person in a suit being chased by pterodactyls and a UFO. It reads, *"Things could be worse."*

"Looks like it's just you and me tonight," she whispers to her potted plant. But Root Bader Ginsburg isn't much for conversation.

On the desk sits a box of personal possessions left to her by her grandmother. She hadn't expected anything beyond the unwanted wedding ring. Until tonight, she couldn't bring herself to open it. Grief always won out over love, loneliness, and curiosity. But right now, she needs to connect.

Lifting the lid, she finds an embroidered handkerchief, a silver Santo Niño pendant, an old woven coin purse, and a faded rosary. She grins at the polaroid from the 70s of her grandmother and a friend flashing peace signs in bell-bottoms. But something at the bottom catches her eye—a manila envelope with her name on it.

She opens it, pulls out a glossy travel pamphlet. The cover shows a riverboat gliding across the Seine at sunset, with soft pink light reflecting on the water. "Bonjour, Paris!" reads the title.

Paris, thinks Pearly. *Hmmm...*

Reyna flips it open. It's a ten-day guided group tour—museums, markets, sunset cruises, pastry tours, the works. Tucked inside the fold is a handwritten note:

> *My Reyna,*
> *If you're reading this, I didn't make it to Paris. But*
> *I hope you will. The ticket is paid for. The room is*
> *booked. A grand adventure awaits in the City of*
> *Love.*
> *I'll be with you in spirit—and who knows, maybe*
> *in the background of a few tourist photos.*
> *With love,*
> *Lola*

Reyna smiles, eyes glinting. She sets down the note, exhales.

Pearly feels it—the hesitation, the longing, the war inside her charge. Reyna wants to say yes. To honor her Lola. And also, let's be honest, who turns down a free trip to Paris? The fashion, the food, and the history would all be incredible. But then the anxiety closes in. There's work after all—she hasn't taken a day off since scoring her new gig—and having to speak French. And then of course there's the City of Love part. She's heard Paris described as the most romantic city in the world. Most people find that a selling point. Not Reyna.

As she paces in tight, fretful circles, something clicks in Pearly's mind.

An idea. The kind that could get her promoted. Or banished.

What if... she got all three of her charges on that trip? Same group tour, same ten days, same divine timing. And what if she went with them as a "fellow tourist," to guide the journey from within? No meddling, all very incognito. Just... nudging. Companionship. Some strategic sparkle.

It isn't the worst idea she's ever had. But that's not saying much.

Reyna's trip is booked. Lillian just dreamed of Paris. That can't be nothing.

Now what about George?

She pulls his file, skimming through decades of dusty memories. Rejection letters, baseball games, Beckett's birth, his late wife's smile—

Wait. There. 1982.

George stops at a mailbox, looking sharp in his old mail carrier uniform. There's a postcard in his hand—Paris at night. Notre Dame in all its medieval glory, its twin towers glowing gold against the dark. Something about it catches him off-guard. The beauty. The majesty. The soul of a thing with so much history.

It captures a life, a world, so different from his own small-town existence.

And then—he pockets it. Doesn't deliver it. Keeps it. Hides it.

He never did make it to Paris. But Pearly, watching with growing excitement, remembers. He's been wanting to surprise Beckett with something special for the kid's eighth grade graduation. And, come on, Beckett reads French *Vogue*...

Some might call that coincidence. Pearly calls it fate. A once-in-an-afterlife chance to get Mildreth Snaggs off her back and maybe—just maybe—change three lives at once.

But first, she has to decide.

Now it's Pearly who's pacing. She's torn between impulse and caution, purpose and fear. Then her eye lands on a thick, dusk-colored volume on the shelf—an astral replica of her most famous work.

The Last Violet.

She pulls it down. Flips through its well-worn pages. And dissolves into memory...

***

Paris, 1877

Evelyn Ashcroft sits at her writing desk, gazing through the rain out the cracked dormer window toward the white dome of Sacré-Cœur. The hustle and bustle of Montmartre filters in from the street, but she isn't listening. Her mind is tangled in the final pages of her masterpiece, her magnum opus. She can feel it in her bones. Watery Parisian light spills into the room, catching the gold edges of book spines and the floral damask wallpaper. The shelves sag under the weight of literary classics, scandalous French poetry, and every novel she's ever written—some very popular, some not so much.

She's made her name turning yearning into an art form. And *The Last Violet?* It might just collapse a lung. Preferably someone else's.

With ink-stained fingers, she hunches over the page and begins the final scene.

Étienne staggered back from the door, regrets still ringing in his ears. "It's nothing, mon cher," she told him. "Just a little chill."

But it wasn't nothing. His Marguerite—his beautiful, selfless, stubborn Marguerite—she'd collapsed in the village green while tending to the fevered child of a laundress too poor to pay for help. He felt he could see her now for the first time—now, when it was too late. Oh, what a fool he was! What a blind fool!

He'd spent months telling himself she deserved more than a broken man like him, months pushing her away, months lying to himself about love. He thought that if he let love bloom, it could only turn to rot beneath the bitter weight of the shrapnel in his leg and the men he left dead on the fields of Austerlitz. Now he was staring down the most terrible loss of his life. And he never told her the one thing he knew beyond all doubt:

He loved her. He always had.

He fumbled for his coat. The rain came down in droves, but no storm could stay him now. He would reach his Marguerite, even if it killed him too.

"Madame Ashcroft?"

Evelyn startles. The scene fades, and she finds herself staring up at her maid, Celeste, holding out a silver tray with a single envelope.

"I know you said not to interrupt you, but the gentleman was—" Celeste hesitates, searching for the right word. "He was very insistent."

Evelyn sighs. "I'm sure he was."

She takes the letter from the tray, glances at the handwriting. Laurent, of course. Gentle, brooding, and ruinously sincere. One of many who'd tried—and failed—to crack the glass around her heart. Men adored her. So did women. And Evelyn had adored being adored. The attention was a balm, a thrill, a spotlight she was loathe to step out of. But real intimacy? That was another matter.

She unfolds the letter. Laurent, as ever, wears his heart on expensive stationery: a proposal of sorts. A villa in Nice. A season of sun, sea, and "perhaps something more."

Evelyn closes the letter. "Decline it," she says, waving a hand. "Graciously."

Celeste curtsies and leaves. Evelyn turns back to her desk, tapping the nib of her pen against her lip.

Was she a fraud of a Romantic? Perhaps. Spinning tales she could never bring herself to live. But what of it? This was not confession—it was craft. And she knew precisely what the people craved: slow-burn love, noble suffering, an epic kiss at the edge of the grave. Very well. She would give it to them.

The storm had soaked him to the bone. Every step was a rebellion against the ruin of his body, every breath a prayer that he was not too late. Candles cast ghostly shadows on the walls of the sickhouse, filled with the moans of the dying. A maid opened the door and gasped at the sight of him—mud-splattered, panting, drenched.

"She's upstairs, Monsieur," the maid whispered. "But she—"

He didn't wait. His hand gripped the banister to steady himself. Every step sent fire through the old shrapnel lodged in his leg. But on he climbed, one stair after another. For her, he would climb a thousand.

His lungs burned when he finally reached her bedside. The sickhouse reeked of vinegar and damp straw. Rows of iron cots stretched into the shadows, each with a tragic figure swaddled in blankets. Marguerite lay pale and still, a sheen of sweat on her brow.

"Forgive me, mon petit oiseau," he choked, taking her hand. "I was a coward. I thought I was protecting you, when I was only protecting my fear."

His little bird's eyes fluttered open. "Then be brave now," she murmured. With trembling fingers, she pressed something into his palm—a small, crumpled packet of violet seeds.

For a moment, he couldn't speak. Months ago, in the orchard, he'd told her the only happy memory he had from childhood. Lying in a field of violets his mother planted.

Even as she lay dying, she'd remembered. She truly did deserve better than him. But that didn't matter anymore. He could no longer dwell on guilt with so little time left for love.

He kissed her. This was no chaste farewell, no careful brush of the lips. No—this was a desperate, defiant kiss that tasted of salt and rain and every unspoken confession. He kissed her like it might rewrite time, like it could fuse their fractured souls, like the gods themselves might pause to watch.

Her hand curled in his hair.

She exhaled. And then Étienne was alone.

***

The book falls shut in her hands.

Pearly sits there, blinking hard. The room is quiet. No rain, no violins, no deathbed confessions. Just the silent strain of a soul sitting it out for too long.

She used to write women who risked everything for love. Who staggered through storms and bared their hearts—and, yes, sometimes their bosoms. How would Evelyn Ashcroft tell *her* story?

"Well, shit," she says. "Might as well make it interesting."

Eight

"Snatch, no—bad girl, bad! That's not a snack, that's my pitch!"

The creature freezes—flame-tipped tail twitching—then resumes chewing on the cord of Pearly's holo-projector with the dead-eyed glee of a toddler ripping up the family will.

"Dumb Pearly!" Pearly scrambles forward, flapping a folder at her like it's going to help. "Get in here before she short-circuits my career!"

She tries to yank the cord away, but it's slick with acid-slobber and hissing softly.

"Sorries!" Dumb Pearly skids into the living room, her hazmat suit half-zipped and one boot missing. "She woke up early and got into the coffee again. Oh, and I think she ate your muffins too."

"Are you kidding me?!" Pearly races to the kitchen counter. An overturned tray reveals one uneaten spore muffin. This was a back-up plan, in case Mildreth responds to carbs.

Pearly wants to say something snarky, but pauses. There's glitter in Dumb Pearly's hair, soot on her cheek, and a hopeful look in her eyes.

"Snatchy-poo," Dumb Pearly coos, crouching low. "Want a Boom-Boom Biscuit?"

Snatch perks up—eyes glowing, feathers puffing—and bolts across the floor, knocking over a mirror propped against the wall. The mirror crashes onto a beanbag with a clang and immediately begins yelling: "YOU'RE NOT A MISTAKE—YOU'RE A LIMITED-EDITION COSMIC EXPERIMENT!"

Pearly frowns. "What the hell is that?"

"Motivational mirror! Found it at the garage sale on the floaty street. Nobody wanted it!"

Pearly picks up the mirror, turns it upright. "YOU'RE GOING TO KILL THIS PRESENTATION DEAD, GIRL! WOO!"

Pearly rolls her eyes, though she can't help but smile. "Fine. Whatever."

She smooths the front of her boring-ass White Robe. She's only wearing it so Mildreth can't ding her on technicalities. It drapes like a sack, especially on someone full-figured and fabulous, but she's done what she can. Her fire-opal bouffant is stacked to high heaven, gold streaks flaring like sunrise, along with glittering shrimp cocktail earrings complete with faux lemon wedge and a dab of rhinestone "cocktail sauce."

She turns to Dumb Pearly. "Just keep Snatch out of my way, alright? I'm nervous enough as it is."

"Okie-dokie. Roger that." Dumb Pearly salutes.

Behind them, the mirror pipes up again: "REMEMBER—YOU'RE NOT TOO MUCH. THEY'RE JUST UNDER-SEASONED."

***

The mirror's mantras are still running through Pearly's mind as she approaches Mildreth's office with a dry mouth and a sweaty aura.

You're not too much. You're gonna kill this presentation dead, girl. Woo.

In one hand, she's clutching her holo-projector, only slightly melted from slobber. She's got a folder of backup materials slung under one arm, clutching the surviving spore muffin in a paper bag.

Pearly's cubicle is sandwiched in the middle of the 22nd floor at the Department of Human Relations, while Mildreth gets a corner office. Perks of management. But hers has tinted windows, so you can't see in. Why? What does she *do* in there? Is her soul just more sensitive to light after so many incarnations in the undercanopy of Mycotia-7?

Pearly stops at the frosted glass door. She smooths her robe, steels herself, and knocks.

"Enter." The voice is muffled.

Pearly steps inside.

Holy shizzle.

The room is dim and dewy. There's moss on the ceiling, and an ergonomic desk made of polished petrified lichen. Pearly thinks she sees something that might be a filing cabinet, but it's hard to make out through all the slime.

Behind the desk sits Mildreth's spore chamber, doubling as an office chair—a sealed orb glowing bioluminescent green.

Pearly stops in the threshold, unsure whether to proceed.

The chamber hisses and the orb splays open like a giant flower. Mildewy mist spills across the floor and into Pearly's hair. She takes an instinctive step back.

"Pearly Gates," sighs Mildreth, and the fungus around the office seems to sigh with her. "To what do I owe this displeasure?"

Pearly tries on a smile. "Mz. Snaggs. Mildreth—"

"Mz. Snaggs will do," she rumbles. "Or you may refer to me as Supervisor."

"Oh, werk," Pearly snaps her fingers, which only seems to confuse Mildreth. "I, uh, have a proposal I'd like to run by you. If it's a good time." Pearly fumbles with the holo-projector. "I can come back if, uh... you're in the middle of..." She gestures awkwardly toward the still-hissing spore chamber. "...Fermenting?"

A long, damp silence. Pearly's aura flickers.

"Get it over with," says Mildreth.

"Right." Pearly presses play on the projector. Glittery 3-D animated text explodes across the room: *Operation Vibe Rise: A Limited-Term Soul Optimization Protocol (Paris Pilot Program)*. Behind the words, the Eiffel Tower shimmers at sunset. Fireworks erupt, then morph into sparkling croissants.

Pearly clears her throat. "Welcome, Supreme Supervisor Snaggs," she announces, "to my proposal for a bold new approach in afterlife mentorship!"

Mildreth does not react.

Well, what was Pearly expecting really? She forges ahead. "Next slide, please!" She says it like she has an assistant, but she's just pressing the remote.

Slide two comes in from the right with a whoosh-click.

Objective – Let's Talk Auras!

Three bullet points appear in glittering text:

- Current charges = stalled growth

- Vibes = low-to-lukewarm

- Potential accelerator = Paris

Below the bullets, a color graph fades in, showing three cartoon soul avatars—Lillian, George, and Reyna—whose auras hover in the muddled territory between orange and yellow.

Pearly gestures at the graph. "As you know, aura progression is the best quick-read for a soul's evolution. Red is survival mode. Violet's full enlightenment. These three?" She points. "Emotionally constipated. Stuck somewhere between blah and burnout."

Mildreth steeples her clammy feelers. "So you admit it, then. Your charges are underperforming."

Pearly stiffens. "I'd say they're poised for a breakthrough."

"You would. You'd also describe an extinction event as a 'teachable moment.'"

"Exactly!" Pearly beams, playing dumb. "Anyway..."

She clicks the remote. The projector sputters, glitches—then suddenly blasts a rainbow explosion with a sound effect so loud it rattles the ceiling moss. A holographic banana wearing sunglasses and a polka-dot bikini flashes the room, giving a double thumbs-up.

Pearly scrambles to click again. The banana vanishes in a puff of glitter, replaced at last by:

What's Blocking the Glow-Up?

She clears her throat. "Slide three."

This one features grainy video feed of all three charges in a moment of spiritual stagnation: Lillian scolding the grocery store staffer, George hesitating as Beckett gets shamed by his parents, Reyna silently accepting the ring she doesn't want.

"Fear of vulnerability," says Pearly, pointing to Lillian. "Guilt," she gestures at George. "Pressure to follow a script she never chose," she adds, nodding toward Reyna. "They're all good people," she says. "Just... stuck."

A shimmering rainbow road appears, only to be blocked by caution tape, traffic cones, and a giant spectral hand stamping everything with a firm red "DENIED."

Before Mildreth can interject, Pearly clicks to the next slide.

The Vibe-Rise Plan

The words "10-Day Immersive in Paris" slide in with an enthusiastic *whoosh*, accompanied by a glitter trail and the faint pop of a champagne cork.

"I've arranged for all three charges to end up on the same guided group tour of the City of Love. The perfect opportunity for subtle synchronicities, shared breakthroughs, and a croissant-based epiphany or two."

In fine print at the bottom:

I will also be going, disguised as a fellow tourist.

And in even finer print:

Please note my prior success with this approach. While not explicitly sanctioned in the current Guide Manual, it is also not technically illegal. Anymore.

A new visual unfurls—Pearly in a trench coat and beret, trailing sparkles behind her charges like a French Mary Poppins.

"But how do we measure growth?" she says, clicking to the next slide.

Success Metrics

"It's simple," declares Pearly. "Aura advancement. Each soul must shift up one vibrational color by the end of the trip."

That seems to get Mildreth's attention. Or at least that's how Pearly interprets her leaning over her desk, beginning to ooze out of her chamber. Whatever it is, Pearly's running with it. The slide shimmers into view: a thermometer labeled **VIBE-O-METER**, ranging from *Meh* to *Practically God*, with cartoon sparkles rising through the spectrum.

"And as an added bonus," she adds, "we might even get group cohesion and a little existential clarity."

A staged selfie pops up—Pearly and her charges in front of Notre-Dame, all grinning with extra-white teeth. Pearly throws up a peace sign. Reyna's mid-blink. Lillian's smile looks aggressively Photoshopped.

She clicks again.

Terms of Engagement

"Now I know what you're thinking, Esteemed Overlord Supervisor Snaggs. What's in it for me?"

Mildreth scowls at Pearly, as a golden scale appears with "Free" on one side and "Fucked" on the other.

"Here's the offer," says Pearly. "If I succeed in raising all three charges' vibes by the end of the trip, you grant me full autonomy to guide my way—forever."

Pearly squares her shoulders and meets Mildreth's eyes.

"And if I fail? You can transfer me, demote me, or send my glittery ass back to waste management. Then I'll be out of your spores for good. Well? How does that sound?"

Mildreth doesn't speak. The mist in the room hangs unnaturally still, like it too is holding its breath. Pearly shifts her weight, resisting the urge to wipe her palms on her robe. The silence stretches. She can't read Mildreth's expression—she never could—but the subtle stiffening of her head-lichen is probably not a good sign.

Pearly swallows. This was a bad idea. What was she thinking? She basically just asked her boss to gamble away her job. It all sounded better from the comfort of her living room. Now, it all comes down to whether Mildreth smells a statistical advantage—or just blood in the water.

Mildreth's spores puff, casting a cool fungal haze across her desk. She taps one gnarled appendage against her scroll. Once. Twice. The third tap freezes mid-air.

"Proposal accepted," she says.

"Wait... what?" Pearly blinks. "Seriously?"

It takes a second to sink in. Then her aura sparkles so hard it practically pops.

"OMG, OMG. Mildreth—Supervisor Snaggs—I promise, you won't regret this! Or wait, I guess one of us will, but it might not be you! Anyway, I'm gonna do it, and thank you, thank you, thank you. OK, I'm gonna leave now before you change your mind."

Pearly grabs the holo-projector, does a little spin, and books it out of the office.

As soon as she closes the door behind her, she strikes a victory pose, pumps her fists, and breaks into a celebratory booty shake.

"Suck on *that*, statistical inevitability."

A junior guide passing by gives her a look. She doesn't care.

She's doing this—really doing this.

And she's going to slay Paris.

***

Mildreth waits until the door clicks shut and Gates is halfway down the corridor before releasing a victory puff of confetti-like spores. The mush of her mouth curls into what some might call an evil grin. But Mildreth isn't evil. She's practical. Her department is a balanced ecosystem, and Pearly Gates is an invasive species. If the renegade guide insists on spreading the spores of her own demise, who is Mildreth to intervene? Let nature run its course.

She swivels her chair back toward her desk. All her files are in order, her notes complete. She exhales, warming the room with the humid scent of decay, and lowers herself into the spore chamber's embrace. The bioluminescent glow deepens to a slow, predatory pulse.

There's no way Gates will deliver. Ten days to uplevel the auras of all three charges? While in disguise in a foreign city, no less. It's an absurd proposition.

And yet...

She's going to have to keep a close eye on this. Pearly Gates is a wildcard. Her methods cannot be determined by an algorithm, and while Mildreth is optimistic Gates will fail, she needs real-time data to ensure desired results. It may be necessary to adjust some policies. Tighten some reins. Create a pressure-cooker in which every flaw and misstep rises to the surface—until Pearly collapses under her own instability.

An idea starts to take shape. It's... out of character. In fact, it's the sort of impulsive maneuver Gates herself might attempt. But you don't become Supervisor without learning to adapt. And if this is what it takes to get Gates out of her lichen—so be it.

It wouldn't be comfortable. But Mildreth has endured discomfort before. She'd once weathered a decade-long infestation of creep-mold, a mycoparasite so invasive it could hollow a soul from the inside out.

She leans back, letting the notion settle.

Yes. A little proactive intelligence gathering might be just what the situation calls for.

NINE

Pearly rolls her glittering luggage to the curb and looks up at the hotel. A shiver of excitement runs from her red vinyl heels to the tip of her sequined beret. This has got to be a thousand percent improvement over her afterlife cubicle. A gem tucked away on a leafy little street in the 8th arrondissement, it's far enough from the tourist mobs to feel exclusive, but close enough to catch a wink of the Eiffel Tower if you tilt your head just right. The building is one of those Parisian paradoxes of classic and modern. Tall windows. Wrought-iron balconies. Creamy stone façade. A burgundy awning with scalloped trim droops over the entrance, and a brushed-gold plaque announces *Hôtel Lumière* in elegant, looping script. Très chic.

Somehow, she managed to nudge all three of her charges into signing up for the ten-day Paris tour. Reyna was easy. She already had the ticket—she just needed a cosmic nudge not to cancel it. George, meanwhile, took one look at a Paris postcard that mysteriously reappeared on his kitchen counter and declared it fate. His big idea: a graduation trip to Paris with Beckett.

Convincing Beckett's parents, though? Above Pearly's pay grade. They weren't her charges, so she couldn't interfere. But when George suddenly gave the world's most persuasive speech about "educational opportunities" and "bonding before college," and the parents nodded along like hypnotized ducks, Pearly had to wonder if someone upstairs was freelancing. Either way, she wasn't complaining.

Lillian was a full production. Pearly tried heartfelt messages from departed loved ones, nostalgic Edith Piaf songs piped into her car radio, even rigging the Tuesday morning Wordle to spell *BERET*. Nothing worked—so Pearly had to resort to subterfuge and gave a nudge to a few of Lillian's estranged family members. After three calls asking for a piece of the insurance money, Lillian stomped and fumed and booked a ticket to Paris.

Now, they're all about to meet for the first time.

Pearly sashays into the hotel, tossing a flirty "Merci!" to the doorman on her way through the gilded glass doors. She pauses at the concierge desk, where a neatly pressed man in his fifties smiles at her.

"Bonjour, madame," he says.

"Bonjour! Comment vous appelez-vous?" It was only one lifetime ago, but Pearly's French is already a little rusty.

"Luc."

"It's a pleasure, Luc. I'm Pearly."

She makes her way into a bright lobby that smells vaguely like espresso. She loves the velvet armchairs in jewel tones clustered around the fireplace and the mirrored elevator doors that give her a glimpse of her grinning reflection.

Heels clicking against the checkered tile, she wheels her luggage toward the fireplace—the designated meeting spot for her tour group. They'll be gathering here any minute, along with their "official" guide. Pearly finds the whole thing deliciously ironic: she's the one with the spiritual mission, but someone else gets to wear the lanyard and rattle off facts. A "vacation" was fine by her, even if it was a working vacation. That gave her plenty of wiggle room to focus on the real shit – the subtle magical shit.

George and Beckett arrive first. She notices them just inside the entrance, looking around a bit lost, and waves them over with enough enthusiasm to scare a passing bellhop.

"Bonjour!" she practically screams. "Bucket List Travel?"

"Yes, ma'am," says George. "I'm George, and this is my grandson, Beckett." Up close, his smile has a hitch in it. The kind people get from years of reassuring everyone else first. His thumb brushes the ring on his right hand, a compromise between memory and moving on.

Pearly beams and extends both arms, bangle bracelets jingling. "Do we handshake, or are we huggers?"

George offers a polite handshake. Beckett just nods.

Pearly clocks the contrast. George wears a button-down and polished Oxfords that have seen better days. His old leather mailbag is slung across one shoulder like he's still making rounds. His eyes gleam as he takes in the fancy surroundings. Beckett slumps beside him, all sharp angles and teenage awkwardness in patchwork pants and a T-shirt he clearly designed himself. It's an abstract pattern that looks sort of like a bird and a flame, depending on the angle. The only thing he's looking at is his phone. "I'm Pearly. Pearly Gates," she says, striking a pose like she's expecting applause.

George blinks. Beckett looks up.

While Pearly can take on any form she wants, she tends to favor full-figured, big-haired, flamboyant female types. So what they see is a woman around the age of forty with a glittering pink beret over teased violet hair. She's rocking a cropped faux-fur jacket in pale lavender and an embroidered belly-dancing skirt that jingles when she moves. Her lipstick is bold. Her cheeks are rouged. Her lashes are visible from space.

"Cruise ship entertainer," she continues, like that explains everything. "Recently retired. Too much drama with a conga line-related incident in the Caribbean. I'm pivoting into food and travel blogging. First assignment? Finding the perfect croissant. Blog title: *Let's Get Flaky.*"

"Well now," says George. "That's creative. Isn't it, Beckett?"

The boy just shrugs.

"Silent type," she says lightly. "That's okay. I talk enough for both of us."

Beckett doesn't smile, but she swears one eyebrow shifts a millimeter. It's a start.

Pearly hears Lillian before she sees her.

"You call this air conditioning? I've had hot flashes with better ventilation."

Lillian marches through the sliding doors in a cloud of beige—the tailored slacks, the sensible cardigan, even her suitcase. She looks like she's been color-corrected out of her own life.

Pearly clocks the details. Every button is fastened, every crease ironed sharp enough to draw blood. The woman radiates control like it's oxygen. But control, Pearly knows, is just panic in good posture.

Lillian fans herself with a travel neck pillow like she's trying to put out a fire.

When Pearly offers to help with the luggage, Lillian's fingers tighten on the handle. "I've got it." Her tone is crisp, but her knuckles whiten.

For a split second, Pearly catches it—the tiny tremor in Lillian's jaw before she lifts her chin again. Then the mask slides back into place. "I don't know what I was thinking," she says.

"Booking this trip. Could be my first senior moment. I should probably get that looked at."

"I don't know." George chuckles. "In my experience, some of the best decisions started with bad ideas."

Lillian side-eyes him. "That's what they said about flared jeans and New Coke."

Pearly claps once. "Okay! Why don't we all go around and—"

"So, are you supposed to be the guide?" Lillian shifts her annoyance to Pearly. Is there a hint of recognition in that penetrating glare? One of those moments where someone feels familiar, even if you don't know them?

"Oh lordy, no." Pearly emits a high-pitched laugh. "I'm just another eager tourist with a dream and Duolingo."

"Speaking of," says George, "where is the guide? Isn't he supposed to be meeting us here?"

Pearly shrugs. "Running late, I guess. Not exactly a stellar start." Interesting how much judgment she can cultivate when someone else is in the hot seat.

The glass doors swing open and everyone turns to look. Reyna steps inside, dragging a rolling suitcase with one errant wheel. She looks exhausted, all flushed cheeks and frizzy hair. The army-green utility jacket and thrift-store maxi dress are par for the course. And, of course, the trademark Doc Martens. She bites her lip while scanning the lobby. "Bucket List Travel?" she asks, hopeful.

"Bullseye!" says Pearly. "Welcome to the party, or as the French say, *Bienvenue bitches!*"

The awkward silence dissipates as Reyna exhales, then joins them with a sheepish smile. "Hi. Sorry. My flight got delayed, and then there was this crisis at work... it was a lot."

"No apologies," Pearly says, stepping in to relieve her of the suitcase. "You made it. Now you can relax. Here, sit." She directs Reyna to one of the plush velvet armchairs.

Reyna sinks in. "Ohhh." Her eyes widen. "This is way better than seat 47E. Ten hours wedged between a screaming toddler and a guy eating boiled eggs out of a Ziploc. If I ever get hired to design Hell, I know exactly what I'm doing."

Pearly and George chuckle at that, and even Beckett cracks a hint of a smile. Only Lillian remains impenetrable. "Is this it?" she says. "I thought there were supposed to be two more. Maybe they came to their senses and canceled."

The ding of the elevator answers her question.

Two men step out together.

The first one's got that low-key magazine-model energy. Crisp button-down. Dark jeans. Medium-brown skin. Short black locs with a few silver threads catching the light at his temples. He looks like the kind of guy who's never rushed, even when everyone else is running late.

The second one's a walking exclamation point—mid-thirties, maybe, and dressed to impress. A silk shirt in royal blue drapes against high-waisted, pleated trousers, and a slim scarf flutters at his collar. His highlighted hair is artful, almost impressionistic—like a Monet rendered with mousse. His eyes gleam when they lock onto the group. "Bonjour, friends!" he says. "It appears destiny has slotted us together for the next ten days."

Pearly likes him immediately. "Lucky us!" she says with a wink. She knew there would be a couple extra tourists in the group, but she had no say as to who they would be.

"I'm Austin," says the younger one, "and this is my husband, Lamar. We're here to celebrate our tenth anniversary."

"Ooh-la-la!" Pearly grins. "How romantic."

As soon as the words are out, she catches a subtle shift in Reyna's expression. The way she wilts in her chair. Pearly files that away for future conversation.

While they wait for the guide, the group takes turns introducing themselves. Lillian offers nothing beyond her name. Beckett mostly scrolls on his phone. Just as they run out of small talk and Pearly's about to suggest a game of Twister, a disheveled young man lumbers into the lobby in a wrinkled striped shirt and slightly-too-short khakis, juggling a cross-body bag, a clipboard, and a baguette wrapped in butcher paper.

"Sorry!" he mumbles, mouth full of bread. "There was a... pigeon situation." He sets the baguette—still warm and slightly dented—on an armchair and flashes the group his best headshot smile. "I'm Michel, your guide through the iconic City of Love. I'll be coordinating logistics, showing you the sights, and providing special access tours with—" he winks, "all the insight of a true Parisian."

Lillian squints. "You don't look Parisian."

"Well, I'm actually from Philly." He shifts his weight, brushing a breadcrumb off his shirt. "But I've been living in Paris for a long time now."

"And how long is 'a long time,' *Michel?*" Lillian presses.

"Oh jeez, feels like practically forever. Anyhoos!" Michel clicks his pen nervously as he scans his clipboard. "Welcome to Paris! On behalf of Bucket List Travel, I'm so glad you're here. I'm sure you're all beat from the flight, so tonight we're keeping things chill. Just dinner in the hotel restaurant. Nothing too fancy, but a great way to break the ice!" He waves the clipboard. "Tomorrow, we hit the ground running, Eiffel-style. You're all checked in, so feel free to freshen up or explore. Just be back down here by seven."

Just as the group's about to disperse, Michel holds up a finger.

"Oh, and one other thing—uh... Lillian? Reyna?" He squints at the clipboard. "Looks like there was a little... mix-up with your rooms."

Pearly hides a smug smile. She may have caused a tiny magical "glitch" in the hotel's booking system. Just enough to ensure her two most emotionally constipated charges would have to—ahem—bond.

Lillian crosses her arms. "What kind of mix-up?"

Michel winces. "The hotel accidentally double-booked one of your rooms, and... well, there aren't any other vacancies. How would you feel about sharing?"

Reyna glances at Lillian. "I mean, I'm okay with it, if you are."

Lillian blinks. "I am not."

"So, uh," Michel flips a page. "I asked about other options. The hotel's totally full."

"Then *un*-book someone," says Lillian. "I will not be bunking like a Girl Scout. Not at my age. And not after paying full price."

Michel runs a hand through his hair. "I get that. I really do. But you'll get a discount. And there's just... no other space."

"Surely someone else has a single." She turns to Pearly, eyes narrowing. "What about you?"

Pearly's jaw tightens. She can't exactly say, *"Sorry, doll, I've got to astral-project back to the afterlife while you're sleeping to fill out my paperwork and make sure my roommate and her pet haven't blown up my house."*

"Oh, I would—believe me, I'd love the company," she says. "But I've got this... condition. Sleepwalking. Night terrors. Paranormal snacking. It's a whole thing." She adjusts her beret. "Not fair to subject anyone to that. Liability-wise."

Lillian scowls. "Fine," she grumbles, "but if she films dance videos for the TikTok while I'm sleeping, you're going to hear about it."

"I have earplugs," Reyna offers. "And I'm lights-out early. You won't even know I'm there."

Pearly gives herself a mental high-five. Score one for meddling.

Later, in her hotel room with the claw-foot tub and the fresco painted with angels, Pearly flops back onto the mattress with a dramatic sigh.

Dinner had been about what she expected. A little strained, with Michel dominating the conversation telling everyone about his plans to write a gender-flipped version of *Emily in Paris*. But nobody bailed, and nobody cried. She'd take it.

The bed is bigger than she expected, with far too many pillows and no one to share them with. She lies back and stretches one arm across the empty space beside her.

Old habits.

For years—lifetimes—Thunder had been there. Warm and steady. Sometimes she was the big spoon. Sometimes he was. She liked to sleep curled against him, one leg slung over his hip like a seatbelt. Just in case the world tried to take him away.

But it wasn't the world in the end. It was her.

So why does he want to grab coffee? And why hasn't he texted? Maybe he's been busy. Maybe he's expecting her to take the lead. Or maybe he's changed his mind.

She composes a mental message:

Pearly: *Hey...just checking in about coffee. I heard there's a new place in Sector 41. Wanna try it?*

But she doesn't send it. Not yet. Not when she's finally back on Earth with her job on the line and ten days to work miracles.

At least, that's what she tells herself.

She gets up and pulls back the curtain, revealing the city at night. Glowing rooftops. A hazy moon. The Arc de Triomphe framed like a movie still. *C'est magnifique.*

Tonight, she rests and resets. Tomorrow, she makes magic.

TEN

I t's the first official day of the tour, and Pearly's ready to put her lipstick stamp on it. The Eiffel Tower has always been one of her favorite human creations—bold and dramatic and a little bit extra. Today she's ready to see it through fresh eyes.

They shuffle forward in the security line, surrounded by a crush of other tourists. Different languages swirl around them. Somewhere nearby, a kid drops a scoop of ice cream, and a woman yells at her husband for not reading the map. Above them, the brown metal tower rises up, up, and away into the afternoon light. The chestnut trees along the lawn are full and green, still clinging to a few pink blossoms from late spring. Pearly takes it all in—the sights, sounds, and smells. She's missed this pulse, the glorious mess of being alive.

Reyna shifts from foot to foot. "Are we going all the way to the summit?"

"We sure are!" says Michel. "Best view in the city."

"Right." Her throat tightens as she tears her gaze from the top. "It's just that, I mean, I'm not exactly besties with heights."

Ahh, that's right. Pearly remembers the time Young Reyna fell off a carnival playground slide and broke an arm. She tried so hard not to cry. The pretty pink cast never quite made up for the trauma. "No worries," says Pearly. "I'll stay with you if you'd rather not go all the way up. There's plenty to see on the first and second level."

"Yeah?" Reyna's eyes gleam, then cloud over. "But what about you? Won't you miss it?"

Pearly waves a hand. "Eh, I've seen it before. I'd rather make new memories with new friends."

Reyna smiles. "Thanks, Pearly. That's really kind of you."

"No problem."

Pearly turns to Lillian, who's watching a group of tourists bust a gut over a pigeon stealing someone's sandwich. "What about you?" Pearly asks, all cheer. "Any requests?"

Lillian snorts. "What are you, a fairy godmother?"

"Depends. You looking for glass slippers or revenge?"

Lillian nods at the tourists. "I'd like to make those squealing imbeciles disappear."

"I *could* do that," says Pearly. "But it'd mess with free will, and the last time I ruptured the space-time continuum, the paperwork alone took six months."

Lillian opens her mouth to bite back, but nothing comes out. "Hmmmph," she says, though Pearly swears she sees a tiny hint of a smirk. She'll take it.

As the group inches forward, Pearly watches Beckett watching Austin and Lamar.

"...so there we were, five hours into this hike," Austin tells George, "before Lamar finally admitted he had no idea where we were."

"Excuse me, I had a *strong directional instinct*." Lamar fake bristles. "I just didn't know which direction."

George chuckles. "And you're still married?"

Austin grins. "Ten glorious years and only mildly traumatized."

Beckett's trying not to stare, but Pearly catches the way he looks at the couple. Maybe it's their ease. Their banter. The way Lamar casually rests a hand on Austin's shoulder. Beckett looks like he's trying to understand a language he doesn't speak yet, and maybe afraid to admit he wants to. He might not technically be her responsibility, but Pearly's pleased. He needed something to shake him loose from those tight-assed parents. And what's good for Beckett is good for George.

They finally make it to the elevator and ride up to the Ferrié Pavilion, first level. Pearly takes in the wide walkway lined with railings and benches offering panoramic views of Paris. Inside, there's a handful of interactive exhibits, some kind of VR "experience," and a bunch of souvenir shops offering steel rivets, mini bronze Towers, and tacky decorative plates.

Pearly trails behind Michel, half-listening as he rattles off factoids like "It was the tallest structure in the world until 1930!" and "Parisians hated it at first—they used to call it the Metal Asparagus!"

Pearly rolls her eyes. "If people don't sneer at you at first, you're probably not doing anything worth remembering."

Then they reach the Glass Floor, and Reyna freezes. Her eyes bulge. She goes perfectly still, like she's just realized she's standing on nothing but air.

"Hey," Pearly approaches her. "It's okay. We'll walk out of it together."

"I can't," Reyna whispers. "I can't move."

"Okay. Then let's start with this." Pearly gently clasps Reyna's hand. "Focus on the sensation of warmth, of connection. Just that. Nothing else."

Reyna nods, closes her eyes.

Pearly rifles through her case file, then calls on a bit of spirit magic. A breeze curls around them, laced with hints of ube halaya and lavender—Lola's comfort dessert and the flowers she always kept in the bathroom. Reyna inhales without meaning to, and her shoulders ease. Her hand softens in Pearly's.

It's enough.

Pearly guides her gently off the glass and over to a nearby bench.

Reyna exhales. "So much for the summit," she says, shaking out her hands. "I couldn't even make it past the first floor."

Pearly sits beside her. "Doesn't matter. You made it to this view." She gestures out toward the city.

Reyna follows her gaze—and finally sees it. The rooftops. The river. The bridges. The glory of Paris.

"Wow," she murmurs. "It really is beautiful. I get why Lola wanted to come here." She sighs, pressing her palms into the bench. "It makes me sad that she didn't get the chance before she passed."

Pearly turns toward Reyna. "I bet wherever she is now, she's happy to experience it through your eyes."

"You think she's still around?" She makes a vague gesture upward. "Heaven and the afterlife and all that?"

"I do," says Pearly. "And I bet she's proud of you for saying yes."

Reyna lets that settle. "Yeah," she says. "Maybe she is."

Pearly leaves Reyna to do some solo reflecting while she continues to explore the pavilion. Something shiny on the floor catches her eye—what is that? Looks like a silver sticker worn down by thousands of tourist sneakers, shaped like two foot-prints. A QR code sits next to it, promising a smartphone-guided tour hosted by none other than Monsieur Gustave Eiffel himself! Curious, Pearly steps into the outlines.

Her phone lights up and an image of a man appears with white hair, a black suit, and an old-timey beard. "Bonjour!" he says.

"I'm Gustave Eiffel. Allow me to take you back in time... to 1889, and the Exposition Universelle."

Pearly perks up. The World's Fair—oh yes. A big showstopper to celebrate the centennial of the French Revolution, and to brag about France's industrial progress on the global stage.

"My tower," says Eiffel, "was meant to be its crown jewel. In June 1884, two of my chief engineers imagined a structure unlike anything the world had ever seen. Four iron columns rising up into the sky, joined by latticed girders, converging at three hundred meters. That's a thousand feet of modern audacity."

The image on her screen shifts: pencil sketches, patent filings, notes scrawled in elegant cursive.

"We had the math. We had the means. What we lacked... was imagination."

That's when Pearly feels it. The tug of a memory. Her vision clouds. Her gaze lifts from the phone.

And just like that, she's not Pearly Gates anymore.

***

Paris, 1886

Evelyn Ashcroft turned heads. She always had. Usually, it was on account of some scandal, the latest whispered rumor she floated to the society columns. But tonight, Evelyn meant to make a different kind of statement. It was the tenth anniversary of her triumph, *The Last Violet*, and she felt uncharacteristically bold.

So she commissioned a headpiece.

From a theatrical milliner near the Palais-Royal, she had asked for something that felt both regal and ravaged—a crown and a cage. That, she said, was how it felt to write. Powerful, yet never entirely free.

The headpiece rose almost a foot above her brow. Four spires of dark bronze, twisting upward in an open framework. At the crown, a single amethyst caught the chandelier light and burned violet. Gaudy? Perhaps. Striking? Undeniably.

From her box seat, Evelyn noticed them staring—two young men near the back of the opera hall. They had that slightly rumpled look of scientists. Engineers? No. Architects.

They weren't looking at *her*, not really. They were looking at the headpiece.

She shifted in her seat, letting the light catch the stone again. Let them study it. She'd worn it to be seen.

One leaned in and murmured something to the other, who pulled out a notepad and began to sketch.

She didn't know what they were saying. But she recognized the look. The seed of an idea taking shape...

***

"Are you done, lady?"

Pearly blinks. She's still standing in the footprints, now with a line of irritated tourists behind her.

"Sorry," she steps aside. She's tempted to tell them to have a little respect for the muse behind the monument, but shrugs it off. She doesn't need credit for *everything*.

The group reconvenes for the ride to the summit—minus Reyna, who's perfectly content journaling from the bench. From the top, Paris unfolds in every direction. Tiny boats drift along the Seine. The golden dome of Les Invalides gleams in the distance. Pearly squints at the Trocadéro and grins. Is that couple breaking up? No better place to get your heart broken than Paris.

Thunder would love this.

The thought arrives before she can censor it, so she lets it hang out in her mind. It's true. Thunder wasn't with her during the Evelyn Ashcroft life, but he's always had a thing for Paris.

Actually, Dumb Pearly would love it, too. The thought pinches a little. Her roommate never gets to enjoy Earthly delights like this.

Back on the lower level, they reconvene with Reyna and browse the gift shop. George picks out a set of coasters. Reyna chooses a tin of fancy tea bags. Lillian, to no one's surprise, gets nothing. "Who needs a bunch of tchotchkes?" she says.

By the time they leave the tower, it's turning to dusk. Michel leads the group across the Champ de Mars, waving them toward a patch of grass in between a family playing frisbee, some Italian kids filming TikToks, and a busker playing an accordion. Pearly follows, swinging a newly-acquired picnic bag, ready to trade steel and sky for something a little softer.

They spread everything out on a checkered blanket and dig into cheese, fruit, and baguettes picked up from Madame Brasserie. It's all very vintage travel poster. Pearly takes off her shoes and lets her toes settle between blades of grass.

"This is soooo swoony!" Austin pops a grape into his mouth. "I wish everyone could experience Paris with a lover."

Pearly watches Reyna pause mid-bite, then pull out her phone and check her work emails, sending out a barrage of messages.

"I don't," says Lillian. "Why ruin it with fights about where to eat and whether your tone was *really* necessary just now?"

George chuckles. "Oh, I don't know. The arguments come and go. But I bet that couple kissing in front of the Tower will remember today forever."

Lillian swills a glass of wine. "I'll take that bet."

"I still remember the day I met my wife," says George. "Feels like it was yesterday."

"How long were you married?" asks Lamar.

"Thirty-eight years before she passed. Each one better than the last." George softens, turns to Beckett. "Remember when Nana used to sneak you extra marshmallows in your hot cocoa? Even when your mom said no?"

Beckett nods, eyes a little misty. "She used to say rules didn't count if you were wearing pajamas."

Austin smiles, then gestures to Pearly and Reyna. "What about you two? Any sweethearts back home?"

Pearly feels a little pang in her chest, but she brushes it aside. "Nope," she says. "I'm a free-wheeling gal these days. Broadening horizons, learning to love myself, yada yada. I'm calling it my Miss Independent Era." She picks up a piece of baguette, takes a big bite. "Who needs a partner when you have a vibrator?"

That gets a laugh. Lamar nearly chokes on a grape, and even George lets out a surprised snort.

But it's Reyna who looks the most surprised. "Did you really just say that out loud?" she marvels. "I think you're my hero."

All eyes turn to her. She puts down her phone, shrugs. "No one back home. Things, uh, haven't worked out too well in that department. I don't..." She swallows, running her hand through the grass. "I guess it's just not a priority."

"Give it time," says Lillian. "I have makeup older than you."

"That's right!" Michel pipes in. "You probably just haven't met the right person yet."

Reyna offers a tight-lipped smile. "Maybe."

Pearly reaches over, rests a hand over Reyna's. "You don't have to know what you want. That's what adventures are for: self-discovery and carbs."

The group eases into silence as they finish their meal. The sky's putting on its evening blush. Apricot, then rose, then that weird in-between color you only see in vacation photos.

Pearly reaches into her tote. "Alright, mes amis," she says, pulling out a box of Pierre Hermé macarons. "Eight tiny miracles of sugar and air. And because I am both generous *and* insightful, I've chosen the perfect one for each of you."

She examines the first. "Raspberry and chocolate. Tart on the outside, sweet when you least expect it. Lillian, darling, that's you."

Lillian snorts but takes it.

Pearly digs into the box once more. "Hazelnut crunch. Solid and dependable, but with a hidden snap. George, this one's got your name on it."

George accepts his cookie with a grin.

"Salted butter fudge," announces Pearly, brandishing the richest looking piece. "Sticky, a little bit dramatic, impossible to ignore. Beckett, sweetheart, this screams tortured teenager."

"Fair enough," he says, taking the macaron.

"For Reyna..." Pearly peers into the box. "Milk chocolate passion fruit. Classic comfort with a tropical surprise. Because under that quiet exterior, you're braver than you let on."

Reyna blushes, hesitating only a second before taking it.

She holds up a golden biscuit. "Honey and bergamot. Bright, floral, a little flamboyant. Austin, honey, I see you."

Austin preens and accepts it with a flourish.

"For Lamar," Pearly says, holding up a pale treat. "Madagascar vanilla. Understated, timeless, the backbone that holds the whole box together."

"Well, now..." Lamar smiles warmly and takes it.

Pearly selects another macaron. "Pistachio," she says. "Refined, mysterious, with just enough bite to leave you clamoring for more. Naturally, this one's mine."

Michel raises an eyebrow. "What about me?"

"Oh. Right." Pearly fishes out the final rose-lychee-raspberry. "This one smells like Marie Antoinette's bubble bath, so I suppose it suits you."

"Err... thanks."

"Okay, everyone," says Pearly, holding up her macaron. "Take a bite on the count of three. One... two... three!"

She sinks her teeth into the pistachio—pale green with a shimmer of edible gold dust.

Ohhhhhhhhhhhhhh.

Time slows. The shell gives way with the gentlest crackle. So crisp, yet delicate. Then comes the center: soft, chewy, impossibly light. The ganache inside is all cool and velvety. It's got just enough salt to make the sweetness sing. Almond, cream, and whatever crazy culinary magic the French seem to conjure out of thin air. She closes her eyes. Perfection.

When she finally looks up, the Eiffel Tower takes its cue and begins to sparkle. Just like her headpiece, all those years ago. First a shimmer, then a full symphony of lights. The whole lawn seems to hush. Even the TikTokers take a beat.

Pearly doesn't say anything. She's too full—with French food, yes, but also with hope. A sense that maybe—just maybe—they're starting to see the magic she sees.

She's still basking in it when her gaze drifts past the Tower to a nearby blanket. It's oddly bare—no wine, no baguette, no tourist clutter—just a single woman seated cross-legged. From a distance, she could be any Parisian enjoying the view. But the longer Pearly looks, the more... *off* it feels.

The woman's features don't quite line up, as if she'd tried to sculpt a human from memory. Her skin tone has a weird, earthy undertone. The wide-brimmed hat she wears curves like the cap of a portobello, shadowing her face—but Pearly catches a glint of electric-blue eyes behind black cat-eye glasses. Her trench coat is the deep mossy green of a rain-soaked forest floor, and something about the way her hair springs from beneath the hat—wild, unkempt—makes Pearly's stomach flip.

No. It couldn't be.

The woman stares at Pearly. It's the kind of pointed, withering assessment she's used to getting at department meetings, usually right before her lunch break gets canceled.

Pearly blinks.

When her eyes open, the blanket is empty. In its place, a single, perfect mushroom has sprouted through the grass, its cap still beaded with evening dew.

Eleven

"**Y**ou're home!"

Dumb Pearly flings herself at Pearly, wrapping her in a sequin-caped bear hug. "How's Par-ee? Do the dogs speak France? What did you wear? How are your humans? Did you get five gold stars? When do you go back?"

Pearly laughs, disentangling herself from her roommate. Snatch rubs up against her legs and singes her fishnets with a smoky purr. That, Pearly doesn't find so laughable. "I missed you, too," she says—and realizes, a little surprised, that she means it. In the beginning, she put up with Dumb Pearly because her double served a purpose. But things are different now. She's glad not to come back to an empty house. And in a lot of ways, no one knows her better than her spiritual clone. Not even Thunder.

"Come sit," says Pearly, patting the sofa. "I'm only here for a quickie." She sets her knapsack on the coffee table.

Dumb Pearly sits down, and Snatch jumps on her lap. They both look at the knapsack like it might harbor treats. *Oops.* She forgot about Snatch. But what do you buy for a lightning-poop-ing Franken-pet at a Parisian gift shop? She thinks for a moment, then summons her manifesting powers as she reaches into the bag. When her hand emerges, it's holding a squeaky Eiffel Tower. Pearly's not sure which of her two companions loves it more.

"And this," she says, turning to Dumb Pearly, "is an assortment of treasures from my first day of sightseeing." She pulls out a tower-themed snow globe, yo-yo, and coloring book.

Dumb Pearly's eyes light up. "For me?" Her voice trembles a little.

Pearly feels her heart catch. This might be the first time Dumb Pearly's ever been given anything that wasn't a work-issued hazmat suit or a training manual.

"Yeah," she says. "For you."

Dumb Pearly swallows, running her fingers along the snow globe. "Thanks, Pearly." She sets it down and picks up the yo-yo. "Ooooh, look Snatchy!" she says, turning it over in her hand. Snatch comes over and sniffs it.

"GENEROSITY LOOKS GOOD ON YOU, GIRL! WAY BETTER THAN THOSE JEGGINGS FROM LAST WEEK!"

Pearly gives a spirited finger to the Motivational Mirror. By the time she turns back, Dumb Pearly and Snatch are having a *Lady and the Tramp* moment with the string. Pearly can only assume they split the plastic like an Oreo and each ate half. She sighs. *Whatever.* Who's to say there's one right way to yo-yo?

They sprawl on the floor to color and catch up. Dumb Pearly regales her with a dramatic retelling of how she and her coworker Abathur chased a toxic leak all the way to the Crooked Harp, Pearly's favorite afterlife watering hole.

"It was a doozy!" she says. "Drank all the Spirit 'n' Tonic and started singing Enochian sea shanties. We had to wait for it to pass out before we could bag it!"

Pearly grins and shakes her head. She does *not* miss waste management—chasing down smelly blobs of negative energy that souls shed upon entering the afterlife isn't exactly her idea of fun—but she's thrilled her roommate loves the job.

"And you?" asks Dumb Pearly. "Did you raise the vibes and save your booty?"

"Maybe a little," says Pearly, coloring in a shark—or possibly a dolphin—looking up at the tower from the Seine. "But I have a long way to go, and only eight more days. I guess I should've factored travel time into my deal with Mildreth. A ten-day trip includes two international flights, and I doubt anyone's having breakthroughs on the plane."

"Shizzle." Dumb Pearly looks up from the rainbow-colored tower. "Who's the toughest nut to crunch?"

Pearly considers. "Probably Lillian. She's the retiree whose house burnt down, and she seems determined to have a miserable time. I don't know how to get through to her, but it'll take more than a macaron and a pretty sunset."

"Is she ugly?"

"What? No. Anyway, what does that matter? It's beauty on the inside that counts."

"That's not what *Gossip Girl* says."

Pearly rolls her eyes. "You gotta stop watching that crap. It'll rot your soul."

Dumb Pearly shrugs. "I like my soul rotty. So what about the others?"

"Well, no one's exactly ripe for spiritual awakening." Pearly sits up, rubs her palms against her forehead. "George is a sweet guy, but he needs to take a stand for what he believes in. And his relationship with his grandson is... not as close as it could be. I'm hoping that'll change." She sighs. "As for Reyna, she's still figuring out who she is. There's some stuff going on internally that she doesn't want to look at. I think she's scared."

Dumb Pearly's brow creases. "Did you give her a cookie?"

Pearly smiles. "I did actually. It helped a little."

"Course it did." She lifts her chin, satisfied with her own guidance. "And Thunder?"

Pearly sets down the red pencil. She forces herself to loosen her jaw before responding. "What about him?"

Dumb Pearly gives her a look. "Girrrl."

Pearly sighs. "I almost reached out yesterday. But, like, shouldn't he be the one to do it? I mean, he brought it up—the coffee catch-up. I don't want to seem desperate."

"That's bananas."

"Is it though?"

Dumb Pearly shakes her head, like Pearly's the dumb one. "Look, beefcakes. I don't know homeboy." It's true. Dumb Pearly didn't even come into existence until after Pearly and Thunder broke up. "But you're..." She pinches her lip. Looks to sky and cocks her head. "Unfinished. And scared."

Pearly blinks. "I'm not scared."

"Oh yeah?" Dumb Pearly looks her dead in the eye. "Then message him right now."

"Like—*now* now?" Pearly sits up. "Nope. Definitely not. I need to find the right moment."

Dumb Pearly rolls her eyes. "Whatevs." She shakes the snow globe, sets it upside down on the floor. They watch glitter swirl around the tower. "Also, P.S., your boss is cooking up something stinky."

Pearly tears her gaze away. "Mildreth? How would you know?"

"Heard it at the Harp. The little White Robe with the big toes was all in a tizzy. Blabbed about 'Personnel' and 'cracking down.' It was all very sus."

"Huh." Pearly thinks back to the spectator at the picnic, the one with the mushroom-y hat. "You know, I might've seen her."

"Boss lady? In Par-ee? Ooooh, stalker vibes."

Pearly shrugs, but the back of her neck prickles. "If it was her, she was in disguise. Sort of. Not a very good one."

"Uh-huh. Told you. Stinkville." She stands up, crosses her arms. "So you'd better crank up the genius."

"Yeah. I guess so."

Dumb Pearly scrunches her nose. Then she snaps her fingers. "Werk! I know what you need." She bends down in front of a cabinet and pulls out a boombox—the same one they used for the lip-sync smackdown back when she got possessed by a toxic leak. Now, it's practically sacred.

She presses play. A thumping synth beat fills the room, followed by the first cocky, impossible-not-to-dance-to line of "SexyBack."

Pearly grins. She gets up and joins her double. They shimmy. They shake. They twerk. They grind on the furniture. Even Snatch gets in on it, chasing her tail in time to the beat. Pearly cracks up when Dumb Pearly does a death drop on the coffee table. It's ridiculous. Glorious.

And for a moment, all is well.

Because sometimes, the most spiritual thing you can do... is get your sexy on.

TWELVE

"**H**ey there Pearly Girlies!" Pearly's in full selfie-mode, camera angled high for maximum cheekbone drama, with the Louvre's glass pyramid gleaming behind her. "This is Pearly Gates, coming atcha live from the world's most glamorous triangle with the very first installment of the *Midnight Croissant Diaries*, a daily vlog showcasing the nitty, the gritty, the magic and the mystery that put the ooh-la-la in this Parisian adventure."

She's dressed for an art date in a feathered bolero and sequined leggings depicting Delacroix's *Liberty Leading the People*, with the colorful French flag trailing down one leg. She was tempted to go topless, like Liberty, but she figured the museum probably had rules against nudity.

"And I've got a crew of eager compatriots with me." She turns the camera to Lillian. "Say hi Lillian!"

"Hey there Pearly Girlies," Lillian snarks in the driest tone imaginable. "Our tour guide's late yet again, and this seemed like a decent way to waste some time—"

"Michel, hiiii!" Pearly spins the phone to catch Michel in the distance, flashing his skip-the-line passes as if they'll make up for his incompetence.

She lowers her voice to a conspiratorial whisper. "That's him. Look, waving those passes around like they're Wonka golden tickets."

She swings the camera toward Beckett, who jumps at the sudden attention. "Beckett, darling, is that cringe?"

He blushes and tugs the brim of his handstitched denim pageboy cap. "I mean... a little?"

"Aesthetic honesty. Respect."

Pearly stops recording and pockets her phone. Not that it matters. She doesn't have any followers. She's not even really streaming. It's all just part of the ruse. "So," she says, looking around at the group. "What's everyone excited to see?"

"The Venus de Milo," says Beckett. "I saw a pic once and couldn't stop staring at the drapery. I mean, can you imagine carving all those folds in marble? It's, like, early couture."

"Nice," says Pearly. "You've got an eye for fashion, kid."

He shrugs, but he's smiling.

"I don't know," says Reyna. "Maybe that painting of the scandalous shipwreck? I can't remember what it's called."

"The Raft of the Medusa," says Lillian, brushing off everyone's surprise. "What? I minored in art history."

"I want to see the really old stuff," says George. "Egypt, Mesopotamia. I always watch those documentaries on PBS. Something about those civilizations just sticks with me."

Now it's Lillian's turn to be surprised. "Really? Me too."

Interesting, thinks Pearly. She files it away for future reference.

Austin elbows Lamar. "You know what *I'm* excited about?"

Lamar raises a brow. "Every statue with a gluteus maximus?"

"Well, yes-and, Lamar. But specifically queer-coded history. I did a little research. Some pre-gaming, if you will. Wanna see if we can find Antinous?"

"Who's Antinous?" says Reyna.

Austin grins. "Emperor Hadrian's boyfriend, of course! After Antinous died, Hadrian made his lover a God. Isn't that romantic?" He puts a hand to his forehead.

"Antonio will have to wait," Michel steps in, "until after the *Mona Lisa*. She's our first stop, Instagram demands it." He takes them down beneath the pyramid, into the cool stone belly of the building. "Fun fact," he says, pointing vaguely at the walls. "Before the Louvre was a museum—or even a palace—it was a fortress. With a moat and everything. Very, uh... defensive."

Pearly trails her fingers across the rough stone blocks, halting when she spots a handful of carved hearts. "Okay, wait. Tell me I'm not hallucinating."

Michel peers over. "Oh, yeah. Those are stonemason marks. Like signatures."

Pearly gasps. "Excuse me, monsieur, but these are clearly medieval love doodles. Somebody was crushing hard while digging a moat."

"That's so romantic!" says Austin, snapping a photo.

Lillian sniffs. "If I'd hired someone to build my fortress, I'd prefer fewer doodles and more cannons."

Pearly grins. "Spoken like a woman who's never carved initials into a desk."

"Why," says Lillian, "would I vandalize perfectly good furniture?"

They follow Michel toward the Denon Wing, but Austin slows at a side gallery with sparkly glass cases. "Wait—are those the French crown jewels? We can't just walk past those!"

"Oh honey," Lamar rubs his partner's shoulder. "You know some of those are fake. They're just rhinestones on steroids."

Austin waves a hand. "Let me dream."

"Okay," Michel groans. "A very quick detour."

The room dazzles with tiaras, scepters, and royal bling so over-the-top even Pearly feels under-accessorized. But it's a dragon-shaped decanter that stops her cold, its jeweled tongue sliding in and out like a panting dog.

"Oh my god," she breathes. "That is either the tackiest thing I've ever seen or the most brilliant. Imagine pouring your Bordeaux while this guy does tongue calisthenics."

Beckett's already got his phone out, getting shots from every angle. "This is going to be my new lock screen." He zooms in, snickering when the tongue pops out again.

Even with their special passes, there's still a line for the world's most famous painting. The gallery is loud and crowded and maybe a little overrated. Pearly can appreciate the technical brilliance and the enigmatic smile, but she isn't exactly living for it. Maybe if girlfriend had a beauty mark and a forty-inch wig, she'd feel differently. But she still respects a fellow icon, so she snaps a photo.

After exiting the line, she flips her phone back into selfie mode. "Okay, moment of truth. Hot takes only—go. Becks," she says, turning the camera to him. "First impression."

Beckett tilts his head. "Okay, I guess. But I like those memes with her holding a cat better."

Then he glances past Pearly to the enormous *Wedding Feast at Cana* dominating the opposite wall. He narrows his eyes, zooming in with his phone. "Wait. Guys. Forget Mona. That is an *actual cat* painted into the corner over there."

Pearly gasps. "Shut up, you're right! Louvre Cat has entered the chat."

Beckett grins, filming. "This is going viral. Cat steals spotlight from world's most famous smile."

Austin clutches his heart in mock horror. "Kids these days! No appreciation for culture. You know, this is how Rome fell." He fans himself with his museum brochure. "Well, I for one think Mona's got secrets. And I want them."

"Nah, I'm with the kid." Lillian crosses her arms. "I've seen better smiles at the DMV."

Reyna shrugs, hands in pockets. "I don't know," she says, glancing back at the painting. "There is something mysterious about her. And, I don't know—self-assured? I think it's beautiful. Like, there aren't many examples out there of unsexualized female beauty."

"I think she looks lonely," says George, forehead wrinkling. "You know how sometimes you can be surrounded by people but feel totally alone? Like everyone's looking but no one sees you?"

Reyna steps up, rests a hand on his shoulder. "Yeah, George," she says. "I know that one."

He smiles at her, and Pearly feels them both soften. She pats herself on back for her ingenious Paris idea.

"Damn, Gramps," Beckett nods. "That was deep." He holds out his hand for a high-five. George looks only too happy to oblige.

"Yeah," Pearly says. "I want to take art history with y'all."

Michel leans in, ruining the moment. "Aren't you going to ask me?"

Pearly sighs. "Sure, Michel. What's your hot take?"

"I mean, I've seen her a lot. We're besties now," he confides. "She told me so telepathically."

"Err, right." Pearly takes him by the shoulders. "Blink twice if you're being held hostage by a Da Vinci."

Michel leads the group through some of the Louvre's greatest hits, including the Venus de Milo, the statue of Nike, and "Liberty Leading the People," which Pearly has to admit is even more spectacular in oil than in sequins.

They break for lunch at the Pyramid Café. For once, Pearly doesn't have much to say—she knows when to shut up and savor. The chickpea stew is buttery and tender. The brioche croque monsieur is scandalously decadent with its layers of warm baked ham and creamy Gruyere. And the chocolate mousse with the candied citrus marmalade? To die for. Like, "cross your heart and call the hearse." Yum.

"One-hour free time," says Michel, when they're finished. "Go explore, and we'll all meet back at the gift shop in an hour."

Austin leans back in his chair, spreading out a marked-up map. "Who's in for the Bootleg Gay History Tour?"

"Define bootleg," says Reyna, already rising.

Austin points dramatically toward the neoclassical galleries. "DIY, unsanctioned, and proudly homosexual. Statues, scandals, secret lovers—it's like a soap opera carved in stone!"

"Cool," she says. "I'm in." She turns to Beckett. "How about you?"

Beckett hesitates. He looks at George, who catches his eye.

"Why don't you go with them?" says George. "I would, but I've got my heart set on the Mesopotamian wing."

"Yeah?" Beckett swallows. "Okay. I mean, just to check it out."

George rests a hand on Beckett's shoulder. "Good. I look forward to hearing about it."

"I'll join you, George," says Lillian. "If you don't mind."

He smiles, eyes sparkling. "Not at all."

"How about you, Pearly?" says Austin.

She wants to go. She's lived a lot of queer lives, and it's always interesting to see how history represents them. But her spirit guide instincts are louder, and they're telling her that her best opportunity lies elsewhere. "I'm going to tag along with George and Lillian," she says. "Make sure they don't get trapped in an ancient curse or a poorly lit hallway."

Austin mock-salutes. "See you in an hour."

Beckett gives Pearly a shy smile, then follows Austin, Lamar, and Reyna into the marble unknown.

Pearly watches them go. Then she turns to George and Lillian. "Alright, my fellow time travelers. Let's get dusty."

The Near Eastern Collection features art from a historical area covering modern day Syria, Lebanon, Jordan, and Israel. Pearly marvels at the sculptures, ivory boxes, golden cups, and ancient jewelry, some dating back to 7,000 BC. "Hey guys, look at this." She calls George and Lillian over to a human figure with thick legs and hand-carved eyes and toes. "This is the oldest sculpture at the Louvre! It used to have painted-on clothes and a wig." A kindred spirit of Pearly's, for sure.

Lillian leans in, examining the figure. "This is from 'Ain Ghazal, right? Neolithic Jordan. They think these statues were ritually buried after use. Maybe ancestor worship, maybe fertility rites. No one really knows." She straightens. "But look at the eyes—wide, stylized. They're not trying to show realism. They're going for presence. Like the figure's meant to watch you."

George gives a low whistle. "You really know your stuff."

She shrugs, but her eyes light up just a smidge. "Yeah, well, I paid attention in class. You know, back when we used to chisel our notes into stone."

He chuckles. "I'd still take your tour over Michel's."

Wait, thinks Pearly. *Are they... flirting?*

The trio moves past a bowl with a hunting scene and a carved woman carrying a baby in a crib to land at a statue of a group of people around a trough, hands bent as if kneading or shaping. "Making Bread or Beer," says the description.

"Hmm," says Pearly. "Which do you think it was?"

"Beer," they say simultaneously. Like, without hesitation.

They turn to one another. Lock eyes. Something flickers.

Pearly watches them, curious.

Poof. An ancient memory floods her vision. It's not her memory. It's theirs.

Ugarit. 2nd millennium BC. A sun-drenched courtyard behind a clay house. Earthen walls, baskets of barley and emmer wheat, a woven baby sling hanging on a peg. Half a dozen workers in linen and headscarves grind barley into fermented mash.

One of them—that's Lillian—is pregnant. Another—that's George—stops what he's doing to wrap his hands around her stomach. The baby. It's kicking. His eyes widen. She laughs.

They return to the trough, moving in rhythm with the others, elbows brushing as they work the grain into something that will feed and uplift their people. Someone starts to sing. Then another. Then they all join in, voices weaving together in a chorus of shared labor and communal identity.

The scene blurs. The courtyard melts into the stone-and-glass air of the museum, the centuries collapsing as Pearly takes a breath.

These two have a history. And possibly a future as well. Maybe that's why Pearly was assigned to them? To help them reconnect. The notion makes her aura tingle. Nothing like a second-chance romance to add a little spice to the mission.

George shakes his head. "That was... weird." He takes a step back.

"Weird how?" says Lillian. There's an edge to her voice.

"I don't know," George shrugs. "Déjà vu or something. Maybe it was an old movie I saw."

Lillian's still focused on the statue. "Huh," she says. "Same here." She glances at George, as if searching for something. Then the armor returns. "Well... there were mushrooms in that duck confit. Could've been the trippy kind."

"Oh, I don't know," says Pearly, aiming for cheery. "History is squirrely. Sometimes it likes to rise from the dead and plant one on you."

Neither of them answers. Lillian clears her throat and drifts toward the next display. George lingers a second longer, then follows, his hands shoved deep in his coat pockets.

Pearly trails after them. She'd meant to spark connection, not drive them farther apart. This can't be good. The silence feels heavy, and for a moment she wishes she were somewhere else. Somewhere easy, familiar.

That's when her eye catches on a small stone slab in the corner. She excuses herself to go check it out. Carved into the slab is an intense, muscly dude that the title card says identifies as the god of storms. He's thrusting a lance into the ground that's meant to look like thunder striking the earth.

Thunder.

A smile tugs at her mouth. He'd get a kick out of this. Maybe it's time to prove Dumb Pearly wrong and just reach out already. She takes a mental snapshot of the carving and frames the telepathic message in her mind:

Pearly: *Alter ego? Or the look on your face when some dude leaves the toilet seat up.*

Pearly exhales, slipping the thought back into her mental drafts folder. Timing, as ever, is a diva. There's no need to rush this. She's working on being less impulsive.

By the time she reaches the gift shop, with George and Lillian in tow, Beckett is holding up a glossy poster of Antinous. He looks up at George. "I don't know what Mom would say. I mean, he is naked, even if he's marble."

George studies the poster, then nods. "Get it. Let me worry about your mother."

Yes, George! Pearly's pretty sure his aura just brightened.

Beckett's fingers tighten around the poster. He smiles and heads for the register.

Pearly's still basking in the glow of guiding-gone-good when she hears a ping in her mind, followed by a telepathic text:

Thunder: *Hey you. How about that coffee? I'm buying. You're spilling the beans.*

Her heart lurches. She grins so hard she almost breaks her face. She's tempted to answer right there between the art posters and the miniature statues, but... no. She should compose herself before she composes a response. Ensure she's coming from a centered state of mind. And anyway, she doesn't want to appear overeager. That was the old Pearly—ready to abandon herself at the first sign of affection. They've waited an entire lifetime. Another day couldn't hurt.

She lets the anticipation build in her chest as she follows the others out of the Louvre and into a light spring rain that makes the cobblestones shimmer like stardust.

Ah, Paris...

THIRTEEN

Lillian's on a rampage. Pearly barely has time to admire the Seine when her charge hooks her by the arm and drags her behind a stack of champagne crates at Port de la Bourdonnais. The others wait in line for the iconic river dinner cruise alongside dozens of chatty tourists.

"Pearly," says Lillian. "You've got to swap with me. Take Reyna. At least for one night. Preferably the whole week. Please. I'm begging you."

Pearly raises a brow. "Is this why you nearly dislocated my shoulder?"

"I'm serious." Lillian glares at her roommate, hard at work excavating the depths of an overstuffed tote. First, it's a pashmina. Then something that might be a spare phone battery. A folded paper map of Paris follows, and two water bottles—no wait, one is filled with iced coffee—before an umbrella and what looks suspiciously like a mini first aid kit join the pile. She finds a tube of Chapstick and puts it on before cramming everything back in.

"When we got back to the hotel to freshen up," says Lillian, "I thought we'd been robbed. But no, it was just Reyna's 'lifestyle.'

Which apparently does not include the use of hangers." She shakes her head, reliving the trauma. "And don't even get me started on the beds," she adds. "They call it 'two twins.' Ha! The room's so tiny they just shoved 'em together and put a line down the middle. As if a sheet could convince me I wasn't being slowly absorbed into Reyna's chaos. I woke up this morning practically welded to her elbow."

Pearly snorts. "Romantic."

"Criminal," snaps Lillian. "If Paris is the City of Love, someone needs to tell the hotels that not everyone came here to play footsie at two a.m."

Pearly bites back a smile. "Sounds like an adventure."

"This is not an adventure! This is a crisis!" Lillian grips the railing to steady herself. "I haven't lived with anyone since 1993—and there's a reason for that!"

"I'm sure there is," says Pearly. "But I think this could be good for both of you." She leans in. "Did you know Reyna told me earlier she admires you? Said you don't take shit from anyone, and she could benefit from being around a confident, mature woman who's not afraid to speak her mind." This may be... a euphemistic repackaging of what Reyna actually said, but Pearly goes more by vibes anyway.

"Well," says Lillian, standing up a little straighter. "I suppose that's true."

"And honestly," says Pearly, "there's a lot you could learn from her, too. If you eased up on the barbs, and—I don't know—got curious about other people. Maybe you find them disappointing because you expect them to be."

She sweeps a hand toward the glimmering water, where the city lights ripple in gold and silver. "There's magic out there, Lillian. And goodness. I swear there is. You just have to be open to it."

Lillian sniffs. "I'm here, aren't I?" She says it like a defense, but Pearly can feel her words penetrating. Lillian glances at the waves lapping against the dock, then back at Reyna. "Fine," she says. "I'll give it another night." She turns to give Pearly a scrutinizing gaze. "I didn't know cruise ship entertainers were so insightful."

Pearly shrugs. "You learn a lot when you have to break up buffet-line fistfights and comfort grown men who lost the limbo contest." She loops an arm around Lillian. "Come on. Let's join the others."

They meet Michel and the group on the boat, a double-decker glass-walled *bateaux-mouches* with a fancy dining room and an open-air rooftop deck. Pearly dressed for the occasion – flowing palazzo pants in midnight blue satin over a tailored bodysuit with a deep "v" covering just enough to avoid a minor scandal. She's accessorized with oversized sunglasses, a faux-fur stole, and chunky pearls to match her name.

Everyone else looks nice, too. Beckett's especially snazzy, sporting a tailored vest in peacock brocade that looks like it waltzed off the set of *The Gilded Age*.

"Wow," says Pearly. "Did you make that?"

"Yeah," he says, brushing his fingers over the fabric. His eyes cloud over, and his shoulders sink a little. "I had to sneak it into my suitcase. There's, uh"—he swallows hard—"kind of a dark history behind it."

She waits to see if he wants to share more, but he doesn't. Not yet anyway. And since he's not one of her charges, she can't peek inside his mind. That's fine. They have time, and she's learned not to force things.

"Group photo!" says Michel. "For the website."

Everyone poses. Pearly more dramatically than the others. "Oooh," she says. "We're serving 'classy international tourists' so hard we just might set the internet on fire."

Click!

They settle into a table. Pearly fakes a bout of window-induced sea sickness—river-vertigo, she claims—to swap seats with George. Now he's next to Lillian. A mustachioed server in a bright blue tie sweeps in with champagne flutes. He reminds Pearly a little of her old boss, Mr. Mustard, minus the cockroach bolero. Outside, the sun is just starting to set, and waves ripple under the glass walls like an evening gown made of endless layers of blue-black silk.

The boat eases away from the dock, and the captain introduces himself over the PA with a sultry French accent. Pearly smirks. This isn't her first Parisian captain, and she knows how they like to seduce an audience. He encourages them to drink in the sights, savor the food, and "allow the music to penetrate their hearts." (And yes, in French, it feels somehow filthier.)

A live singer takes the stage. Red hair. Red dress. A spitfire, like Pearly, with a velvety voice and charisma for days. She opens with a smoky "C'est Si Bon," and Pearly cocks her head, watching her the way another performer watches the competition.

"Do you miss it?" asks Reyna.

"What, performing?" Pearly smiles, thinking of her days in drag, and all the other stages she commanded across her lifetimes. "Sometimes," she says. "Maybe more if I had a gig like this."

The first course arrives, and everyone digs in. Pearly revels in the duck foie gras with apricot chutney and the escargot bathed in garlic butter so decadent she's tempted to dab it on her wrists.

"I, uh, still haven't tried snails yet," Michel pokes at the shells. "I think I might pass for now. But, uh, y'know. Bon appetit."

Beckett eyes his portion with considerable suspicion, but after one tentative bite, he's all in. George smiles. Pearly tunes into his thoughts. He's happy to be broadening the kid's horizons. Maybe if someone had done that for him, he wouldn't have been small-minded for so long. Or passed it onto his daughter, who took it and ran with it. He still feels partly to blame for Beckett's parenting.

Through the glass, the Musée d'Orsay slides past, its massive clock faces glowing rose-gold in the setting sun.

"Oh yeah, that's the fancy old train station," says Michel.

"Former train station," says Lillian. "It's been a museum for nearly forty years. Houses the largest collection of Impressionist and post-Impressionist art in the world. But you're only a tour guide," she snarks. "Why would you know that?"

The second course lands—sea bass with root vegetables and a sauce so good Pearly asks for three extra servings. They drift under Pont Alexandre III, and suddenly everyone's crammed at the windows, snapping shots of the city's flashiest bridge with its Art Nouveau lamps, cherubs, nymphs, and those giant winged horses looking like they're ready to fly off. When the singer transitions into a slower number, Pearly sings along. It's just loud enough for the nearest tables to hear. Someone gives her a thumbs up. The singer notices.

"Uh-oh," says Pearly. "She's clocked me."

A beat later, the DJ kicks things off with the unmistakable "Uh-huh, uh-huh, uh-huh." The singer grins, gesturing to Pearly to join her.

"Do it!" says Austin. The room perks up.

Pearly stands—because of course she does—and sashays to the stage. The singer hands her a mic, and without missing a beat, they launch into a razzle-dazzling duet of *Lady Marmalade*. Pearly hams it up, pointing toward George during "Voulez-vous coucher..." just to watch him blush. Beckett laughs. Austin films. Even Lillian taps her foot under the table.

As the music crests, Pearly feels her aura flare—bright, glittery, and just a little unhinged, like a disco ball exploding. She sees the shimmer spill outward in threads of light, brushing against the auras around her.

Each time it makes contact, something shifts. A stressed-out Millennial mother stops fretting over her five-year-old and starts dancing on her chair. A bickering couple forgets their argument and starts spanking each other with forks in time to the beat. A bored waiter lets go of his ennui and shimmies down the length of the boat clacking lobster claw castanets.

This is not French restraint. It's messy, joyful, contagious: hips shaking, arms flailing, the kind of dance floor chaos you'd expect at a Midwestern wedding with an open bar. The singer beams, catching the energy, and belts even harder. Pearly grins, fanning the glow as it spreads.

They bring it home together in a who's-topping-who finale, and Pearly flips her hair and blows a kiss before strutting back to her seat. "Well," she says, fanning herself with the dessert menu, "you can take the girl out of the cruise ship..."

The final course does not disappoint. Pearly pretends to snap pics for her fake following before nibbling her way through a popcorn-and-morello cherry finger—*OMFG*—then an elderflower-raspberry cheesecake so good it ought to come with a halo. She licks the last bit of raspberry from her fork just as the boat glides past Notre-Dame, its golden reflection wavering in the dark water. Everyone "oohs" and "aahs."

"If y'all don't mind," says George, standing up, "I'd like to see this one from the rooftop deck."

Pearly gives him a minute, then follows behind. "I'm gonna go film some footage for my vlog," she lies.

She finds him at the railing, holding up his old postcard as he looks out at the cathedral. A light wind ruffles what's left of his hair as he takes in the twin bell towers, the famous rose stained-glass window, the elaborate flying buttresses and stone gargoyles. The boat has timed it just right to pass by the cathedral as a light show projects onto the façade. One moment it's a spring garden bursting into bloom, then a swirling gust of powdered snow, then a crush of soldiers moving through a battlefield in 1917.

"Stunning old broad, isn't she?" says Pearly, stepping up beside him. "Especially now, after the fire and restoration."

"Sure is," he grins. "I grew up Southern Baptist. We're not exactly known for our pomp and pageantry." He shakes his head. "But it's hard not to look at that and think there's a higher power behind the scenes."

"Yeah." Pearly rests her arms on the railing, wondering what George would think if he knew she was his spirit guide. She hasn't always embraced concepts like that when she was incarnated. A lot depended on the beliefs she was born into, or bucked against. But with every death, she remembered. And despite the laugh-so-you-don't-cry red tape of afterlife bureaucracy, she has no doubt something intelligent and loving sits at the center of it all.

"You know," says George, "I always thought I'd take my Maggie to Paris."

"Your wife?" asks Pearly, even though she knows the answer.

"Yes. She passed five years ago. Damn virus took us all by surprise."

"I'm sorry."

"It's okay. We had forty years together. That's more than most."

Pearly leans against the railing. "Tell me about her."

"Well, she baked a mean peach cobbler." They watch the light show shift to a glowing, red-pulsing heart. "She loved to paint, but she was terrible at everything but clouds. So we had cloud paintings in every room in the house, and dozens more in the attic."

"Just clouds?" says Pearly. "No thunderstorm period? No 'angry sky over the barn?'"

"She tried a sunset once. It didn't go well." He goes inward for a moment, and Pearly sees him replaying the memory. There's Maggie, stomping across the yard with a slashed pink canvas while George mows the lawn. She holds it like its diseased. He stops the mower, watches her toss it into the trash with angry tears. Then he goes to her, wraps her in an embrace.

The memory fades. George shifts his attention back to Pearly. "When she smiled," he says, "which was constantly—it was like spotting one of those double-rainbows. You just... felt good. And couldn't look away. Not that she was hard to spot in a crowd. She liked to say 'the bigger the hair, the closer to God.'"

"Preach," says Pearly. "We would've been friends for sure."

"I don't doubt that." He smiles at Pearly. "Hmm, what else? She put up with all my tinkering, even got a kick out of it, I think." He pauses, considering. "And she understood Beckett, better than his parents—or me. They had a special bond. He and I... well. His folks can be so hard on him sometimes. And I haven't always known how to show that softer side for him. It's not how I was raised. Not how I've always been, either. I'm hoping to make up for it if it's not too late."

"It's not." Pearly moves closer, rests a hand on his shoulder.

He swallows, shifting his gaze to the water. "How do you know?"

"Kids are resilient," says Pearly. "And anyway, I see it. He's already starting to warm up to you. Give it time."

He nods. They watch as the cathedral's golden lights grow smaller, swallowed by the night and the curve of the river.

"So why didn't you?" asks Pearly.

"Didn't what?"

"Take Maggie to Paris."

He shrugs. "Got busy raising kids. Grandkids. When you're paying a mortgage and saving for college, priorities shift. And Maggie, she was a homebody. Loved our porch swing more than the prospect of adventure."

"But not you."

"I'm just here for my grandson."

"You sure about that?"

He waves off the question, glances down, rubbing a thumb over the crease in his knuckles. "My story's already been written," he says. "Sometimes, I catch myself in the mirror and I say 'who is that guy?' Seventy sounds so ancient. I don't feel ancient." He holds up his hands, dotted with constellations of age spots. "These are old man hands."

Pearly arches an eyebrow. "I think that's a crock of shit, George. You've got wrinkles, not rigor mortis." She gestures out to the glittering skyline. "You finally made it to the city of your dreams. It could write you a new chapter—if you let it."

He doesn't say anything. But when he looks out over the water, she notices a gleam in his eye that wasn't there before. It's not an aura shift—not yet—but it's a step in the right direction.

A voice crackles over the PA. "If you'd like to join us for one last toast to Paris, please make your way to the dining room. We've saved the bubbles for the end."

"You coming?" he says.

"In a minute."

George nods and disappears down the stairs, leaving Pearly alone at the railing with a jumble of thoughts.

The boat drifts past Île Saint-Louis, where a young couple sits on a bench beside the river, framed by the glow of the streetlamps. They're kissing like they've forgotten the rest of the world exists—hands tangled, laughter caught in the night air. Pearly exhales, letting the sight wash over her. She tells herself it's just human chemistry, that they'll probably argue about dishes by next Tuesday. But the truth lodges beneath her ribs, that longing to be seen and safe and wanted all at once.

She thinks of Thunder. He used to look at her like that, like she was both the question and the answer. The memory hurts in the sweetest way.

A new chapter, she told George.

Could she get one, too?

She knows why she's been dragging her feet with Thunder—she doesn't want to repeat the past. Who they were, how they related. There was magic between them, but also plenty of dysfunction. She's afraid if they reconnect, they'll just slip back into old patterns.

Who says it has to be like it was before though? The future's a blank page, and they can fill it in however they want.

Right?

She doesn't even know if he still has feelings for her. Maybe he just wants to connect as friends. Maybe that would even be for the best.

All she knows is that these what-ifs aren't getting her anywhere. Pearly prides herself on being an action-taker, a soul who writes her own story. And it's time to pick up that proverbial pen.

She pulls up her telepathic text from Thunder.

Thunder: *Hey you. How about that coffee? I'm buying. You're spilling the beans.*

She thinks for a moment, then composes a response.

And before she can change her mind, she sends it.

Pearly: *Mais oui, chérie.*

***

The rooftop deck is nearly empty when Pearly Gates skips down the stairs, humming some ridiculous tune. Human music in general is woefully unrefined compared to the fungal variety. Mildreth eyes Gates from afar but does not follow. She stays at the railing, her human disguise itching in all the wrong places.

She has seen enough. The gaudy duet was to be expected. Spectacle is Gates' natural element. But watching the widower open up at Notre-Dame? His aura blossomed, like a mycelial thread searching for new ground. That was dangerous—for Mildreth. If this continues, the wager could spin out of her control. Unacceptable.

The Department is a balanced ecosystem. Pearly Gates is blight. A glittery contagion. Left unchecked, she will spread.

Fourteen

Pearly most definitely does not try on twenty-two different outfits for her coffee date. Check that—coffee outing.
No one said it was a date. Anyway, she stops counting after a
couple failed experiments with "moderately slutty librarian" and
"girl-next-door realness," but it can't be that many.

At least she's got time. Her charges are tucked into their
hotel beds, blissfully unaware their undercover spirit guide has
slipped back to the afterlife for a date. Outing.

Let's just call it coffee.

In the end, she opts for what she calls simplicity. Rainbow
sherbet hair, an off-the-shoulder sweatshirt over metallic blue
leggings, and four-inch heeled glass slippers.

"Not bad, Miss Thing," she says to the mirror, giving her curves
an approving once-over.

"BREAKING NEWS: PARIS CANCELS CROISSANTS BE-
CAUSE YOU'RE THE ONLY SNACK THEY NEED!" Oh, right.
It's *that* mirror.

"Hot stuff!" Dumb Pearly calls from the doorway, flashing a
thumbs-up. "You're gonna turn heads like the Exorcist!"

"Umm... thanks? The hair's not too much, is it?"

"No way. It screams 'lick me!'" Dumb Pearly comes in and sits at the foot of the bed. "Nervous?" she asks, watching the original fuss with her lipstick.

"Of course not. Why would I be? I've known Thunder for, like, thousands of years."

"Yeah, but you haven't hung out since he dumped you."

Pearly balks. "He didn't—" She hesitates. "Okay, I guess he did." She meets Dumb Pearly's gaze in the mirror. "What if..." she swallows, starts again. "What if he's disappointed?"

"Then he doesn't deserve you." Dumb Pearly shakes her head. "Girl, you talk like he's Mr. Perfect, but hello—you said he eats cereal with a fork. Takes two to limbo."

Pearly frowns. "Yeah. Right. Uh, what are you saying exactly?"

Dumb Pearly stands up. She takes Pearly by the shoulders, turns her away from the mirror. "Look at me. What do you see?"

"Me? Only nicer?"

Dumb Pearly snorts. "I'm the you that stuck around. The you that got a bedroom instead of a broom closet. The you that you didn't toss to the curb when the Higher-Ups gave me soul-hood." She gives Pearly's shoulders a hearty shake. "So don't act like you're not good enough. Cuz you're me. And we slay."

Pearly feels her aura brightening. She smiles. "Yeah. Okay. Thanks for the reality check."

"Anytime, girl. Now go git it."

Pearly turns away from the mirror—

"POV: YOU'RE SHINIER THAN A FRESHLY WIPED BOWL-ING TROPHY!"

***

On the way to Perkatory, Seraphina makes it abundantly clear she wants in on the Paris Adventure. First, she blasts *"Voulez-Vous"* by ABBA at full volume. Then she squirts *"Paris or Bust"* across her windshield in wiper fluid. Finally, she transforms herself into a sparkly pink Vespa and refuses to budge until Pearly promises to "think about it." With all the walking tours and group activities, she's not sure where Seraphina would fit in.

When they descend into the parking lot, Pearly sees Thunder's winged motorcycle gleaming against its kickstand. Of course he's already here. At least she isn't late for once. She gives her reflection a final check in the rearview and strolls to the entrance with what she hopes passes for casual cool.

Perkatory is the kind of place that knows it's hot and flaunts it. Neon script coils above the door, promising "afterlife-changing lattes" and "coffee to reincarnate for." Inside, astral hipsters with constellation tattoos sip, chat, and argue about oat milk as the barista staff clatters from table to table—because the staff *are* the mugs. Sentient cappuccino cups balance milk pitchers in their handles. Espresso demitasses bark orders in tiny-but-bossy voices. A ceramic mug with lipstick stains makes glowing latte art while sloshing along to the beat of ambient techno.

And there—halfway up the line—is Thunder.

He's easy to spot, with his motorcycle helmet in hand. But Pearly would know him with her eyes closed. That familiar aura—deep blue threaded with sweetness and generosity—and just enough "bad boy" to keep things interesting in the bedroom. Not that Pearly is thinking about sex. Absolutely not. No ma'am. Couldn't be farther from her mind.

This is just coffee.

"Hey," she says, sidling up next to him.

"Hey." He grins, perfect white teeth flashing against his tight white t-shirt. Pearly goes a little weak-kneed. Who wouldn't, when Thunder smiles like that? No wonder everybody loves him. "I've been checking out the menu." He holds out a laminated card and taps the top entry. "Looks like this one's their claim to fame."

Singularity Latte – Perkatory's Signature Sip. Brewed with beans aged in the event horizon of a pocket black hole, this cosmic creation is topped with self-orbiting foam that will swirl for eternity (or until you drink it). Side effects may include minor time dilation and/or slight gravitational pull toward the nearest point of interest.

Please sip responsibly. Management is not liable for emotional entanglements or existential crises.

"Oooh, danger coffee. I'm in."

Thunder grins. "I figured."

When they arrive at the counter, a stout white diner mug with a chipped rim and a faded green logo takes their order. "Two singularities?" it rasps in a Jersey accent. "Coming right up."

"I love how committed to coffee y'all are." She puts a hand on her chest. "Souls after my own heart."

The mug chuckles. "Helps me remember why we're all on this hamster wheel. Last life I was a housewife in Toledo. Abusive husband, the whole sob story. First thing I did after I finally walked out—no suitcase, no plan—was stumble into an all-night diner. Vinyl booth, four a.m., trying to hide my tears. The waitress poured me a cup. And that first sip..." A giant silver spoon stirs within the mug, echoing its emotions. "That was freedom. The first thing I ever did just for me."

"That's beautiful," says Pearly. "And honestly kind of genius, embodying your story like this."

The mug shrugs. "Marketing, honey. I know a good brand when I see one." It sets two steaming cups on the counter, gives them a once-over. "And I know a good pairing when I see it. You two lovebirds enjoy."

"Oh, we're not—" Pearly stammers. "We're, uh. Friendbirds."

The mug just smiles. "If you say so."

Pearly tries to shrug off the awkward as Thunder leads them to an empty table. He looks totally unflustered, of course. But she knows he always looks that way, even when he's not calm on the inside at all. Maybe he was doing the same thing she was, just trying to look cool. They sit across from one another and set down their lattes. Foam swirls at the top like cosmic debris orbiting an event horizon. Might be a latte, but somehow it's dark as a black hole.

"Cheers," he says, holding up his mug. "To a long overdue catch-up."

"Cheers."

Their fingertips brush as their cups clink. Pearly takes an extra-long sip, mostly to stop herself from blurting out something ridiculous. She's not sure how they managed to make a latte that tastes like chaos and possibility, but something inside her begins to loosen.

"Wowza," she says. "They're not kidding around." They set their mugs down and watch them begin to creep closer to each other like magnets.

Thunder arches a brow. "Side effects."

"Mm-hm. Totally normal. Just gravity having a crush on us." She tries to joke, but her aura is sparkling, and she can feel herself leaning toward him. "So..." She drums her extra-long French-manicured nails on the table. "What's the tea? Where are you living these days?"

"I got a place by the Nursery. It's nice enough, I guess. The soul who manifested it had these glow-in-the-dark gargoyles. They're motion activated, so every time I open a door, they belt out 'It's Raining Men.' I keep meaning to change it, but I've been busy. And I think they're starting to grow on me. They make things more interesting. Colorful."

He looks up at her with—what? Is that longing? Is he saying he misses her making things colorful and interesting? *Speculation, Your Honor.* She pushes away the thought.

"And you?" he says. "Things working out with the room-mate?"

"Honestly, yeah. You'd think a house with two Pearlys would be a Twilight Zone episode. But it's actually been great watching her become her own person. Sometimes, when I'm having a hard day, just seeing the best parts of me reflected back gives me hope. Maybe I'm not a lost cause after all."

"You don't really think that, do you?"

She takes a sip of her latte, considering. "Not anymore. Pretty sure I did when you and I were together." The mugs edge closer together. Pearly grabs hers to keep it from colliding with Thunder's. "About that," she says. "I want to apologize for... well..." She wipes a bit of foam from her lip. "I don't think I was a very good partner. I was too wrapped up in myself to see it, and you deserved better."

Thunder leans over with his elbows on the table. The table's gotten smaller, the space between them shrinking. "You know, Pearly," he says, "I've had a lot of time to process everything. And sure, there were some aspects of our relationship that weren't the healthiest, especially toward the end. But it wasn't just you. I think we both got complacent. Eternity is a long time. And after thousands of years, we were relying on our soulmate bond to do the work. So I owe you an apology, too."

Their faces inch closer together. Suddenly she can feel the warmth of his breath on her cheeks. The gentle tingle of his aura pressing up against hers. Must be the lattes. She meets his gaze, and her mind replays their last kiss. The one that broke their soulmate cord. Would there ever be a do-over? Is she even allowed to want that? She grips her chair under the table, feeling the heat simmer between them. He's got to be feeling it, too.

Thunder clears his throat. "So, uh, how's the job?"

"Mixed bag. I do love being a guide. Hard as it may be to believe, I'm actually good at helping people."

"I believe that. Any classic Pearly stories?"

She takes a sip, reflects. "Hmm. Once, I helped a girl get over her fear of the ocean by appearing as a dolphin. Swam right up, gave her a nuzzle. Someone snapped a photo. It's still framed in her bedroom."

"I love that," says Thunder. "I bet you're pretty cute as a dolphin."

"Thanks!" Pearly steamrolls forward to cover up her flushed cheeks. "Then there was Lillian. Ten years old, clutching her mama's hand at the Bakersfield Mall, saving their pennies for a birthday perfume sample set. The clerk took one look at her mother's Goodwill coat and said they'd 'probably feel more comfortable at the outlet across the street.' I made the lights flicker, the register jam, alarms wailing until the manager came running. That clerk learned real fast who didn't belong."

He smiles. "Sounds like a good use of guide privilege."

"I thought so." She grins. "There was of course that one time I magicked mold onto a rival's muffin so my charge got hired for a job instead. Didn't exactly write that one in the report."

Thunder chuckles. "Sounds like you're doing great."

"Yeah," she says, "except my boss. Let's just say she makes Mr. Mustard look like Mr. Rogers." She sips her latte again, swallowing with a flourish. "But I have a plan."

"Of course you do," he grins.

"It's a little risky."

"Do tell."

She looks around to see if anyone's listening, then she remembers she's not actually breaking any rules this time. "I kind of made a bet," she says. "If I can uplevel my charges' auras before the end of a ten-day tour of Paris, she has to promise to leave me alone. Otherwise, she can fire me or transfer me to the Null Region or whatever."

His brow furrows. "The Null Region—that's practically banishment. I heard telepathy doesn't even work out there."

She bristles. "Well, I don't expect to actually get sent there. I'm already making progress."

"Yeah, but... I mean, ten days isn't a lot of time. It can take an entire lifetime—or more—for a soul's aura to advance. What you're doing sounds like a hell of a dice roll." He crumples the napkin next to his mug like it's some kind of stress ball.

"Yes," Pearly raises an eyebrow, "a dice roll I intend to win." Studying him, she can tell she's poked a nerve, but she refuses to back down. "You always play it safe."

He leans back in his chair, popping the bubble of intimacy. "You say that like it's a curse word."

"It's not!" She bites her lip. "I mean, not necessarily. But... haven't you ever wondered what—or who—is on the other side of all that caution?" She lays both hands on the table. A challenge. "I have."

He winces, looks down. "This—this isn't about me. Look, I'm just... I'm worried about you, Pearly."

She sighs. "Couldn't you try trusting me instead? I'm not the freewheeling soul you remember. I mean, I am, but a lot has happened since we broke up. I've actually become responsible. Ish. And I'm willing to take a risk to get what I want." She forces her jaw to unclench. "I thought you'd be supportive."

"I am," he says. "I mean, I support you. But I can't be your cheerleader on this. Not with that much at stake. It's just not worth it. Please, Pearly. Try and find a way out of this, and you can still—"

"Look," Pearly pushes back her chair and stands, fighting the effects of the singularity latte. "Maybe this was a bad idea." The anger's bubbling up now, and she's afraid she's going to make a scene. She's been known to do that. "I have to get back to my charges anyway. Before Michel-the-joke-of-a-tour-guide accidentally reroutes the itinerary to Euro Disney."

"Pearly..."

She tosses her hair, aura sparking like a live wire. "Next time maybe order the Decaf of Doom. This much gravity's wasted on someone too scared to fall."

And with that, she walks out, glass slippers clacking all the way to the door.

FiFTEEN

P early's back in Paris, but her mind's still obsessing over that failure of a non-date. And if that wasn't bad enough, there's Mildreth's latest absurdity: the brand-new Karmic Expense Report system. Now every hint of intervention has to be logged like a cosmic tax return—who the charge is, what Pearly does, the so-called "spiritual cost-benefit analysis," and whether it fits under an "approved category." Pearly feels the reins tightening. She's been around the block enough to smell an excuse to get rid of her.

By the time she drags herself to the hotel curb for their Versailles day trip, she's not exactly her usual dazzling self. Still, she manages to manifest what she considers a proper tribute to Marie Antoinette: a hot-pink tulle skirt, sequined jacket, pearls looped like a lasso, and a feathered tiara perched atop a three-foot powdered wig. History buffs might quibble, but Pearly's pretty sure that if the doomed queen had been handed a Bedazzler, she'd have gone just as hard.

"Well," says Lillian, sidling up to Pearly, "if they run out of chandeliers, you can always hang yourself from the ceiling."

Pearly laughs, the knot in her chest loosening a little. "You know, Lillian," she says. "You've got a real gift for throwing shade. You'd make a damn fine drag queen..." She pauses, glancing at Lillian's beige pant-suit. "If you stopped dressing like a designer file cabinet."

Lillian makes a noise that sounds suspiciously like a laugh. She covers by scanning the curb. "No van yet, apparently. Big surprise – Michel's late again."

"I'm sure you're already composing a scathing Yelp review."

Lillian nods, like the instrument of justice she tries to be. "The public must know."

Over the next few minutes, Reyna, Lamar, Austin, and George trickle in. Reyna's only half present, doing something on her phone that looks work-related. Beckett lingers at the periphery, phone clamped to his ear, his face pinched tight. Pearly lets her guide-hearing drift closer and catches snippets of his mother's voice: *"You sound different—are you keeping something from us?"* and *"Just remember, you live under our roof."* Pearly groans, watching Beckett shut his eyes and breathe through it. George is watching too.

"Hey." Pearly rests a hand on his shoulder. "This is good for him. You're doing the right thing. I promise."

"I hope so." His gaze stays fixed on Beckett. "I used to be like them, you know. No margin for any truth but mine."

"What happened?" she asks. "To change you."

He shifts, finally looking at her. "I got old. Realized something was wrong with my principles when they didn't allow for loving my grandson." As he says it, his aura glows a little brighter. Pearly feels her own aura brightening in response. This is really working. And it's moving to see. She gets a little choked up.

"That's inspiring, George. Thank you."

As they turn back toward the curb, a sleek black Mercedes van pulls up, all polished chrome and tinted windows. The engine rolls to a stop.

"So that's what he's been up to." Lillian rolls her eyes. "Getting a hot new ride."

From the driver's seat, a figure steps out.

Except it's not Michel.

It's Thunder.

Her Thunder.

Of course, she'd know that aura anywhere. Grinning beneath a vintage leather chauffeur's cap, he looks like some impossible mash-up of French James Dean and movie-star tour guide—motorcycle jacket, dark jeans, and just enough of a silk scarf knotted at his throat to make it all très chic. Pearly's heart hammers.

What? How?

"Bonjour, mes amis!" he calls out, sweeping into a little bow as though he's been doing this his whole afterlife. "I regret to inform you that Michel is indisposed, and I'll be your guide for the duration of your trip. My name is Thomas—though most people call me Thunder." He flashes a grin. "And as a fellow American who fell hopelessly in love with Paris many years ago, I promise you an experience you'll never forget."

The sliding door eases open, and Thunder gestures inside. "All aboard for Versailles! Does anyone have questions before we pull a Louis and move in with ten thousand of our closest friends?"

"What happened to Michel?" asks Austin.

"Ahh..." Thunder shakes his head with mock gravity. "An unfortunate run-in with a gas station quiche."

"How unfortunate," Lillian snickers.

"He'll live," says Thunder, "but not happily." He winks at Pearly.

The muffin. He'd taken her story about hexing Danielle's competition with mold and ran with it. The nerve. The gall. She's supposed to be the hellion, the rule-breaker—not gentle, 'babies love me' Thunder. Pearly can't decide if she wants to throttle him or jump his bones. Possibly both.

Thunder helps each passenger into the van, exchanging pleasantries and checking off names. Pearly dawdles at the end of the line. When he finally gets to her, he takes her hand. Her skin tingles.

"Madame," he says. She feels a little woozy. "You must be the legendary Pearly Gates."

"Legendary? I didn't know I had a reputation."

"Oh, I've seen your vlog. Didn't they stamp it on your passport? *Warning: liable to inspire outlandish schemes.*"

She shakes her head. "Must've gotten lost in the paperwork. Typical."

Her knees wobble, but she yanks herself onto the seat beside Austin.

"Do you two know each other?" he says.

"What? You mean, me and him? Ha! Why would you say that?"

"You're flustered."

"I am not," she snaps, fanning herself with exaggerated dignity. "This wig is just making me overheat."

"Nope." Austin crosses his arms. "Not buying it. I am an expert in detecting chemistry, and there is definitely something bubbling between you two."

Pearly grumbles but doesn't argue. She's still in shock. What is Thunder doing here? He isn't even a spirit guide, which makes the whole scenario that much more unsanctioned. He said he'd be leading them for the rest of the trip. But what about his work at the Nursery? Did he conjure up a Dumb Thunder to take over? Okay, that seems unlikely. But then again, so was this. Maybe Pearly isn't the only one who's changed.

Thunder clears his throat and starts the van. "Versailles wasn't built for comfort, or even beauty," he says, as they pull into traffic. "It was politics. Louis XIV wanted the world to know he was supreme. He drained a third of the treasury to create a palace so dazzling that foreign ambassadors walked into the Hall of Mirrors and left convinced they'd seen the center of the universe. His vassals had to spend their time begging for the chance to put on his shoes in the morning instead of plotting against him at home. Versailles was propaganda in stone and gold—and it worked."

Pearly stares at the back of his head, still trying to work it out. More importantly, *why* is he here? Is this about his so-called self-development as a soul... or is it about her? Maybe he really does want to reconnect. As friends. Or...

Thunder grins, tapping the wheel. "Of course, the reality wasn't all gold leaf. Versailles reeked. No plumbing. Nobles relieved themselves in stairwells and behind curtains. People carried pomanders and drenched themselves in perfume just to breathe. Rumor has it Louis hated warm water and only took three baths his entire life, but that's probably an exaggeration. Still, the place stunk. But to be fair, most places did."

Lillian wrinkles her nose. "Gold on the walls. Crap in the corners. So basically a royal litter box."

The van erupts in laughter, and even Lillian cracks a smile, but Pearly's too busy obsessing to pay much attention. Of course he'd go and do something epic—heroic and, okay, maybe a little swoony—right after she'd sworn him off. Pearly squirms, crossing her legs under all that tulle, trying to settle the nerves in her stomach.

"Then came Marie Antoinette, everyone's favorite."

"Yes!" says Austin. "I must know every scandalous detail. No censorship!"

Thunder chuckles. "Well, let's start with the basics. She arrived from Austria at fourteen, a teenager expected to save a dynasty. She quickly gained a reputation for excess—lavish parties, rampant gambling. By twenty, her hairstyles were the most famous in Europe. Towering constructions shaped like ships, gardens, even entire battles." He shifts his gaze, finding Pearly in the rearview mirror. "Though I must admit"—he winks—"your wig would give her a run for her money."

Pearly arches an eyebrow. "Bring it on, darling. I'm ready for that lip-sync smackdown."

"In any case," Thunder continues, "for all the spectacle, she longed for escape. So she commissioned a private hamlet—a little village where she could show her kids how farming worked. People said she played a milkmaid while peasants starved outside the walls. Didn't exactly go over well with the public. You'll see it yourselves, after we tour the main palace."

Pearly exhales, her grip tightening on the seat cushion. She needs answers. And before this day is over, she'll get them.

***

As soon as they spill out of the van, Pearly angles herself in front of the palace gates, tall spikes of gilded iron glittering in the morning sun. She flips her phone into selfie mode.

"Hey Pearly Girlies," she says, sweeping her free arm toward the sprawling façade. "Reporting live from Versailles—the place where subtlety checked out centuries ago. Behind me? Twenty years of construction, enough gold leaf to blind a small country, and a front gate that says, 'Yes, peasants, your taxes are working hard.' If excess had a zip code, babes, this would be it."

She puckers a kiss toward the camera. "Say hi to France famille! And say hi to our new tour guide and a fan of the channel, Thomas—oh, sorry! I mean Thunder! Say 'bonjour,' Thunder!" She angles the camera at him. He waves and tips his hat.

The gates creak open and they cross the gravel courtyard, shoes crunching in rhythm. Thunder launches into more historical context. Pearly only half-listens. She's still fighting Thunder's magnetic pull. By the time they step into the palace, she's swallowed whole by chandeliers, frescoes, and more gilt than a drag queen's dressing room. *Perfection.* Pearly could definitely live here. And she likes the idea of ruling the world with the power of glamour. Maybe she'll manifest some of this for her afterlife home. Dumb Pearly would surely approve.

Pearly's less impressed by the King's Bedchamber. Glitz is one thing, but having your sleeping rituals—and sex life—on full display? No thanks. The bed sits on a raised platform like a throne draped in gold and crimson velvet. Chairs for the highest-ranking courtiers are arranged in stiff rows at the foot of the bed, explains Thunder, because even sleep was political theater.

"This wasn't just a bedroom," he says. "It was a stage. The king's 'rising' and 'going to bed' were public ceremonies. Nobles elbowed each other for the honor of handing him his shirt or holding the candlestick. Imagine dozens of people packed in here, watching you brush your teeth—because proximity to the king was power." Thunder gestures toward the bed. "And for Louis XVI and Marie Antoinette, this room got even more awkward. They were married at fourteen and fifteen, and it took them seven years to produce a child. The court obsessed over it. Pamphlets mocked them, rumors flew. Was he impotent, was she uninterested, was there some medical issue? Nope. They were just teenagers under the crushing weight of an empire, with zero Sex Ed."

The group laughs and moves on, but Pearly notices Reyna hanging back, a disturbed look on her face. She snaps a photo, but it's more like the way someone would document a crime scene than show off a piece of history.

"Hey," says Pearly, sidling closer. "Whatcha thinking?"

Reyna lowers her phone, gaze fixed on the bed. "It's wild, isn't it? Turning the most private part of your life into public property. I mean, I know that producing an heir was politically important, I watched *Game of Thrones*, I get it. But the lack of body autonomy is just... ugh." She shakes her head. "And honestly? That hasn't really gone away. People still make assumptions. They want you to want what they want, because obviously that's the only way you'll be happy."

Pearly lets that settle, then nods. "You're right. Folks love to write other people's scripts. But let me ask you—if you get to write yours, what's in it? What would make you happy?"

Reyna blinks, like no one's ever asked her that before. She takes a moment, really thinking. "Honestly? I haven't thought about it much. I've been so focused on work and getting ahead." She bites her lip, looks up. "I feel like I'm supposed to want to find 'my person.' Fall in love, build a life together. And I guess that sounds okay in theory, but in reality it's felt like putting on a scratchy, too-small sweater. So maybe what I want..." Her voice wavers. She looks up at Pearly. "I'd like to find a way to fall in love with the world."

Pearly leans in, gently takes Reyna's hand. "Sweetheart, that line should be embroidered on a pillow and sold at Anthropologie."

Reyna laughs despite herself, the heaviness breaking just enough.

"How about we start with Paris?" says Pearly. "Redefine the City of Love on your terms."

Reyna smiles, and Pearly feels a brightening in her aura. "Yeah," she says. "I'd like that."

The group drifts down another corridor, heels clicking on parquet, when suddenly the hallway detonates into brilliance. Seventeen windows flare against seventeen mirrors, chandeliers scattering firelight across marble and gilt. Pearly stops dead. If Versailles had a thesis statement, this was it. She pulls out her phone once again. Even if it's a fake vlog, there's something satisfying in describing what she's seeing.

"The Hall of Mirrors," she says. "AKA the world's longest runway. Two hundred and forty feet of marble fabulousness, gardens on one side, infinity mirrors on the other. And the ceiling? Louis XIV's victory scrapbook in oil paint. Honestly, babes, the only thing missing is Donna Summer."

Satisfied, she pockets her phone and rejoins the others. Thunder's in the middle of a history lesson. He gestures upward, voice echoing through the gallery. "And here's the flex: mirrors were insanely expensive in the 1600s. Venetian mirrors were a trade secret, so Louis XIV bribed the glassmakers to defect. A few of them got hunted down and killed when they tried to sneak back. All so Louis could line up seventeen windows with seventeen mirrors and show the world that he was richer than God."

"Wasn't the furniture in here originally silver?" asks Lillian.

"That's right," says Thunder. "But it didn't last long. Louis had them melted down in 1689 to pay for a war. Imagine redecorating your house by funding an army with your coffee table."

"Dude," says Austin. "You are so much better than Michel." He turns to the group. "Right? Sorry not sorry, Michel."

Nods all around. Pearly has to admit, Thunder is nailing it—knowledgeable, funny, magnetic. She wonders how he knows so much about Versailles. She doesn't remember living that life together. Another mystery that needs solving.

As the others wander off to snap photos, Pearly lingers. She tilts her head, admiring her reflection in the world's most epic mirror—sequins blazing, wig feathers bobbing, tiara a starburst of rhinestones. For once, she actually looks like she belongs.

Thunder drifts up beside her, eyes twinkling. "The fairest of them all. I think Louis would've loved you."

She grins, meeting his eyes in the glass. "Which one?"

"Fourteenth for sure. Fifteenth too, though his mistress might've angled for the guillotine."

"Ah yes," Pearly says. "I missed the beheadings. France was already a republic by the time I incarnated here."

His hand brushes her waist, casual but electric. In the reflection, it almost looks like they're posing for a portrait. Two spirits framed by chandeliers and endless lights.

And then the mirror ripples.

The surface wavers, as if heat is rising off marble. Pearly gasps as their reflections stretch and multiply, expanding into an infinite corridor of selves.

On the left, she sees their past lives: stolen dances in candlelit halls, sunburnt laughter in desert markets, long nights at war clinging to each other in the trenches. Their lives were joyous and brutal and shallow and deep. And always, they found each other. Always, they loved.

And always, at the end—in a quiet corner of the afterlife—one of them broke the bond. The soulmate cord severed. The pattern reset.

To the right, futures unfurl: glimmers of possibility stacked like glass panes. In most of them, the cycle repeats—love found, life lived, cord cut. But a few shine differently. In those, the cord remains intact, pulsing brighter in enduring intimacy. A future rewritten.

Her stomach twists. Is this prophecy, or just her fear and longing refracted back at her?

She steals a glance at Thunder's reflection, but his eyes are unreadable. Is he seeing it too? Or is it just her?

The mirror shudders and collapses, the visions folding into plain marble and glass. Just their two reflections remain, side by side, captured like a portrait that history forgot.

"Well, that was weird." Pearly forces a laugh. "We should probably move on before some evil witch sends a huntsman for us."

She peels herself away, pulse racing. She still wants to corner him, demand answers, but not here. Not with that vision clinging to her.

"Right," he says. "I should, uh, go check on the others."

She moves away from the mirror, but her pulse won't slow down. She still wants to talk to him, to find out what the hell is going on. But she needs a moment after... whatever that was.

By the time they reach the Queen's Hamlet, Pearly's ready to engage. She forces herself to push down the impatience and look around. The Hamlet is storybook quaint—thatched roofs, pastel cottages, ripe orchards, and lots of cute farm animals. It's giving rustic fantasy, a countryside set with a costume budget. Everything's too neat, too polished. It's mud without the mess.

Austin crouches next to a goat, grinning at Lamar through the phone camera. "Hey babe, can we get a goat for our anniversary?"

Lamar arches a brow. "I thought you wanted that Cartier watch?"

"Now I want a Cartier goat."

The goat bleats. Everyone laughs.

"Okay, so it's a farm," says Beckett. "What's the big deal?"

"That's the paradox," says Thunder. "On one hand, it *was* just a farm. Real crops, real animals, food for the palace table. For Marie Antoinette, it was an escape. A place to walk, to breathe, to live a simpler life. But the flip side?" He shakes his head. "Versailles poured insane amounts of France's money into projects like this while ordinary people went hungry. That tension made the Hamlet infamous. Was it a refuge? Yes. Was it extravagance in the face of suffering? Also yes."

The group disperses to walk the grounds, meandering between the cottages and surrounding gardens. Pearly sees her chance—Thunder alone—and grabs it.

"Hey," she says. "Can we talk?"

He studies her for a moment, then nods toward a narrow path leading past the orchards. They cut across the grass toward a low stone building with whitewashed walls and a tiled roof—the Dairy. Inside, the air smells of milk, marble walls gleaming pale in the filtered light. They climb a winding staircase to a fairy-tale tower overlooking the estate. It's the perfect setting for a kiss. But Pearly's no Disney princess, and she's not ready for Happily Ever After. She has questions.

"Thunder—"

"I'm sorry." He swallows hard, then takes a deep breath. "You were right. At the café. I do play it safe. I could incarnate a thousand more times, making all the right choices, working my way up the spiritual ladder. But..." He gestures to the orchards, the cottages, the whole manicured fantasy around them. "What's the point of all this? To get an 'A' on the Higher-Ups' report card? Or to have the fullest possible experience of life?" He turns back to her, the vulnerability etched on his face. She can tell this has been eating at him. "I don't pretend to have all the answers,

Pearly. But you poked at something that needed poking. So—" his mouth curves into that familiar grin— "here I am."

Her heart compresses. That grin could undo empires. "How exactly did you pull this off? There's no way you got permission from the Department of Human Relations."

"Nope." He leans against the cool stone wall. "I told the Nursery I was going on vacation. I just didn't tell them where."

Pearly lets out a low whistle, shaking her head. "Impressive." And so unlike him. This little stunt is reckless and terrifying and maybe the bravest thing she's ever seen him do.

Silence stretches between them. Through the open window, sunlight glances off the thatched roofs below. It's a little too golden, too perfect.

"You know," he says at last, "I worked here once. As a dairymaid. Met the queen herself a couple of times."

"I suspected as much," she smirks. "You're a little too good."

His eyes flash, teasing. "I don't think you've complained in the past."

Pearly flushes, clearing her throat. "So what was the Queen like? She didn't really say 'let them eat cake,' did she?"

He shakes his head. "She meant well, I think. Wanted a taste of the simple life. So she had us pour milk into gold cups for courtiers in silk hats. I remember feeling..." His forehead creases. "It was exciting, at the time. To be close to her. But she was always a million miles away." He exhales. "The only thing that felt real was caring for the animals. Once, I held this scrawny little goat that wouldn't stand on its own, and for a second—just a second—I felt like I was holding the whole world together. That was enough."

Pearly can't help but laugh. "Classic Thunder. Always nurturing the newborns."

His eyes cloud over. "Not always. There were other lives, you know. Ones that weren't so nurturing."

"I know."

His shoulders soften. "Pearly, I've been thinking..." He steps closer, close enough that she can smell leather and burning leaves and vanilla with a hint of tobacco. "Maybe this is a chance for us to start fresh. Get to know one another as if we're meeting for the first time. No history. No assumptions. No hiding. Just you, me, and Paris. We've both been here, but never together. What do you say?"

She'd never let herself dream of a proposition like this. Yet here it is, dangling between them like one of Versailles' glittering chandeliers. Should she trust it? The mirrors said they were doomed to repeat the past. Maybe they were. Pearly's never let the odds stop her, but seeing all those unhappy reflections—it makes her wonder. Every time they cut that cord, the pain was almost unbearable. Does she really want to risk putting herself through that again? Maybe it's better to keep him at a distance.

But she wants this. It feels right. There has to be a reason they keep finding one another. There has to be a real chance to get it right.

The bigger question: does she deserve it? She's certainly screwed things up enough, on Earth and in the spirit world. Put herself first. Made bad choices. Blamed others for her problems. She's lied and manipulated to get what she wants. Most of the cord-cutting between her and Thunder resulted from her own unwillingness to grow. But she has grown.

And she does deserve this. That's the difference between New Pearly and Old Pearly—this one knows her worth.

"Scares the shit out of me." She takes his hand. "Let's do it."

Sixteen

The Palais-Royal courtyard looks like a set of checkers possessed by Beetlejuice. Designed in the 80s, its black-and-white striped columns jut out from the stone, clashing playfully with the golden arcades and shuttered windows of the palace surrounding them. Pearly poses for photos with the gang as they wait for Thunder to emerge from the waffle joint, the first treat on today's food tour. But her heart's not really in the poses. She feels a little tingly, and she's pretty sure it's not due to the morning breeze. More like she's carrying a secret—no, not a secret. A seed of possibility.

Still, her job comes first. She can't get so distracted by the Thunder Situation that she forgets why they're here in the first place. Mildreth would love that. She'd be playing right into Mildreth's hands. (Or her vines, or whatever.)

Thunder comes out of an arched doorway carrying a tray of golden-brown waffles dusted with powdered sugar. The smell alone hushes the group mid-selfie. He sets the tray on a nearby bench and beckons them closer.

"This," Thunder gestures to the striped columns, "is the Palais-Royal. Once the playground of cardinals and kings. Later, the hub of artists and revolutionaries. And today, a place to catch up, to gossip, to watch the passing parade. People come here to linger—to eat, to argue, to flirt, to gamble. To live." He takes a bite of his waffle, leaving a powdery residue on his upper lip. Pearly is tempted to lick it off. "Now, compared to the rest of France," he explains, "Paris is go-go-go. But compared to us Americans, even the Parisians are masters of slowing down. It's about appreciating what's in front of you. So if there's one thing I'd like to ask of you today, it's to follow their lead. To savor. I hope you brought your appetites," he says, as plates of waffles disappear into waiting hands. "Because these? These are perfection."

Crunching sounds fill the air as everyone digs in, one by one until only Reyna's left. She's off to the side, thumbs flying, eyes glued to her phone. Thunder notices and gives Pearly a pointed look. She nods, grateful to have him as "sous-chef" of guide work. And it's true, Reyna has been glued to her phone. Not exactly optimal conditions for spiritual awakening.

"Hey Reyna!" She swivels toward her charge, phone already in hand. "This deserves a reaction shot. Can I film your first bite for the vlog?"

Reyna laughs, cheeks flushing. She looks embarrassed to have been caught work-texting, but also grateful that Pearly didn't call her out directly. "Sure. But seriously, it's a waffle. How life-changing could it be?"

Pearly just smirks and hits record. "Okay, Pearly Girlies—welcome to *Pearly Slays Paris*, Food Tour Edition. Stop one: we got waffles dusted with magic sugar, and we got Reyna here about to give us a review. Ready? Steady? And... bite!"

Reyna freezes as the waffle hits her mouth, eyes widening. "Oh..." She swallows, then smiles. "This is... it's kind of like otap. My Lola used to make those. Flaky, sugary, so messy you'd end up with crumbs all over your shirt." She glances at the powdered sugar dusting her fingers. "Except this is softer. Warmer. Like if otap was just a little bit extra."

"Like me!" Pearly gushes, before returning to reporter mode. "So, what's your glitter rating?"

"Huh?"

"Zero to five—how sparkly is that waffle?"

Reyna facepalms, holding the half-eaten waffle up to the camera. "Ten."

"Ten?! Sure sounds life-changing to me! Well, you've heard it here first, folks: waffles are the new psychedelic gateway drugs. And... bon appetit!"

When she finishes eating, Reyna excuses herself to use the restroom. Afterwards, she catches up to Pearly, a scandalized look on her face. "What is *up* with the toilets here? No lids! None! Do people just... squat?"

Pearly grins. "It's supposed to be more hygienic."

Reyna blinks. "For who?"

"Anyone with good aim and strong thighs."

Their next stop is no less divine: Alain Ducasse, the legendary Parisian chef who also dabbled in chocolate. But today isn't about chocolate—not yet. Today is about gelato. Italian, yes, but this is the French version. While the others swoon over rich flavors like hazelnut praline hibiscus and Peruvian chocolate, Lillian orders the herb sorbet.

"Really?" says George. "What's in it?"

She takes a spoonful, eyes half-closed. "Basil... cilantro. Mmmm. Thyme, I think. Orange peel. Ginger." She nods, satisfied. "Bright, sharp, completely unexpected." Then, all serious: "If I were ever foolish enough to ruin my life by marrying again, it would be to Alain Ducasse."

George steps up. "I'll have what she's having."

Beckett goes basic with vanilla, and when George offers him a taste of the weird green scoop, he makes a face. "Pass."

"You sure?" says Lillian. "Travel is supposed to expand your horizons. Not much of that back home, I'd imagine."

"God, no," Beckett mutters. He eyes the sorbet again. "Alright, Gramps, give me a bite." One taste, and his eyebrows shoot up. "Whoa. That's actually amazing. Like... garden Sprite." He turns to Lillian. "Okay, you were right. Thanks for pushing me."

"My pleasure," she says. Pearly notices the faint brightening in her aura—and George's too. She only wishes Mildreth would give bonus points for Beckett's growth, but that seems unlikely.

As they wind their way through the 1st arrondissement to the next stop, Thunder slips back into tour guide mode. "Anyone can call themselves a bakery," he says, "but boulangeries can only use four ingredients in their baguettes: flour, water, salt, and either yeast or sourdough starter. No preservatives. No freezing. And everything has to be made on-site." He parks them at an outdoor table under a sycamore tree, the late morning light dappling under its leaves. "Wait here," he says. "This one might take a little longer, but I promise it'll be worth it."

Pearly watches Beckett snap photos of the scenery, crouching low to frame the shot just so. He isn't aiming at the postcard view of the street. He's zeroed in on the way a bicycle's red basket pops against the gray stone wall, or the way sunlight gleams on a row of pastry tarts in a window. "Kid's got a good eye," she says to George, sitting beside her.

George nods, pride registering across his face before something darker chases it away.

Pearly raises her voice. "So what do you want to do with all that creative mojo, Beckett?"

Beckett shrugs without looking up from his camera. "Design stuff. Fashion, maybe. If I ever make it out of Tennessee." He tries to make it a joke, but there's an edge to his voice.

"Hey, not if," says Pearly, "but when? There's a big world out there, Becks, and it's waiting for you."

He fiddles with the lens cap, buying time. "It's... complicated." He lowers the camera. "Let's just say not everyone back home thinks runway shows are a noble calling. Dad thinks if I can't tackle him in a football jersey, then something must be wrong with me."

George shifts in his chair, eyes fixed on the cobblestones.

Lillian glances over. Her gaze narrows, but her voice is softer than Pearly's heard from her before. "Beckett, none of that is your fault."

Beckett just waves a hand. "Try telling him that." He snaps a photo of the tabletop, as if the pattern in the wood grain is suddenly fascinating. "He's got this way of making it sound like every problem in the world is mine. Wrong shirt, wrong friends, wrong everything."

Pearly leans in. "Sounds like maybe the problem isn't you."

That lands. Beckett swallows, working his jaw, but he doesn't argue. He just shrugs.

The silence hangs heavy. Pearly looks to George, willing him to ask more questions, or affirm the kid, or even just hug him. George finally clears his throat, but whatever words he means to say dissolve before they reach his lips. He just pats Beckett's shoulder once, awkward and brief. Pearly has to work to keep her face neutral.

Before the moment can collapse under its own weight, Thunder reappears balancing a tray of steaming quiches. "Hope you saved room," he says cheerfully.

The quiche is still warm, its golden crust flaking at the touch of a fork to reveal a silky custard laced with cheese and caramelized onion. Steam rises in buttery spirals, rich enough to make Pearly's stomach growl. But as Thunder passes out the plates, he must notice the underlying tension as Pearly gets a telepathic ping.

Thunder: *Uhh... what'd I miss?*

Pearly: *Family drama. Everyone's uncomfortable but no one's talking. Like when you get a haircut so bad people start complimenting your earrings.*

Thunder suppresses a smirk and retreats to safer ground, refilling water glasses. Beckett, meanwhile, shrugs and spears a hefty bite of quiche.

"Let's just eat," he says, trying to sound casual. "New foods, new experiences, right?" He takes a bite, then points his fork like it's Exhibit A. "And this one? Totally worth it."

As the group digs in, Pearly tunes in to George's inner world.

He's still spinning from Beckett's words, replaying them over and over in his mind. Was it just a teenage exaggeration, or something darker he'd been too cowardly to see? And if it's the latter, what on earth is he supposed to do about it?

Pearly would like to rest a hand on George's knee, to say, "Hey, this is good. He's opening up..." but the kid's right there.

As they finish off the quiche, Pearly watches Beckett. He's quiet again, back to photographing the pastries in the window. She reminds herself that progress doesn't come in a single confession, but in crumbs. She just hopes those crumbs become a whole quiche by the end of the trip.

After that, it's on to Jeffrey Cagnes for what Thunder swears is Paris's best croissant. "They're known for their tarts," he says. "But their croissants... let's just say if I were planning my last meal on Earth, this would be on the tray."

"That's a lofty claim," says Lillian.

"You're not wrong," Thunder agrees. "So what's your criteria?"

"Hmm, let's see…" Lillian holds up a hand, ticking off points. "Buttery. Flaky. Tender inside, golden outside. Pretty enough to seduce you, sturdy enough to survive the first bite. And most importantly—how do you feel while you're eating it? Because a Parisian croissant isn't just food. It's an experience."

"You're damn right," echoes Thunder. "So, Lillian. Since you're the connoisseur, how about you get us started? This one's all you."

Lillian slides her croissant out of the bag with a skeptic's eye. It's a work of art: crescent curves perfectly arched, the crust lacquered in gold, layers so fine you can see the air between them. She turns it over in her hands as though testing for weak points.

"Well," she says, with a dry look to camera. "It certainly looks nicer than the frozen crap I burned at two a.m. last week. But looks can be deceiving. Don't get your hopes up, Pearly Girlies."

"Thank you, Lillian," says Pearly. "Always prudent to keep our joy in check."

With exaggerated caution, Lillian breaks the croissant in half. A sigh escapes her before she can stop it. The interior is a honeycomb of delicate layers, glistening with butter, the scent rising warm and rich. "Well, damn," she murmurs despite herself. Then she takes a bite.

Her eyes flutter shut. A soft, incredulous laugh slips out. "Oh… oh my." She covers her mouth as if embarrassed, but the damage is done. Her smile breaks wide, unguarded and luminous. It's the first flicker of real happiness anyone has seen from her the entire trip. Then she actually giggles. "This is wonderful," she says, tearing up. "Just as I remembered."

"Yeah?" says Pearly. "From when?"

"My semester abroad." Her smile turns wistful, nostalgic. "A lifetime ago." She looks into the camera, holds up the croissant. "This," she says, aura sparkling, "is worth the plane ticket."

Pearly lowers the camera, grinning. "And there you have it, folks. Croissant: one. Lillian's cynicism: zero."

George, who's been watching the whole thing with an amused smile, leans closer. "Careful," he teases. "If Paris can get you giggling over a croissant, who knows what else it'll talk you into."

Lillian shoots him a sideways glance, eyes narrowing as if to scold—but her lips are still curved, betraying her. "Don't tell anyone. I have a reputation to maintain."

"Your secret's safe with me," he says.

She waves him off, but Pearly catches the faintest blush. Oh yeah. Something's brewing between those two.

Across the table, Reyna tears off the last bite of her croissant a little too fast, flaky crumbs dusting her shirt. She fumbles for a napkin, muttering under her breath.

"You okay?" Pearly asks.

"Yeah." Reyna shrugs, brushing a strand of hair from her face. "I mean, it's cute—the old people flirting. But also a little... triggering, I guess?" She turns away, focusing a little too hard on folding the napkin into sharp creases. "I'm used to it though."

Pearly raises an eyebrow. "Triggering how?"

"Oh, you know." Reyna smirks without much humor. "My anxiety about dying alone. All that good stuff." She dunks the last shred of croissant into her coffee like it's no big deal.

Pearly doesn't press, but she files it away.

"Time for the next course," Thunder announces, shepherding them down a narrow side street and into a tiny bakery, all warm bread and flour dust in the air. He emerges moments later with a tray filled with slim, crusty baguettes and a sampler of cheeses. There's a soft brie, a tangy comté, and a pungent bleu. The group tears in, trading bites and reactions. Pearly notes the way Beckett arranges his plate into a mini composition, almost like he's plating for a magazine.

"And now, the pièce de résistance!" Thunder presents a tray of steaming mugs, rich cocoa layered with orange peel and spice.

"Careful," he warns, handing them out one by one. "This isn't Swiss Miss. It's closer to liquid velvet." The others laugh, already lifting cups to their lips. Beckett's already Instagramming his while Austin and Lamar debate whether it tastes more like mousse or hot pudding.

As the argument rages on, Thunder turns to Pearly, one mug still in hand. "Walk with me a sec?"

He guides her a few steps aside, away from the bustle. When he finally offers her the cup, he doesn't just hand it over. He keeps hold of it, inviting her to lean in for the first sip.

The chocolate coats her tongue—dark, silky, almost overwhelming. Pearly shivers, and not from the autumn air. Thunder watches her reaction with warmth in his eyes.

"Remember?" he says.

And then a trapdoor opens and she's falling backward through memory.

***

Madrid, 1692

The convent is silence and sameness. Prayers at the bell, work at the loom, a crust of bread at supper. In this life, Pearly and Thunder go by Sister Magdalena and Sister Theresa. God has called them to simplicity—at least that's what the Church tells them. But for them, the convent is full of hidden glances, half-smiles, and secret laughter that makes the fasting hours bearable.

That night, after Compline's final prayers, Magdalena slips into Theresa's narrow chamber with something hidden in her sleeve. She unwraps a small bundle of linen to reveal a dark, pungent paste. The scent of roasted beans and spice fills the little room.

"Chocolate?" Theresa's eyes widen. "You'll have us excommunicated."

Magdalena grins, reckless and unrepentant. "So what if the Pope says no?" She leans closer, lowering her voice. "Let him keep his decrees. We'll keep our secrets. And our chocolate."

She fetches a small earthen cup, pours in the hot water she smuggled from the kitchen. The paste softens, then melts, frothed with a wooden stick until steam curls between them. The drink is thick and bittersweet, laced with cinnamon and sugar. Magdalena takes the first sip, savoring the richness against her tongue, then presses the cup into Theresa's reluctant hands.

Their fingers brush on the rim. Theresa tastes, and her expression softens despite herself. "If we're damned for this," Magdalena muffles her laughter in her sleeve, "let us be damned."

Theresa shakes her head, though she can't hide her smile. "And may the angels forgive us."

They pass the cup between them, giggles hushed in the stone chamber, lips touching where the other has just sipped. Each taste is a rebellion. Love, whatever name it bears, must taste like this: impossible to confess, and all the more glorious for being shared.

***

Pearly blinks, the world sliding back into place—the chatter of the group, the clink of mugs, the cold Paris air nipping at her nose. She exhales, grounding herself.

"Yes," she says at last. "I remember." She looks up, meets his gaze. "Falling in love with you was never the hard part." Her hand lifts almost of its own accord, brushing his cheek. "The hard part was not blowing it up."

"Maybe so," he says. "But we're not the same souls we were then. Otherwise, what's the point of reincarnation? Have some hope for us, Pearly Gates." He turns the cup in his hands, then places his mouth over the place where Pearly just drank. He takes a long, slow sip, then returns the cup to her and rejoins the group.

Pearly's knees wobble. She forces herself to breathe. Still, after all this time...

"Ummmm... what was that?"

Pearly freezes. She whips around to find Austin leaning against a lamppost, Lamar perched on the curb beside him, both grinning like cats who've cornered a canary.

She shrugs in mock innocence. "What was what?"

"Oh, please," says Austin. "Don't tell me you two don't have some kind of torrid history."

Pearly huffs. "Okay, okay. Fine. We..." She trails off, considering how to frame it. "Used to be together."

"I knew it!" Austin flings a hand skyward. "Spill the tea, girl. Illicit affairs? Boardroom-to-bedroom betrayals? Secret children? Deadly duels at dawn?"

"Nothing that dramatic," she lies, though she feels her cheeks flushing. Honestly, Austin's just scratching the surface.

"Could've fooled us," Lamar teases. "Looks to me like lover-boy's ready to rekindle the flame."

Austin claps his hands together. "Girlfriend, you need to get. On. That."

"Maybe. I don't know." Pearly shifts her weight, feeling suddenly sixteen for the millionth time. "It's complicated." She realizes that this is the same brush-off Beckett gave to her.

"Honey," Austin says with exaggerated gravitas, "love is always complicated. That's what keeps the fanfic spicy."

"Okay, okay," Pearly laughs, "but if you two start a ship name, I'm cutting you off."

"What, like Punder?" Austin grins. "Or Thurly."

"Oooh, Thurly," says Lamar. "I like it."

"Really? I like Punder better."

"Y'all are incorrigible." Pearly walks away before they can wheedle more out of her. She's not used to being on this side of the dynamic. But she has to admit, she kinda likes being doted on, even in a teasing way. All in all, the day's gone well. But just as she's about to give herself a pat on the back, a telepathic message comes through that ruins whatever's left of her appetite:

Mildreth Snaggs: *All guides are required to report in person for a daily department meeting. Effective immediately.*

Suddenly all those pastries aren't sitting too well in her stomach.

SEVENTEEN

The mandatory morning meeting is about as useful as seatbelts on an escalator. Pearly fidgets in her chair, half-listening to Mildreth drone about accountability circles and good spiritual hygiene. The agenda: five-minute updates on each guide's charges. It really could've been an email. Pearly's fairly sure Mildreth only mandated in-person attendance to mess with her. Teleporting back and forth from the spirit world is exhausting.

"Hylonome?" she says. "Please share your update."

Everyone turns to the white-robed centaur at the far end of the table. The one sporting the gold sticker on her aura, awarded from Mildreth for "administrative excellence." Pearly struggles not to roll her eyes.

Hylonome shifts her hooves under the table, clears her throat. "My charges are responding beautifully to the subliminal gratitude prompts I seeded in their morning routines. One of them paused to admire a sunrise yesterday—precisely on schedule—which correlated with a measurable uptick in aura coherence. I've documented everything in a growth-tracking meta-chart, which I've shared with the group drive."

Her share receives a chorus of appreciative murmurs.

"Excellent work as always." Mildreth's electric blue eyes gleam with satisfaction. "Thank you, Hylonome. How about you, Seth-Squared?"

A lanky soul in a short-sleeved button-down pipes up. It's hard for Pearly to focus on him due to the shadowy mirror image overlapping with his form. "Steady progress," he says. "I've fine-tuned their subliminal nudges so they now default to choosing whole grains over refined sugars, and early indicators suggest a 9% improvement in long-term health trajectories. I'll circulate a spreadsheet after the meeting."

Heads nod. One guide manifests a glowing thumbs-up.

"Very good, Seth-Squared." Mildreth preens, smoothing a patch of lichen. "This is the kind of diligence that elevates the entire department." She turns to Pearly. Not that she'd been smiling before, but something in her expression definitely wilts. "Pearly Gates. What do you have to share with the group?"

Pearly grits her teeth. There's no universe in which Mildreth is impressed by anything she says, and anyway, Mildreth practically salivates at the thought of Pearly failing. It looks like her boss is already watching behind the scenes, so why bother dressing it up? She leans back in her chair, crosses her feet up on the table, and addresses the room.

"I ate the most glorious croissant," she announces. "In Paris. With my charges. Who think I'm a retired cruise ship director."

Gasps ripple down the table. One drops a scroll. Another manifests a string of pearls just to clutch them for dramatic effect.

"It's all unfolding exactly as I envisioned," Pearly continues. "I'm pretty sure Lillian experienced her first moment of genuine joy in forty years. George is finally starting to connect with his grandson. Reyna is seeing the world—and herself—through new eyes. It's been kind of magical, honestly." She almost mentions Thunder, then thinks better of it. She might be officially on the job, but he isn't. Best not to drag him into this.

Silence. Pearly watches as frowns form and brows furrow.

"Wait," says Seth-Squared. "So you're... *there*? In Paris? With your charges?"

"As we speak! It really is lovely this time of year. Five stars. Highly recommend."

"That's—unprecedented!"

"Not true," says Pearly. "I did it once before. Only this time, it's all above board."

"But..." sputters Hylonome. "You're supposed to nudge from a distance. What about aura contamination? The cosmic code of ethics!"

The room dissolves into whispers. A holographic chart flickers to life over the table, one guide already sketching out potential karmic disruptions from "excessive croissant exposure."

Pearly crosses her arms. "Relax. Nobody's aura has been harmed in the consumption of baked goods."

"Mz. Snaggs?" says Hylonome. "Did you really approve this?"

All eyes turn to Mildreth. She pushes up her glasses. "I did. As a one-time experiment in immersive field engagement. Gates knows the risks, as do I. We'll all be watching her results with considerable interest." The words sound harmless enough, but Pearly hears the subtext: *the bet is on, and the clock is ticking.*

Papers shuffle. Heads shake. Smirks abound. Pearly flashes a beauty pageant smile, but under it she feels that familiar, hot little coil of stubbornness. It's exactly the kind of thing that makes her want to prove them all spectacularly wrong.

Eighteen

Pearly's never met a flea market she didn't like. Why buy new when you can find treasures marinated in someone else's drama? And the flea market at Saint-Ouen is supposed to be legendary. But first, there's the metro ride — perfect cover to study her charges' auras, and to track her own progress.

All three auras hover stubbornly between orange and yellow, survival mode with a flicker of mild optimism. Not terrible, but nowhere near what Pearly promised Mildreth: *"One full vibrational color upshift by the end of Paris."* Which means Pearly needs to see them edging toward green in the next five days. Five. Days. She shakes her head, astounded by her own audacity. Most souls take lifetimes to climb that far.

Aura growth follows the color spectrum. Red to violet, with each step a little more wisdom, a little more expansion. Which puts Pearly herself in the blue zone. Higher, sure, but not because she's a paragon of virtue. Blue just means she's been incarnating a hell of a lot longer than her charges, collecting scars like frequent-flier miles.

Across from her, Reyna is glued to the glowing metro map above the doors, watching the little bulbs flash with each approaching stop. Pearly has to admit it's genius, way more efficient than the transit roulette mortals play back in the States. Still, Reyna watches with bated breath, as if one missed stop will doom her entire existence. Has her aura shifted? Maybe a little. Definitely not an entire level.

What about Lillian? Obviously, no—although something did break open as she ate that croissant. There's potential, but it needs time to simmer. Time, and maybe a few more flirty exchanges with George. An unexpected late-in-life romance could be just the thing to tip the scales.

And speaking of George? He's warming with Beckett, but he's still not sure how to break through the guilt and step up his game. Pearly drums her gold-glittered nails on the metro pole. *Get it together, people!*

At least one person seems to be making progress—Beckett. Across the car, he scrolls through his camera roll, grinning. "This one or this one?" he says to Thunder, sitting beside him. "For my Insta." This trip's been really good for the kid. Too bad he doesn't count for Pearly's quota.

Thunder studies the shots for a few moments, then taps one. "This one screams 'brooding artist.' The kind who sketches strangers in cafés and never pays for his own coffee."

"Or, you know," says Pearly, "like Timothée Chalamet's younger cousin who eats carbs."

"Yeah?" says Beckett, looking pleased. "Cool." He posts the pic.

They walk the ten minutes from Garibaldi, cafés giving way to antique shops with mirrors and art prints spilling onto the sidewalk. Then the street folds into the covered alleys of Saint-Ouen, and the shift is immediate. It's like stepping through a portal into a vintage *Star Wars* junkyard run by aliens with French accents and good taste.

The ceiling soars above them in glass and iron, strung with massive silver spheres that dangle in clusters, disco-ball planets reflecting fractured light. Stalls branch off in every direction, cluttered with strange juxtapositions: a pair of ceramic bulldogs guarding a porcelain vase, a velvet chair upholstered in neon pop-art faces, a medical mannequin with half its skull missing and its plastic heart forever exposed.

In one courtyard, an orange UFO squats between buildings, its porthole eyes daring passersby to climb aboard. Around the next corner, a shop brims with retro comics and toy robots, *Tintin* adventures stacked beside glass-eyed dolls and miniature racecars. It's chaos masquerading as commerce, a surreal museum where treasure and trash rub shoulders.

Thunder and Beckett linger at the toy shop, Beckett already elbow-deep in a bin of vintage action figures. Thunder picks up an Angry-Garfield-in-Golf-Attire and does a French impersonation.

"Casse-toi, Jon, où est ma lasagne?"

Pearly leaves them to it, drifting toward George and Lillian as the group begins to scatter through the maze.

Lillian slows at a stall arranged like a jewel box: antique velvet chairs, brass lamps, lacquered tables. She drifts toward a carved walnut chair upholstered in bold peacock blue, her fingertips grazing the wood.

George leans in, squinting at the frame. "That's real craftsmanship. You can see it in the carving."

"Oui, monsieur!" The shop owner appears at his elbow, a wiry man in a scarf. "Nineteenth century, but solid enough to last another hundred years!"

Lillian lingers, her hand still on the chair. "It is beautiful," she admits. "But not exactly practical."

George tilts his head. "Why don't you try it out? Just to see."

She hesitates. "It's not mine."

"Not yet," says George. "But it should be."

"Please, madame." The shop owner gestures grandly. "A chair only lives when someone sits."

Lillian still hovers, wary. Pearly can't help herself. "Lil, this is the first thing not-beige that I've seen you consider this entire trip. I don't know what happened to make you monochrome—" she does, of course, "—but I am very much in favor of you purchasing this chair."

Lillian flinches, then lowers herself into the seat. The velvet sighs under her weight. She smooths the fabric, eyes distant.

"My old house..." Her voice catches. "It was full of color. Rugs from Florence, paintings on every wall. I filled it with things that made me feel alive. And then one day it all went up in smoke. Since then, I—" She swallows. "I couldn't look at color without thinking about what I lost in the fire. So I just... moved to a condo and made everything beige. Easier that way."

George's expression softens. "I'm so sorry, Lillian. I can't imagine losing my home. Mine's not much. Just a little house in Tennessee. But it's got creaky floors, a porch swing, walls covered in family photos, and the smell of cedar in every room. It's... lived in."

Lillian lets out a slow breath. "That sounds nice." She steals a glance at him, then looks away. Her fingers tighten on the chair's carved arms. For a moment, Pearly swears she sees her charge's aura flare greener. But then Lillian stands, smoothing her skirt. "Thank you," she says to the shopkeeper, her voice brisk again, "but shipping it would be a nightmare."

The vendor shrugs, accustomed to browsers who fall in love and walk away.

Pearly lingers just long enough to see George's eyes follow Lillian into the crowd, his expression caught somewhere between admiration and regret. It tugs at her, but she doesn't press. Instead, she pivots to go find Reyna, leaving George and the chair behind.

Pearly drifts down one of the quieter lanes. Here the market feels different—curated, hushed, as if each stall guards its own little museum. She slows at a shop window where velvet trays glitter beneath the glass.

That's when she sees it.

The garnet necklace.

Her stomach flips. Delicate gold chain, oval pendant, the stone still glowing even in the dim Paris light. It shouldn't be here, not a century later, staring at her from behind the case. But every curve of the setting, every facet of the garnet, is unmistakable.

Her hand rises, pressing against the glass. And in an instant, the market dissolves—

***

Paris, 1873

Evelyn Ashcroft steps into a jeweler's on Rue de la Paix with her publisher's advance folded crisp in her purse. Her second novel has just sold out its first run. The critics call her "the next Brontë," or at least the enlightened ones do. She's twenty-five, unmarried, and for the first time, flush with money she earned by her own pen.

The necklace gleams from a velvet tray, garnet set in gold. It's not the grandest piece in the shop, but it's one she can afford. Something about it calls to her.

"A timeless piece, mademoiselle." The clerk lifts it up like some holy artifact. "For a woman who wishes to be remembered." No matter the century, salesmen know how to sell.

Evelyn meets her own eyes in the mirror as he fastens the clasp. The garnet burns at her throat, a talisman announcing to the world—and to herself—*I have arrived.* She's not just someone's daughter or someone's wife. No. She is Evelyn Ashcroft, published novelist, and her own woman.

When she leaves the shop, she walks taller than she ever has. The necklace warms against her skin, like it's getting accustomed to her. Proof she's claimed her own place in the world.

***

The vision dissolves, and Pearly blinks at her reflection in the boutique window. The garnet looks smaller than she remembers, its setting cracked, its shine dulled. She smiles, shakes her head. Memory is a funny thing. It's like going back to your old school auditorium and realizing it only held two hundred seats when your kid-eyes swore it was a stadium. But her affection remains. She hasn't bought anything so far on this trip. Surely, she deserves a little memento.

She enters the shop. The vendor wears a fitted blazer and what others who are not Pearly might call too much eyeliner. "Bonjour, madame. Aimez-vous le grenat?"

Pearly leans on the glass case, giving the necklace another once-over. "Oh, certainly," she says, in perfect French. "How much?"

"Three thousand euro."

Pearly laughs, tossing her hair. "Three thousand? At that price, it should cook dinner too. Two thousand."

"I cannot," the woman balks. "Lowest I could go is 2500."

"Deal." Maybe if Pearly was alive, she'd push harder. But there's really no point if you can just manifest the money anyway. Probably a little steep for her expense reports, but it's not like it's going to collapse the French economy.

She leaves the hush of the covered stalls and steps into daylight with the necklace tucked into her bag. The market changes tempo instantly—louder, tighter, more chaotic. The outdoor lanes stretch ahead in a crush of bodies and stalls. Tables are stacked with what look, at first glance, like luxury goods: Louis Vuitton sweaters folded in neat piles, Converse sneakers lined up in military precision, Gucci belts gleaming under the sun. From a distance, it's the Champs-Élysées. Up close, Pearly can see it. Some of the leather's a little stiff, the logos a little too loud, the kind of almost-perfect that tips into counterfeit.

It's a whole ecosystem. Buyers pretending not to notice, sellers pretending not to care, everyone getting what they need. The din is relentless: vendors calling out in rapid-fire French and Arabic, zippers rasping, plastic bags crackling. She cranes her neck, searching for a flicker of her charges' auras in the crowd.

Then she hears Reyna—her voice sharp and panicked, cutting through the noise.

Pearly pushes past a wall of handbags and finds her on the ground beside a stall, backpack upended, its guts scattered across the pavement. Lip gloss rolls under a rack of belts. Crumpled receipts stick to the sole of a passing sneaker. A balled-up scarf, half a sandwich, and a paper map of Paris fan out around her.

Reyna is on her knees in the middle of it, rifling through the pile again and again, eyes panicked, breath coming too fast. Shoppers are forced to step wide around her, muttering as they detour, a traffic jam building in the narrow lane. Vendors glare. Someone yells at her in French.

"It's gone!" Reyna gasps, shaking out the empty backpack. "My phone, my card—someone took them!"

Her aura crackles, jagged and raw. Pearly feels the heat of it. Reyna's chest heaves, her eyes glassy. She's spiraling.

"Reyna," says Pearly. "It's gonna be okay."

Reyna shakes her head, tears spilling out of her. "My whole life is in there. My job—I can't—how am I supposed to—"

The words dissolve into sobs. Pearly lets her own aura ripple outward, a gentle brush of calm to take the edge off. But it's not enough, not even close. Reyna breathes in frantic gasps, on the verge of collapse.

"We'll figure this out." Pearly takes Reyna by the shoulders, tries to catch her eyes. Reyna looks back at her, but she's somewhere else, mind spinning. "You're safe," Pearly tells her. "You're not alone. Okay?"

Reyna clutches the edge of her bag, knuckles white, but she nods. Barely.

Pearly exhales, the blue thread of her aura already fraying against Reyna's panic. When she tunes into Reyna's thoughts, she hears the thing she fears most:

I want to go home.

Uh-oh.

For half a second, her fingers twitch with the urge to fix it. A phone, a credit card—easy enough to manifest. She could hand Reyna a shiny replacement in seconds. But guides have rules, and this one is ironclad: never manifest anything that might shortcut a charge's karma. Money for herself? Harmless. Spirits don't rack up debt. But a mortal's lifeline—her connection to work, relationships, responsibilities? That's sacred territory. Swap it out, and you don't just replace an object. You erase the lesson that comes with its loss.

And karma, like Mildreth, does not forgive paperwork errors.

The market presses in on them again. Voices, heat, counterfeit logos gleam in the sun. Pearly straightens, her mind already leaping ahead. To answers. To options. She can't conjure a fix, but she might be able to trace one. She's got to find that pickpocket.

There's only one place in the afterlife that keeps records of every moment lived and lost.

It's risky, but what choice does she have? If Reyna is going to make it through Paris, Pearly will have to break the rules.

Nineteen

"I'm just going to state for the record... again..." Thunder folds his arms across his chest. "That I think this is a terrible idea."

Pearly kicks up a sandaled foot onto Seraphina's dashboard. "Noted," she says. "Let the record also show that Thunder cannot distinguish folly from genius."

"Pearly, if we get caught—"

"What happened to 'I'm tired of playing it safe?'" Her tone is casual, but the forced smile betrays her anxiety. She tried so hard to downplay her usual excess: manifesting the dull brown archivist's robe, pinning her hair into a bun, clipping on the glowing book-shaped brooch. But restraint only goes so far. A glance in the rearview shows off her sole concession—an extra layer of metallic copper eyeliner. If anyone got that close, the jig was probably up anyway.

Thunder bristles in the passenger seat. "Breaking into the Department of Records isn't exactly what I had in mind." Yet there he is, looking like a snack in his very own archivist disguise. Maybe he should wear those sexy reading glasses more often.

"But if Reyna goes home, I lose my White Robe—" she throws her hands wide for emphasis, nearly whacking the glovebox—"or worse! Mildreth could reassign me to the Null Region. Do you know how remote it is there? It's like the Antarctica of the afterlife. I heard there's not even coffee—" she leans in dramatically—"or telepathy." Pearly shudders at the prospect.

From the backseat, Dumb Pearly cups her hands around her pet's leathery ears.

"GUYS! Your drama's upsetting Snatchy-poo."

Snatch honks, half-cat purr, half-ostrich screech, sparks glowing beneath trembling tail feathers. Pearly didn't want to get Dumb Pearly wrapped up in her own scheming—again—but it was the only plausible option. And anyway, her roommate was only too happy to come on board.

Even Seraphina's in disguise tonight, trading her usual bubblegum-pink dump-truck form for something less conspicuous. She's now a silvery sedan with angel-wing mirrors and faintly glowing hubcaps. But the glitter still leaks through her seams in motes that drift around the cabin like impatient fireflies. Pearly had to agree to let Seraphina return with her to Paris in order for her emotional support vehicle to agree to the heist—er, outing.

The astral highway curves, and the Department of Records swells on the horizon. At first it looks like nothing more than a circle of pointy spires. But the closer they get, the higher it stretches, rising into a sprawling complex that's half-cathedral, half-municipal library. It looks like a fancy crown, only instead of jewels it's made of light. Pearly's seen it countless times, and it never fails to impress.

A parking lot spreads out at its base, neatly striped and nearly empty except for a couple of hoverboards, a broomstick, a carriage driven by invisible horses, and a glowing orb hovering patiently in a handicap spot. Manicured hedges curl in spirals, trees with parchment-thin leaves rustle without wind, and stone benches line the walkway. Pearly pulls into a spot close to the exit. Just in case they need a clean getaway.

The book return chute gleams in the wall. Above it, a plaque in bold font clarifies the rules: **BORROWED VOLUMES ONLY. LIFE LOGS MAY NOT LEAVE THE PREMISES.**

Pearly twists toward the rearview mirror for a final check. The bun is suitably severe, the robe acceptably drab, the brooch tolerably old school. But her glamour refuses to settle. She's doing it on purpose: nose sharper one moment, rounder the next, eyes shifting from green to violet to brown. A face no one could ever describe the same way twice.

"See?" she says, striking a pose. "Serving totally forgettable."

Thunder raises an eyebrow. "You look like a magic eye poster."

Pearly beams. "Exactly. Nobody stares at those for long."

"Yeah," Thunder shrugs, "unless they're trippin'."

She glances at Dumb Pearly in the rearview. "You remember what to do?"

"Aye aye, Captain!" She clips a leash on Snatch's collar, then looks up. "Can I have a code name?"

"Uhh, sure." She turns to Thunder, hoping to facilitate bonding between her roommate and her... whatever he is. "Sergeant Thunder—can you please assign Dumb Pearly a code name?"

Thunder studies Pearly's double. Unlike him and Pearly, she's supposed to stand out. And she certainly does, in her neon yellow unitard. And her caution-sign sash. And black go-go boots. And, naturally, her sequined pirate's hat. He exhales. "How about Jolly Roger?"

"Werk!" Dumb Pearly holds out her hand for a high-five. He slaps it. Pearly smiles.

"Okay people," she says. "Let's do this."

***

They step into the atrium.

It's grand in the way only the afterlife can be: marble arches soaring into infinity, chandeliers glimmering like constellations frozen mid-orbit. Golden light pours through tall stained-glass windows, but the scenes in the glass refuse to stay still. A birth dissolves into a funeral, a soldier's march ripples into a child's first steps, a political debate turns into a dance party. The shifting colors spill across the marble floor, painting a kaleidoscope of stories in progress.

At the center is a circular welcome desk staffed by archivists in brown robes just like Pearly and Thunder's. All visitors must stop here to present their energy signature if they want to venture deeper into the Library. Tonight, it's the first obstacle Pearly and Thunder need to get through.

The Library hums with quiet activity. Souls sit at long wooden tables, bent over glowing tomes. Some murmur to each other, reviewing the wreckage or triumphs of their most recent lives. Soul school students research papers about karma or soul contracts or the role of technology in spiritual evolution. Rolling carts glide silently between the tables, self-guided like those sidewalk delivery robots. On the far wall, carved plaques point into the wings: *Incarnations A–M | Incarnations N–Z | Reference.*

Pearly and Thunder hang back, hugging the shadow of a column, while Dumb Pearly waltzes in with Snatch on a leash. She struts right up to the welcome desk, where an archivist in reading glasses—for show, of course—types something onto a screen reflecting blue light onto his ageless face. Pearly pegs them as an old soul. You can usually tell by the eyes, or the haircut, or the way they cinch their robe. But the giveaway is the pin on their chest that says, "*Ask me about my 1,327th incarnation.*"

They pick up the scanner, a handheld chrome device. "Energy signature, please."

The scanner beeps as Dumb Pearly puffs up her chest like a show pony, threads of light spiraling out to map her aura. The archivist frowns, tilts the device, waits.

Pearly squeezes Thunder's hand. *Please, please, just let it clear.*

"It'll be fine," he murmurs, though his other hand is clenched in a fist.

Another beep. The screen flashes green. The archivist nods. "You may proceed—" His gaze finally drifts lower, landing on Snatch. The little creature blinks up with wide, ember-bright eyes. The archivist's frown deepens. "But pets are not permitted in the Library." He gestures toward a nearby plaque: *NO PETS, FOOD, OR KARMIC BAGGAGE BEYOND THIS POINT.*

Pearly holds her breath behind the column. This is the moment. Would her double remember the script?

Dumb Pearly tilts her head, all guileless innocence. "But she's my emotional support animal! I mean, wouldn't *you* need one if you were nothing but a copy-paste who spends her afterlife mopping up stinky energy leaks?"

Pearly swallows hard. That part wasn't in the script. Does Dumb Pearly actually believe that?

The archivist blinks. Sympathy flickers across his lined face. "Well..." He exhales, clearly against his better judgment. "I suppose it would be alright. If she behaves."

"She might," Dumb Pearly says brightly, "if you gave her a treat."

A long pause. Then, with the smallest flick of his wrist, the archivist manifests a glowing cube of light.

Dumb Pearly beams, snatches it, and pops it into Snatch's waiting beak.

For a long, terrible beat, nothing happens. Snatch chews happily, purring like a kitten. Pearly's stomach knots. Thunder's hand tightens on hers.

Then Snatch squats, tail feathers trembling.

FLASH. BANG.

A ball of lightning explodes across the marble floor, leaving a smoking crater where a footnote cart had just been. Snatch flaps her stubby wings, careens sideways into a reading table, and sends tomes scattering like frightened pigeons. Students shriek and dive for cover. An archivist yelps as his robe sleeve catches fire. Sparks ricochet into a chandelier, setting the constellations spinning.

"SNATCHY-POOOOO!" shrieks Dumb Pearly, sprinting after the creature as if this isn't perfectly normal. Back home, lightning-poops and spontaneous combustion are just part of the daily routine.

The Library is less forgiving. In the chaos, Pearly seizes Thunder's hand. "Now," she hisses, and together they dart past the welcome desk into the endless shelves of life logs. Each soul has their own "series," with one log per incarnation.

The noise fades behind them as they dive in. Here the hush is deeper, almost alive. Towers of books rise in endless, glowing spirals. Every title shimmers, shifting to reflect the soul's name across lifetimes.

After several twists and turns, they find the shelf they need: Reyna's stack. Most of the books bear other names—her prior incarnations, closed and complete. But the one Pearly wants is the *active* volume, the life in progress. Its cover trembles, as if still being written by an unseen hand.

That's why they had to sneak in. No one's supposed to touch a life book until the story is finished. That's the rule. An unfinished volume shifts with every choice, every heartbeat. Peek too soon and you risk more than spoilers. You risk smudging the ink. A nudge here, a bias there. It's enough to tangle karma and throw the whole thing off course.

But Pearly doesn't need Reyna's future. What she needs is barely in the past — the moment with the pickpocket. Life logs show more than what their protagonist saw; they hold every angle. You can study an argument from both sides, see through the eyes of the liar and the lied-to. Even if Reyna never noticed the thief, the omniscient record did.

Still, it's illegal. Pearly knows that by cracking it open she's flirting with disaster, but she's already doing that anyway with the Mildreth gamble. Might as well buy disaster a drink, slip on the sexy negligee, and take it to bed.

She glances at Thunder, heart thudding. She'd have conjured Reyna a new phone if she could, but a SIM card's a lot harder to manifest than a bucket of popcorn. At least this way, no one has to know. Probably. Hopefully.

"Well," says Thunder, squeezing her hand. "Here goes every-thing."

Pearly hesitates, palm hovering an inch from the cover. "Un-finished books are jumpy," she whispers. "Every volume has its own vibration, perfectly tuned to the soul it belongs to. The second I touch it, my energy bleeds into the mix. If the rhythm spikes, the wards will flag it and the front desk will get an automatic readout. I won't just be reading Reyna's story—I'll get written into it. My signature stamped across her record forever."

Thunder crosses his arms. "I'm not even officially a guide, and I know that can't be good."

"Which is why I need you as my anchor." She gestures at the quivering pages. "I hold the book, you hold me. Keeps my signature steady, out of the ink. No imprint, no trace."

His jaw tightens. "You do realize this isn't bending rules—it's breaking the spine clean in half."

She flashes him a grin. "Only if we fuck it up. Seatbelt me."

For a heartbeat he doesn't move, eyes locked on the trembling cover. Then, with a sigh, he steps close. "You know, you're impossible."

"And yet," she says sweetly as she lowers her hands to the book, "you keep showing up."

The instant her palms touch the cover, light ripples outward and the book shudders, sensing a new vibration. She can feel it under her skin: Reyna's pulse, then her own, trying to sync. Thunder's hands fall over hers, warm and solid, and the pulse steadies a notch. But it's not enough. Threads of light lash up her wrists, hungry for her experiences.

"Not holding," she hisses.

He steps in fully, arms wrapping around her from behind, pressing her into him. His hands flatten over hers on the cover. His chest anchors against her back. Her breath stops, and she feels a little woozy from the sudden intimacy—but it seems to be working. The mixed beats slow, then align, the glow drawing taut until the book vibrates a contained, steady energy.

For a heartbeat or an eternity, she's not in the Library at all. She's in a candlelit chamber centuries ago, his lips finding the crown of her head after a battle. Then again on a crowded train in another life, their bodies crushed together with every jolt of the tracks, the heat between them sharper than the steam outside. Then again in the bedroom of their afterlife home, silk sheets, loosened auras, his hands running up the length of her—

NOPE.

She jerks herself back, pulse hammering. *Not now, Miss Thing. You're on a job. And it's dangerous.*

Thunder's grip tightens slightly. "You good?"

She tries to find words that won't give her away. "Is Donna Summer the most legendary disco queen?"

"Uh...yes?"

"See? Answered your own question." She flips the cover open before he can press further. The table of contents unfurls in glowing script—each chapter a year in Reyna's life, titles shifting faintly as if the ink hasn't finished drying. Pearly drags her finger down the list until she finds the one she wants: *Twenty-Five.*

The page ripples open at her touch. Light bursts, and suddenly she's behind Reyna's eyes. The flea market slams around her: counterfeit luxury goods piled high, leather too stiff, logos too loud. The outdoor lanes crush with noise and bodies, vendors shouting in French and Arabic over the rasp of zippers and the crackle of plastic bags. Her knees hit pavement. Her hands scrabble through the spilled guts of her backpack—lip gloss, scarf, half a sandwich, paper map—everything except the phone.

Her chest heaves. Her vision blurs. The panic claws up her throat. *It's gone. My whole life is gone.*

Pearly grits her teeth. "Too narrow."

She presses harder against the page, and the scene shudders, then expands. No longer bound to Reyna's panic, she rises into an omniscient sweep of the crowd. Auras flare like fireflies. The counterfeit lanes churn. And there—just over Reyna's shoulder—a figure slides close, hands quick as smoke, plucking the phone and card free before vanishing back into the tide.

Pearly narrows her focus even further. The book obliges, overlay text flickering into being above the thief's head like a cosmic Netflix trivia card.

"Claude Mercier — soul name 'Guzzle.' Cameo role: Swipe-and-run at the Saint-Ouen Market. Five incarnations as background extra."

She yanks her hand back, pulse hammering. The glow flares once, then settles—quiet, for now. Pearly grins. "There you are, you little shit."

Thunder leans in, lips almost brushing against her ear. "We've got a name?"

"Affirmative," she grins. "Now let's blow this joint."

Thunder's arms are still around her. For a second, neither of them moves. The danger has passed, but the press of his chest against her back, his hands still covering hers—if she could stretch out this moment for eternity, she would. But every moment they stay is another chance to get caught, and anyway she's worried about Dumb Pearly.

She clears her throat. "You can, uh... un-seatbelt me now."

Ever so slowly, Thunder lets go, fingertips brushing against her hips as they disentwine. He's barely touching her, but she feels every micro-sensation—like she's being buttered by some hot cosmic knife. She has to focus so as not to melt straight into the floor.

They slip out of the stacks, through the lingering chaos of archivists shooing sparks from chandeliers and students retrieving scattered tomes. No one stops them. Somehow, impossibly, they make it out the front doors. Seraphina's waiting at the curb, engine idling, with Dumb Pearly and Snatch in tow. They pile in, and Seraphina screeches out of the lot with a little more drama than necessary.

From the backseat, Dumb Pearly leans forward, eyes shining. "Did it work, Captain? You get the baddie?"

Pearly twists in her seat, still buzzing from the heist. "Yeah. What did we miss? You get into any trouble?"

"Nah, they kicked me out, but I think they felt sorries." Dumb Pearly pumps a fist. "Team Snatch for the win!" She hugs the still-smoking creature to her chest. "Who's a good girl?!" Then she looks up, finds Thunder's eyes in the rearview. "Thanks for helping," she says. "Guess you're not a judgy goody two shoes after all."

"Uh..." Pearly makes the 'shut-up' gesture, slicing a finger across her neck. She turns to Thunder. "I only said that one time. Right after we broke up. You know how it is... crazy flies outta your mouth, you know? I didn't really mean it."

Thunder's mouth twitches, but he lets it go. Pearly catches the flicker of amusement in his eyes.

From the corner of her eye, she sees Dumb Pearly watching how close she's sitting to Thunder. There's curiosity in her gaze, edged with something else Pearly can't quite pinpoint. Seraphina takes a corner too fast, glitter spraying from her seams as they speed away from the Library. Pearly sinks into the seat, finally letting her body unclench. She can still feel the echo of Thunder's arms around her, the steadiness of his hands over hers. It felt... safe. But safety can be an illusion.

"Well, that was a fun outing." She blows out a shaky breath.

"Barrel of laughs," says Thunder. "But maybe next time, less crime, more gelato."

Dumb Pearly giggles, and Pearly tells herself everything is fine.

Outside, the astral highway unspools in streaks of light. Inside, her heart feels like a book still being written—pages trembling, ink uncertain, the ending undecided.

TWENTY

It's late when Pearly returns to Hôtel Lumière. She almost forgets to manifest a manicure, her excuse for bailing on the group. It's easy to pickpocket a pickpocket when you can turn invisible between blinks. She even feels a sense of karmic justice, even if "An Eye for an Eye" was repealed ages ago. She bubbles with glittery optimism as she sashays through the front doors, clutching Reyna's phone.

The lobby's still lively. George and Beckett are locked in a pool game against Austin and Lamar, laughter mixing with the crack of cue balls. A couple of tourists drift toward the elevator, fancy cocktails in hand. For a moment, it feels like just another ordinary Paris night.

Then the elevator dings.

Reyna steps out, suitcase rolling behind her, shoulders tight, eyes locked on the exit.

Pearly freezes. Her entire afterlife flashes before her eyes. No matter what, she can't let Reyna leave. Not yet. "Hey!" she calls, forcing brightness into her voice. "You weren't gonna give us the slip, were you?"

Reyna stops short, cheeks reddening. "No, I—I would've texted you guys on the plane. I mean... I would if I had a phone." She frowns, gaze falling to the suitcase handle. "Look, I don't want to disappoint anyone. Especially not my Lola. It's just... this isn't working out."

"I know you've had a hard day. But I've got good news." With a flourish worthy of a stage magician, she reaches into her trench coat and pulls out Reyna's phone, with the credit card tucked inside the case.

Reyna's eyes widen. "Where—how did you—?"

"It's the strangest thing," says Pearly. "After my manicure, I went back to the flea market. Followed the vibes. Dug around a little. Found it wedged under a carpet sample next to three counterfeit Prada belts and an empty crêpe cone. Who knows how it got there? Who cares?!"

She presses the phone into Reyna's hand.

Reyna clutches it like a lifeline, then bursts into tears. "I'm sorry," she gasps. "I'm not usually this dramatic."

"Oh, honey." Pearly smiles softly. "If drama were an Olympic sport, I'd be up there with a gold medal, a bouquet, and an endorsement deal." Pearly gestures toward the almost-empty hotel bar. "Why don't we sit down? Talk things out. After that, if you still want to leave, I'll even pay for your Uber. There's always another standby flight."

Reyna takes a couple of deep breaths, wipes her eyes. "Yeah, okay." She bites her lip. "You mind if I check my messages first?"

"Whatever you need."

Pearly drags Reyna's suitcase to one of the tiny round tables circling the bar. She doesn't know if the French make everything small to foster intimacy, but it certainly has that effect. Pearly orders them each a glass of wine while Reyna scrolls frantically. Pearly props her chin on her hand, watching her charge across the flickering tealight. Just a businessman nursing a whiskey, a couple flirting on swivel stools, a bartender wiping the countertop as French jazz plays in the background. It's the kind of setting that begs for confessions.

Reyna's scrolling slows. Eventually she pockets the phone with a shake of her head.

"What?" asks Pearly, as the bartender brings their wine.

Reyna shrugs off her jacket. "When I got back to the hotel, I was, like, out of my mind for the first couple hours." She takes a sip of wine, collecting her thoughts. "I told myself it was because I might be missing some emergency at work—there's always some emergency at work—but that wasn't it. Not really." She sighs, leans back in her chair. "I mean, I know we're all addicted to our phones, right? But when I didn't have it, I realized how much I rely on it to drown out the silence."

Pearly notices the dim light reflecting through her glass, creating the perfect shade of red. "What's so bad about silence?"

Reyna makes a face. "It's terrifying. It means I'm all alone." She picks up her glass again, but she doesn't drink. She just stares into its depths. "I didn't worry about it as much when I was younger. I had a big family and a lot of friends, and when you're in school, there's always reasons to connect, you know? But then I graduated and got a job and my friends started coupling up and moving out and... I guess I felt like what I had to offer wasn't as important anymore. They'd forget about me until they had a breakup or needed to vent about their relationship. I could see this future stretching out before me, and it seemed so lonely. So quiet. I felt—I don't know—irrelevant? And I hated it. So I'd reach for my phone. Doomscrolling, work crises, whatever. Anything to fill the void."

Pearly rests her elbows on the table. "That doesn't make you irrelevant, Reyna. It just makes you human. And maybe a little too good at pretending you don't need anyone."

"Yeah, maybe."

"Silence can be brutal sometimes," Pearly nods. "Feels like it's pointing a big neon arrow at every crack in your life. And lord, do I know cracks! I've fallen off the wall so many times I make Humpty Dumpty look good." She leans in. "But silence can be more than a container for your self-destructive thoughts."

Reyna frowns, chewing on the thought. "Yeah, I guess." Her fingers toy with the stem of her wineglass, twisting it back and forth. Pearly senses her charge is eager to return to lighter territory. "So," she says, "wanna see what I got at the flea market?"

"What?" Reyna blinks. "Yeah, sure."

Pearly digs into her handbag and slides a small bundle wrapped in crinkled tissue across the table. "Go on," she says.

Reyna peels back the layers until the antique garnet necklace catches the candlelight. "Ohhhhhh." Her breath catches. "That's exquisite." She glances up at Pearly. "It looks practically made for you."

Pearly smiles. And suddenly, something inside her begins to shift. "Why don't you try it on?"

"Me?" Reyna laughs, shaking her head. "I don't exactly think it goes with my Docs." She stomps her combat boots for emphasis.

"Well, I think it's a delightful study in contrasts," says Pearly, holding out the chain. "Just humor me, okay?"

Reyna hesitates—then reaches for it. The clasp clicks shut at the nape of her neck, and Pearly watches as a subtle warmth settles over her aura, smoothing the jagged edges and shading her orangey parts yellow. For the first time all night, Reyna looks more centered than fractured. Her shoulders drop a fraction.

"Wow," Pearly breathes. "Look at you." She lifts her phone and snaps a quick picture before Reyna can protest. "See? Gorgeous." She swivels the screen so Reyna can glimpse herself, garnet glowing against her collarbone.

Reyna studies the image, almost startled. "Huh." A small, real smile breaks through. "I almost look... I don't know. Elegant."

She does indeed look elegant—even today, it's a statement piece. And Pearly sure does like to make a statement. But more importantly, the necklace carries meaning. It was very precious to her in a past life. Which is why her next move surprises her even more than Reyna.

"Keep it," Pearly says, sliding the box toward her.

"What? No. I couldn't—"

"I insist. It's calling to you, and I must heed the call." Pearly leans back, waves her off. "Besides, I have enough jewelry."

Reyna touches the pendant, fingers lingering. She doesn't argue again. Pearly tunes into her thoughts: the suitcase by her feet suddenly feels less like an escape route and more like dead weight.

Pearly stands, picks it up. "What do you say we take this back to your room, then go challenge the boys to a game of pool? I don't know about you, but I'm a shark in sequins, and I bet they'll never see us coming."

Reyna smiles, a little teary-eyed again, but for much different reasons. "I'm in," she says.

They walk to the elevator together, press the button. Then Reyna turns to Pearly. "You know," she says, studying Pearly's face. "Not everyone would've gone back to look for my phone. Honestly, probably no one. So...thank you."

Pearly forces a smile, her throat suddenly tight. Maybe she's not the selfish soul she once was. The truth here is a little messier: she went back because if Reyna bailed, then Mildreth wins. But didn't she also go back because she couldn't bear to see Reyna hurting? She would've done it anyway—wouldn't she?

She wonders what would have happened if she hadn't intervened. Would Reyna have gone back to Seattle and continued her slow spiral into spiritual stagnation, or would she have found her own way to turn things around? Sometimes it's hard to know where "appropriate guidance" ends and codependency begins. Or worse, pure ego. Maybe they go over this in guide school, but Pearly skipped that part and went straight to on-the-job training. She's a trust-your-gut kind of gal, and that's worked out so far. Mostly. But she should probably check in with Malcolm.

The elevator dings, sparing her from all her unanswered questions. For now.

***

The chamber seals with a damp hiss, mist curling through the seams. Mildreth lets the spores settle against her skin. The meeting was routine, but Gates's update lingers, sharp as fungicide in the lungs. Croissants. Cohesion. That insipid metallic lipstick smile.

Mildreth activates her console and Reyna Cruz's file blooms across the bioluminescent screen. Metrics scroll by. Probability of an exit event logged at ninety-two percent. That human should be on a plane by now, aura dimming towards orange. Yet the numbers tick in the other direction. Stabilization. Uplift. That damn suitcase.

Gates sat at her table with unchecked arrogance, spinning blunders into progress, as if probability itself bent to her will. Mildreth presses her filaments flat against the desk, forcing the fungal chamber to still its humid trembling. But the truth glows on the screen: chaos had triumphed over order. Again.

It isn't the numbers that unsettle her. It's what they imply.

One anomaly can be dismissed. Two, explained away. But this—this was a pattern. Pearly Gates isn't stumbling into improbable outcomes. She's generating them.

Mildreth's spores constrict, releasing a bitter tang into the chamber. Variables this unruly aren't supposed to stabilize. They're supposed to collapse, living proof of the natural order.

Yet Gates flaunts her defiance of the rules. That doesn't make her clever. It makes her dangerous.

For a brief moment, before she can suppress it, Mildreth remembers the wanting. The ache that once thrummed through her when she watched the guides-in-training bend close to their charges, nudging human souls toward revelation. She had wanted that more than anything: to feel the weight of a mortal life blossom from her guidance, to shape its trajectory with care and precision.

She can almost see it—the observation hall where students watched guides at work, their interventions projected in streams of light. The way a charge paused before a fateful choice, the nudge invisible to mortal eyes but radiant to hers. *That will be me*, she dreamed. *It must be me.* Yet when the paths were drawn, fate consigned her not to the field but to the desk.

Mildreth jerks herself back from the memory. Gates treats rules as decoration, just like Malcolm used to do. Fumbling her way to a win and calling it destiny. But if failure will not find her, then Mildreth will deliver it.

Twenty-One

Four-and-a-half hours and two bathroom stops from Paris, Pearly decides reincarnation might actually be quicker than road trips. Normandy unspools outside the van windows in waves of apple orchards and pastures dotted with cows munching salted grass. Apparently, that grass makes their butter the eighth wonder of the world. *Very pastoral chic,* she thinks, propping her chin on her neon manicure. She's full of energy this morning, but her charges are still yawning awake. They got out of bed at 5am to see another epic building, but this one's way older than Versailles.

Thunder nods toward the faint shape just off the coast, an island surfacing from the fog. "Many armies have tried to conquer Mont Saint-Michel, but none have succeeded. The tides came in faster than horses. The quicksand swallowed armies whole. For over a thousand years, this abbey never fell."

"More stubborn than me," Lillian mutters. Everyone laughs.

"And that's not even the strangest part," Thunder adds. "It all started because a bishop ignored the Archangel Michael—three times. First two visits, he thought it was a trick. The third time,

Michael poked a hole straight through his skull to make him listen."

"No way," says Beckett.

Thunder shrugs. "You can still see the skull. They keep it at Saint-Gervais Basilica. Some say it's evidence of weird medieval surgery..." Thunder winces. "But either way, he finally built the abbey. And it's been standing ever since."

Pearly presses her nose to the glass as the outline sharpens into spires. Her breath fogs the window, and she traces a heart in it.

"Does anyone live there?" asks George, squinting into the distance.

"Twelve someones!" says Thunder. "A small community of monks and nuns. Everyone else commutes."

Then Reyna gasps. "Oh my God."

The van crests a rise, and there it is: Mont Saint-Michel, floating out of the mist like something a fairy godmother doodled on too much espresso. Spires stab skyward. Granite walls tumble down in terraces of chapels and crypts. A medieval village clings to the rock beneath, its crooked streets curling upward toward the abbey, gulls soaring overhead. A slender bridge links it to the mainland, but with the tide high and the water gleaming, the bridge nearly vanishes, leaving the island adrift like a castle conjured out of the sea.

By the time they park the van and ride the tram across the bridge to the island, everyone is starving. Which makes sense—this is the birthplace of the omelet that launched a thousand postcards. La Mère Poulard is a high-end spectacle of a restaurant: copper pans swinging from hooks, aproned cooks whipping eggs into foamy clouds and beating them over open fires while tourists lean in for photos. The air smells like butter, woodsmoke, and sea salt.

Lamar raises his cider in salute as the massive omelets land puffed and golden on the table. "Fifty euros well spent. Worth it for the drama alone."

Austin rubs his hands together. "This egg knows how to make an entrance."

Meanwhile, George frowns down at his plate. "I don't get it. It's just eggs. Back home you could get this for five bucks and still have change for bacon."

"That's the French way," says Lillian, twirling her fork. "Butter, eggs, salt, and pepper. Simple. Classic. Perfect."

George isn't buying it. "Maybe." He leans in, challenging Lillian. "But then, you've never had one of my omelets. Country ham, sharp cheddar, crispy caramelized onions, sumptuous fried green tomatoes..."

Lillian arches a brow, lips curving into an almost-smile. "Is that an offer, Mr. Mailman?"

"Could be," says George. "If you promise to bring your appetite."

"Oh, I'll bring it."

"Oh no," Beckett whispers to Pearly, hiding his head in his hands. "The old people are flirting." Despite the cringe, he seems happy to see George light up.

But after their leisurely lunch comes the long climb upward. The cobbled lanes narrow as they begin their trek, shops crammed with postcards, snow globes, and miniature spires pressing close on either side. Pilgrims once trudged barefoot up this same incline, Thunder explains, though Pearly doubts medieval pilgrims had to dodge as many souvenir stands.

The steps steepen as they start to leave the village behind, and soon everyone is panting. Two hundred steps later, everyone's sweating, and they're still barely halfway to the abbey.

George presses a hand to his lower back. "Didn't know this trip came with cardio."

"Free penance with every purchase," says Pearly, fluttering her lashes.

Lillian pauses mid-stair, one hand braced on the stone wall. "This is... harder than I expected."

George slows beside her without comment, letting her match pace. "Guess that hoity-toity omelet wasn't enough fuel."

"Oh, please." Lillian shoots him a sideways glance. "You think I'd be walking any faster with a belly full of *country* ham, and *sharp* cheddar, and *crispy* caramelized onions, and those *oh-so-sumptuous* fried green tomatoes..."

Austin fans himself with a guidebook, only a few steps ahead. "If I collapse, bury me in the catacombs. Or somewhere with a panoramic view."

"Think of it as ritual," says Thunder. "For centuries, the faithful climbed these steps. Every ache, every blister, all part of their devotion."

"I don't know," says Pearly, grabbing the handrail. "I'm not sure I need bunions to get closer to God."

The group staggers upward together, laughter and grumbling braided with effort. By the time the village falls away and the abbey looms above them, they're flushed and winded—but a little more bonded, too.

The steps narrow as they push past the last of the souvenir stalls, the smell of frying caramel giving way to damp stone and candle wax. The air cools, quieter now except for the scrape of shoes on stone.

Inside the abbey, the noise of the crowd softens, voices swallowed by the vaulted ceilings. Candles flicker in alcoves, the flames bending in unseen drafts. From somewhere deeper in the stone, a low chant echoes, like the walls themselves are breathing it back.

Reyna slows, glancing around. "Where are the people who live here?" she whispers.

Thunder gestures upward. "They keep to their cloister most of the day, except for prayers. Lauds in the morning, Vespers at sunset. Occasionally, they interact with tourists, but mostly they stay, holding vigil."

They crest the last stair, and the abbey opens around them: massive arches springing upward like ribs, crypts and chapels carved into the rock, the cloister towering above in a crown of green and stone.

George lowers himself onto a pew with a grateful sigh, Beckett flopping down beside him. Pearly slips in too, with Austin and Lamar claiming the other end.

"Does anyone want to check out that courtyard?" asks Reyna, gesturing toward a set of arched openings at the far side of the nave. Through them, sunlight spills onto a patch of green garden hemmed in by delicate columns.

"The cloister," says Lillian. "I would." She turns to Thunder. "Want to give us the tour?"

"Certainly!" Thunder rises, smoothing his jacket. "First bit of trivia: this was the monks' version of a water cooler. Only with more prayer and less gossip." He winks, then gestures grandly for them to follow. "Come along, mes amies."

As they leave, Pearly sits in the hush with the others, light slanting through stained glass in fractured colors.

George leans back, eyes on the high arches. "A little fancier than our church back home. And older. When did you say this was built—eleven hundred?"

"Yeah," says Pearly. "She's an antique, for sure."

"Still though," George muses. "Gives me the same feeling. Reverence, I guess. Comfort. Something about the rhythm of church life—it steadies me. Same hymns every week, potluck after service, Mrs. Blakely's banana pudding gone before you can blink." His gaze shifts to Beckett. "When your grandma got sick, that's where folks showed up. They cut the grass, brought casseroles, prayed with me when I couldn't keep my head straight. Didn't fix the hurt, but I knew I wasn't carrying it alone. I had my community. And I had God."

Austin smiles. "That's sweet. I grew up going to Temple, but yeah—vibe's the same. Just swap banana pudding for latkes and sour cream."

"Not me," says Lamar. He's staring at the flicker of a candle in a side altar, expression stoic. "The message I got from church was: there's something wrong with you, don't talk about it, and maybe you'll be okay—but you'll probably go to Hell anyway." He exhales. "Took a lot of years to shake that shit off."

Beckett lets out a sound somewhere between a laugh and a sigh of relief. "That's... wow. I've never heard anyone actually say that out loud. Thank you."

George's brows pinch, troubled. "I thought you liked church, Becks."

Beckett presses his elbows to his knees, staring at the stone floor. "Yeah. When I was five." His voice hardens. "Same pews. Same hymns. But every Sunday, as I got older, all I heard was what I wasn't allowed to be. Who I wasn't allowed to be with. You got comfort, Grandpa. I got surveillance." He huffs out a sharp breath. "Did you know Mom and Dad won't even let me hang out with anyone who isn't in my youth group anymore?"

George blinks, taken off guard. "Why not?"

Beckett's eyes flicker, then drop. Pearly can feel the tension winding between them—tight, fragile. *Please, George,* she thinks. *See him. Let yourself see him.*

"There was kind of an... incident last year." He clears his throat. "I had this friend, Jordan. He came over after school sometimes. We watched *Project Runway*, talked about moving to New York, becoming designers. He was terrible at sewing, but he made me laugh. And, uh, he was pretty cute too." He glances briefly at George, who gives a slight nod of approval.

Austin squeezes Lamar's shoulder. "Both very important qualities in a man."

Beckett blushes. "Yeah, well, anyway. We were reading *The Great Gatsby* in class, and I got obsessed with twenties looks. That vest I wore the other day? From that. I also made a flapper dress—sequins, fringe, the whole thing." He glances up, daring someone to laugh. No one does. "When it was done, we wanted to see it move. So I put on my vest, Jordan put on the dress, we cranked up a jazz playlist and tried the Charleston. Then a slower song came on, and we were just... dancing. That's all. Just dancing." He swallows hard. "Until my dad came home early from the bar."

Pearly's stomach drops. She knows where this is going.

"All he saw was a boy in a dress, and my hand around his waist. He, uh, didn't take it well." He shrinks in his seat, staring down at the floor.

George regards his grandson with concern, as old memories from his own childhood flash through his mind. "Did your dad—did he hit you?"

"No, nothing like that." Beckett kicks at the stone floor with his sneaker. "But he burned the dresses. He was pretty drunk. He might not even remember."

"Oh, Becks," says George. "Why didn't you tell me?"

"It was right after Grandma died. You had enough going on."

His words hang in the air. The chant from the upper chapel infiltrates the space.

"No," says George. "That's not an excuse. I should have known something was wrong. I should have been there for you."

Pearly doesn't disagree, but she's hoping he'll do more than drown in his own guilt. "You didn't cause it," she says. "Neither of you did. Sometimes good people get crushed under someone else's fear."

Beckett's eyes glisten. "Then what's the point, if life's gonna suck for no reason?"

"That," Pearly says, exhaling, "is the oldest question there is."

Beckett lets out a dry laugh. "You know what's funny? I actually Googled that once. 'Why do bad things happen to good people?' I only had one night before Mom checked my history and put on parental controls, but I didn't find anything super helpful."

Pearly turns to him. "And what answer were you hoping for?"

"I don't know." Beckett shrugs. "Something that didn't sound like a press release for divine indifference."

"Fair enough." She considers what to say that won't get her Voided on the spot—she's already been on thin ice for revealing her true nature to past charges—but in all honesty, she has a lot of the same questions. "Wanna know what I think?" she says.

Beckett brushes his mop of bangs from his face. "Sure, I guess."

She takes a breath, spreading her hands out in front of her. "I think the universe is like a cake."

"A cake?" Beckett is very close to an eye-roll.

"Yes, and we—you and me and all the other people on Earth—we're in the jelly layer. And because of that, we've learned a lot about jelly. And maybe we even know a little about the chocolate layer or the icing layers, too. But it's impossible for us, as jelly, to step outside our layer and have the perspective to say 'oh, that's a cake!' And even more incomprehensible to understand the concept of 'birthday party.'"

"What about, like, the Baker?" says Beckett. "If there is something out there, it doesn't seem like it gives a damn about us."

As a soul who's lived many lives, Pearly has more perspective than most, but even she can't claim to know what God is up to in Sector Zero. "I don't pretend to have access to the kitchen. I just know the recipe works, and that the ingredient everything holds together with—the one you can taste even when you can't name it—is love. I know that the times I've tasted it directly are the only times I've been sure of anything."

"Now that's a spiritual philosophy I could get behind," says Lamar. "Dessertology. Better than astrology. I don't want anyone telling me who I am just because I was born in January."

"That is a very Capricorn thing to say, sweetie," says Austin.

This gets a few chuckles, even from Beckett.

"Exactly." Pearly smiles. "The point isn't whether bad things should or shouldn't happen. It's that they don't cancel the sweetness underneath."

Now Beckett does roll his eyes—but he's sitting less hunched, his energy lighter.

George clears his throat. "That sounds a lot like what Jesus said, in his own way."

Everyone turns to him. Pearly holds her breath. As a soul, she falls into the "spiritual-but-not-religious" category, but she's practiced just about every religion there is over her many lives. She's seen it used for faith, hope, community, and manipulation. Fortunately, she's never seen George use it for the latter.

George looks up, eyes shining. "He didn't promise safety. He just said, 'Love anyway.' Even when it hurts. Even when it doesn't make sense. Especially then."

Pearly smiles, feeling the words resonate in her chest.

Beckett sighs. "Kind of a hard sell, Gramps."

"Yes," says George. "But maybe it's the only thing that makes the rest survivable."

Lamar leans back against the pew. "Paul had a version of that too, didn't he? 'Suffering produces perseverance, perseverance character, and character hope.'" He glances toward Beckett. "Translation: make meaning from the wreckage."

Austin snorts. "That guy would've gone viral on TikTok."

Beckett raises an eyebrow. "So let me get this straight: one says we can't see the whole cake, one says love anyway, and one says recycle your trauma into hope merch?"

"Pretty much," Pearly says. "But that's the thing—they're all the same answer. You don't get to know the pattern yet. You just keep loving and creating and being your most authentic self, and maybe someday it'll be revealed."

Beckett glances at George. "Do you think there's a pattern?"

George hesitates. "I don't know," he admits. "But I think maybe it's enough to believe there's *room* for one."

"Yeah," says Beckett. "Maybe."

The wind moans through the abbey's old stones. The candle flames bend and right themselves.

Pearly studies the two of them—the hesitant grandfather, the hurting grandson—and feels that ache she's come to know too well: the knowledge that grace can start here, but it won't be finished here. Not yet. Back home, there will be fallout. Conversations. Maybe a reckoning that's long overdue.

If George can step up. If Beckett can stay open.

Sometimes, it feels to Pearly like the cake is one bite away from collapse. But for now—just for now—it feels like the jelly layer is holding. And maybe that's enough.

TWENTY-TWO

After a hike back down through the village, the group huddles up where the bridge to the mainland meets the sand. The abbey rises behind them like a stone diva posing for a pilgrimage calendar.

Thunder stands before them, sweeping an arm out to the sea. "The locals call this the pilgrim's path," he says. The tide has gone out far enough to reveal the flats—a gleaming plain of wet sand and shallow pools that stretch almost to the horizon. "For centuries, people crossed the bay on foot to reach the abbey at low tide. It's tradition to walk a small part of it. Barefoot, if you're feeling brave."

"Define brave," says Lillian, eyeing the glimmering expanse.

"Well, there's quicksand," he shrugs. "But we won't be going far enough in to find any." He gestures toward a row of wooden stakes jutting from the sand. "That line marks the safe loop. Stay within it, and we'll make it back before the tide returns. It's about a mile round trip."

Pearly stops fake-filming Thunder and swivels her phone to selfie-mode. "You hear that, Pearly Girlies?" she says into the lens. "Package deal: adventure and exfoliation, all in one."

"Can't we just go to a spa?" says Austin.

"Where's the drama in that?" Lamar takes his partner by the hand. "I thought you'd relish the prospect of getting swept away in the tides."

"Tempting," says Austin, giving Lamar a peck on the cheek, "but I prefer my tragic romance on the screen."

"Agreed," says Reyna, rolling up her pant legs. "Let's not trend for the wrong reasons."

They take off their shoes and step onto the sand. The first touch is cool and silky, giving just enough to feel alive beneath their feet. Water laps over their toes and pulls back, leaving the abbey's reflection rippling in the shallows.

Pearly lingers behind for a moment, watching Thunder stride ahead, all confidence and borrowed authority. They're both pretending—he with his counterfeit lanyard, she with her fake vlog—but together, they almost pass for one honest guide.

Pearly breathes it in, content. The abbey gleams in the background, its spire mirrored in the flats, suspended between two worlds. She does a quick aura assessment and determines that all three of her charges are developing some golden-yellow tones. Not bad for a group that started the week in the spiritual dumpster.

As they move farther from shore, the light changes. A silvery mist curls over the water. Shadows melt, and it begins to rain. The only sound is the soft squish of their footsteps and the distant whistle of wind moving over the sea.

"Weather sure moves fast out here," says George.

"Sometimes," agrees Thunder, but he shoots Pearly a look. She hears his voice in her mind.

Thunder: *Is it just me, or does something feel off?*

She nods at him. There's a charge in the air—a sharp, static quality—that makes her aura prickle. The rain thickens into a fine, cold drizzle.

"Wish I'd brought my umbrella," says Reyna. "I don't want to get stuck in a downpour."

Thunder squints through the mist, then clears his throat. "Alright, gang. Let's start heading back."

"Good idea," says Lillian. "This fog is making my hair frizz, and my knees are about ready to unionize." She sidesteps a tangle of marsh grass—and immediately sinks to her ankle.

There's a beat of silence as everyone stares at her like they're watching a science experiment unfold.

"Wow, you weren't kidding," says Lamar. "I didn't expect to see quicksand outside a Saturday morning cartoon."

"Don't just stand there!" huffs Lillian, tugging uselessly. "Help me before I become a cautionary tale."

Thunder crouches beside her, examining the sinkhole. "Okay, no sudden moves," he says. "Rock your foot a little, slow and steady. The bay—she likes gentle."

"Fantastic," mutters Lillian. "Another man projecting."

The group chuckles, tension easing, until George offers a hand. Lillian takes it, but she still doesn't budge. Any nervous laughter begins to die.

"Okay," she says. "Less cute now." Her face looks strained, and Pearly sees a hint of panic in her eyes.

"Let me help you, George," she says, and takes Lillian's other arm.

Even Beckett and Reyna set down their phones to join the effort. Everyone heaves, but it's like the bay is holding her there on purpose. When she finally frees one leg, the other sinks deeper.

"Is it supposed to do that?" asks Beckett.

"Guys, stop!" says Thunder. "What did I just say? Slow and gentle." He turns to Lillian. "I want you to lie down and distribute your weight as evenly as possible. Everyone, help her."

"Okay," she says, with a tremor in her voice. They all lower her to the ground, and she splays out like a sand angel.

Thunder frowns, pressing his palm to the sand. "It's thicker than it should be. Like the composition changed."

"Thunder," snaps Lillian, "I am *composing* a meltdown. Do something."

"Sorry." Thunder starts digging around her ankles. "Okay, Lil, try to wiggle your legs side-to-side. We're going to create pockets around your limbs that'll fill with water and loosen the quicksand's grip."

They get to work following Thunder's lead, but every time they make progress, the sand reclaims it. Pearly feels Lillian's anxiety skyrocket and her breathing become ragged. She stops digging and crouches beside Lillian's head. "Hey," she says. "It's gonna be okay. We've got you."

Lillian looks ready to spit out a retort, but Pearly rests her palms at the base of Lillian's skull and projects calming energy into her charge. It isn't easy—like trying to pour water into a clenched fist—but it does seem to work. Whatever words were about to surface sputter out and die. Pearly continues to anchor Lillian, gently massaging her temples to relax and distract her. She focuses on maintaining a stable, welcoming aura. Lillian's breathing slows, along with her racing heart. Pearly hears the fleeting thought pass through Lillian's mind—it's been a long time since anyone's held her. One by one, the worry lines in Lillian's forehead diminish.

The sand loosens with a wet sigh, releasing Lillian all at once. She collapses backward into George's arms. "Erm...thanks," she says, flushing. She turns to Thunder. "What are you, some kind of sand whisperer?"

Thunder shrugs. "Something like that."

Pearly sniffs the air. She thinks she detects a lingering mycelial odor, but she can't be sure. What she does know is that Thunder just saved the day—and possibly her job. She reaches out to him in her mind.

Pearly: *That was incredible. How'd you know what to do?*

He stands up, brushing sand off his pants.

Thunder: *Oh, I died in quicksand once.*

Naturally.

Thunder helps Lillian up, then scans the horizon. "Okay, gang. We've gotta move—now."

They slog back across the sand, but the fog only thickens, obscuring the abbey. The rhythmic rumble of the tide grows louder.

When they reach the bridge, the last trolley car is already gliding away toward the mainland, its red taillights vanishing into the mist.

"Wait—hey!" Beckett calls, breaking into a jog, but the sound is swallowed by fog.

Thunder exhales. "That was the last run."

"Meaning?" asks Reyna.

"Meaning the next trolley isn't until morning. And walking that bridge in this fog would be asking for trouble."

Pearly glances toward the abbey, its lights flickering through the haze. "Guess we're sleeping with the saints tonight."

***

The monks and nuns are surprisingly gracious, considering they just got shoehorned into a sleepover for eight. Apparently, it's a thing that happens now and then. But it's still awkward. They've been ushered through a warren of stone corridors to the abbey's guest refectory—a narrow room carved right into the rock, where candlelight wobbles against salt-streaked walls and the windows rattle from the wind outside. The tide has swallowed the bridge, and fog presses close to the glass like a nosy neighbor.

Dinner comes in hearty bowls of lentil soup, coarse brown bread, and freshly brewed cider. But for once, Pearly isn't hungry. She's still stewing over the likelihood of sabotage from Mildreth. She can't prove anything, of course, which makes it all the more infuriating. But it seems perfectly on-brand that her boss might "nudge" events just enough to derail the trip—and her charges along with it.

Sister Claire had insisted they change out of their wet clothes, producing a mismatched stack of spare robes from the laundry. The effect is... mixed. George looks saintly. Beckett looks like he's about to start a medieval boy band. Lillian looks annoyed, as usual. Pearly, of course, cinched her robe with a sequined ribbon from her bag. Only Thunder looks right at home. Pearly swears he could blend in anywhere. She clears her throat, surveying the table. Her poor, damp pilgrims.

"So," Pearly says. "What do y'all do for fun around here?"

Brother Mathieu furrows a brow. "Fun?"

"We bake," says Sister Claire, in heavily accented English. "The brothers are very competitive about scones."

Brother Mathieu sets down his spoon. "Because Sister Claire cheats. She uses an air fryer."

Sister Claire smiles sweetly. "It's not cheating. It's divine convection."

"That sounds nice," says George. "What else?"

"Gardening," says Brother Mathieu. "Long walks up and down a mountain of stairs—and over to the mainland for a pack of gum."

A few laughs break out around the table. Even Lillian looks mildly amused.

Brother Mathieu continues, warming to his own list. "There's also reading, of course." He pauses, then adds matter-of-factly, "And Netflix, when the Wi-Fi cooperates."

"Wait," says Beckett. "You get Wi-Fi up here?"

"Sometimes," concedes Sister Claire. "We call it the miracle of Saint Router."

More laughter. Pearly starts to relax. This isn't going so badly. "And dance parties, I hope? Wouldn't be a celebration of the divine without a little booty shaking..."

Sister Claire's mouth twitches. "Well," she says. "We sing sometimes."

The meal winds down, conversation tapering to a contented murmur. Cider glasses half-full. Spoons scraping the last of the stew. The storm outside has softened to a light drizzle that taps against the stained-glass windows.

Reyna sits between Pearly and Sister Claire, watching a curl of steam rise from her bowl. "Can I ask you something?" she says, fidgeting with a cloth napkin.

Sister Claire looks up. "Of course."

Reyna hesitates. "Don't you ever get... lonely? All this solitude, all the quiet—it would drive me crazy."

Sister Claire smiles, setting down her spoon. "At first, it nearly did. When I took my vows, I thought the silence would swallow me whole. I hummed during chores just to hear something human." She shakes her head, as if recalling those early days. "But over time, I realized the quiet isn't empty. It's alive. It listens."

Reyna tilts her head. "Listens?"

"Mm." She folds her hands, thoughtful. "When I stopped trying to fill the silence, it started to feel like a companion. Someone who... who never interrupts and always tells the truth."

Reyna's brow furrows. "That sounds peaceful. But kind of sad, too."

"It's not sadness," says Claire. "It's privacy. And I say privacy is the new rebellion."

"Wow," says Reyna. "I love that. Tell me more."

Sister Claire's eyes crinkle at the edges. "Everyone's out there shouting into the void—posting, confessing, performing. But real connection starts here." She taps her chest. "In the quiet."

Reyna nods, studying the nun. "Well, I have to say, you certainly don't look lonely."

"I'm not. And it isn't just silence that keeps me company." Sister Claire gestures around the room. "I have my brothers and sisters. I have God. It's more than enough." She pauses, then releases a soft exhale. "I chose this life. It may not be conventional, but it's mine. And I wouldn't trade it for anything."

Reyna smiles, a little wistful. "I've spent so much of my life trying to want what everyone says I'm supposed to want. But hearing you talk about your unconventional path—it's inspiring. Maybe I can let go of some of that pressure."

"You're off to a good start," says the nun. "A little permission goes a long way."

The chapel bell tolls. Sister Claire rises, brushing crumbs from her habit. "Time for rest," she says. "Come, I'll show you where you'll sleep." She gestures for the women to follow her down a narrow stone corridor. The air grows cooler, saltier. They pass through an arched doorway into a modest guest chamber lined with rough-hewn bunks and woolen blankets that smell of lavender and salty sea air.

The men's quarters branch off in the other direction. Pearly watches Thunder and the others disappear through another door. Then she turns to help Reyna untangle her robe and claim a spot by the wall. The wind rattles the windowpanes, but the space feels warm now, steeped in laughter and candle smoke.

By the time they've settled, the room has gone dim except for a single taper flickering on the windowsill. The others are already asleep. The only sounds are soft breathing, the rustle of blankets, the distant sigh of the tide. Then Reyna, too, drifts off.

Pearly lies awake a while longer, turning over thoughts of solitude, companionship, and love. Reconnecting with Thunder has been good—they share such a long history, and yet somehow they're discovering each other anew—but so has watching her charges bloom. It's not just a job. It's her purpose. Thunder still holds her heart, and maybe he always will, but she no longer needs his love to feel whole.

That realization lands softly in her chest, like a tide settling after a storm. She exhales, long and deep, and smiles to herself. *This,* she thinks, *is freedom.*

Then a trace of movement catches her eye: a figure near the window, half-lit by silver. Lillian—still in her borrowed robe, arms wrapped around her chest, gazes out toward the dark water.

Pearly hadn't realized anyone else was awake.

For a long moment she just watches. Then she swings her legs off the cot and crosses the cold stone floor.

Lillian doesn't turn when Pearly approaches. Her reflection wavers in the window, the sea behind her a blur of silver fog. "I can't stop thinking about that quicksand," she says. "How it pulled at me, wouldn't let go. It felt... familiar. Like a chain I've been dragging for years."

Pearly moves closer, so she and Lillian are shoulder-to-shoulder. "Yeah? How so, Lil?"

Lillian lets the silence hang. Pearly waits.

"When I was twenty-two," Lillian says finally, "I'd just started law school at Emory. Newly married. Newly pregnant." She lets out a brittle laugh. "I remember thinking, well, at least the tuition insurance will cover one of us."

Pearly's brow knits. "That's... darkly practical of you."

"Story of my life." Lillian presses her palm to the cold glass. "I told my husband. He said it wasn't 'good timing.' Then he said he'd met someone else. He was moving out that weekend."

Pearly winces. "Oh, sweetheart..."

Lillian's breath fogs the pane. "He didn't even have the decency to check on me after he left. Said he couldn't handle the 'drama.' This from a man who couldn't talk to me for a week every time we argued."

"Oof," says Pearly. "You didn't deserve that."

Lillian shakes her head. "No one does. But it happened anyway." Her gaze drifts to the horizon.

Pearly folds her arms, leaning on the glass. "What did you do?" she asks.

"A week later, I started bleeding in class. At first, I thought it was stress. Then the cramps hit." Her voice wobbles, and she purses her lips. "I drove myself to the ER because I didn't know who else to call. I remember the smell of antiseptic and burnt coffee. The waiting room chairs were vinyl—the kind that sticks to your thighs when you sit down. I kept my coat buttoned even though it was eighty degrees. I didn't want anyone to see the blood on my skirt."

Pearly's throat tightens. She doesn't want to interrupt, so she simply reaches out and squeezes Lillian's hand.

Lillian rocks back on her heels, then rests her head against the window. "The nurse was kind. She wore fuchsia lipstick and told me to squeeze her hand when the contractions came. I did."

The wind picks up, smacking against the stone and glass.

"When it was over," she continues, "they gave me a cup of apple juice and a list of follow-up appointments I never went to. I walked outside, and everything was just—too much. Too bright. Too clean. Too heavy. I got in my car and sat there with the engine running for an hour, just... waiting for something. I don't know what. Forgiveness, maybe. Whatever it was, it didn't come."

She glances at Pearly then, eyes glinting in the dark. "I told myself I didn't need anyone after that. And for forty years, I made damn sure no one proved me wrong. Built a career. A reputation. A fortress, kind of like this one. But the foundation was resentment, and it's been sinking ever since."

"Ahh," says Pearly. "That's why the quicksand was so hard for you."

"Yes." Her gaze returns to the window. "I think that's what it was showing me. What I've been stuck in all this time."

Pearly lets this land. They both look out over the dark water below. Then she turns to Lillian. "Sounds like he broke something sacred," she says. "And you did what people do when that happens—you built armor from what was left."

Lillian shakes her head. "I did. Titanium-grade."

Pearly smiles. "And that's okay. It's kept you upright. But armor's heavy, sugar. Sooner or later, you've got to put it down if you want to hold anything else."

Lillian's gaze shifts toward her reflection in the window. "Like what?"

Pearly shrugs. "Oh, I don't know. A conversation. A hand. Maybe even a certain retired mailman with a thing for whittling ducks."

Lillian gets all huffy, then her shoulders drop, resigned. "It's that obvious, huh?"

"Glaringly," says Pearly. "He's into you, Lil. And for what it's worth? He's a good man."

Lillian studies the glass as if it might give her an excuse to say no. Eventually, she sighs. "It's been a long time since I trusted myself to choose someone good."

"I get that," says Pearly. "Maybe start by choosing to be open. That's the only part you can control. The rest..." She gestures toward the tide. "You let it come when it's ready."

Lillian turns away from the window, locks eyes with Pearly. "I'm scared," she whispers.

"I know." Pearly gently takes Lillian's hand. "And that's okay. It means you're not numb. Look, I can't promise you how it'll turn out. But I don't want to see you on your deathbed chained to a lifetime of could've-beens."

Lillian lets out a wry laugh. "You make a persuasive case, Counselor."

"Good," says Pearly. "Then consider this cross-examination adjourned."

TWENTY-THREE

Pearly isn't sure what's suckier—killer quicksand or Mildreth's passive-aggressive interrogation tactics. The latest department meeting didn't go so well, big whoop, nothing new there. But now that her boss was actively trying to sabotage her mission, things had officially gone from "annoying" to "career-ending with a side of cosmic humiliation." Mildreth was testing how far Pearly would bend before she breaks.

The smell of burnt toast forces her back to the present. Some kind of whipped-cream concoction oozes out from under the front door. Never a good sign. Dumb Pearly insisted on a "breakfast debrief," and Pearly agreed. She felt too guilty for roping her clone into her schemes to say no. And for not being home much lately.

She pushes the door open to find her roommate in a sparkly chef's hat and an apron that reads *Kiss the Doppelgänger.* A tower of heart-shaped pancakes teeters on the counter, syrup cascading down in sticky rivulets. The blender whirs a death-chant. Snatch perches on top of the fridge, fur puffed and eyes glowing like emergency exit signs.

Dumb Pearly wields a blowtorch in one hand and flips pancakes with the other. Behind her, the Motivational Mirror leans against the toaster, shouting encouragements between sizzles.

"YOU'RE A GASTRONOMIC GODDESS!" it hollers.

"I know, right?" Dumb Pearly beams, singeing a strawberry. "I call this one *The Garden of Eatin'!*"

"YOUR INNER CHEF IS A LIMITED-EDITION MIRACLE!"

"Um… good morning?" Pearly sidesteps the trail of whipped cream and walks fully into the kitchen.

"Roomie!" Dumb Pearly drops the blowtorch and rushes Pearly like a linebacker. The torch ignites the whipped cream like a line of gunpowder, sending Snatch screeching out of the room.

Pearly sighs as she manifests a fire extinguisher and gets to work on the flaming hardwood. "I guess that's one way to start the day."

"You're welcome! I always wanted to caramelize the floor."

"Next time maybe just coffee."

Dumb Pearly takes a taste of the firefighting foam. "Tangy! Anyway, coffee's so yesterday. I'm giving breakfast a narrative arc."

"YOU'RE NOT BURNT OUT," shouts the mirror, "YOU'RE FLAMBÉED WITH PURPOSE!"

Pearly groans. "Can we shut that thing off while we eat?"

"Party pooper," scowls Dumb Pearly, scooping up the mirror. She carries it out of the room, where it can be heard muffled through the wall shouting, *"YOU'RE STILL ENOUGH—JUST LESS AUDIBLE!"*

Pearly exhales and starts dismantling the pancake tower, trying to serve them both without triggering an avalanche. When they're finally sitting at the table, she reaches across and takes her double's hand, smiling. "Thanks for doing this," she says. "I've missed you."

Dumb Pearly grins, stabbing a fork into her flapjack pile. "Me too, OG."

"So…" says Pearly, swallowing a surprisingly decent pancake, if you eat around the foam. "What's new with you?"

Dumb Pearly chews thoughtfully, eyes drifting. Pearly's expecting work-related stories, or some new show her clone's binging. "I think I wanna go to Soul School."

Pearly blinks. "What? Why? I thought you liked waste management."

"I do! But… I've missed a lot. You and Thunder and everyone else—you got to learn things I didn't. Sometimes I feel like there's a secret no one's telling me."

Pearly feels a tug at her heart. She never realized how much responsibility she'd have to take for her clone. In a way, Dumb Pearly was one of her charges too. "I get it. I never went to Guide School, just started in the field. It's probably one of the reasons Mildreth doesn't like me. But it doesn't make me any less of a guide—or a soul."

Dumb Pearly pushes her plate away, quieter now. "It's not just that."

"Then what?"

"I dunno. Maybe I just wanna be ready." She pokes the pancakes again. "In case things change."

Pearly studies her. "Things like… what?"

"Forget it." Dumb Pearly forces a grin. "So! Tell me about the meeting. Did boss-face sprout something new?"

Pearly laughs, but something's shifting in her double. She's just not sure what. But she doesn't want to force Dumb Pearly to talk about it. So she lets it go—for now.

"Something like that," she says. "Mildreth is trying to throw me off, but I can't prove anything. And meanwhile I have to go to these stupid meetings that I think she invented just to mess with me. It's taking me away from Paris, and every time I go, I start doubting myself."

Dumb Pearly's eyes light up. "Well next meeting, I can sub for you! I'll wear your robe, your hair, your uh... aura. Nobody will know the difference! It'll be just like old times."

For a moment, Pearly considers it. Dumb Pearly is her clone, after all. She was created for pretty much this purpose in the first place. And they do have the same energy signature...

What's the worst that could happen?

In Pearly's imagination, the kitchen dissolves into the Department conference room.

"Pearly Gates," says Mildreth, adjusting her glasses, "since you seem so prepared, by all means, proceed with your update."

Dumb Pearly stands at the head of the table with a manic grin and a crayon agenda labeled, *Ooh-La-La-Bitches!*

"Oh, Glittercakes." She fans out Pearly's robe with a flourish, "It was a *show.* Mont-Saint-Michel? Pure drama. Mud, miracles, a little mid-life crisis. But I, the legend—the queen—the sparkle boss of saving the day—pulled off a surprise happy ending!"

"Hmm." Mildreth glances down at her agenda. It features a drawing of the abbey covered in heart stickers. "And what was the nature of the challenges you encountered?"

"Oh, that?" Dumb Pearly waves a hand. "Nothing Pearly Gates couldn't handle. Which is me! I'm Pearly Gates. Funky fog with an attitude, some killer quicksand trying to drag the old lady down, but I ate that challenge. We even had... um... a dance break! With the locals."

Mildreth folds her hands. "A dance break."

It wouldn't be too far-fetched, thinks Pearly. *That's something I would do.*

"That's right!" Dumb Pearly beams. "Have you ever seen a nun twerk? Seriously divine, hundred percent recommend. Look, it went viral on TikTok!"

She cues up a video on Pearly's phone and broadcasts it onto the conference room's wall screen. Gasps abound as some manufactured video—*where did she even get that?*—scandalizes the other guides.

Okay, Pearly frets. *Now we're crossing a line...*

"And this... improvisational choreography," says Mildreth, "was in your mission outline?"

Dumb Pearly waves away the question. "Twerking is the mission, Moldlykins! Can I get a hallelujah?"

The air goes out of the room as the other guides exchange stares of condemnation. Mildreth looks Dumb Pearly up and down, then pulls something up on her scroll. "Tell me, *Pearly*. What were the stops on your group's food tour?"

Dumb Pearly swallows. "Food tour? Oh! Right! Uh... croissants. Obviously. And, um, coffee. In those little cups. And that place with the cheese. Or was it soap? It *smelled* like cheese."

Mildreth exhales, a faint puff of spores releasing into the air. "So... you don't know."

"Of course I know!" Dumb Pearly shouts. "I'm just... in a food coma. From all the food! But yeah, we went to a lot of boo-lown-jer... boo-lawn-ger... bakeries! And then—oh!—the big tower thingy with the pointy top! Very inspiring. Did you know dolphins swim in that river? Well, they did in my coloring book anyway."

Mildreth's twig-like lips flatten into a thin line. "You're certain this report is accurate?"

"Totally! Pinky-promise accurate."

"You realize what we do here is serious? I will not tolerate field work that tampers with a soul's aura, reversing centuries of work and making a mockery of the profession. What do you have to say in your defense?"

Dumb Pearly stops, scratches her head. "I, uh... did all my own stunts?"

"Mm-hmm." Mildreth taps her scroll. "Security."

Two cherubic interns in tiny blazers step forward, each holding a clipboard.

Dumb Pearly gasps. "Wait! No! I can fix it! I can make a chart!" She grabs a crayon and scribbles frantically on a napkin. "See? Pie chart. For the pies. We ate pie!"

The interns each take one of her elbows.

"Okay, okay!" Dumb Pearly yelps as they drag her backward. "I regret everything except the outfits!"

The conference room fades in a puff of sparkles and shame—

—and Pearly blinks, back in her kitchen, coffee steaming in her hand.

"No, yeah." She exhales. "That's the worst that could happen."

Dumb Pearly grins. "So that's a yes?"

"Not if my afterlife depended on it." She leans on the table, a spark lighting in her eyes. "But you did help me to realize something. If Mildreth Snaggs is playing dirty, the only way I'm gonna win is if I play dirty, too."

***

Pearly's still mulling it over while waiting in line to get into Shakespeare and Company, Paris's most famous bookstore, at least among English-speakers. She glances at her charges, only half-listening to Thunder explain what's so cool about the place. At least Reyna isn't on her phone—and is it Pearly's imagination, or is Lillian standing closer to George than usual?

"...so technically," Thunder's saying, "this isn't the *original* Shakespeare and Company. Sylvia Beach opened that one in 1919, but it closed during the war. Then an American named George Whitman reopened a new one in 1951—same spirit, same mission. He even let writers sleep among the stacks if they helped around the shop."

Austin sighs. "That's so romantic."

"Sounds like a fire hazard," says Lillian.

Thunder chuckles. "Whitman called it a socialist utopia masquerading as a bookstore. It was, in essence—" he winks at Pearly "—a reincarnation of Beach's shop."

Pearly smiles. *Cute.*

The group filters through the narrow doorway, ducking beneath strings of postcards and handwritten quotes. George lingers near the entrance, running a hand along a wall of biographies, while Lillian browses a stack of literary fiction and pretends not to watch him. Beckett drifts toward the LGBTQ fiction in the corner. He glances around first—checking who might be looking—then starts pulling books, one after another, the tension in his shoulders softening just a little.

Reyna heads upstairs, and Pearly follows behind—Reyna's made a lot of progress in the last few days, but she still seems a little untethered. Up they go, up a set of narrow wooden steps painted with a quote from Hafiz: "*I wish I could show you when you are lonely or in darkness the astonishing light of your own being.*" Her aura brightens reading the words. Unlike some of her colleagues, Pearly's not into judging one soul as more enlightened than another. But Hafiz—he sure was tapped into something.

The second floor gives off "secret attic" vibes. Low wooden beams cross the ceiling and mismatched chandeliers dangle like antique jewelry. Every inch of wall is covered in books—leaning, double-stacked, sliding sideways into little paper avalanches. Someone's left a half-finished espresso on the armrest beside a paperback that's been underlined to death. It's sparsely populated, but everyone here has really settled in. Reading nooks abound, with one guy even lying on his back, feet propped up on an old writing desk.

Reyna paces the floor, scanning the spines for something that calls to her. She picks up a slim poetry collection, flips it open, frowns, and sets it back down. Near the window, a tabby cat sits on a round table covered in a yellow cloth, bathed in morning sun. It turns to Pearly as she approaches, tail curling into a perfect question mark.

"*Ah,*" the tabby says, its voice lazy and Parisian. "*You are not like the others, n'est-ce pas?*"

As everyone knows, cats have a unique ability to exist in multiple dimensions. If you can tune into their frequency, you can hear their thoughts.

"*No, monsieur,*" Pearly curtseys. "*I'm just visiting the mortal plane on a work trip. How's life as a shop cat?*"

The cat licks his paws with a look of disdain.

"*It was acceptable,*" he muses, "*until they unleashed a beast called 'vacuum.' Barbaric. No respect for delicate natures.*"

"*Would you like a head scratch to ease your suffering?*"

The cat huffs, but leans forward anyway.

"*Fine. But only briefly. Behind the left ear. And do not muss the whiskers.*"

"*Merci.*" Pearly obliges. Somehow, cats always make it seem like they're doing *you* a favor. Nevertheless, the tabby purrs.

"*De rien,*" the cat stretches out on the table. "*Now move along. You're blocking my light.*"

He shuts his eyes. Conversation over. Pearly glances around for a less judgmental audience. That's when she spots the bookseller—young, mop-haired, sliding a new stack of paperbacks into place with reverent care.

"Excuse me," she says, approaching. "You wouldn't happen to have any copies of *The Last Violet*? It's an old novel by—"

"Evelyn Ashcroft!" His accent is British, his eyes gleaming. "Of course. We've got a few vintage editions tucked away. Hard to believe she ever fell out of fashion. "Come on, I'll show you."

He leads her through a maze of shelves to a corner display, where she finds three copies of her past life's greatest hit.

"Thank you," she breathes, plucking one off the shelf. "You have no idea how much this means to me. It's been a long time since I've seen this book." She turns it over in her hands, reads the description on the back cover. There were no blurbs back in the day, and it amuses her to feel the old author within get all huffy at reducing her masterpiece to a short pitch and a stupid tagline: "She went to France to heal a soldier—and found herself in the crossfire of love."

Whatever.

She looks back to the bookseller, suddenly noticing the flag pinned to his sweater—black, grey, white, and purple. Her eyes light up. *Well, universe, you sure done it again.*

"You see that young woman over there?" She nods at Reyna, still browsing the shelves with the glazed look of someone grappling with choice overload on an extensive menu. "I think she could use a little guidance."

"Of course," he says. "Cheers. I hope you enjoy the read."

Pearly turns up her guide hearing so she can witness the exchange. Reyna stands awkwardly by the shelf, grimacing over the back-cover blurb she's been reading. The bookseller sidles up next to her.

"Looking for something in particular?" he asks. "Or just taking in the ambiance?"

"Bit of both," Reyna admits. She puts the book back on the shelf. "All I know is I'm *not* looking for anything with a shirtless man and a dragon."

He nods, feigning concern. "No spicy romantasy for you then? Tragic, really. That's half our export economy."

"Yeah, no thanks," says Reyna. "My libido doesn't have a fantasy life."

He breaks into a grin. "That belongs on a tote bag."

"Yeah? Maybe I got into the wrong career."

"Could be worse," he says. "I sell other people's dreams for a living. Pays the rent—barely."

They share an easy laugh. Her eyes shift to the pin on his sweater. He notices her noticing.

"You look like you want to say something," he says. "Go on, then."

"That's a pride flag, isn't it?" Her brow wrinkles. "Not trans, that's pink and blue..."

"Ace," he clarifies. "For asexual. More specifically, I identify as biromantic, asexual."

"Ahh, I see." She bites her lip. "I've heard of ace. I didn't realize there were subcategories."

"Lots of them," he says. "For me, it means I experience romantic attraction to others but not sexual attraction."

She rocks back on her feet, considering. In her mind, she reviews the few crushes she's had over the years. She'd never fantasized about having sex with them. But she has a libido. She masturbates sometimes. So that couldn't be her.

Could it?

Anxiety quickens her pulse. She forces herself to take a breath. "How... when did you figure that out? If you don't mind me asking."

He smiles. "Not at all. My mother likes to tell the story of how I announced when I was five that I was never going to kiss anyone. But I don't think it started to click until my late teens.

And it wasn't until one of my exes suggested it that I did some research and realized that was me. I had to sort through a fair amount of shame and confusion to get there. When I finally did, it was a relief."

"I bet it was. That's great to hear." But internally, she's even more confused. Were her crushes even romantic? She'd always assumed so, but what she admired was their beauty or their songwriting talent. She wants to ask more questions, but it's a lot to take in and she's starting to feel overwhelmed. "I wish I was as together as you," she says. "I'm always questioning whether I'm doing it right. You know. Life."

"The way I see it," he says, "if you're being authentically you, you're doing it right. And that's a gift to yourself, along with the people who care about you."

They stand there in silence for a moment, but it's not awkward silence.

"I don't usually feel this comfortable with people," she admits. "Definitely not ones I've just met. It's... refreshing."

"It is," he says. "Rare, that. Like finding a good cup of tea abroad."

She smiles. "Exactly. I mean, except I drink coffee. I'm from Seattle."

"Seattle," he says. "That's U.S., yeah?"

"Yeah," she blushes. "Sorry, that was presumptive."

"No worries. So what brings you to Paris?"

"My grandmother," she says. "She always wanted to visit, but she died before she could. She left me her ticket. I thought if I followed through, I'd feel closer to her."

"Has it worked?" he asks.

Reyna hesitates. "Sometimes. Other times, I just feel like an imposter. Like I'm borrowing someone else's dream."

He nods, thoughtful. "That's still part of the story, though. You're writing your own chapter now."

She smiles, shaking her head. "You're good at this."

"Occupational hazard," he says. "Some people sell souvenirs. I deal in introspection." He studies her a moment, then reaches for a nearby display. "Actually..." He holds up a slim leather-bound journal emblazoned with the Shakespeare and Company logo. "Might as well start that new chapter properly. Perfect for secrets, sketches, and the occasional rant about humanity."

Reyna laughs, taking it. She flips it open, shuffling through the blank pages. "You know," she says. "This is perfect. I met a nun the other day who told me privacy is the new rebellion."

He smirks. "You should put that on a tote bag, too."

"I don't know..." Reyna pretends to think about it. "Maybe we should diversify, make some mugs."

"Brilliant," he says. "Coasters too. Nothing says quiet defiance like a matching set."

They both chuckle, then settle into another non-awkward silence. It's Reyna who eventually breaks it. "Hey, um, if I wanted to read more about asexuality... do you have any suggestions?"

"I do!" He grins, exposing a set of dimples. "Angela Chen's book, *ACE*, is a great start. And if you want more, I'm happy to provide other recs." He pulls out a business card from a battered wallet and hands it to her. "Or if you'd just like a friend to explore the city with—feel free to reach out."

"Thanks. I just might." Reyna glances at the card. "Ollie," she says. "It's nice to meet you. Really nice. I'm Reyna."

They shake hands, and she pockets the card with a smile.

Thunder nudges Pearly. She startles, not realizing he'd been standing beside her, witnessing the exchange. "You're a good guide," he says.

"What?"

"A good guide," he repeats. He shifts his weight, like he's considering how much to reveal. "When I first heard you changed jobs, I wasn't sure you'd stick the landing. I mean, you're not exactly the poster child for this line of work."

She snorts. "Ya think?"

"But now watching you down here?" He smiles, his thumb brushing over her knuckles. "I see you. I don't care what anyone says. You were made for this. And those souls—" He nods to Reyna. "They're lucky to have you."

She swallows, eyes glistening. "Thank you. That's probably the nicest thing anyone's ever said to me."

"Really? I think you need a bigger sample size."

They descend back down the stairs. Reyna and Ollie are admiring a painted inscription above the archway.

Be not inhospitable to strangers lest they be angels in disguise.

Pearly stares at it, a laugh catching in her throat. If they only knew.

TWENTY-FOUR

Pearly follows the group out of Shakespeare and Company into the watercolor light of late afternoon. Along the Seine, the green stalls of the bouquinistes stretch for blocks, attached to the old stone walls. Beckett moves from one to the next snapping pics of antique books and maps, vintage postcards and art prints. They keep walking until they smell roasted chestnuts and perfume, the streets widening into the chic swirl of Saint-Germain.

Pearly slows as the green-gilded awnings of Café de Flore come into view. The café is hopping, with waiters in bow ties balancing silver trays through a maze of tiny terrace tables. She smiles, a wave of nostalgia washing over her. The café has been a hotspot since the dawn of the Third Republic, when it was a crossroads for artists, poets, and dreamers. She can almost feel it thrumming beneath the modern-day bustle, that pulse of freedom and creation that once made this quarter the heartbeat of Paris.

"Can we stop here?" asks Beckett, eyeing the Insta-worthy café.

"Sure," says Thunder. "Good eye."

The group finds a trio of tables on the terrace beneath the awnings. Pearly orders a round of café pots and pastries, because no one argues with her when she's decisive about carbs.

Pearly raises her phone. "Okay, everyone—book haul time!"

Austin groans. "Can we at least eat first?"

"Nope." Pearly points her camera at him. "Documentation before digestion."

Lillian pulls a small paper bag onto her lap. "I found this. *Women Who Painted in Secret.* Apparently, half the Impressionists were women with bad PR."

Pearly gives a thumbs up. "I'd read that."

George clears his throat, setting a hardback on the table. *Letters That Changed the World.* "Seemed fitting. Carried a lot of letters in my day. Figured I'd finally see what was in some of 'em."

Austin fans open an absurdly thick tome. "*Les Misérables.* Tragic, dramatic, French. I figured if I don't finish it, I can always use it to start that weight-lifting regimen."

Lamar puts an arm around his partner. "Good plan, sweetie. At least it'll be lighter than your emotional baggage."

Austin swoons. "God, I love it when you tease me. What did you get?"

Lamar holds up a book entitled *Swearing in French.* "In case anyone tries to rob us again."

"Well," says Pearly. "Speaking of tragic, dramatic, and French..." She pulls out her copy of *The Last Violet.* "I have it on good authority this fits the bill. Oh, and I couldn't resist this..." She extracts a blue trucker hat embroidered with the phrase **UNRELIABLE NARRATOR** and puts it on. Everyone chuckles.

Reyna shows the group her journal. "Mine's for writing things down before they explode in my head. A first step in befriending the silence."

"I love that." Pearly points her phone at Thunder. "And you? Buy anything?"

"Nah," he says. "I carry everyone else's enlightenment."

All eyes slide toward Beckett. He's been quiet, nursing his hot chocolate, paper bag untouched.

"What about you?" George asks. "Find anything good?"

Beckett hesitates, then slides three books from the bag. *Love in Exile*—its cover still bearing a gold "Coup de Cœur" sticker. Then there's *Cemetery Boys* and *Letters to My Younger Queer Self.* His hands tremble as he places them on the table.

"I almost chickened out at the register," he says, blushing. "But the cashier..."

"Ollie," says Reyna.

"Yeah. He was so enthusiastic that I ended up getting all three."

"I'm glad." Reyna smiles. "He had some recs for me too. Those look amazing."

"They do," Pearly adds gently. "Solid taste."

At the next table, a burst of teenage laughter breaks through the café's chatter. It's harmless enough, but something in Beckett's posture changes. He goes very still, shoulders tightening as if bracing for impact.

Pearly follows Beckett's gaze. Just a group of teens at the next table, laughing and talking in hushed tones. But something in the air shifts. It feels charged, the kind of static that prickles before a storm.

"Let's just go," Beckett mutters, shoving the books into his bag.

Behind him, the teens snicker—one laugh cracking louder than the rest.

Pearly tilts her head, extending her hearing to catch bits of conversation. *Relax,* she tells herself. *They're not laughing at him.*

The words drift over in slangy French, quick and jumbled. Something about a party and a forgotten shoe. Ordinary, harmless.

"They're just talking about their night out," she assures him. "Nothing to do with you."

"Yeah, sure," Beckett snaps, slinging the bag over his shoulder. "I don't want to talk about it, okay?"

Pearly's stomach knots. She glances at Thunder. His eyes meet hers. They can both feel it. The air is thicker now, damp and sour. A faint trace of mildew curls around the edges of her senses.

Of course. Mildreth. Whispering rot into Beckett's mind, amplifying every doubt until it echoes like truth.

George leans in, laying a steady hand over his grandson's. "Becks," he says softly, "you didn't do anything wrong."

Beckett yanks his hand away. "Don't." His voice cracks, which only seems to rile him up further.

"Hey, I'm just trying to help."

"You're a little late." Beckett's eyes flash. "Where were you when Dad threatened to send me to conversion camp? Or when Mom said I was embarrassing the family? That's when I needed your help."

Austin and Lamar share a look. They turn toward Beckett, compassion in their eyes.

George's mouth opens, then closes again. Around them, the café's chatter continues, but the group falls silent, witnessing the heated exchange. Pearly senses Mildreth is up to something—amplifying Beckett's fears, lowering the vibration in the room.

She leans in, ready to intercede, when she hears Thunder's voice in her mind.

Thunder: *Are you sure? Maybe they need to work this out on their own.*

Pearly: *Didn't you just tell me I was a good guide? Have some faith, mon chéri.*

But he does have a point. Pearly takes a moment to tune into George's thoughts. *He's right. God, he's right. I just sat there and let them steamroll him.* The shame is so raw she almost looks away.

"Look, Beckett," Lamar offers, "I've been there. I get it—"

"No, you don't get it!" Beckett's eyes flash. "None of you get it!"

The café goes still. Even the air seems to hold its breath.

Pearly feels the tug in her chest. The unmistakable pulse of a soul spinning too fast. She shouldn't. She *knows* she shouldn't. Beckett isn't her charge. It's not just frowned upon—it's illegal to interfere. But Mildreth's presence lingers at the periphery, feeding on the ache. Growing on it, like mold. Pearly can't just watch it poison him.

Alright, Snaggs, she thinks. *You make it stink, I'll bring the air freshener.*

She closes her eyes, tuning in to Beckett's energy field until she finds the channel—angry, unstable, like a radio station fighting through static—and sends her thoughts through.

Pearly: *Hey, kid. You're okay. You are not broken.*
You're just... becoming.
The noise in your head isn't truth—
it's fear in a bad disguise.
Breathe. Look up.
Find one thing in this room that's safe.

Beckett's shoulders twitch, almost imperceptibly. His gaze snags on Austin, who hasn't looked away. The tension in his throat loosens a fraction. He blinks hard, and when he speaks again, his voice trembles but doesn't shatter. "I just... I need a minute, okay?"

Austin nods. "Take all the time you need."

The storm in Beckett's aura calms to a dull, uncertain glow. Pearly exhales, the connection snapping like a pulled thread. Her pulse is racing, her palms damp. She knows she crossed a line, but she can't bring herself to regret it.

If Mildreth wants to fight dirty, she thinks, *then fine. I'll meet her in the mud.*

And hey, it seemed to work. The tension in the air has softened, just a little. Beckett no longer looks ready to bolt, and George has shifted from paralyzing guilt to quiet contemplation.

"You're right, Becks," he says. "I should've said something. I didn't know what to do, and that's not an excuse. I just froze."

Beckett blinks, the anger melting into something else. Hurt, disbelief, maybe relief. He doesn't answer, but he doesn't look away either.

"I promise to do better," says George. "If you don't trust me right now—well, that's okay. I hope to earn back that trust."

Beckett looks at George for a long moment. Then he nods.

Thunder squeezes Pearly's hand under the table, and her heart swells a little. For herself, for Thunder, for George and Beckett, for the fragile grace of a universe slowly earning back her trust—one messy human moment at a time.

***

By the time they finish up, the sun has set, the twilight is ripe with possibility, and Pearly intends to squeeze the juice out of it. With only three nights left in Paris, she's got to step things up. Her charges are all doing well—certainly compared to where they started—but the level of progress Pearly promised Mildreth is almost unheard of in such a short amount of time.

They stroll through the narrow cobblestone streets, past shuttered bookshops and cafés and daredevil Parisians on bikes and motorcycles who must have guides watching out for them. Pearly keeps an eye out for experiences that might inspire bonding *and* spiritual revelation. Sometimes those are the same thing.

She hears it before she sees it—a jazz melody drifting through the night like a spell that forgot where it parked its car. She follows the sound to a corner where warm light glows against red velvet curtains. Wide windows reveal silhouettes leaning close over candlelit tables, and a chandelier throws shards of gold onto a glossy black piano. Above the awning, the sign reads *La Note de Grâce*. Grace Note.

Well, if that isn't a sign...

The music grows clearer as she pushes open the door, ushering the group inside. The place is drenched in color—crimson walls, gilt molding, mirrors that double everything: candles, faces, wine-fueled applause. A mural sprawls across the ceiling, angels mid-debauch, their trumpets catching the light from a low crystal chandelier. The bar is polished mahogany with bottles glowing behind glass. Red velvet banquettes line the room, already full of patrons pressed shoulder to shoulder. Waiters in white shirts and black suspenders weave through the maze of tables, balancing trays of wine. But the centerpiece of the room is a gleaming black piano.

The pianist—a young guy with a loosened tie and a close-cropped goatee—plays with easy confidence, some French melody that sounds vaguely familiar to Pearly. A microphone stands nearby, waiting for the next singer to take her turn.

The song shifts into Sinatra's "Fly Me to the Moon." George's fingers start tapping the tablecloth, muscle memory at work.

Pearly leans toward him. "You play?" She knows the answer of course, but she can't exactly tell him she's written his case file.

He chuckles. "Used to bang around on a piano in the rec hall. Army base in Georgia, long time ago. We had this upright that was mostly held together by prayer and duct tape."

"Oh yeah?" says Lillian. "What'd you play?"

"Whatever I could remember from church, mostly. The guys liked it when I did Elvis or Jerry Lee. The chaplain, not so much."

The pianist modulates into a final refrain, and Lillian sings along without thinking. Softly, but with surprising range. Pearly senses Lillian doesn't want to draw attention to herself, and yet Pearly knows how much Lillian loved singing in her youth—at church, and then in her college days.

When the song ends, the singer leans into the mic, beaming. "All right, who's feeling brave tonight? We always make room for a guest or two. Don't be shy—Paris loves a debut."

Austin elbows Pearly. "How about you? You've never been shy a day in your life."

Pearly laughs, half rising from her seat. The pull of the spotlight is instinctive—the unabashed pleasure in belting out a banger, not to mention the thrill of applause. For a heartbeat, she almost does it.

Then she looks at her charges. She sees George's fingers still tapping the table. Lillian's lips still forming the last line of the melody, too shy to finish it aloud.

Pearly exhales. The moment crystallizes.

"Actually," she says, "I think Paris has waited long enough to hear *these two.*"

George blinks. "What?"

Lillian sputters. "Oh, absolutely not—"

But Pearly's already waving at the stage. "Trust me, I have impeccable instincts."

The singer grins. "A duet! Perfect!"

Laughter and good-natured protests circulate through the room, but the crowd is clapping now, urging them forward. Lillian's cheeks flush pink. George looks like he'd rather face artillery fire—but he stands.

The pianist slides over, gesturing to the keys. George sits, flexing his hands. "I'm pretty rusty," he says. "Hope these arthritic fingers remember what to do."

"They will," promises Pearly.

George and Lillian confer in hushed tones. They seem to be arguing about what to play. She keeps shaking her head—not that, not that—but eventually, he makes a suggestion that produces a tiny smile.

"Okay, okay," she says, then turns to the group. "Set the bar low, okay?"

"Too late!" teases Reyna. "Give it to us, diva!"

"Yeah, Lillian!" cheers Beckett.

Austin whoops. "Break a heart, not a hip!"

Lillian rolls her eyes. "You all are incorrigible," she says into the mic. This earns a chorus of laughs and whistles from the group.

She nods at George, and he begins to play. The opening notes of "At Last" ripple through the space—tender, soulful, timeless. Conversation fades. Wine glasses hover midair. Lillian swallows hard, catching her reflection in the polished black of the piano lid.

When she starts to sing, her voice is almost too fragile to carry, as if she's testing its weight. She closes her eyes and lets the melody pull her in. By the next phrase, she's steady. Pearly can feel years of restraint slipping off her shoulders like a mink stole.

Thunder leans closer. "She's good," he murmurs.

"She's magnificent," Pearly whispers back, her throat tightening.

George finds his rhythm, fingers caressing the keys like an old lover. When he finally looks up at Lillian—just once—it's enough to cause a flare in both their auras. Lillian doesn't look away.

She sings about finding love after a long, lonely road—about peace that finally feels like her own. Her voice opens fully now, raw and unguarded, and George answers with a tender echo from the keys. When she reaches the part about smiles that feel like spells and love that feels like home, Pearly risks a glance at Thunder.

Of course, he smiles at her—casting the same spell that first enchanted her back in Soul School. The effect is powerful as ever, but her response has changed. Once upon a time, she'd have leaned into the heat and chaos of it. But now that she and Thunder aren't trying to impress or prove anything, there's... space. And in that space, something new is forming—something softer, steadier, maybe even *holy*. She always assumed stability was dull. But stability, she realizes, is what lets you drop the act. For a soul who's spent lifetimes performing, that might be the sexiest thing of all.

The final refrain swells and settles. A last trembling note lingers, suspended between heartbeats—then fades into silence.

The room erupts in applause. Pearly tears her gaze from Thunder and joins the others, clapping hard enough to sting her palms. Lillian's cheeks are flushed, her eyes bright, as if she's surprised by what she's unleashed. George stays seated, one hand still on the keys, grinning like a schoolboy who's just learned his crush likes him back.

Pearly joins the applause, her heart full and glittering. Tonight, she remembers why they call Paris the City of Love.

TWENTY-FIVE

Pearly hates exercise, but she loves Montmartre. Climbing the hill to reach her favorite neighborhood is worth the thigh-strain. She refuses to wear sensible shoes on general principle, so her concession is a pair of rubber-soled platform boots patterned with sequined red lips.

The morning air is crisp and lemon-bright, the steep streets glistening from an early rinse of rain. Behind Pearly, the group climbs at varying speeds of enthusiasm. But everyone stops grumbling when they glimpse the iconic red windmill of the Moulin Rouge. Beckett snaps a selfie and declares, "Greatest musical of all time." Lamar can't help his look of horror.

"A movie musical?!" He fans himself, like he's about to pass out.

Austin rolls his eyes. "Oh, now who's the dramatic one?" He pats Lamar's head. "There, there, you'll be okay," he says. "If it's about the drama, *Phantom of the Opera* wins on sheer chandelier count."

Lamar balks. "Now you're just trying to get a rise out of me. Andrew Lloyd Weber, greatest musical of all time? Not in any version of reality I choose to participate in."

"Alright," says Lillian, "so what do you think it is?"

Lamar straightens his shoulders, adopting a smug look. "It's gotta be Sondheim, of course. *Company* or *Sunday in the Park*."

Austin shakes his head. "Oh sweetie, those are elitist musicals. Where's the glitz, where's the glamour? Where's the fun?"

"Come on, my darlings," says, Pearly, hoping to rope the group back on track. "Culture waits for no one. And for the record—*Cabaret*, hands down."

At the crest of the hill, the Basilique du Sacré-Cœur rises like a frosted meringue against a watercolor sky. The bells start to chime, echoing across the terracotta rooftops. Pearly pauses, pretending she's catching her breath but really just absorbing it—the sweep of Paris below, hazy and infinite.

Beckett lifts his phone, framing the basilica against the skyline. The glare washes the photo almost white, but he clicks anyway. He studies the shot for a moment, frowns, deletes it.

"Keep up, cherub," Pearly calls.

He jogs to catch the group, but glances back once before the curve of the street hides the domes from view.

Pearly tilts her head toward the slope of Rue de l'Abreuvoir, where pastel houses pose like they know they're in a painting. Evelyn Ashcroft once lived halfway down that hill. A shiver of memory passes through her. Evelyn had been so sure her words would outlive her. But she never quite learned that living is an art too, not just writing about it.

She could stay here all day, but the square ahead is calling—*Place du Tertre*, where dozens of street artists have already staked out spots with easels, canvasses, and camping chairs.

"About a hundred-forty licensed artists work here," says Thunder, gesturing toward the rows of easels. "Each one had to earn a spot through a jury. One square meter per person!"

Most of the artists are silver-haired veterans, sleeves smudged with charcoal, alongside a sprinkling of enterprising twenty-somethings. A woman in a striped scarf sells watercolor postcards still damp around the edges. The cobblestones shine with reflected color. Nearby, a musician with a handlebar moustache plays an old French tune on an accordion. He's slightly off-key, but charming nonetheless.

At the next stall, a painter dabs at a half-finished landscape while chatting with Lillian and Reyna. "You like wine?" he asks. "You must try the local vintage—Clos Montmartre, just behind the square."

"Is it good?" asks Reyna.

"Terrible!" he says, grinning. "But the vineyard makes a fine photo, and the walk is better than the wine."

"I like him," says Lillian. "Let's do it."

A moment later the two of them wander off together, arm-in-arm, following his directions. Nothing mends a reluctant roommate situation like a quest for questionable alcohol.

George stops at a stall lined with sketches of families, lovers, and the occasional poodle in a beret. He watches a mother and daughter pose, the older woman's hand resting gently on the girl's shoulder. Their laughter echoes through the square.

George smiles, then turns to Beckett. "What d'you say? One for the old man's scrapbook?"

Beckett grimaces. "Seriously? In public?"

"Posterity waits for no teenager."

Austin applauds. "Do it, dude. Your face screams *Teen Vogue*."

Reyna elbows him. "You just want to flirt with the artist."

"I contain multitudes," he replies grandly, then drags Lamar toward the Dalí museum across the street.

Beckett sighs, but he sits beside his grandfather, shoulders locked in defensive formation. The artist sizes them up. He's a wiry man with paint under every fingernail.

"Family?" he asks.

"Yes, sir," George says, beaming. "This is my grandson!"

Beckett ducks behind his bangs. "Oh god, this can't be real."

"Oh, it's as real as your teenage angst, darling." Pearly claps her hands. "Okay, gentlemen, smile like you actually like each other!"

The artist frowns. "Non, s'il vous plaît. We want a natural look."

Pearly juts out her chin. "What if they naturally smile?"

The artist stares at her, deadpan.

She stares back.

"Okay, okay," she concedes. "No smiling." She watches them sitting next to each other, all stiff and silent. "I have an idea!" she says. "Interview time!"

George breaks his portrait face to raise an eyebrow. "Interview?"

"Obviously. Every great work of art deserves behind-the-scenes commentary." She winks at the artist. "Keep sketching, maestro."

She crouches beside the pair, slipping into her best host voice. "Question one: Beckett, what's it like traveling with your grandfather in the most romantic city on earth?"

Beckett brushes his bangs out of his eyes. "Uh, weird? But... good-weird, I guess."

"Define good-weird."

He shrugs, glancing sideways at George. "We actually talk now."

"Progress!" Pearly grins. "George, same question in reverse. What's it like seeing Paris through your grandson's eyes?"

George chuckles. "I like watching him notice things I forget to see—color, sound, beauty. All the little joys I hurry past."

He glances at Beckett as the artist shades the paper with measured strokes. "Makes me think about what else I hurried past. Back home, I told myself I was being respectful. Letting his parents handle things their way. But 'keeping the peace' just meant keeping my mouth shut when I was scared to speak up."

"So what," says Beckett, "you going rogue now?"

George smiles. "Something like that."

"Go George!" cheers Pearly. "We are here for it." She clears her throat, summoning her faux-host energy. "If you could go back and change one thing about how you handled the rough patches, what would you tell younger-you?"

"Hmmm..." George leans back in his chair. "I'd tell him to speak up sooner. Even if his voice shakes."

"Yeah?" says Beckett.

"Yeah." George breaks into a wistful smile. "And I'd tell him not to beat himself up for stealing that girlie magazine from the gas station that one time."

Beckett's eyes widen. "You *what*? Gramps, you absolute menace."

Everyone bursts out laughing. The artist glances up. "Stay still, please—this part needs precision."

"Final question," she says. "What's something you've learned from each other on this trip?"

Beckett smirks. "That Grandpa can apparently play piano *and* have feelings. Didn't see that crossover coming."

George laughs. "Yeah, well... took me long enough to learn the chords."

When the sketch is done, the artist flips it over, revealing a moment in time captured in charcoal. The likeness isn't exact, more impressionist than literal, but the feeling is right: two figures leaning in, laughter about to break free.

Beckett studies it. "We look like each other."

George nods. "Hope that isn't disappointing."

"Nah," says Beckett. He wraps an arm around George. "It just means you're a good candidate for *Senior Vogue*."

"And cut," says Pearly. "That was perfect. No retakes needed."

Thunder taps her shoulder. "Your turn."

"What?"

He nods toward an older artist in a green corduroy jacket, mustard-colored cap, and silver beard. "I already paid for it."

The man beckons to her. "Madame, it would be my honor..."

Pearly preens, perching on the stool as she fluffs her hair. "Make me look expensive."

The artist chuckles. "Picasso used to say that."

"Well, I taught him everything he knew," she says.

Thunder smirks. "Really?"

She shrugs. "Maybe." No, not really. But it could be true. And mysterious is always sexy.

The artist starts sketching, telling anecdotes about old celebrities and famous locals. His pencil flies across the paper until, mid-stroke, he hesitates.

"I have to stop talking now," he says, "to focus on the eyes."

"Of course, darling," says Pearly. "Windows to the soul."

"Indeed," he nods, looking down at the drawing, then back up at her. Something shifts in his expression. He stops sketching and really takes her in. "You—you have been here before, haven't you?"

"Umm... yes?" Pearly can't be sure what he means, but she senses he's seeing straight into her soul, into all the lives she's lived. All the mistakes she's made.

"You burn so bright, chérie." He smiles at her, but his eyes are filled with… is that pity? Condemnation? "No wonder everything you touch goes up in flames."

The words land like cinders. Pearly's smile holds, but her pulse races. The square around her goes silent as she lets the words settle—her worst fear, slapping her in the face. For one nauseating second, she swears she smells mold.

The artist blinks hard, disturbed by his own words. "I—don't know why I said that." He looks almost frightened, as if realizing the thought wasn't his. "Forgive me."

"It's okay," she says. "You're not wrong." She tries to laugh it off with a hair toss, but her hands tremble in her lap.

Thunder crouches beside her. "You don't actually believe that, do you?"

Does she? She wouldn't say she's hurt her charges, but when it comes to love—yeah, she's left scorch marks.

"I don't know," she admits. "I'm not sure who I am anymore."

He doesn't argue. Just kisses her forehead and hands her the sketch. Her own eyes stare back—bright, defiant, almost daring her. She's risen from her own ashes more times than she can count. But has she changed? Or just learned to pose better in the smoke?

She tucks the sketch away, making a silent promise not to start any brush fires.

By dusk, they've wound down the hill to the *Mur des je t'aime*, the "I Love You Wall." The cobalt wall gleams with those three little words written in 250 languages. The others drift toward crêpes and souvenirs. Pearly and Thunder linger. The setting sun turns the tiles to sapphires.

She's lost track of how many times she and Thunder have said "I love you." A million? Ten million? It's practically their second language by now. But not since their breakup. And it's never meant the same thing twice. Sometimes it's, "thank you." Sometimes, "forgive me." Sometimes it's just code for, "don't you dare die on me yet." They've said it in a dozen centuries and a hundred bodies, between fights and funerals and champagne toasts. They've said it as a joke, a prayer, a promise they both knew they couldn't keep. And somehow, they keep saying it. She guesses that's what love is when you've lived long enough to ruin it a few thousand times: muscle memory with teeth.

Her fingertips graze the tile, and the memories rise like smoke.

Once, beneath an Arctic sky in the year the sea froze solid, she stitched a sealskin tent by the glow of an oil lamp. He slept beside her, frost tangled in his beard. When she whispered *eremeh,* her breath crystallized before it reached him. But he smiled in his sleep, as if it had found its way into his dreams.

Once, in a Honolulu bakery where guava steamed from the ovens and the streets smelled of sugar cane, she shouted *aloha wau iā 'oe* across the counter, laughing as dough exploded from the pan. He laughed too—covered in flour, then covered her in kisses.

Once, in Shanghai's French Concession, rain inked the alleyways black. She was copying poetry for a paper-lantern festival when he returned, coat torn, blood on his sleeve. She pressed his wrist to stop the shaking and wrote the words instead: *w ài n.* He read them upside down, smiled, and ruined the lantern with tears.

Every language, every century—a new translation of the same impossible thing.

Pearly exhales. Thunder's reflection gleams beside hers in the tiles, both faces fractured by a hundred translations of the same word.

For a heartbeat, she almost says it. *I love you.*

Then she remembers the artist's voice. *No wonder everything you touch goes up in flames.*

She steps back before the fire catches. "Ready to go?" she asks, too brightly. "The others are probably wondering if we've eloped."

Thunder offers a hand instead of an answer.

She takes it. The wall glows behind them, a mosaic of promises she isn't ready to make again—at least, not yet.

TWENTY-SIX

S ix days down, two to go. Pearly's busy making plans when the summons arrives mid-espresso.

TO: GATES, PEARLY
SUBJECT: *Urgent Review of Field Conduct*
LOCATION: Dept. of Human Relations, Supervisor Snaggs' office
WHEN: Now

She sighs, setting down the spreadsheet and grabbing her White Robe. "That can't be good."

She has a kneejerk impulse to reach out to Thunder, but what could he do? No, best to deal with this herself. After all, she knows her boss better than anyone—except maybe Malcolm, and she's gotten him in enough hot water already. And anyway, she's fully capable of dealing with Mildreth. Or at least, that's what she tells herself.

For once, she wishes she had that damn Motivational Mirror.

*****

Pearly enters her boss's office like a prisoner awaiting sentencing. She holds her head high and vows not to flinch. She didn't do anything wrong. Well, OK, she did, technically. But it was for a good cause. Surely the Higher-Ups would see that.

Mildreth sits motionless, fingers steepled, expression carved from cold authority.

"Punctual," she says. "Fascinating what a disciplinary summons can do for motivation."

"Morning to you too," says Pearly, sliding into the chair opposite. "Love what you've done with the, uh, growths. Is that a new haircut?"

"No." Mildreth taps a glowing document. "Clause Four, Section Eight-C—unauthorized interference with a soul not under your supervision. Beckett Whitaker. Care to confirm or deny?"

Pearly glances at the file, then back up. "Confirm. But in my defense, he was mid-existential implosion." *Because of you,* she thinks. "I had to do something."

"Did you?" Mildreth leans back. "According to Department protocol, that was not your call to make. Beckett has his own guide, and you had no idea what protocols that guide had in motion."

Before Pearly can respond, there's a sharp knock.

"Enter," commands Mildreth.

A young guide walks in, sporting a pristine White Robe with that "new manifestation" smell.

Pearly blinks. "Oh! Hello. Didn't see that one coming."

"I thought it appropriate," says Mildreth, "to include the directly affected party. Beckett's guide deserves accountability. Gates here will answer for her actions. What she did was inappropriate, illegal, and disrespectful."

Edwina crosses her arms. "Appreciated. Though for the record, I'm not here to complain."

Mildreth's smile tightens. "No?"

"No." Edwina glances at Pearly. "Actually, I'd like to commend her. I'm still pretty new at all this, and sometimes I worry about overstepping. I'd rather do too little than too much, you know? But Pearly showed me there are moments when the right nudge can save a soul."

Pearly can't resist. "You hear that, Mz. Snaggs? Commendable."

"If she hadn't intervened," Edwina continues, "Beckett's frequency might've fractured beyond repair. She stabilized him long enough for me to follow protocol and complete the alignment."

The room buzzes with static. A ceiling fungus emits a nervous puff.

"Well, sounds like consensus." Pearly rises smoothly. "I'll be on my way—unless you need this documented in triplicate?"

"You are not absolved," hisses Mildreth.

"Of course not." Pearly smiles, serene. "But Beckett's doing better—and that's the point, isn't it?"

"Exactly." Edwina nods to Pearly. "Would've been nice to have a soul like you in Guide School. Thanks again for stepping up." She offers prayer hands to both of them, then leaves.

Mildreth's expression curdles. "Let's not forget where we stand. You still haven't fulfilled the terms of our agreement."

Pearly tilts her head. "Working on it. You can't rush enlightenment. Unless you've got a spreadsheet for that too?"

"OUT!"

Pearly glides to the door. The hinges wheeze as she opens it. "Always a pleasure," she calls out, and steps into the hall, leaving Supervisor Snaggs alone with her fury.

***

Mildreth Snaggs steps into the Department cafeteria and instantly feels her irritation spike. Lines of guides and administrators shuffle through brightly-lit buffet stations, chatting about promotion reviews, soul assignments, afterwork gatherings. The scent of motivational meatloaf hangs in the air.

She takes a tray, and scans the options without enthusiasm. They're all designed for palates accustomed to incarnating on Earth. She asked once if the kitchen could make some moldy lasagna. She could always manifest it herself, but it's the thought that counts. They just assumed she was joking.

Mildreth Snaggs does not joke.

At the drink station, she overhears two junior supervisors behind her.

"You heard about Gates?"

"Thought she'd be suspended."

"I know, right? The Higher-Ups seem to have a thing for her."

"Either that or she's just lucky."

"Nobody's *that* lucky. I'd love to know how she does it."

"Maybe she could lead a seminar."

The spoon in Mildreth's hand bends, just slightly, under her grip. She forces it straight again, smoothing the metal between her fingers as if she could iron out the universe's incompetence.

She glances at the seating area. There's an empty spot at the junior supervisors' table. But as soon as they catch Mildreth's eye, they freeze, stopping their conversation.

Mildreth sighs. She takes her tray and chooses the farthest table, devoid of other souls. Better to have peace and quiet than strain to make small talk. Sometimes not understanding a conversation happening around you is even worse than not being included—when everything they say and do reminds you of how alien you are.

She opens her scroll beside a plate of congealing Spore-Loaf Surprise and scrolls through Gates's latest data: three charges trending yellow. The numbers blink in smug alignment. Gates *could* pull this off.

Mildreth will have to keep chipping away at the weakest link. To sink the knife a little deeper.

She swipes over to Beckett's profile. A web of data threads expands across the screen—connections, energy ties, emotional dependencies. Family lines glowing like veins.

Mildreth's lips curl. She knows exactly how to bring down this house of cards.

A burst of laughter erupts from a nearby table, snapping her back to the cafeteria. She turns, watching two junior guides clinking glasses. Celebrating some pointless ritual.

She straightens the bent spoon one last time and sets it neatly beside her tray.

She doesn't need "friends." She needs order. And for that, she's willing to resort to desperate measures. Someday, the universe—and the Higher-Ups—will thank her.

TWENTY-SEVEN

On a scale of one to freakout, Pearly's pacing her hotel room in her thinking wig. Her charges have one day left in Paris, and if they don't uplevel before boarding planes tomorrow, it's back to cosmic sewage duty—at best. She even made a spreadsheet. If she did her auric calculations right, Lillian, George, and Reyna all just need a little something to create the final shift from orange to yellow.

Her kneejerk impulse is to ask Thunder for ideas, but he's already too worried she'll get shipped off to the Null Region. Anyway, he's a nurse, not a spirit guide.

No, the person she needs is Malcolm. He's been a guide for eons. He's got to have some advice. And he always saw her—the real her—when the other White Robes just saw a liability in heels. Pearly stops pacing long enough to shoot an espresso. Then she sends a telepathic message asking Malcolm to please *please* **please** meet her at their favorite afterlife haunt for a chat.

He agrees.

***

Since starting her new gig, Pearly's been too busy to hang at The Crooked Harp, but the place hasn't changed a bit. It's still a semi-seedy dive bar filled with bad lighting, colorful regulars, and questionable decisions. As Pearly weaves through the throng to find a seat at the bar, the self-playing harp in the corner starts twanging a rendition of "Bad Reputation." She gives it the stink-eye, passing a couple of drunken cherubs and a Reaper flirting with a belly-dancing Banshee.

"Hey Diesel," she says, sliding into a stool. "What's shakin'?"

The pony-tailed bartender turns to her. "Well, shit," he grins, "look who's slumming with the locals. Good to see you, Pearly." He sets down a towel and leans across the bar to give her a hug. Pearly still hasn't found out whether Diesel was once actually Jesus in a past life, but she prefers not knowing—keeps things spicy. "What can I get you?"

She wrinkles her nose. "I'm pretty jacked on Earth caffeine, so nothing too stimulating. But if you have anything that builds confidence or produces miracles..."

He chuckles. "I know just the thing."

As he starts mixing, the door creaks open and in walks Malcolm. He's giving "postcard angel" with his White Robe and rosy cheeks. The halo acts like a ring light framing his face.

"Hey Mal," says Pearly, waving him over. "Thanks for coming on short notice. Drinks on me."

"If you insist," he says. "Diesel, a Nirvana Lite when you get a chance?"

"You got it," says the bartender, sliding Pearly a swirling, luminous liquid over ice. "Glow job," he says. "Sip, don't shoot."

"So," says Malcolm, turning to Pearly. "What's this about that required an in-person conversation? Aren't you supposed to be in Paris?"

She nods, samples her drink. It creates a warm, sparkly feeling—not erasing her anxiety, but lending her just enough nerve to spill her guts.

"I have a bit of a... situation," she explains. "I mean, my charges are doing great. But 'almost enlightened' doesn't cut it. If they don't shift to full yellow by tomorrow, Mildreth gets to reassign me to waste management. Or exile me to some celestial backwater."

"What?" says Malcolm. "Why didn't you tell me about this? Are you pulling my wing?"

"No!"

He just blinks at her. "Diesel—something stronger please." He turns back to Pearly. "I thought you were done with the risky schemes."

Pearly slumps down into her stool. "Yeah well, it kinda backfired. I swear Mildreth is trying to sabotage me." She picks up her drink, swirls it around. "Like, I don't get it. Why does she hate me so much? It almost feels personal."

Diesel sets another Glow Job on the counter. But Malcolm doesn't sip. He shoots. "Blahhhh!" He sputters, eyes flashing halo-bright before dimming again. He grips the bar, breathes. "It, uh, may have something to do with me."

Pearly narrows her eyes. "You?"

"I told you we went to Soul School together?"

"Yeah..."

He runs a hand through his hair. "Let's just say I wasn't quite as enlightened then. I wasn't trying to be cruel—I just... disagreed with her ideas. Loudly. In public. I'd poke holes in her theories during presentations, prove to everyone how clever I was. I had friends, influence. She didn't. And I sure as hell didn't make it easier for her."

Pearly gapes. It's not that she thinks less of him; everyone has shadows in their past. It's that he never told her.

"She wanted to be a guide," he continues. "But when the Board opened one training slot, they gave it to me. Not her."

Pearly exhales. "Okay. I mean, I wish you'd told me this earlier."

"I know," he says quietly. "I'm sorry, Pearly."

"It makes sense now," she says. "Mildreth's spent the last few centuries making sure nobody else pulls a 'Malcolm.'"

"Exactly." He meets her gaze. "And you're doing it again—breaking rules, dazzling the Higher-Ups. You're on thin ice. Promise me you'll tread lightly."

"Lightly isn't really my thing, Mal," she says. "I wear stilettos."

***

The sign for **TRAGIC VINTAGE** blinks in pixel-style lights that look like they were salvaged from a 1970s disco. A Greco-Roman statue in a blue toga lounges by the doorway, draped in strands of silver pearls and a pair of aviator shades. Color explodes from the racks rolled onto the sidewalk—tie-dyed tees, sequined jackets, something that might once have been a marching-band coat.

Pearly's conversation with Malcolm didn't do much to ease her nerves. The pressure is on. But she can't make people fall in love. Not with each other, and not with themselves. And as irresistible as the pastries are in Paris, she doesn't think that's going to do the trick.

She could fake a small miracle at Notre-Dame—just a brief halo sighting, nothing showy.

She could break her leg—just slightly—to force everyone to rally around her.

She could manifest a city-wide blackout to make them face their inner darkness.

No, no, no. She can't do any of those things—at least, not without Mildreth dropping the hammer on her.

"How are you feeling?" Thunder asks, stepping up beside her. His brow is creased as he scans her face for clues.

She flashes him a smile that feels like it was glued on by a stagehand.

"Fine. Good. Ready for a little makeover magic!" Her voice is a touch too bright, too brittle.

Thunder glances around, then leans closer. "Do you have a plan? You said you were working on something."

"Yeah… not really. Anyway, I do my best work when I wing it."

"Pearly." He reaches out, taking hold of her wrist. "You know how serious this is."

"I know." She breaks eye contact. "I just… can't think about that right now. If I do, I'll freeze. Just… follow my lead, okay? Please?"

He hesitates—clearly doesn't want to, clearly will anyway.

"Okay," he says finally, letting go of her wrist. He steps toward the others waiting outside the store. "Pearly had an idea," he says, waving her over. "And I thought it was a good one, so we'll be taking her lead today."

Pearly exhales, pasting the smile back on. She sweeps an arm toward the window display, where a faux-fur-clad mannequin is posed like a diva mid-encore. "Today, we embrace color, courage, and questionable fashion choices. Consider it an exercise in self-expression and wardrobe-based healing."

Austin's already halfway inside. "Oh my GOD," he shouts, "it's like if David Bowie and Barbie had a garage sale! Lamar, Beckett—get in here."

Lamar rolls his eyes. With love.

George peers into the window, eyeing a mannequin in a crop top and metallic purple biker shorts. "Do they have a men's section?"

Beckett laughs. "That *is* the men's section, Gramps. Come on." He links arms with George and the two saunter into the store.

Pearly looks at her remaining charges, Lillian and Reyna. "Well...?"

"Yeah, sure," shrugs Reyna. "I love a good thrift store. Maybe they've got rainbow glitter Docs."

Lillian sighs. "Okay, but... do we have to be tacky?"

Pearly puts an arm around her. "Think of it as an excuse to let your inner child out to play—in a sandbox full of sequins." She glances at Thunder. "You coming, chéri? That glitter bomber jacket is calling your name. And maybe the tiara."

He gives her *that* look. "I always did enjoy a little role-play..."

Her stomach does a flip-flop as they all head inside. She sure hopes she'll get a chance to follow up on that flirtation. It would be hard if she's stuck in some interdimensional abyss. *Relax, Miss Thing. Stay open to miracles.*

The shop is a kaleidoscope of color, texture, and sound. Racks line every wall offering everything from leopard print blazers to superhero capes to rhinestone-studded cowboy boots. Somewhere an old stereo plays Bronski Beat's "Small-town Boy." Sequins shed. Feathers drift. Pearly is totally in her element—part stylist, part therapist. A wardrobe change always helped her come up with new ideas. Maybe if she changed her charges' wardrobes she'd know how to help them too. And who knows, they might receive a glow-up so glamorous they'll all become enlightened!

"Remember," she tells them, "you're not shopping—you're *summoning!*"

Austin immediately disappears into a dressing room and reemerges in a gold jumpsuit, arms raised like he just won a gay wrestling title. "How do I look?"

Lamar comes up behind him, wraps his arms around Austin's waist. "Like Studio 54 threw up, but in a good way."

Pearly hands Lillian a bright orange silk blouse.

Lillian wrinkles her nose. "At least if air traffic control goes on strike, I could get off the plane and help out." But she takes it anyway and heads into the dressing room.

George debates between two blazers—a brown corduroy and a navy velvet with beaded lapels.

"Go with the velvet," says Beckett. "Corduroy says 'tax audit.'"

"Velvet says midlife crisis. And I'm seventy!"

"Nothing wrong with a late bloomer," says Thunder, who is indeed wearing a tiara and somehow still looks hot.

Pearly locks eyes with George. "I'm going to suggest a reframe. You're giving me—" She makes a frame with her fingers, squinting at him like a director, "—Mick Jagger goes to confession."

She turns to Reyna, hands her a pair of mirrored heart sunglasses lined in tiny rhinestones. Reyna puts them on, checks herself out, and grins. "Okay, sold," she says. "But what about you, Pearly?"

Pearly quirks an eyebrow. "Oh darling, you just wait..." She notices Beckett heading down a flight of narrow steps to the basement. "Pardonnez-moi," she says. "I believe our young man might need some fairy-godmothering..."

She follows him down the stairs, heels clicking on worn stone. The basement feels like a secret cavern—a curved, low stone ceiling, fluorescent lights buzzing pink against the rough limestone, and crowded racks stuffed with vintage, over-the-top everything. Beckett's already flipping through hangers, selecting items and discarding others. The kid knows his fabric. Pearly leans against a rack of sequined jackets, watching.

"Go on," she says. "Find something that feels like your inside self got invited to the outside."

He smirks. "That's not terrifying at all."

"You'll live. Probably even thrive."

He pulls a psychedelic rayon shirt from the rack, holds it up, then winces. "Too much?"

"Not enough," she says. "You're in Paris. Live large."

He laughs, sets the shirt aside, then grabs a few more pieces that look like they came from a disco's lost-and-found. Pearly cranks the shop stereo to Goldfrapp's "Ooh La La." Upstairs, laughter filters down, then footsteps. One by one, the others crowd into the tiny basement, drawn by the music.

Thunder ducks under the archway. "You're turning this into a nightclub, aren't you?"

"Obviously," says Pearly. "Get your glow sticks." She spins toward Beckett. "All right, Teen Vogue. Runway time. Three looks. Shock, delight, and revelation."

Beckett groans. "You're impossible."

"I'm your favorite aunt's favorite aunt."

She hands him the pile of clothes. A minute later, he steps out in a silver lamé shirt tucked into magenta trousers, sleeves cuffed, collar popped. The fluorescent light makes him glimmer like some disco phoenix.

Austin whoops. "Yes! Tiny Freddie Mercury!"

George snorts. "If Freddie did his homework."

Beckett laughs, loosening.

"Better," says Pearly. "But we're not at 'liberation,' we're at 'school talent show.' Next!"

He vanishes behind the curtain. More rustling. When he reappears, he's wearing leopard-print pants, a black mesh top, and a vintage motorcycle jacket with silver fringe down the sleeves.

Reyna gasps. "That jacket..."

Thunder nods, appreciative. "If you don't take that home, I will."

Pearly beams. "Progress. But let's see what happens if we *really* let go of the armor."

Beckett hesitates. "You mean... something softer?"

She shrugs. "Something that scares you a little—in a good way."

Silence, then movement behind the curtain. Pearly shifts back and forth from toes to heels, anxious to see what the kid's cooking up.

When Beckett steps out again, the room goes still.

He's wearing a charcoal jumpsuit, half-buttoned to reveal a shimmering silver tank beneath, the fabric catching light like liquid mercury. A thin metallic belt cinches his waist, grounding the look. Over it all, he's draped an absurdly long, furry pink scarf, looped twice around his neck and trailing to the floor like the world's most glamorous boa constrictor. The contrast shouldn't work—industrial gray against bubble-gum fantasy—but somehow it does. Brilliantly.

He hesitates at first, tugging at the scarf, but Pearly crosses the space before he can retreat. She dips a fingertip into her own shimmer compact and lightly dusts glitter across his cheekbones.

"There," she murmurs. "Perfect."

The light catches—soft, iridescent—and Beckett straightens, posture easy now, shoulders open.

Austin whistles. "That's not a look—that's a thesis statement."

George's eyes glisten. "Wow. Becks. You look wonderful. Just...wonderful."

"Thanks, Gramps." Beckett looks in the mirror, frowns. "I don't know. You think I can wear this out in public?"

Pearly steps forward, adjusts his collar just slightly. "Honey, this is what 'in public' was made for." She looks at the racks, eyes settling on a floor length rainbow faux fur jacket with an oversized hood. "And don't you worry," she says, "we'll all be backing you up."

They emerge from Tragic Vintage like a Technicolor explosion. Beckett's at the center, scarf trailing like a comet, the others orbiting around him in their own forms of fabulous: Austin in his gold jumpsuit and oversized sunglasses, Lamar with a feathered beret, Reyna rocking her rhinestone heart shades, Lillian in that orange blouse she swore she'd never wear, and George—God bless him—in the velvet jacket. Even Thunder's tiara stays on.

Tourists stare. Locals grin. Someone shouts, "J'adore!" from across Rue Sainte-Croix.

One teenager waves a bright pink flyer. "*Bal de l'Amour!*" they call. "Big street dance at Bastille tonight—DJs, drag, karaoke—come join!"

Pearly stops short.

She takes the flyer. It's advertising a celebration of love and courage for the International Day Against Homophobia and Transphobia. "Perfect."

Thunder comes up beside her, reading over her shoulder. "A public celebration of love," he says. "That could do it. It might be enough."

"Exactly," she says. "If this doesn't raise their vibration, I don't know what will."

He nods, but the worry doesn't leave his face.

She squeezes his arm. "The universe just sent us an engraved invitation. Let's go see what happens."

***

They spend the afternoon drifting through Le Marais—stopping at the farmers market, lounging on the lawn underneath the Place des Vosges fountain, posing for impromptu photos in front of a rainbow-colored graffiti mural entitled "Queer Power." Every interaction feels lighter, easier, like the city itself is conspiring to lift them. Pearly doesn't have to guide. She just watches the glow travel outward, all her charges shimmering in their almost-yellow hues.

As the sun begins to dip, Reyna checks her phone. She smiles at a new message. Pearly catches the mix of curiosity, nerves, and excitement.

"Expecting company?" she asks.

Reyna shrugs, failing to play it cool. "Ollie's meeting us at Bastille."

Pearly's grin is instant. "Oh, good. I liked him. Book boy has excellent taste."

By dusk, they've made it to Place de la Bastille, following the pulse of music and color. The square glitters with flags fluttering from balconies, lights strung from lampposts, and drag performers sashaying across makeshift stages. The crowd is joy incarnate—strangers hugging like old friends, lovers spinning under strings of fairy lights. A tatted DJ in a pink cowboy hat drops Stromae's "Tous les mêmes," and the square pulses in unison, bass vibrating through the cobblestones. It's chaotic, radiant, irresistible.

Ollie spots them first, waving through the crowd, a rainbow bandana tucked into his pocket. Reyna lights up, weaving through the bodies to meet him halfway.

"You actually came," she says, a little breathless.

"Of course," he smiles. "You invited me, didn't you?"

"I know," she says, glancing around at the glitter and chaos. "It's just—this is a lot."

"For Paris?" He shrugs. "Pretty standard Thursday. Besides," he meets her gaze, "it's more fun when you know someone in the crowd."

"Totally." Her smile softens, turning more vulnerable. "Hey," she swallows, "I wanted to thank you for the Angela Chen rec. I've been reading it on my Kindle at the hotel, and, well... it's giving me a lot to think about. I'm still sorting through it all, but I feel seen. And that feels promising."

He brightens. "I love that. Take it at whatever pace feels right. There's no timer on figuring yourself out."

"Yeah."

Pearly feels a swell of pride she tries very hard to pass off as professional satisfaction. Reyna asking real questions, taking real steps toward understanding herself? That's growth. She watches as Reyna introduces him to the others. Beckett produces a sheet of stickers from his bag—hearts, stars, tiny croissants—and presses one onto Ollie's lapel.

"House rule," he says. "Everyone gets branded."

Ollie glances down at the sticker, then back at Reyna. "Guess I'm officially initiated."

Reyna smiles. "Welcome to the chaos." Then, more serious. "I'm really glad you're here."

He smiles back. "Me too."

Pearly feels it then—the warm pulse of connection. Kinship. Belonging. Two people finding each other in the noise and saying, without words, *I see you. You're safe here.*

On the main stage, a drag performer in a glittering evening gown takes the mic. "We fight all day so we can dance all night!" she shouts, voice echoing off the stone. "*L'amour triomphe toujours!*"

The crowd roars. Pearly can *feel* it—an electric pulse that rolls through the square like light, brightening everything it touches.

Lillian laughs first, swept into the rhythm by George, who moves with surprising grace for a man in a velvet jacket. Austin and Lamar are next, dancing loudly and proudly. Reyna and Ollie join them, her rhinestone heart glasses flashing with every spin.

Beckett lingers at the edge beside Pearly and Thunder, half-hiding behind his pink scarf. For a while he just watches. Then a group of teens notice him, waving him over, smearing rainbow paint across his cheeks before he can protest. They hand him a brush and a grin.

Pearly catches the exact second he lets go. The soft exhale, the loosening of limbs, the moment he decides he gets to belong. His scarf fans out as he spins into the crowd, face flushed with exuberance. With freedom.

She doesn't interfere. She doesn't need to. For once, it's not about nudging or fixing or orchestrating divine outcomes. It's about trusting that she's done what she came here to do. The rest—their choices, their light, the degree to which their auras shift—isn't hers to control.

She closes her eyes, lets the bass roll through her, and breathes. For the first time in... well, several lifetimes, she lets herself simply *be.*

TWENTY-EIGHT

The crowd begins to thin, music spilling into the side streets as the group heads back to the hotel. Pearly lets the rhythm fade through her body, still smiling as Thunder steps in front of the group.

"Alright, mes amis," he says. "Before we call it a night, I've booked us one last adventure."

Pearly turns to him, brow raised. She didn't know about this.

"If it involves mud or stairs," says Lillian, "I'm out."

Thunder shakes his head. "Think velvet seats and champagne. Parisian. Glamorous. Mildly scandalous…"

"You're speaking my love language," says Austin.

"Me too," Pearly echoes. *What is he cooking up?*

Thunder turns to Ollie. "You're welcome to join us if you're up for it."

"Thanks," says Ollie. "I'd love that."

"What about you, Becks?" George leans against the wall. "Sounds like nothing we got in Tennessee."

Beckett shakes his head. "Actually, I think I'm gonna sit this one out. Today's been a big day for me, and I kind of need some screentime, you know? Besides, I've become, like, super-emotionally invested in a French reality show. I don't understand what's happening but there are contestants at a castle blowing confetti out of bowls while people in rabbit and cat masks stand ominously behind them. I've gotta see how it ends."

They escort him back to the hotel, the city still bustling with activity. Everything here runs later—meals, music, miracles. In the lobby glow, Beckett's eyes are half-asleep but bright.

"You good?" asks Pearly.

"Yeah. Actually... really good." He glances at his phone, thumb hovering. "Might even post something about today. It was pretty epic."

Pearly grins. "Make sure to tag the universe. It loves attention."

He snorts, heading for the elevator. The doors close on that small, hard-won smile.

Thunder watches him go, then turns to the others. "Now, grown-ups—go put on the most fabulous outfit you've got."

Reyna leans against the wall. "You're still not telling us where we're going?"

"Mystery heightens pleasure."

Upstairs in her room, Pearly gives herself permission to be *extra* extra.

A single snap of her fingers and her suitcase bursts open in a shimmer of light. Sequins, feathers, silk scarves, and stray glitter motes rise into the air. "Alright, my pretties," she murmurs, "show me your potential."

She swipes through the options. Gold lamé (too award season), midnight tulle (too funeral), a black dress that tries to sell her as "mysterious" (too boring to live). Then she exhales and lets her instincts take over.

The light around her bends, threads of rose quartz and champagne gold weaving themselves into a gown worthy of divine scandal. A structured corset cinches at the waist before flaring over her hips, bursting with jewel-toned rhinestones that catch the light. Long sheer gloves fade into blush-pink shimmer, accented by chunky rhinestone bracelets. The skirt spills open into a daring thigh-high slit, revealing a bedazzled garter that matches the bracelets—because of course it does. Her hair is impossibly big and glamorous, her heels unapologetically high. And that brazen red lipstick? It doesn't whisper "kiss me." It dares you.

"Better," she says, turning before the mirror. Her reflection winks back.

She steps back, admiring the full effect. She looks like someone Paris should make room for.

As if on cue, there's a knock.

Thunder leans in the doorway. His leather jacket is slung over his shoulder, shirt unbuttoned just enough to suggest mischief, eyes glinting with a mix of amusement and awe. "Well," he says, "if the show starts before we even get there, we're in trouble."

Pearly grins, brushing an imaginary speck of glitter off his chest as she passes. "Please. I *am* the show. You're just lucky enough to have backstage access."

"Do I?" He stops her in the doorway, hands settling at her hips. "And what does that entail exactly?" His fingertip traces the edge of her corset, feather-light.

Her aura tingles. She swallows hard, pulse climbing. "I don't know," she admits, looking up at him. "Let's just see how things go, okay?"

"Of course, chérie." He offers his arm. "Shall we?"

She takes it.

They descend to the lobby, where the rest of the group is gathered like the glam version of a family photo that finally got the lighting right.

Austin and Lamar are already waiting with Ollie, both in sharp satin jackets—one crimson, one black—looking smug about how good they clean up. Reyna joins them in a silver slip dress under a cropped leather vest, knee-high boots, and metallic eyeliner that could cut glass. Next is George, who wears the navy velvet blazer he got at the thrift store.

The elevator dings. Lillian steps out—and stops the conversation in its tracks.

She's wearing an emerald green cocktail dress. Silky, fitted through the waist, with a square neckline. A pair of simple gold hoops catch the light when she moves. Her hair is in a simple updo, and—wow—is that lipstick?

"I bought it for a wedding years ago," she says, smoothing the fabric like she's making peace with it. "Never thought I'd wear it again."

George goes completely still. "Lillian," he manages, "you look..."

"Stunning," says Reyna.

"Glamorous!" says Austin.

George swallows. "Beautiful."

Lillian blushes. For once, she has no snappy comeback.

Pearly grins. She's not sure if it's their auras or the bling, but everyone is positively radiant.

Outside, Thunder's Mercedes van idles at the curb, headlights spilling across the cobblestones. He gestures grandly toward it.

"Your chariot," he announces, "for our final night in the City of Love. Prepare yourselves for velvet, vice, and some very expensive champagne."

Pearly grins, sliding into the van. "Finally," she says, "a mission I can get behind—and possibly under."

Thunder just shakes his head, grinning as he pulls into traffic.

The city blurs by in streaks of rain-slick reflection—Paris at its most cinematic. Street lamps flash across the windshield like a reel of old film. In the back seat, Lillian and George are laughing about cultural differences.

"Back home," says Lillian, "we're usually in bed by the time Parisians sit down to dinner."

"That's right," says George. "If we waited this long to eat in Tennessee, they'd give us the next day's senior discount."

Reyna snorts. "Please, in Seattle, dinner's at whatever hour your laptop battery dies."

Ollie chuckles. "In London, we eat at six and feel very smug about it. But a lot of us still work late and have no personal life."

Lillian laughs. "Guess we're all learning to live on Paris time. Fashionably late and slightly tipsy."

Pearly smiles, watching the city lights slide across their faces. In the reflection on the window, everyone looks softer, shinier, a little more alive. It's a great distraction from the fear of what her life might look like tomorrow.

Fifteen minutes later, the van glides to a stop beside a vivid red carpet. Above the door, golden letters gleam: **CRAZY HORSE PARIS**, framed by a pair of glowing neon lips.

Pearly steps out first, her jeweled gown catching the marquee glow. "Well," she says, taking in the flashing pink reflections on the brass doors, "this looks promising."

Inside, the warm air embraces them. The lobby is all mirrors and gold bars and red carpet patterned with tiny lips. They follow a tuxedoed usher down a spiraled stairwell. The theater below is smaller than Pearly expects—intimate, secretive, like they've been admitted to a sequin-infused underworld. Velvet banquettes curve around tiny tables, each crowned with a silver champagne bucket and glasses emblazoned with lips. Red and pink sconces give everything a soft, sensual glow.

Pearly slides into a booth alongside Thunder, George, and Lillian. The others are just behind them. She's all too aware of Thunder's presence, his aura sliding up against hers, crackling at the edges, as they pop the champagne and hold up their flutes.

"To second chances," she declares. She meets each gaze in turn, ending with Thunder. "And hundredth chances—because sometimes that's how long it takes us to learn."

They echo her, glasses clinking all around. "To second and hundredth chances…"

Thunder holds her gaze as he sips.

The house lights fade, and a hush fills the room. Pearly feels Thunder's fingers find hers beneath the table—warm and inviting. She exhales, melting into the velvet banquette just as the spotlight blooms across the stage. It slices through the dark, revealing a man in a top hat, sequined pants, lace corset, and mirrored sunglasses.

"Bonsoir, mes chéris!" The emcee's voice floats through the room. "Welcome to the House of Crazy—where art takes its clothes off and everyone leaves a little more enlightened."

The crowd cheers. He prowls along the stage edge, working up the crowd.

"Tonight," he continues, "we give you the gospel according to Beyoncé."

A beat drops—a sultry *Crazy in Love* remix —and he sings with gusto. He works the aisles like a preacher in heels, flirting with a couple up front, mock-scolding a tuxedoed man for clapping off-beat, winking at Pearly's table.

Thunder chuckles. "He's good."

"Excellent," Pearly agrees. The command, the tease, the effortless control. It carries her back to her drag queen life in Chicago, where she once ruled a stage the same way. She feels it again—the pull of the spotlight. The pleasure of performing.

Once, the stage was the only place she felt alive. But surrounded by laughter, love, and a dangerously handsome tour guide, she feels something even rarer. Contentment. In this moment, she realizes how much these people mean to her. She's gotten more than she could have imagined out of being on the sidelines of their lives. And if she got exiled tomorrow, she wouldn't just lose Thunder—she'd lose them too. That fear sits at the bottom of her stomach, gnawing away at her hard-won personal growth.

The medley shifts into *Halo*. The emcee's final note makes the champagne glasses tremble. The room erupts in applause, and with a glittering bow, he disappears behind the curtain.

The music shifts. A single bass line pulses.

In the narrow gap between the curtains, twelve dancers appear, backs to the audience. All that's visible are twelve perfectly framed, perfectly lit butts—yes, butts—each one flexing, tilting, and shimmering in choreographed harmony. The effect is oddly elegant, like someone turned anatomy into abstract art.

Thunder leans toward her. "Reminds me of someone's early work."

Pearly giggles. "Mine never had this much lighting budget."

He laughs softly, and the sound slides under her skin. Thunder was always her number one fan.

Moments later, icy blue floods the stage. A new tableau emerges: topless female dancers in towering fur hats, white tassels swaying over the groin. They march in formation, every step a parody of military precision. The crowd howls with delight. Pearly glances at Reyna to gauge her comfort level. Fortunately, her charge seems to be eating it up, laughing with delight as she brings a champagne glass to her lips.

After a solo number with kaleidoscopic projections creating "costumes" on the naked body and a cheeky striptease by a muscular male dancer balancing on one hand, the lights rise for intermission. Pearly leans back against the banquette and turns to the group. "So," she says, "what's the consensus so far?"

George clears his throat. "I'll admit, I was... skeptical at first. But good Lord—those dancers are athletes."

Lillian laughs into her champagne. "Athletes with impeccable lighting design. It's beautiful, actually. I thought it'd be raunchy, but it's more like watching living sculpture."

Reyna nods. "Yeah. As a visual spectacle, it's incredible. I've never seen anything like it. And the sensuality is delicious."

"Agreed." Austin raises his glass. "And about time someone gave butts the respect they deserve."

They all burst out laughing. Pearly watches the glow ripple across their auras, each one soft, shimmering, open—but not quite there. Not the golden yellow she promised Mildreth. Her teeth start to clench, so she forces a smile.

Thunder nudges her. "And what about you, Pearly? What's your consensus?"

"Darling," she says, "I aspire to this level of tasteful debauchery."

The lights dim again, and a hush sweeps through the room. A low, smoky bass line rolls out—Portishead's "Glory Box." Pearly feels it before she hears it, the vibration thrumming through the velvet banquette and into her spine.

Two dancers emerge—a man and a woman—entwined around a glowing hoop suspended mid-air. The woman hangs upside down, hair trailing like liquid gold, her partner holding her by the small of her back. They move slowly, dangerously. Gravity and grace locked in a lover's quarrel.

To Pearly, it's not lust—it's longing. It's the unbearable ache of wanting to merge with something beautiful that's always just a little bit out of reach.

Thunder's hand finds Pearly's again beneath the table. He squeezes once, then rests his palm on her thigh, fingers brushing the edge of her garter. She doesn't look at him—she can't. The air between them is too charged. Onstage, the woman arches. The man catches her. The hoop turns, their bodies a living orbit.

Pearly's throat tightens. Every past version of herself—the performer, the lover, the guide with something to prove—sways inside her like a chandelier about to fall. She used to think desire was born of drama, chaos, risk. But this—this is different. Desire born of safety. Of warmth. Of being seen, mess and all.

When the song fades, she finally looks at him. Something unspoken passes between them. Pearly wants so badly to savor this moment, to not worry about what comes next. She sees it in Thunder's eyes, too. The question: *Do you love me? Do you want to spend whatever time we have left together, in case it's over after tonight?*

And the answer.

The answer is *yes.*

TWENTY-NINE

The van pulls up to the hotel, headlights illuminating the scalloped awning. Inside, the lobby glitters all welcoming and bright. Too bright for how late it is.

Thunder shifts into park. "End of the line, party people."

Sleepy groans and muffled laughter echo from the back. Lillian lifts her head from George's shoulder. Reyna and Ollie joke about sleeping in the van.

"Don't get too comfortable," warns Thunder. "Breakfast at eight. One last croissant before we scatter to the winds."

"Make it noon," Austin mumbles, slumped against the window. "Croissants taste better with sleep."

"My flight's at noon," says Reyna. "I've got to leave by nine."

"Noted," says Pearly. "Bring your luggage. I'll bring the glitter."

Lillian offers a wry smile. "You always do."

One by one, they climb out—hugs, cheek-kisses, a chorus of "see you in the morning." The hotel doors revolve and swallow them up until the street quiets again.

Only Pearly and Thunder remain.

He glances over. "So... you heading in?"

She pulls her gaze from the boulevard's haze of lamplight. "Eventually."

Thunder cuts the engine. Silence settles. He reaches over and clasps her hand. It's warm. Inviting. Electric. "What would you like to do, madame? May I escort you somewhere?"

She considers. Here they are in luminous Paris, rooftops sparkling like sequins on the horizon. She's been so focused on her charges that she hasn't really asked what *she* wants. This is her last night in the City of Love. And she's sitting beside her favorite soul in the whole universe.

A soft honk breaks the silence. Then a familiar electric purr.

Down the street, a sparkly pink Vespa glows under a lamppost—chrome shining, headlights winking in greeting.

Pearly's eyebrows shoot up. "You have got to be kidding me."

Thunder raises both hands. "I didn't do it."

Seraphina revs her engine, side mirrors giving a guilty little shrug that says "you *said* I could come..."

Pearly chuckles, shaking her head. "After the Hall of Records, she made me promise I'd bring her to Paris. I guess she got tired of waiting."

Thunder grins. "Good for her."

They climb out of the van and walk arm-in-arm across the street. Pearly steps forward, running a hand over Seraphina's curves. "You look cute in this form," she says. "Very bubble-gum chic."

Seraphina bounces on her tires like a low-rider, clearly in agreement.

Pearly slips on the glittery pink helmet dangling from the handlebar and swings a leg over the seat. She glances back. "Coming?"

He doesn't hesitate. "Wouldn't miss it."

He climbs on behind her, hands finding her waist. Seraphina gives an ecstatic *vroom* and peels out, the three of them streaking through the shimmer of midnight rain. And then—because of course she would—a familiar anthem bursts from the speakers: "I Want to Know What Love Is," by Foreigner. The sound is huge, unapologetically earnest, all synths and slow-motion yearning.

Pearly bursts out laughing. "Oh my God, Seraphina, really?"

Thunder leans close, his breath warm against her ear. "I always knew she was a romantic."

Paris rises to meet them. Cobblestones slick with rain, flowerbeds jeweled with dew. They zigzag past a row of terraced cafés, waiters stacking chairs as neon signs blink good-night. The Arc de Triomphe glows ahead, its pale stone brushed with champagne haze. They sweep around it, laughter echoing off the empty traffic circle, then dart down the Champs-Élysées.

The music climbs—so over-the-top it almost begs for an eye roll, and yet it's impossible not to love. Pearly's chest expands. She throws her head back and sings along, Thunder's warmth pressed close behind her. She belts out the song's plea to *finally understand love*, feeling wild, ridiculous, and perfectly free.

When the chorus hits, Thunder joins in, flinging his deep baritone into the wind. He's gloriously off-key, and that imperfection cracks her heart wide open.

Seraphina cruises on past the gleaming windows of designer boutiques, a street busker slow-dancing alone beneath an awning, lovers pressed close in café shadows. The city seems to breathe with them, every window a sigh, every passing streetlamp a pulse beneath its skin.

She curves toward the Left Bank, where timeworn façades lean over the narrow streets like eavesdropping friends. The dome of Les Invalides gleams in the distance, while down below the carousel spins for no one, scattering color across the cobblestones.

Thunder tightens his arms as they whip around a curve, and Pearly stops singing to simply *feel.* The heat of him at her back, steady and real, pricks tears behind her eyes. She hasn't felt this kind of closeness in ages—had almost convinced herself she never would again.

The song hits its peak. Choirs on the wind, a city made of light. They cross the bridge at Concorde, fountains tossing silver into the air, then follow the embankment where the Seine glimmers a silent invitation. Pearly exhales, the wind catching her breath and carrying it away. In this instant, everything feels possible. Every mistake a stepping stone laid by grace toward the life unfolding ahead.

Seraphina coasts to a stop on Pont des Arts, her motor sighing into silence. The pedestrian bridge stretches ahead of them—wooden planks damp with mist, iron railings crowded with padlocks etched with names and initials. Tiny declarations of forever clinging to the city's heart, their keys flung into the river.

Beneath them, the Seine drifts slow and dark, whispering against the stone pilings. Pearly removes her helmet, pleasantly surprised to find her hair windswept but intact. Thunder swings off behind her. Together they step toward the railing, the night air cool against their faces. Beyond the fog, the Eiffel Tower shimmers in the distance, its reflection spilling across the water. Seraphina idles in the background, giving the couple some time alone.

Pearly rests her palms on the railing. The metal is cold beneath her touch, the locks brushing her knuckles. "Didn't they ban these? Too many locks weighing down the bridge?"

Thunder nods. "That's the story."

She sighs. "It's a romantic idea though. Very extra. I respect the commitment."

He puts his hand atop hers, entwining their fingers against the rusted steel. For a few moments, they stand together in silence, watching the water. Pearly's aura hums with aliveness. She's turned on—but also, you know, ON. Lit from the inside out. And it's not just Thunder, though he's definitely a delicious factor. It's everything: her charges, Dumb Pearly, the messy beauty of the week that brought her here. For the first time, she can feel the threads—how they all connect. How she connects.

Her teachers used to say every soul in the divine tapestry is a unique and necessary thread. Pearly always believed the first part. The second felt like cosmic flattery.

Until now.

The realization floods her. She'd already learned she was worthy simply for existing. But this feels different—rooted, radiant. *Useful.* Maybe even *of service.* She still has miles to go on the ladder of spiritual evolution, but her footing finally feels steady. And that vision she saw in the Hall of Mirrors—the one where she and Thunder were doomed to repeat the past—no longer scares her. She creates her own damn destiny.

Pearly turns toward Thunder, searching his face in the soft haze of the bridge lights.

"It was good that we broke up," she says.

He just nods. "I know."

She exhales, a shaky laugh escaping. "We were both choking on that soulmate cord—using it as an excuse not to grow. At least I was. I thought being bound to you meant I didn't have to figure myself out."

Thunder's mouth curves. "And now?"

"I know who I am without you." Her voice steadies. "And I like her. I didn't even know she existed, but she does—and she's solid. She's the one steering now, and I trust her."

"That makes me happy, Pearly. It really does."

She smiles, then frowns a little. "But I've been scared too. Scared that if we got back together, I'd lose her again. That I'd go back to being the version who lived through you instead of with you."

Thunder tilts his head. "And do you still believe that?"

She shakes her head. "No. Because she's part of me now. You can't un-grow something that's taken root." She hesitates, eyes shining. "Being with you here—it's been amazing. Not just fun—though, yes, it has been *obscenely* fun—but grounding. Nurturing. Like that sculpture. You know, the two flower-pot people watering each other?"

He chuckles. "I remember."

"That's what I want," she says. "Not to perform for you. To water you, and be watered in return. To bloom together."

She swallows, the words hanging between them like fragile light. "Is that... what you want, too?"

For a moment, Thunder doesn't answer. A breeze stirs the river, scattering their reflections into ripples of light. Pearly's throat tightens. Her heart thuds—open, exposed. He slides his hand from hers only to trace a thumb along her wrist, sending a shiver through her body and into her aura.

"Coming down here was the biggest risk I've ever taken," he says finally. "You know me—not exactly the rule-breaking type. I'm the kind of soul who'd rather file a bunch of forms than steal a baguette from a restaurant."

Pearly chuckles. "Confirmed."

He smiles. "I used to think that was a strength. But lately, I've realized it's also kept me small. Safe. You... challenge me, Pearly.

In the best possible way. You always have—even back in Soul School."

"Yeah," she says, teasing. "Who knew my stodgy cosmo-ethics tutor would turn out to be kind of hot?"

He laughs, shaking his head. "And as much as that scares me sometimes, it doesn't scare me half as much as what I'd miss if I kept playing it safe. You and I—we're good together. Imperfect, sure, but good. And yes, we've crashed and burned, more than once."

Pearly arches a brow. "Spectacularly."

"Spectacularly," he agrees. "But I don't believe in Happily Ever After—not the kind they sell on greeting cards. I believe in showing up. In choosing each other, day after day, as our most honest, messy selves. I believe it's never too late to start again."

He meets her gaze, something so steady and luminous behind it that makes her pulse skip. "I've always loved you, Pearly. I don't want to erase what we were. I just want to see who we can become. And I don't need us to engrave a lock or throw away a key." He glances at the rows of rusted padlocks beside them. "Real love isn't about being fastened in place. It's about trusting that even when we drift, we'll find our way back."

He squeezes her hand. "So yes, Pearly Gates. I want that too."

For a heartbeat, the world holds still. The river hushes, the lamps seem to dim, even the air stops moving.

Pearly's pulse tumbles. "You do realize," she whispers, "this is all against protocol. You're not even supposed to be here."

He shrugs, eyes filled with mischief. "Then I guess I'll be filing a lot of paperwork."

Her laugh dissolves into a sigh as he leans in.

The first brush of his lips is tentative—after all this time, they still test the current before diving in—but the spark is immediate. It flares through her like sunrise through glass, quick and clean and holy. Thunder deepens the kiss, one hand sliding to the back of her neck, anchoring her. Pearly melts into it, fingers curling in his jacket, the taste of him both new and achingly familiar: smoke, leather, spiced tobacco, a hint of vanilla.

The world tilts. The Seine blurs. Pearly feels herself unravel and reassemble in the same breath—every lifetime, every heartbreak, every ridiculous celestial demerit dissolving into this one impossible, perfect moment. His lips, soft and searching, press gently against hers—then harder, more insistent—as she surrenders the last of her resistance.

And then she feels it. A light tug threading through her chest. Fine gold filaments unfurl, seeking, connecting. The soulmate cord.

Only this time, it doesn't bind. It breathes.

It weaves itself anew—flexible, luminous, alive—vibrating not with ownership, but with harmony. Two frequencies, distinct yet perfectly in tune.

Thunder pulls back just far enough for their foreheads to rest together, breath mingling.

"I stand corrected," he murmurs. "Looks like the universe approved the request after all."

Pearly laughs, breathless. "I guess it did."

He grins, leaning in to kiss her once more.

But just as her lips part and that warm, electric tingle begins to rise, something shifts. A static hiss ripples through her aura, cutting through the haze. She shivers—this time from the sensation of cold. Of something... wrong.

Pearly blinks, disoriented. "Do you—do you feel that?"

Thunder's brow furrows. "Feel what?"

She pulls back fully now, scanning the bridge. The night looks the same, serene and golden—but the unease inside her buzzes sharp, undeniable. Then her phone vibrates in her pocket.

She fishes it out, frowning at the glow of the screen.

1 New Message — Reyna Cruz

Beckett's missing.

Thirty

Missing.

The message burns on the screen, its tiny blue glow reflected in her pupils. She shows the screen to Thunder, heart racing, eyes glassy. She feels a million miles away—disoriented from the state change, wondering what the hell just happened?

"We have to get back." Thunder's already moving toward Seraphina.

"Yeah." The word leaves her mouth, but her feet won't follow. It's like she's the one in quicksand now.

Thunder turns back. "Pearly. Come on." He grips her shoulders, meeting her eyes until everything else drops away. "They need you. You don't have to be perfect or composed. Just *you.*"

That breaks through. Her next breath comes easier. She nods. Gets moving.

Seraphina's engine revs as they swing onto the seat, the night folding open before them. The bridge, the locks, the shimmer of the Seine—all of it drops behind them as Paris blurs into motion again. Rain beads on Pearly's helmet visor, lazy droplets turning to a steady downpour. She clings to Thunder's jacket, fighting the urge to tear through worst-case scenarios.

But the thought still cuts through: if she'd gone back to the hotel after the show instead of taking that ride, would this have happened? She prioritized herself over her charges, and now she's paying for it.

Thunder takes the corners hard and fast. Seraphina shoots through the wet streets like a glittering pink comet, a little too quick for anything human-built. The city's energy has dimmed. The cafés are dark, the sidewalks slick, the night caught between dreams. Or maybe nightmares.

By the time they glide beneath the scalloped hotel awning, they're both drenched. Pearly peels herself off the seat, water running from the hem of her now very heavy gown. Her phone buzzes with another text from Reyna saying everyone's gathered in George and Beckett's room. But Pearly wants to take the temperature first.

She heads for the concierge desk, shoes squelching. "Luc!" she calls out.

Luc looks up from the computer, startled to see them dripping across the marble floor.

"Madame Pearly," he says, half-standing. "You're—"

"The boy in 402," Pearly cuts in. "Beckett Whitaker. When did you last see him?"

Luc blinks, searching his memory. "Not long ago. He came down alone. Said he was bringing an umbrella to his grandfather."

Thunder glances at Pearly, raises a brow. Obviously, a lie.

"He looked…" Luc hesitates. "Upset. But he was polite. I thought, maybe they argue?" He gestures toward the doors, where rain still beads against the glass. "He took the pink flamingo umbrella."

Pearly exhales. "Merci, Luc. We'll let you know if we need anything else."

The elevator creaks upward. Pearly wipes her sleeve across her cheek, but it's no use. She's soaked through. Thunder stands beside her, jaw set. Their reflections swim in the mirrored walls.

"We're going to find him," he says.

She nods, swallowing hard.

"Are they all in the room?" he asks.

"Yes," she says, reading Reyna's latest text. "George wanted to go out looking, but the others convinced him to wait."

When the doors open, the hallway light feels too bright. Artificial and sterile after the day's vibrant blur of color and laughter. She knocks once on 402, and the door opens immediately.

Reyna's the first face she sees—eyes puffy, mouth set in a firm line. "Thank god you're here," she says. "We were just discussing what to do."

Pearly steps inside, followed by Thunder. The others are scattered through the room. Austin's by the window. Ollie's pacing. Lillian's perched on the second bed, with Lamar near the door. George sits at the desk, head in his hands, the lamplight cutting deep shadows across his face.

He looks up as they enter. "He's not like this. He wouldn't just disappear." He rubs a hand across his face. "I shouldn't have left him alone."

Pearly crosses the room before he can spiral. "You couldn't have known," she says, resting a hand on his shoulder.

Thunder scans the room. "His things?"

"Still here," Reyna says. "Bag half-packed. Charger plugged in."

"Look, there's his phone." Austin points to the foot of the bed. "Weird he didn't take it."

Pearly moves closer. The phone sits facedown, still glowing faintly. She flips it over. All she can see is the first line of a text from his mom:

We'll talk when you're back. We found a place...

Pearly's heart pounds. Whatever came after that must've set him off. It would be easy enough to unlock his phone. She knows she shouldn't, but what's a little more unauthorized magic at this point? Besides, it could provide a clue to where he is...

She takes a breath and taps the phone. The screen unlocks.

> **MOM (10:24 PM):** *We'll talk when you're back. We found a place that can help you think clearly about all this. The camp starts on Tuesday.*
> **BECKETT (10:31 PM):** *i don't need a camp mom. there's nothing wrong with me*
> **MOM (11:55 PM):** *Your father says don't come home if you're going to live like that.*

Pearly shows the others.

"But," says George, "why now? What happened?"

"Guys," says Reyna. "Check this out." She's on Instagram, scrolling to Beckett's feed. A reel plays: the makeshift runway at Tragic Vintage. Beckett laughs, struts, spins for the camera. The caption reads:

> **Le Marais basement runway debut**
> **Today's fit: one pink scarf and zero apologies.**
> **Never thought Paris would be the place I finally liked the person in the mirror.**
> **#marais #baldelamour #moulinrougecore #comingoutishotterinparis**

The reel loops—Beckett laughing, twirling, striking a ridiculous pose while Reyna cheers behind the camera. He looks so alive. So free. Pearly's heart aches.

Now it all clicks. The texts. The missing phone. The silence.

"He came out," says Pearly. "And somehow his parents found out about it." This troubles her. How could Beckett's guide let this happen? Edwina seemed competent enough, and from what she said in their last meeting, she was open to direct intervention. It doesn't add up.

***

"Edwina," says Mildreth. "Thank you for coming in on such short notice."

Edwina stands stiffly in the doorway, robe slightly crooked and her aura giving off a nervous flicker. "I don't understand. My charge is in crisis, and I really should be with him."

"That's exactly what I wanted to talk to you about." Mildreth gestures toward the dripping chair opposite her desk. "Your... methods have raised concerns."

"Methods?" Edwina perches on the edge of the chair. "You mean talking to Beckett? Listening?"

"I mean interference. Unstructured emotional contact. Improvised empathy. You're a new guide, Edwina. This case requires a more seasoned hand."

Edwina drops the ingratiating smile. "You're taking him from me?"

"I'm assuming temporary supervision." Mildreth laces her tendrils together. "It's a delicate—" she pauses, searching for a palatable term, "—configuration. Multiple souls intertwined, karmic parameters overlapping. We can't afford improvisation."

Edwina frowns, forehead wrinkling. "But only a guide can manage an active charge. You're an administrator."

Something resembling a smile creeps across Mildreth's face. "I am whatever the Higher-Ups require me to be."

Edwina squares her shoulders. "I'm filing a complaint."

"With the Higher-Ups?" Mildreth's chortle releases a puff of luminescent spores. "Who do you think authorized this reassignment? Sometimes the decisions above our pay grade are ineffable. Our duty is to trust and comply."

Edwina swallows hard. "And what am I supposed to do in the meantime?"

"Nothing." Mildreth rises from her chamber, mist curling around her like a cape. "Stand down. Take a break. We'll notify you when your services are required again."

Edwina hesitates, fists clenching around her robe. "He's scared," she says. "He needs someone who actually sees him."

"Then consider him fortunate," Mildreth says, turning back to her console. "I see *everything*."

The chamber seals with a hiss, dismissing her.

Mildreth waits until Edwina exits. Then she exhales, long and slow. She knows she's crossed a line. But decay spreads fastest when left unchecked—and she's merely pruning the rot before it reaches the roots.

***

Pearly feels a weight in her chest. She can't name it, but the universe feels a few degrees off-kilter.

George pushes back from the desk, eyes blazing. "Of course it's them. Their beliefs matter more to them than their son ever will."

"How did his parents even see his post?" says Reyna. "They don't strike me as the type to be on Instagram."

Pearly and Thunder exchange a look. *Mildreth.* Could she have gone that far?

Thunder steadies the lamp before it topples. "Then we find him before they do more damage." The rain outside pounds harder, the neon from the street bleeding pink across the curtains.

"George," Pearly says gently. "We're angry too. But right now, Beckett needs us calm."

He exhales, shoulders shaking. "Fine. Where do we start?"

Thunder steps forward beside her. "We split up, cover ground fast." His voice cuts clean through the room. "He left his phone. Means he knows they can track him. He's scared, but he's thinking."

Pearly nods, catching his rhythm. "Reyna, Ollie—you know Le Marais. Check the places he loved, even if they're closed: Tragic Vintage, the café with the red awning, that record shop. If he wanted to feel safe, that might be where he'd go. Austin, Lamar—stay here. If he tries to come back, someone needs to be waiting." She turns to George, crouches down beside him. "You and Lillian check the metro stops. He might've gone underground to stay dry and invisible."

Lillian rests a hand on George's arm. "We'll find him, George." For once, there's not a hint of cynicism in her voice. "He's level-headed. Good instincts. Like you."

George nods, blinking hard. "Let's hope that's enough."

Thunder's already grabbing his jacket. "And us?"

Pearly glances toward the rain-slick streets beyond the glass. "I don't know," she admits. "I just need to *do* something. Get out there, look around." She turns to him. "Will you come with me?"

He stops, reaches out, and wipes a streak of mascara from her cheek with his thumb.

"Always."

***

She doesn't know what she's hoping to find. Movement in an alley, a flash of Beckett's jacket, some tiny cosmic breadcrumb. Anything. But the city gives her nothing. No leads. No flashes of intuition. Just rain and silence.

Finally, Pearly pulls to the curb beside a shuttered bakery. They both take off their helmets.

"I did this." She turns to Thunder. "I did this."

His eyes search hers. "Did what?"

"If I hadn't made that bet with Mildreth, she wouldn't have tried to sabotage me. And Beckett would be sleeping soundly in his bed right now. I'm the one who couldn't resist making a gamble, who wasn't above endangering other people so I could win."

"Pearly—"

"I thought I was doing better," she pushes on, voice cracking. "Raising the energy, giving them hope, whatever. But I just... I just made it easier for her. I left the door wide open, and Mildreth waltzed right in."

Thunder rests a hand on her arm. "You didn't make her do this. Or Beckett's parents. Everyone has free will."

"But I'm a guide, Thunder! I'm supposed to help people. Not..." She waves a hand at the chaos. "Ruin their lives."

He lets that sit for a moment. Rain drips from an awning nearby, steady as a clock. Somewhere down the street, a car splashes through a puddle, headlights cutting briefly through the night.

"You can't close the door by punishing yourself," he says.

She swipes rain—or tears—from her cheeks. "Then how?"

"Maybe start by listening to your heart. I bet it's got better advice than your runaway mind, or me for that matter."

The words hang between them. For once, she doesn't argue. She just breathes.

Then, from somewhere above, the faint toll of a bell breaks through the mist. Pearly looks up. Through the thinning fog, a soft white glow crowns the hill—the basilica at Sacré-Cœur. Something about it calls to her.

She slides her helmet back on and revs Seraphina's engine. "I think I know what I need to do," she says.

Thunder leans closer. "What's that?"

She almost laughs as the words escape her. It's probably not what he expects. "Pray."

***

The journey feels longer than it should. Seraphina gives it her all as they wind up the empty streets. By the time they reach the steps of Sacré-Cœur, the rain has stopped. The air is cool and damp, heavy in Pearly's lungs.

She parks the scooter at the base of the hill. Thunder doesn't say anything. He just falls into step beside her as she starts to climb. Each stair feels heavier, as if the weight of the whole day has settled in her bones.

At the top, the basilica looms silent and luminous. The city flickers far below, a million tiny lights pulsing like the newborn souls Thunder tends in the Nursery. Pearly walks to the railing, water beading on the iron.

She doesn't fold her hands or bow her head. She just looks out at Paris—soaked, shimmering, heartbreakingly alive. Up here, she feels vulnerable. Exposed. Like the universe could read her pulse if it wanted to.

"Okay," she says finally, to no one in particular. The Higher-Ups maybe. The Baker. Or that secret love ingredient that keeps the cake from collapsing. "I know we don't talk much. I figure if I stay out of your way, you'll stay out of mine. And mostly... that's worked out."

Her voice catches on the last word. She laughs, shaky. "Until now."

Thunder lingers a few steps behind her, silent, arms crossed against the chill.

Pearly grips the railing, knuckles whitening. "Maybe that's the problem. I keep trying to do it all myself. Hold everything together with charm and chaos and glitter and caffeine. But I think I finally hit the edge of what that can fix." She exhales, long and uneven. "Because asking for help? That terrifies me. It means admitting I'm not in control. And if I'm not in control, then what's stopping the whole cake from sliding off the counter and face-planting into the void?" She shakes her head. "I guess that's why I like causing chaos. It's safer if I'm the one making the mess."

The wind gusts, tugging at her hair. A lone taxi crosses the square below, its headlights smearing gold across the cobblestones.

"But this time," she says, "my chaos hurt people. People who trusted me. And if I could take it back, I would. Because Beckett deserves better. So does George. If you could've seen them—seen what they've fought through these past eight days—you'd be rooting for them too."

She pauses, swallowing hard. "So I'm asking. Not for a miracle. Just... a nudge. A sign. A little guidance. Or maybe a map with an 'X' on it, if you're feeling generous." Her voice drops to a whisper. "Please. I need help."

She closes her eyes.

For a long moment, there's nothing. Just the soft drip of rain from the basilica's stone shoulders, the distant swish of tires on wet pavement, the faint smell of sugar from some late-night patisserie down the hill.

She exhales. And in that breath, she finally lets go—of the guilt, the grasping, the endless need to fix everything. The surrender settles into her bones. Into her heart. Her soul.

Only then does the air shift.

A breath of wind moves through the square. Pearly's shoulders loosen for the first time all night. The tightness in her chest unspools, replaced by something warm and still and terrifyingly peaceful.

Her eyes flutter open. The city lies quiet beneath her. A break in the clouds lets moonlight spill down the steps, tracing a soft, silvery path toward the overlook.

She frowns. Something moves at the far edge of the light.

At first she thinks it's a trick of reflection—rain pooling, catching the glow. But then the shape shifts slightly, forming a hunched silhouette: small, still, heartbreakingly human.

Pearly's heart stops. "Thunder," she whispers.

He steps closer, following her gaze. "What is it?"

But she's already moving down the steps, careful at first, then faster, her heels clicking against the wet stone.

Halfway down, the figure resolves. It's Beckett, sitting cross-legged near the railing, hair plastered to his forehead, jacket soaked through. A flamingo umbrella lies folded beside him—his last small act of defiance against the weather and the wiles of the universe.

He's staring out at the city with a blank expression, like he's simply run out of emotion.

Pearly slows. Every sound around her goes soft—the rain, the wind, even her own heartbeat.

And then she remembers.

The moment on the hill days ago. Beckett had lifted his phone, the basilica glowing behind him. He'd frowned at the picture before deleting it, like it hadn't captured what he was really feeling.

Now she understands why he came back. He'd been called here too.

The sound of her footsteps must reach him, because he turns. The instant he sees her, the blankness cracks. His lip trembles. His shoulders cave.

And then he just... breaks.

She's there before he can fold in on himself, wrapping him up, holding him as he sobs. Loud, ragged, everything he's been swallowing spilling out into her coat. She doesn't need to read his thoughts to know what it is: a lifetime of holding back, of pretending he's fine while the people who are supposed to love him keep asking him to disappear.

Thunder crouches behind them, one steady hand on Beckett's back, the other grounding Pearly.

None of them speak. There's nothing to say.

The three of them stay like that—holding one another under the watch of the white basilica, and the stars above, and a universe that might not be so indifferent after all.

THIRTY-ONE

The elevator dings before Pearly can even exhale. Luc barely glances up. One look at Beckett's blotchy face is enough for him to wave them through.

Fourth floor. 402.

The hallway lights are still dimmed for night mode, but a seam of pinkish-red leaks in through the window at the end of the corridor—the kind of light that means too early for breakfast, go back to sleep.

Pearly knocks. The door flies open.

George stands there in his rumpled shirt, bare feet, hope and panic tangled in his eyes. The second he sees Beckett, his shoulders drop, then rise again, trembling with everything he's been holding back.

"Thank God," he says, pulling the boy in.

Beckett folds into him, wordless. Pearly feels the static drain from the air—and with it, any lingering trace of mildew. Somewhere, in the back of her mind, she knows Mildreth Snaggs will not be happy.

Lillian's at the table too. Her hair's still perfect, but her face seems open and vulnerable in a way Pearly's never seen. The others are present too: Reyna and Ollie, Lamar and Austin. Thunder stays by the door, a quiet wall of presence.

Pearly doesn't say anything. She doesn't need to. The energy in the room is rearranging itself just fine.

Beckett pulls back first. His eyes are red, his voice wavering.

"I'm sorry," he says. "I didn't mean to make everyone worry. I just—I guess I freaked out. My parents..."

"We saw the texts, kiddo," says Lillian.

George tightens his hold on Beckett's shoulders. "What they said—about the camp? That's not gonna happen. I promise I won't let that happen."

Beckett shakes his head, voice cracking. "I shouldn't have left. I just... couldn't stay in that room. I couldn't hear their words in my head anymore."

"It's okay," says Lillian. "You didn't do anything wrong. You survived a moment that would've broken most adults. And you came back. That's brave."

Beckett swallows hard. "Then why does it still hurt this much?"

Pearly moves closer, kneeling beside the boy. "Because you love them," she says.

"We're going to sort this out, Becks." George pulls out his phone. "Right now."

Beckett blinks. "Wait—are you sure that's a good idea? Maybe they just need time."

George meets his gaze. "You asked me the other day where I was when they talked to you like that. And you were right. I wasn't there for you. Let me be here now."

Beckett glances at all the people around him, taking in their faces. Part of him seems embarrassed by the attention, but mostly he looks grateful for the show of support. "Okay."

George takes a breath, dials. The room goes still. He scrolls to his daughter's number and hesitates.

Lillian comes up next to him, touches his wrist. "Keep it simple," she advises. "Don't let her bait you. Just state what's true."

Pearly's grateful for her charge's background in family law. Once again, she wonders if the universe didn't conspire to arrange this exact lineup of souls in one Paris hotel room.

He nods, jaw tight, and hits call. It rings three times before George's daughter picks up.

"Daddy," Marla says. Her tone is clipped, almost businesslike. "I assume this is about Beckett."

"That's right," says George.

"Then I'll save you the speech. We meant what we said last night. Unless he's willing to get help, he's not welcome here."

"Help," George repeats. "You mean that correctional circus you call therapy."

"Don't start," she snaps. "We prayed on this. It's what's best for him—"

"I think you mean it's what's best for you, Marla. Have you ever thought about what might really be best for Beckett?" His grip tightens around the phone.

"He's confused, Daddy. It's not who he really is."

"No," says George. "He knows exactly who he is. You're the ones who are confused."

There's a sharp inhale on the other end. "If you're calling to argue, we're done."

"I'm not calling to argue," George says. "I'm calling to tell you he's not going to that camp. Period."

"That's not your call."

"Actually, you made it my call." His nostrils flare, and Pearly can see him working to keep his tone civil. "You told him not to come home. Fine. Say what you want, but that's on record. And I'll fight you for it. So here's what's happening: Beckett's under my care from now on. Until and unless..." He looks up, like he's asking the heavens for help. "Unless you find some love in your heart."

Silence. Long enough for Pearly to feel the fear and anger dressed up as righteousness crackle on the other end. The only sounds are the soft hum of the minibar and the collective heartbeat trying to catch up.

Then the line goes dead.

Beckett blinks hard. "So that's it?"

"For now," George says.

"So I don't..." Beckett swallows. "I don't have to go to the camp?"

George kneels, coming eye-to-eye with his grandson. "No, Becks. You don't have to do anything that isn't true to who you are. My house might be different from what you're used to, but we'll make it ours. Deal?"

Beckett searches George's face for any signs of his parents' cruelty. But all he sees is kindness and acceptance. "You think I could use Grandma's sewing room? To make stuff?"

"Oh, absolutely. She'd be thrilled."

The smallest smile breaks through. It's fragile, but it's there.

Lillian steps closer, all calm precision again. "And you've got me on logistics," she says. "We'll handle guardianship, school, anything you need documented."

George glances up at her, relief and gratitude tempering his exhaustion. "I don't even know what to say."

She just smiles. "It's okay, George. I'm happy to help."

Pearly lets her awareness drift toward George, tuning into the stream of his thoughts. Beneath the fatigue and adrenaline, a reckoning is taking shape. He knows now he'll never be able to "fix" his daughter. He can't rewrite what was missed when she was small, or what twisted in the dark while he looked away. It pains him to accept that Beckett may never find the love and approval he deserves from his parents—but he will find it here, with George. The past can't be repaired, but the present can be redeemed. And for now, that has to be enough.

The understanding settles into him, sorrow and grace intertwined. Pearly feels the warmth spread outward, sees the last trace of orange in his aura melt into a calm, unwavering yellow. It fills the room like dawn after a long, dark night.

Thunder steps up beside her, gives her shoulder a light squeeze. "That's it," he says. "You helped him turn the corner."

Pearly watches the small constellation of souls who just weathered the storm together. George kneeling beside Beckett, Lillian close behind, the others hovering in a loose circle of relief and support.

"No," she whispers. "They did."

THIRTY-TWO

Everything looks different in daylight—including the prospects for Pearly's future. Everyone's aura looks brand-spanking-new, but it's not enough to fulfill her end of the bargain. Only George has gone full yellow. Maybe the Null Region won't be so terrible? Maybe Thunder could find some way to sneak in for a conjugal visit. Maybe she'd discover some glamorous new shade of nothingness.

She stands at her hotel window, watching the sky paint a brilliant blue over the rooftops of Paris. The air's still damp from last night's storm and everything glistens. Below, a bread truck rattles past, and a woman in a red coat walks her dog while eating a baguette. Even the pigeons have a little extra spring in their step.

Pearly exhales, fogging the glass. It's hard to believe the trip is coming to a close. She feels like an entire lifetime happened over the last eight days. In a way, it did. She's watched resentment give way to vulnerability, loneliness turn to belonging, and a fractured family find its first thread of healing. She's seen souls—hers included—begin to trust that love doesn't have to follow the rules to be real.

For the first time since taking this job, she doesn't feel like a fraud or a fixer. She feels... present. Tired, yes, but alive in the way only Earth can make you—chaos, heartbreak and all.

A knock breaks the quiet. Thunder steps through the adjoining door, holding two coffees.

"Café crème," he says, handing one over. "They were out of glitter sprinkles. Civilization continues to disappoint."

Pearly takes the cup, still watching the rooftops. "Thanks. I was starting to think you'd abandoned me for the pastry cart."

"Tempting," he says. "But I figured I should check on the hero of last night's redemption arc."

She smirks. "Let's not call it that until the paperwork clears."

Thunder leans against the window beside her, their shoulders nearly touching. "Still worried about the meeting?"

"Hard not to be," she says. "Technically, I haven't fulfilled my end of the bargain. Mildreth's probably oiling her gavel as we speak."

"Listen," he says, "you've already done more than anyone could've expected. "If they—if they hold you to the letter of the law, then I... I don't even know..." He crumples, runs his hands through his hair.

"You know." She rubs his back. "We were supposed to have our big reunion moment. Champagne, questionable decisions, cosmic fireworks. Then Beckett went missing and the universe hit pause."

Thunder smiles. "Yeah. We're so cliffhanger."

"Still time for a sequel," she says, the corner of her mouth curving up.

He tilts his cup toward her in a half-toast. "Count me in."

For a moment, they just stand there—two spirits in borrowed skin, coffee cooling, the city yawning awake beneath them.

Then Pearly exhales, straightens her jacket. "All right. Before I spiral into sentiment, we should get downstairs. The goodbye breakfast isn't going to emotionally regulate itself."

Thunder grins. "After you, Ms. Gates."

***

The basement dining room is modeled on the old metro station it once was. Arched ceilings curve low and white, tiled in glossy subway brick that reflects the soft halogen light. Framed black-and-white photos of Parisian street scenes line the walls. At the far end, a sign salvaged from the metro—*Miromesnil*—hangs over a narrow exit door.

A long buffet counter gleams beneath sleek black tile. Silver trays full of sausage, eggs, pastries, and fruit strut their stuff alongside freshly-squeezed orange juice and a coffee machine offering a variety of espresso concoctions.

Pearly and Thunder step inside, cups in hand. Everyone else is already there. Austin is feeding Lamar sliced strawberries. George and Beckett are clustered at one end of the table with Lillian, scrolling through photos of the trip. Reyna's chatting with a server about regional and specialty sausages. Pearly breezes through the buffet line taking one of everything—except for croissants, she obviously needs two—and sits down smack in the middle.

Pearly studies the group for a long moment, then clears her throat. "All right, sparkle brigade," she says. "Before we scatter back to our various mortal and metaphysical realms, I propose a new tradition."

Austin looks up. "Oh, is this where we form a book club? Because I'm still recovering from the Louvre gift shop."

"Close," Pearly says. She picks up a croissant, and sets it in the center of the table like a holy relic. "Pass the Croissant. Each person shares one favorite memory, or something they're taking with them from the trip. Heartfelt or ridiculous—dealer's choice."

Reyna arches an eyebrow. "Is this for the vlog?"

Thunder snickers.

"Nah," says Pearly. "Some things aren't meant for the highlight reel."

That earns a few smiles and couple of orange juice cheers. Pearly folds her napkin, scoots closer to the table. "All right," she says. "Let's have our illustrious tour guide start."

The Croissant flakes in Thunder's hands as he considers. "You know," he says, "tour guides talk about landmarks and history and where to get the best espresso. But the best part of any trip isn't the itinerary. It's the people."

He glances around the table, meeting each set of eyes in turn. "I've seen how you all showed up for one another. In little moments and big ones. Whether it was cheering someone on, or dragging someone out of quicksand—"

Lillian groans. "You people will *never* let that go."

"Nope," he says. "Sorry Lillian, your tale will forever be told within the hallowed halls of the abbey—and probably on my next tour." He pauses for laughter, then continues. "But seriously, every day, there was something. A kindness, a joke, a hand offered when it wasn't required. You all took care of each other. That's what makes travel worth it. And since the guide's usually the one asking for reviews, I figured I'd give one instead: ten stars across the board."

Austin clasps his hands. "Oh, we're never topping that. Group photo and credits, everyone."

Thunder passes the Croissant toward him, but his eyes linger on Pearly. She hears his thoughts in her mind:

Thunder: *And an extra glittery star for you, my love. You were sensational.*

Pearly hides her smile in her coffee cup. If her aura could preen, it would.

Austin catches the croissant midair. "Well," he says, "obviously my favorite memory was Versailles." He sets the pastry on his plate and fans himself with a napkin. "The grandeur. The chandeliers. The unapologetic opulence. Oh, and besides that, how could I forget? The lovely man who did the one-handed striptease at Crazy Horse."

Lamar covers his face. "Dear God."

Austin grins. "Anyway! We've been to Paris before, back when we first started dating, but this time felt different. I think it's because we saw it through new eyes—ours, older and wiser now—and yours." He gestures to the group with an expansive sweep. "You know, we live in West Hollywood, which is its own little planet of sequins and therapy. The rest of the world isn't always as welcoming. It's easy to take that for granted sometimes." He glances at Beckett, gives a nod of solidarity. "This is a good reminder that I need to keep throwing open doors—and maybe the occasional disco ball—for anyone who doesn't feel like they belong."

He raises his mimosa glass. "So if any of you find yourselves in L.A., come visit. We'll go big. Full rainbow. All the drama—well, the *good* kind."

Clinks all around. Beckett glances at George, a spark of hope in his eyes.

"We'll make it happen," George promises.

Lamar takes the croissant from Austin and clears his throat. "Speaking of drama…"

Austin groans. "Here we go."

Lamar ignores him, eyes sparkling. "Did you know today is officially our tenth anniversary?"

A collective gasp rises around the table.

"It got a bit lost in the chaos," Lamar continues, "but I didn't want to let the moment pass. Austin, my love, you amuse me to no end and remind me daily that life isn't meant to be taken too seriously. You light up every room you walk into—sometimes literally, depending on your wardrobe—and I can't imagine sharing a life, or a tiny hotel bathroom, with anyone else."

From his pocket, Lamar pulls out a small velvet box and flips it open to reveal a ring that glints like the crown jewels had a love child with Rocket Man.

Austin gasps, hand to chest. "Is that—?"

"It's an anniversary ring," Lamar says. "Because I'm not waiting another ten years to prove I'm still utterly besotted with you."

The table bursts into applause, cheers, and a few sniffles. Austin, naturally, milks it for all it's worth—hands over heart, dabbing his eyes with the napkin like a silent film star.

"You see?" he declares, sliding the ring on. "This is what happens when you survive a ten-hour flight without reality TV. Romance *blooms.*"

Laughter fills the room again, bright and buoyant.

Pearly feels it radiate through her. The joy, the safety, the love for these beautiful, flawed, messy, perfectly imperfect humans.

Lillian eyes the croissant like it might bite her back. "Well," she says, "I guess I didn't realize how small my life had gotten. And yes, drab. Literally and figuratively beige."

Austin gasps. "Say it ain't so."

"I know," she says. "Tragic. But true. It wasn't just color either. I think I was afraid to enjoy my life because I couldn't bear to lose anything again. Even after arriving in Paris, I was perfectly prepared to dislike everyone and everything. Especially my unplanned roommate."

Reyna snorts. "You mean the one who left wet towels on every available surface?"

"Exactly," Lillian deadpans. "But apparently, you're not as insufferable as you seemed. Paris cracked me open a little. You all cracked me open a little. Turns out there's still some color left under all the gray."

She pauses, staring at the steam curling off her coffee. "I don't want to just sit around waiting to get old and die. Well—older, anyway. Even if my knees complain, there's so much more of the world to experience. And yes, it's better with company. I'd forgotten that part. Sometimes it's good to... duet."

A beat. She looks up, glancing at George, who's already watching her. The contact holds a moment too long to be casual.

Pearly feels like her charge is on the cusp of saying more. She leans forward ever so slightly, as if proximity alone could coax the confession out of her. *Go on*, she thinks. *Say it.*

But Lillian only exhales, lips twitching into a wry smile. "Also," she says, "the croissant on that food tour? Life-changing. I saw God, and he was laminated in butter."

"Lillian," says Pearly. "If you ever want a second career as a stand-up comic, I would totally help you get gigs."

Lillian rolls her eyes, but Pearly can tell she doesn't hate the idea...

George clears his throat, takes the croissant from her with a nod. "Well," he says, "that's a hard act to follow. I don't have any profound reflections about color palettes or divine pastry encounters, but—"

"Coward," coughs Lillian, just loud enough for him to hear.

He chuckles. "—but I'll give it a shot."

He clears his throat, eyes sweeping the table. "When I thought about a meaningful graduation gift for Beckett, I figured I'd show him a little history, a little culture, a glimpse of the world outside our small Tennessee town. I thought it would be educational.

You know, museums, architecture, cows with better pedigrees than ours."

That earns a laugh from Beckett. "Who knew it was the salt?" he says.

"But I had no idea," George continues, "that it would be so much more. I'm grateful to every one of you for showing my grandson what belonging can look like. For reminding me what it feels like to see someone's light come back on." He smiles at Beckett. "You've handled yourself with more grace and courage than most adults I know. You made me proud before we ever got on that plane, but now... well, kiddo, you're the bravest person I've ever met."

Beckett blushes. "Okay, Gramps, embarrass the kid." But beneath the awkward, he's beaming.

George smiles, then looks down at the croissant in his hands. "And as for it never being too late for second chances..." His gaze lifts to Lillian. "I heartily agree."

The words hang in the air. Lillian meets his eyes, like they're locked in a love duel, each waiting to see who goes for the holster first. Her fingertips tap her coffee cup once, twice, hesitating on the edge of confession.

Pearly holds her breath, sending every ounce of Cupid energy she can muster across the table.

But George only smiles. He slides the croissant toward his grandson.

"Your turn, Becks."

"Uh," he says, fiddling with the pastry, "I mean, the fashion show was pretty epic. Even if it did, you know..." He gestures vaguely. "Cause the whole parental meltdown thing. Still worth it. For like ten minutes there, I felt—" He stops, bites his lip. "I don't know. Like all my stupid dreams maybe weren't so stupid after all."

"Oh honey," says Pearly, "I think great things are in store for you."

Beckett shrugs. "Yeah, well, the internet seems to agree, mostly anyway. A lot of the comments were actually nice. Like, from other kids at school."

"That's great, Becks," says Reyna.

He turns the croissant over in his hands, unconsciously tearing off a layer. "But honestly?" he says. "I think my favorite memory is getting that portrait done with Gramps."

George tilts his head, surprised.

"It's funny," Beckett says. "At the time, I was kind of mortified getting sketched in public with my grandpa. But now, when I look at it, I just feel proud. Like, I'm proud to be your grandson." He smiles at George. "You think we could hang that up when we get home?"

George ruffles his grandson's hair. "Yeah, Becks," he says. "Front and center. Next to Grandma's needlepoint."

"The one with the snowman riding the deer?"

"That's the one."

"Sweet." He passes the croissant to Reyna. She tears off a chunk, stuffs it in her mouth, chews.

"Well," she says after swallowing, "I didn't even want to come on this trip."

A few eyebrows rise around the table.

"I mean, it wasn't even supposed to be mine. My grandmother left it to me, and I figured I'd honor her memory, take a few pretty photos, maybe eat something decadent and call it a day. But even once I got here, I wasn't really *here*. I was anxious, distracted—always trying to manage something. My job. My schedule. My own nerves."

She exhales, gaze dropping to her coffee. "The truth is, I was scared to be alone with my own thoughts. Because if I stopped long enough to listen, I'd have to face how lost I felt. I kept waiting for the world to make space for me, but *I* wasn't making space for me."

A-ha! Pearly smells a breakthrough…

Reyna lifts her head again, and for the first time her voice doesn't waver. "Over the course of this trip, I got clear about something important, and I wanted you all to be the first I shared it with. Becks," she says, "your bravery really moved me, and I figured if you could do it, I could too." She takes a breath. "So here's my truth: I'm aro-ace. That stands for aromantic-asexual. It means I don't experience romantic or sexual attraction to other people. I'd heard of it before, but I had a lot of wrong assumptions and didn't think it could apply to me. I was wrong. It turns out you can be ace and still have a libido! Who knew?"

A few soft chuckles—not at her, but with her. Reyna's shoulders drop, and she lets out an audible exhale.

"And it was confusing," she continues. "I liked the idea of sex and romance, but not the experience. I kept trying to make it work, but it was like forcing myself into a genre that wasn't written for me. I thought there had to be something wrong with me. Like being ace was a glitch rather than a setting. But actually, it's kind of liberating just to put it out there. To say out loud there's nothing wrong with me at all. This is just who I am."

She stops, glances around the room. Lots of sympathetic faces. Pearly's heart is practically exploding with pride.

"That's cool," says Beckett. "One of my online gaming friends is ace. So is the author of *Heartstopper* and Maya from Borderlands 2 and 3. She's this badass Siren with cosmic powers and zero patience for flirty NPCs."

Reyna flashes Beckett a grateful smile. "I didn't know about Maya. I'll have to check her out."

"You should," Beckett says. "She punches stuff with galaxies."

"Anyway," she continues, "once I started to let down my own defenses, everything shifted. Paris looked brighter. People felt closer. Even I felt different—like maybe I'm not outside of everything, just standing in my own doorway waiting to walk in." She pauses, fingers moving to her neckline. "And apparently I look killer walking in with antique jewelry."

That earns a laugh from the group. Pearly's eyes catch the glint of the necklace at Reyna's throat—the one she gave her earlier in the week. It seems to shimmer brighter now, alive with her newfound ease.

Reyna takes a breath. "Anyway, you asked what we're taking home from this trip. My answer's 'nothing.' Because I'm not going home. Not yet."

That gets everyone's attention.

"I've decided to stay in Paris for a while. Ollie said I could crash with him. I think I want to see who I am when I'm not on a deadline—or running from silence."

She looks around the table, eyes shiny but sure. "You all helped me get here. So thank you. For making space for me... until I learned how to do it myself."

Thunder raises his glass. "To Reyna," he says. "And to making space."

The table clinks and cheers. Pearly watches Reyna drink in contentment, and with it the final shift in her aura from orange to yellow. Pearly's elated—but she can't help feeling a twinge of disappointment. She's so close, and yet so far. Two out of three won't be enough to appease Mildreth.

Reyna passes her the croissant. "Your turn, Pearly."

Pearly raises an eyebrow. "Excuse me? I organized the emotional catharsis. I'm exempt."

"Democracy of crumbs," says Austin.

"Fine," she sighs, twirling the poor, mostly-eaten pastry between her fingers. "My favorite memory? Honestly... this. Right here. Not because the lighting's perfect or the company's easy on the eyes—though both are true—but because this is what it looks like when people actually *show up* for each other. Messy, tired, covered in pastry flakes—but real. You've all been spectacularly human. And that's my favorite kind of magic."

"Cringe," says Beckett. But he's smiling.

Pearly winks at him. "Oh, you love it."

"We do," says George.

She sets the croissant on the table. "You know, I've spent years traveling with strangers. Cruise ships, food tours, the occasional questionable karaoke night. Most people come and go faster than a buffet refill. But you? You stuck. And that's something worth toasting."

"Yes!" says Reyna. "More toasting!" Everyone raises cups of coffee and glasses of orange juice and mimosa. The table erupts with joyful clinks.

"And since we're addressing heartfelt truths," says Pearly, "let's also address the elephant in the room."

Austin gasps theatrically. "Oh my God, are you two—?"

"Yes," Pearly interrupts, "Thunder and I *do* have a history. And that history is about to get a new chapter..."

"I *knew* it!" Austin pumps his fist, triumphant. "Sorry, carry on."

Pearly turns to Thunder. "My love—you are the best travel companion on this wild and wondrous cosmic journey. Thank you for putting up with me, for believing in me, for calling my bullshit, for surprising me by actually taking my advice to stop playing it safe—and for being a steady compass when I was spinning in circles. Also," she adds, smiling, "for wearing those hot little motorcycle pants. That's a true public service for us all."

Thunder bows his head, mock-humbled. "We all serve in our own way."

"Some of us more heroically than others."

He tilts his glass toward her. "To Pearly—who keeps finding the light, no matter how many times the world tries to dim it."

He leans in, brushing her lips with a kiss that sends confetti bursting through her chakras.

When she breathes again, Pearly looks around the table. Austin and Lamar leaning shoulder to shoulder. Reyna glowing with newfound peace. Beckett showing George and Lillian the photos he took from Sacré-Cœur.

And then—faintly, beneath it all—a telepathic whisper.

Mildreth: *Time's up, Gates.*

The meeting. The cosmic audit waiting beyond this perfect morning.

Pearly straightens her napkin, finishes her coffee in one graceful sip.

Not yet, she thinks. *Paperwork can wait. The Null Region can wait. People can't.*

THIRTY-THREE

Most of the group's already scattered like glitter after a drag brunch.

Austin and Lamar caught the morning flight to London, where they planned to see a show, raid Harrods, and make it back to L.A. before their jet lag catches up with them. Reyna hugged everyone before heading off to Ollie's new sublet, promising to start a WhatsApp group so they could all keep in touch. Even Thunder's gone, having run out of "vacation time" from the Nursery and needing to return to his actual afterlife job as Head Nurse.

"Are you gonna be okay?" he'd asked. "What if—"

She'd silenced him with a kiss. "It'll all work out," she'd said, considerably more confident than she'd actually felt. "And I have no regrets. Seriously. I wouldn't trade these past ten days for anything."

It was enough to send him home, but he'd made her promise to update him as soon as she met with Mildreth.

That just leaves the stragglers—George, Beckett, Lillian, and Pearly herself—lingering in the hotel lobby, suitcases in tow. Pearly leans against the concierge desk, watching George and

Lillian finish checkout. Both sneak glances at one another, but neither seems willing to say what's in their heart.

Well, she thinks, *this is it. The final boarding call for Denial Airlines.* Pearly's out of magic tricks. If these two want to be stubborn, there's nothing else she can do.

Beckett hugs Lillian first, all teenage elbows and genuine sincerity.

"You know," he says, pulling back, "you're pretty cool for—"

"Don't you dare say old lady."

He grins. "I was gonna say for someone who pretends not to care, but totally does."

"Hmmph." She ruffles his mop of bangs. "If anyone gives you shit, you send them to me."

"Copy that."

Then George turns to her. He takes her hand and presses a quick kiss to it, old-school Southern gentleman to the bone. "Lillian," he says, "you are extraordinary."

She swallows, glances up at him. "Thank you, George. You're... not so bad yourself."

For a heartbeat they just stand there, studying each other, two people realizing they've run out of reasons to pretend they don't care. Then he releases her hand.

"Safe travels," he says.

"You too," she replies—too quickly.

He tips his hat, gestures to Beckett, and the two head for the cab idling at the curb. The bellhop loads their bags, the driver waves. And just like that, they're gone.

The lobby settles. Pearly sighs. It's not an unhappy ending—just not the one she'd been hoping for. But there's that pesky free will doing its thing.

Lillian stays rooted to the marble floor, expression neutral. Her aura, too, has gone a little dull.

Pearly drifts closer. "You okay?"

Lillian exhales. "Of course. Why wouldn't I be?"

Pearly's tempted to say, *"Because your heart's doing jazzercise."* Instead, she shrugs. "You just look a little... unsettled."

"I'm fine."

"Okay. So tell me—what's the first thing you're going to do when you get home?"

"Laundry," Lillian says after a beat. "And maybe... buy a paint sample. Something reckless, like eggshell."

Pearly feigns shock. "Lillian, you rebel."

Lillian's lips twitch. "I might even spring for semi-gloss. Live dangerously."

Pearly feels the flicker of the thought Lillian isn't saying out loud. *What's the point if I'm the only one who sees it?*

The revolving door spins. A new family steps into the lobby. Jet-lagged parents, two wide-eyed kids clutching stuffed animals, the father already consulting a map as if he might outsmart Paris. Their excitement fills the air, bright and buzzing. Pearly feels it brush against her like static, the unmistakable shimmer of beginnings. She wonders what imprint the city will make on them.

Lillian moves toward the front desk, making a dry remark about minibar prices. Pearly half-listens until the doorman clears his throat.

"Madame?" he says, holding out a small envelope. "He leave something for you."

Lillian blinks. "For me?"

The handwriting on the front is neat, familiar. Lillian slides a finger beneath the flap and unfolds a single sheet inside.

Her eyes skim the page once. Then again. For a moment she just stands there. Then she swallows, hands the note to Pearly.

Pearly takes it, feeling George's energy still clinging to the paper. She reads:

> *For the woman who almost*
> *bought the blue chair at the Saint-Ouen market—*
> *you said shipping would be a nightmare,*
> *but some things are worth the trouble.*
> *It'll be waiting for you when you get home.*
> *– G.*

Pearly looks up. Lillian's blinking too fast, her chin set like she's trying to keep something from spilling over.

"Why..." Lillian looks around for someone, or something, to blame. "Why would he do that?"

Pearly rests a hand on her charge's arm. "I think you know why, Lil."

Lillian lets out an incredulous laugh that breaks halfway to a sob. Then her gaze drifts toward the revolving door, to the street beyond. Pearly feels the shift, the decision starting to take shape in her mind.

"You know," Pearly examines her fingernails. "His flight doesn't leave for another hour."

Lillian's eyes widen. "You mean—"

"I mean we're about to do something you'll remember for the rest of your life." Pearly grabs her tote, already striding toward the door. Then she stops, glances back. "Or something you'll regret for the rest of your life if you don't. Choice is yours, babe."

Lillian takes a long breath. Her fingers tighten around the strap of her purse. It looks like she might talk herself out of it. Then her eyes narrow, and her resolve hardens. She hands her suitcase handle to the doorman. "Could you hold this for me?"

He blinks. "Of course, madame. But—your taxi—?"

"Change of plans," she says, already hurrying toward the door.

Outside, Seraphina waits at the curb in her Vespa form—pink, polished, and purring. Pearly hands Lillian a spare helmet, then pulls on her own. "Hold tight," she snaps down her visor. Time for some of that late-for-the-staff-meeting energy. "Next stop, Charles de Gaulle. Traffic laws optional."

Seraphina rockets out of the roundabout like she's been waiting her whole afterlife for this joyride. Pearly leans forward, grinning into the wind as Paris unfurls ahead in all her chaotic glory. Honking taxis, delivery vans, a bus blocking half the street just because it can.

"Alright, sweetheart," Pearly murmurs, "show me what you've got."

Seraphina answers with a throaty rev that could qualify as a battle cry. "Holding Out for a Hero" bursts from her speakers as she squeals into traffic, weaving between lanes, dodging a garbage truck and cutting off a very offended man on a Ducati.

The driver shouts something colorful in French. Pearly blows him a kiss.

"Do you even know where you're going?" Lillian clutches Pearly's shoulders.

"Not exactly!" Pearly shouts back. "But don't worry, the Vespa does."

Seraphina honks, missing someone's side mirror by a whisper. They hit the Seine, darting along the embankment as a pack of scooters tries to overtake them. Seraphina flashes her headlights in challenge. The lead rider smirks—until the Vespa growls, surges ahead, and leaves him choking on exhaust and indignation.

Pearly whoops. "That's my girl!"

Traffic snarls near the Arc de Triomphe, the mother of all roundabouts. Horns blare, pedestrians scatter. Pearly doesn't even ease up. "You ready?" she calls over her shoulder.

"No!" Lillian yells.

"Perfect!"

Seraphina dives into the swirl of chaos like a sparkly torpedo. Taxis brake. Cyclists curse. A delivery driver crosses himself. Pearly and Lillian loop the monument twice before shooting out the other side victorious, slightly illegal, and spectacularly alive.

By the time the highway signs for Charles de Gaulle appear, Pearly's cheeks ache from smiling. Lillian's laughter rings out behind her, wild and free.

"Paris," Pearly announces, easing back on the throttle, "you've been a worthy opponent. But I declare us the winner."

Lillian gawks at the crowd of travelers streaming through the sliding doors. "Now what?"

"Now," Pearly says, yanking off her helmet, "we run!"

They charge through the sliding doors, dodging rolling suitcases and jet-lagged tourists. Pearly scans the crowd, tuning into George's energy—it hums faintly ahead, steady and golden.

"Security," she mutters. "He's at security."

"Then we'll never make it!" Lillian pants.

Pearly grins, eyes sparkling. "Sure we will."

She commandeers one of the airport wheelchairs lined up at the wall. "Hop in."

Lillian huffs. "Absolutely not."

"Fine," Pearly says, already grabbing her by the elbow, "then trip gracefully into it."

And they're off, Pearly push-sprinting through the terminal, weaving between window displays and disgruntled travelers.

"George!" Lillian calls, clutching her purse in one hand and Pearly's armrest in the other.

He's up ahead—front of the security line, shoes off, boarding pass in hand—one step from disappearing through the scanner.

Pearly focuses her energy and snaps her fingers, casual as a hair toss. A shimmer ripples through the air. The walk-through alarms start shrieking, the x-ray belt grinds to a halt mid-bag, and a laptop tray tips over like a domino.

"Oops," Pearly says, utterly unconvincing.

Lillian's eyes widen. "Pearly—"

"Go!"

Lillian scrambles out of the chair and hurries forward as chaos blooms behind her. Officers wave their arms in the midst of flickering lights and shouting passengers.

"George!"

He looks up, startled. "Lillian?"

She stops a few feet away, breathing hard, hair slightly wild from the sprint (and Pearly's questionable driving).

"You—" Lillian pants, trying to catch her breath, "—you bought the chair."

He grins. "Didn't want you coming back to an empty condo. And... it suited you. The real you."

Her jaw drops. "But—you don't even know me."

"I think I do."

Lillian exhales, shaky. "Maybe you do," she says. "And that scares the hell out of me." She laughs under her breath. "Dammit, George, I thought I was prepared for anything after the fire. I built my whole life around that idea. Be ready to leave at a moment's notice. Don't get attached. Don't collect things you can't fit in a suitcase. Don't love anything you can't list on an insurance form."

Over by the security gate, a toddler drops a stuffed giraffe and wails. A gate agent makes a last call in three languages. Pearly can feel the tension in the air. This is a place of constant arrivals and departures, perfect for last chances.

Lillian's voice wavers, but she keeps going. "I had this mental checklist of survival: keys, phone, passport, painkillers, exit plan. I thought that was enough. But then you—" she gestures weakly toward him, "—you showed up with your jazz and your omelets and your calm, infuriating kindness, and suddenly I realized I was missing a few things. Like laughter. And music. And the kind of quiet that doesn't feel lonely. You reminded me what it's like to be... seen. And not for what I've lost, but for what's still here."

Behind them, a chorus of frustrated French erupts as three TSA agents argue over which machine short-circuited first. One bangs on the x-ray belt with the heel of his hand. Another waves a metal detector like a wand gone rogue. The scene is kind of a clusterfuck—wires sparking, alarms hiccupping, an entire system frantically trying to put itself back together. Pearly tries to convince herself all the missed flights are also part of the universe's plan.

Lillian takes another breath. "And the way you show up for Beckett—it floors me. I saw so many broken families over the years, so much fallout, but that's not what I see with you. I see a man who shows up even when it's hard. Who stays. Who listens."

Her voice drops to almost a whisper. "And I see something else. I see a future I want to build. With you. If you'll have me."

A few people turn away from the pandemonium to eavesdrop on the soap opera unfolding before their very eyes. George steps forward until they're close enough that she can feel his breath against her hair.

"You've always been the brave one, Lillian," he says. "Took me a while to catch up."

He reaches for her hand. She hesitates just long enough to feel the weight of the choice, then threads her fingers through his.

And then he kisses her.

It's not polished or planned. It's the kind of kiss that knocks the air out of old ghosts and makes the living remember they're still allowed to want things.

A few travelers applaud. Someone whistles. Beckett groans, "Oh my God," but he finds himself clapping too.

Pearly feels the glow before she sees it. Lillian's aura brightens, the orange softening into pure yellow, warm as morning sunshine. George's, too, flares in harmony.

And suddenly Pearly realizes that all three of them—George, Lillian, Reyna—have found it. The color, the shift, the choice to live open-hearted again.

She did it.

She won.

But what she really won wasn't a bet. It was faith—simple, shining faith—in the ridiculous, relentless grace of second chances.

THIRTY-FOUR

Pearly Gates waltzes back into the Department of Human Relations like she owns the place. After all, she just pulled off a triple aura shift—in ten days, no less. That deserves fireworks, or at least a commemorative plaque. Just in case they name her Employee of the Month, she's even wearing a photo-friendly outfit: a pink taffeta floor-length gown patterned with holographic cat heads and fish bones. It doesn't exactly go with her robe, but whatever. Someone's gotta show a little spunk.

When she gets to her cubicle, there's someone waiting for her. "Malcolm!"

Pearly's eyes light up. Her mentor sits at her desk clutching a string of balloons shaped like different French-themed objects—a baguette, a pigeon, the Arc de Triomphe.

"Congratulations, Pearly!" He offers her a latte. "Word is you nailed the assignment. Everyone's talking about it."

"Please. The auditors are just mad they can't quantify charisma."

"Well, actually, they can—"

"Come on, Mal. Don't rain on my parade."

"So..." Malcolm rubs the back of his head. "How'd it go?"

"You mean with Mildreth? Hasn't happened yet." Pearly takes a sip of the latte. It's fine, but not by Paris standards. That's the problem with the afterlife—they never figured out espresso. "I have a meeting with her in..." she checks her scroll. "Five minutes. And for once, I will not be late. Walk with me?"

He frowns, worry-lines clouding his cobalt eyes, then picks up his coffee. "Sure."

They head down the main corridor, weaving through the maze of cubicles. Holo-screens hang overhead, each broadcasting its favorite flavor of bureaucracy: *Soul Productivity Up 3%*, *Aura Optimization Pilot Expanding to New Sectors*, *Reminder: Empathy Metrics Due by Noon.*

Malcolm keeps his voice low as they pass a group of junior guides pretending not to eavesdrop. "You know she's not going to take this well, right?"

Pearly waves a hand. "She'll take it exactly how the universe dictates. We made a deal, Mal. The terms were clear, the cosmos witnessed, and I played by the rules."

He gives her a look. "Did you?"

"Ish." She notices Hylonome, Mildreth's teacher's pet, watching them. "But she broke 'em first," Pearly whispers. "And the only way she'd be able to call me out is to admit her own tampering. So I'm safe. And hey—three souls just upleveled. That's cosmic progress. If anything, she should thank me."

Malcolm winces. "I don't think that's gonna happen."

"Don't worry, she can't touch me." Pearly slows down as they approach the executive wing. "She's a bureaucrat. Bureaucrats may bluff, but they don't break contract. Besides"—she flashes a grin—"she'd never risk the paperwork."

"Maybe," Malcolm concedes. "I'm just looking out for you."

She stops, stands on her tip-toes, and plants a quick kiss on his cheek. "I know, and I appreciate it. You really are the best, Mal. Oh! Wait—I got you something."

She rummages through the folds of pink taffeta and pulls out the **UNRELIABLE NARRATOR** trucker hat from Shakespeare and Company. "Thought you might appreciate the irony," she says, handing it over.

Malcolm grins, resting it atop his halo. "Thanks, Pearly. Does this make me a hipster?"

"Totally. You'd fit right in at Perkatory."

At the end of the hall, Mildreth's corner office glows green behind tinted glass. Pearly pauses to fluff her gown and smooth her hair. "How do I look?"

Malcolm appraises her. "Like you're about to start a revolution at a cat-themed prom."

"Perfect."

"Pearly..." He stops, glancing at Mildreth's door. "Good luck."

She winks. "Luck's redundant when you've got style." She knocks twice.

"Enter."

She steps through. The door seals behind her with a soft hiss.

"Gates," Mildreth says without looking up from her desk. "You're on time. Miracles do happen."

"Trying something new," says Pearly, flouncing up to the desk. "You know how the living are always going on about personal growth."

Mildreth pushes up her glasses, gives Pearly's outfit the once-over. "And was that what Paris was? Growth?"

"Three humans in the yellow, no violations, no spiritual casualties." Pearly spreads her arms. "Call it what you want. I call it results."

Mildreth taps a pen to the desk. She sighs, releasing a puff of spores. "I suppose you have fulfilled your end of the proposal. And therefore, the Department will—reluctantly as it may be—acquiesce to your terms."

She manifests an updated guide contract. It's filled with cosmic legalese, but it does stipulate Pearly's right to guide souls as she sees fit, with no interference from Mildreth or anyone else in the Department. *Is this actually happening?* Pearly wonders. *Is Mildreth Snaggs waving the white flag?* Sure enough, Mildreth signs the contract with her energy signature, and Pearly does the same.

It's official.

Woozy with victory, Pearly sinks into the chair opposite the desk. "So, what's next? My own assistant? A raise in celestial credit? I'd settle for a shout-out at the next Department meeting and my name on the Inspiration Board, honestly."

Mildreth opens a file cabinet and places the contract in a folder. "If I were you," she says, shutting the drawer, "I'd be saying goodbye to my soulmate."

Pearly's heart stops. "What do you mean? We just..." She leans forward. "We just signed the contract. You can't send me away."

"That is correct." Mildreth taps a few keys on her console. "But we made no such deal for your partner. Thunder, I believe? Evidence confirms that he accompanied you to Earth without clearance, interfered in mortal guidance, and accessed restricted archives. These actions constitute violations of Interincarnate Transit Protocols 2.1–2.4 and Archive Security Statutes 7.3–7.5. In consequence, he is to be transferred to the Null Region..." Mildreth looks up with a gleam in her eye. "Indefinitely."

Pearly's stomach churns. She rises from her chair. "You can't do that! You—"

"In fact, I can—and I have. The transfer is currently under review and should process within the hour."

Pearly seethes, white-knuckling the edge of her boss's desk. "This is a low blow. Even for you."

Mildreth tsk-tsks. "Maybe you should've considered all possible outcomes before coming to me with your proposal."

"Okay, fine," Pearly concedes. "I messed up. But don't punish Thunder for my mistakes. If you have to banish someone, do it to me. He doesn't deserve this."

Mildreth shakes her head. "Even if I wanted to, I couldn't. Not with the contract you just signed." She flashes something that might be a smile at Pearly. "You made this bed. Now go lie in it. Alone." She picks up a stack of papers, gestures to the door. "If there's nothing else—"

The door bursts open, and Malcolm tumbles in. "Dammit, Mildreth, this has gone too far! You're punishing her because you can't punish me."

Fuckety Fuckerton! Pearly can't handle all these plot twists. They're turning her insides into a rollercoaster.

"Malcolm?" Mildreth bristles. "Were you listening at the door? I'll have to add that to the list of protocol violations."

He marches toward the desk, the trucker hat still dangling precariously on his halo. "I just saw the transfer request," he says.

She sets down the papers. "Then you understand I'm maintaining departmental integrity—"

"No." He shakes his head. "You're angry, Mildreth. And you have every right to be. At me. Not at her."

"Don't you lecture me," she snaps, as angry spores begin to choke the room. "I'm not the youngling I once was. I refuse to stand for it."

"Please," he says, "just hear me out." He takes a breath, glancing at Pearly then back at Mildreth. "When we were in Soul

School, I was—well, I was a bully. I laughed at your presentations, undercut your ideas, made you the punchline so I could be the prodigy. I thought it was competition, but it was cruelty." He looks down at his hands, face flushing. "But I'm not that soul anymore. I know I used to mock your approach as too by-the-book, but I've actually come around in a lot of ways."

Mildreth frowns. "I find that hard to believe."

"It's true!" says Pearly. "He's the biggest rule-follower I know. Do you have any idea how hard it was to convince him to let me sub for him? He was all 'what would the Higher-Ups think?' I swear, you're like two peas in a pod."

"How dare you," Mildreth scoffs. "I'm not a legume."

"The point is," says Malcolm, "I never apologized. Not in school. Not when they chose me over you for guide training. Not when I built a career as a guide, and you built armor thick enough to make sure no one could humiliate you again. You became the system that crushed you. I recognize it, because I was a part of it."

Mildreth's aura crackles. "Why bring this to me now?"

"Because I saw your memo," he says. "And I realized you were about to do to Pearly what I did to you. Hurt someone bright because their light made you remember what it felt like to be dimmed. And is that really you? Bending the rules to get your way?"

Mildreth looks... unsettled. Like this was the one thing she hadn't prepared for. "Gates broke the rules," she manages, but it sounds brittle. "So did her partner."

"Maybe so," says Malcolm. "But they did it for something bigger than themselves. And isn't that more important than protocol? The thing about Pearly—chaotic as she is—she helps people. She believes in them. And that makes her a good guide. I hope you can see that. And I sincerely hope my idiot mistakes in the past won't jeopardize her future. Or yours. Because once you go down this road, it's hard to go back."

Pearly watches Mildreth studying Malcolm. She can't be sure, but her boss looks brighter. More vulnerable. She wants to say more human, but that wouldn't be fair. More soulful, maybe.

Mildreth clears her throat. "You've carried that guilt all this time?"

"Every assignment," says Malcolm. "Every time I told a new guide to be kind."

Mildreth taps her appendages on the desk. Then she turns back to the console. The screen glows in her glasses, but Pearly can't see what her supervisor's typing. Finally, Mildreth taps a key, and an automated voice responds. "Are you sure you'd like to cancel this transfer request?"

"Yes," says Mildreth. "Supervisor Snaggs. Authorization code 467-Alpha-2."

A chime sounds. "Request has been cancelled."

She leans back in her chair. "Done," she says. "He stays."

Pearly and Malcolm exhale simultaneously. "Thank you," says Malcolm.

"Don't thank me," she says. "You were right. I was about to repeat your mistake."

He nods. "Then maybe we both learned something."

They all sit in awkward silence. Pearly wants to express her gratitude, but she doesn't want to ruin the moment by sticking her foot in her mouth and causing Mildreth to reconsider.

"Well," says Mildreth. "I should probably…"

"Right," says Malcolm. "Come on, Pearly. Let's let Mildreth get back to work."

She nods. They turn to leave, but halfway to the door Malcolm stops. Turns back.

"There's, uh, a place called the Crooked Harp," he says. "Pearly swears by their Glow Jobs. Maybe you'd like to join us for a pint sometime. Just to, I don't know, catch up."

Her brows lift. "You're inviting me to... socialize?"

He smiles at her. "Yeah."

She cocks her head. "I will consider your offer," she says.

"Great. And Mildreth—thanks again."

He turns back, heads out the door. But now it's Pearly who hesitates. Digging into her taffeta once again, she pulls out a small, pink-glittered Eiffel Tower and places it on Mildreth's desk. "It, um, lights up," she says. "Like the real one. I thought it would go nicely with your..." She glances around the slime-covered room. "Decor."

Mildreth eyes the souvenir. She sits very still. Pearly wonders if she somehow offended her boss. Then she notices something shifting. The spores around Mildreth pulse, then glow pale pink. A single white bloom unfurls from her shoulder, delicate and luminous, where once there was only mold.

Mildreth glances at it, amused. Then she does something she hasn't done in centuries.

She smiles.

THIRTY-FIVE

*H*ome, sweet home.

Pearly is pooped—in all the best ways. She gave her all to the Paris assignment, recharged her charges, and beat the bad guy with the power of love. OK, maybe Malcolm beat the bad guy. But she helped! Now she's ready for a bath, a manicure, and an uninterrupted date with Thunder. But first, she needs to have a talk with Dumb Pearly.

Her roommate is still at work when Pearly returns to the house. Snatch is there, and she bounds up to Pearly with an excited honk-purr, breathing fire onto Pearly's gown. She pats out the flames, gives the pet a decadent belly rub, and realizes—yes—she actually missed the little monster. Then she gets up and walks around the living room. It used to be a shrine to her and Thunder, filled with mementos from all their lives together. But when they broke up, those reminders became painful and Pearly unmanifested them.

Now the room reflects her new life. There's the framed photo of her and Dumb Pearly in front of the afterlife aquarium. And the weird plant her roommate insisted they buy at the floating farmer's market after watching it throw its own fruit at potential buyers. And of course, the Motivational Mirror.

"WELCOME HOME, YOU RADIANT DISASTER! YOU WENT TO PARIS, BROKE SEVENTEEN RULES, AND STILL GOT A PROMOTION. TELL ME YOU SLAYED WITHOUT TELLING ME YOU SLAYED!"

Pearly grins despite herself. It's true—she did slay.

The house feels different now. Lighter, maybe. But it still holds her memories, like the rings of a tree. For a moment she just stands there, breathing it in, half expecting Thunder to walk through the door. Instead, she hears another sound entirely. Footsteps, clomping across the yard.

Pearly hears her roommate before she sees her. "Snatchy-poo! I have treats for you..."

The door bursts open and Dumb Pearly breezes in, hazmat suit half-zipped, clutching a bag labeled in Sharpie: **"LIVE SNACKS (PROBLY)."** She freezes when she sees Pearly.

The bag wiggles. Then it bolts, scuttling across the floor. Snatch lets out an indignant honk and tears after it, claws skittering on the tile.

"You're back!" Dumb Pearly launches herself into Pearly's arms. "Are you, like, back-back? What did Boss-Face say? Are you in trouble? Do I have to cut a bitch?"

Pearly laughs, hugging her tightly. "I'm back-back. And thank you for the offer, but I don't think that'll be necessary."

Behind them, a triumphant squawk echoes from the kitchen, followed by the sound of enthusiastic chewing.

"Okay, but the scissors stay pre-sharpened," she says. "Just in case. You can never tell with management."

Pearly raises an eyebrow. "Um... what exactly was in that bag?"

"Oh! Snatch's new favorite snacks. Schrödinger's crickets. Ethically sourced. They're only sentient if you open the bag." Dumb Pearly beams. "Anyway, we missed you! The mirror got depressed and kept yelling affirmations at the toaster."

"Sounds about right." Pearly smiles. "I missed you too."

"Good! Now sit and spill. Don't skip anything. I want all the details and all the drama." She drags Pearly to the sofa. Snatch reappears a moment later, licking her claws, and hops onto Dumb Pearly's lap.

Pearly sits cross-legged on the couch, cup of celestial chamomile steaming between her hands, as she fills Dumb Pearly in on everything that's happened since their breakfast debrief.

Her roommate's eyes go wide at the part where Beckett goes missing. She gasps when Pearly shares the miracle at Sacré-Cœur. She stands up and applauds when Pearly describes the madcap ride on Seraphina to reunite Lillian and George.

But when Pearly gets to Thunder—how he showed up in Paris, how they found their way back to each other—Dumb Pearly goes quiet. Too quiet.

Pearly finishes the story and waits. She sips her drink and embraces the silence, broken only by Snatch's tiny snores in Dumb Pearly's lap.

"So..." Dumb Pearly says finally, eyes fixed on Snatch's fur. "What happens now?"

Pearly shrugs, unsure whether to laugh or sigh. "I don't know. Thunder and I haven't had a chance to talk it out yet. We might—"

She stops when she notices Dumb Pearly's expression—a brave little smile trembling on her lips, the kind people wear when they're trying very hard not to cry.

"Oh, honey," says Pearly. "What is it?"

Dumb Pearly strokes Snatch's back. "Nothing. It's just... when you and Thunder were together before, this was *your* house. I was kind of the, you know, emergency clone. Temporary roommate. I figured once you two made up, you'd want your old life back." She tries to laugh, but it's more of an almost-sob. "I'll be fine. I can crash in the shed for a while. Or the attic. Or maybe Seraphina needs a glove compartment roommate—"

"Wait—no!" Pearly sets down her mug and scoots closer. "Is that what you think? Sweetie, no. I would never kick you out. You're my family. I love you."

Dumb Pearly blinks hard, eyes shining. "You... you mean that?"

"Of course I do." Pearly takes her hands. "Reyna helped me see something over there. We keep talking about love like it's a pyramid, with romance at the top and everything else below. But that's not how it feels anymore. Not to me."

Her throat constricts. She didn't realize how much she needed to say this out loud.

"When I was with Thunder, I thought loving him was, like, the purpose to my whole existence. When we broke up, I thought losing him meant I'd failed. But these last lives, these last *lessons*—they've shown me that love isn't a ladder you climb to reach happily-ever-after. It's more like..." She looks around the cozy chaos of the room—the weird fruit plant, the photo, the stupid mirror. "It's more like light. It just keeps expanding, filling every corner. If you let it."

Dumb Pearly's tears spill over. Pearly squeezes her hands.

"There's room in that light for Thunder," Pearly continues, "and for you, and for me. For the parts of me that screw up, or fall apart, or forget how to believe. There's room in this house for all of it. And if we ever need more space—" she glances up with a wry grin "—well, Thunder's great at manifesting square footage. I'll make him do an addition."

That finally cracks Dumb Pearly's composure. She laughs through her tears, collapsing against Pearly's shoulder.

Snatch lets out a jealous squeak, then climbs onto Pearly's head, nesting in her hair like a tiny, cozy crown.

This time, she doesn't mind.

"THAT'S RIGHT, LADIES!" shouts the mirror. "LOVE ISN'T A TRIANGLE—IT'S A WHOLE DAMN CONSTELLATION!"

They both laugh, and cry harder. Pearly leans her cheek against Dumb Pearly's glitter-streaked hair, feeling the warmth of two hearts that are somehow, weirdly, gloriously, the same.

Maybe it isn't a traditional family.

But it's hers.

There's only one member missing—and it's time to go see him.

Thirty-Six

Pearly slips through the Nursery doors, its glow bathing her in soft, iridescent light. She pauses in the atrium, clutching a white paper bag and smoothing the skirt of her holographic cat gown. She reflects on the last time she was here. It was, literally, another lifetime ago.

After her first attempt to be a guide almost blew up in her face, she came here to get perspective. Holding a newborn soul had shifted something in Pearly. Some part of her had recognized her own innocence, and how everyone—even her—was worthy of the universe's Unconditional Love.

That was a moment of healing, of inner transformation. She discovered she didn't need to cling to Thunder for validation. To prove she was loveable. But now she's taken another step on her journey. A "yes, and." To be open to love—to give and receive it without conditions—is the next chapter she wants to write.

She's calling it her Grown-Up Era.

That's right, Miss Thing. Own it.

She sees him before he sees her.

Thunder stands a few feet back from an incubator, arms crossed over silver-white scrubs, supervising two trainees who are doing their absolute best. Which is still not great.

The newborn soul inside the incubator is having a full cosmic meltdown. It pulses in frantic bursts—bright, dim, BRIGHT, dim—like it's trying to Morse-code its distress to the universe.

One aide is waving a resonance chart at it like he's trying to fend off a wasp. The other clutches a tuning fork she clearly does not trust, holding it at arm's length like it might explode.

"Okay, sweetheart," pleads Chart-Waver as the newborn flares again, rattling every mobile in a three-incubator radius. "Can you dial it down like ten percent?"

"Alright, that's enough," Thunder slips in between them. He plants his hands above the incubator, closes his eyes, and begins to hum. Low. Soothing. Grounding.

The room responds instantly. The mobiles quiet down. The helpers sag with relief as the newborn soul settles into a steady, even glow.

"How does he make it look so easy?" whispers Tuning Fork.

Chart-Waver shrugs. "Maybe it's a charisma thing."

Thunder cracks a smile, still watching the newborn. "You have to meet them where they are."

He gives the incubator a gentle tap, an affectionate little "there you go." The newborn pulses once, content.

"Okay," Pearly calls out. "That was stupidly attractive."

Thunder whirls around. His eyes land on her, beaming with joy and relief and just enough roguish charm to send a ripple of desire through Pearly's soul.

"Alright, kids. You can take it from here." He walks toward her, his grin expanding with every step. "Hi." He stops just a few feet away. His brow wrinkles, and he suddenly looks nervous. "Does this mean..."

Pearly nods. "It's over. We signed a contract and everything." She considers telling him how Malcolm just saved both their asses from lifetimes of misery and separation, but decides to save it for another time. This moment is about the two of them.

"Oh thank god." He sweeps in and envelops her in a warm embrace. Tears cloud her vision and she lets them fall down her face as she relaxes into his strong, welcoming arms. His hands find the small of her back, and her cheek presses up against his. Her pulse slows, just like the newborn's did. For the first time since she proposed the deal with Mildreth, she feels really and truly safe.

When they finally pull apart, she holds out the bag. "Brought you something."

He runs a finger down her tear-stained face. "Let's go somewhere more private," he says. "Follow me."

He leads her through a narrow, winding hallway. The glow on the walls shifts from white to pink to red, and the air gets warmer as they progress. Eventually, they emerge onto a small balcony that seems suspended in nothingness.

Pearly's breath stops.

The Great Cosmic Womb expands beneath them, vast and shimmering, the birthplace of all life. It glows with a deep, rhythmic pulse—an ancient heartbeat she feels in her astral bones. Red and violet currents of starlit energy swirl through its center, and from that slow-moving vortex, tiny newborn souls rise in spirals, curious bits of consciousness breaking off from All That Is to experience the universe from a particular set of circumstances.

"So," says Thunder. "What do you think?"

The background hum isn't a sound so much as a vibration of pure love, familiar and foreign all at once. As if the universe is singing her own name back to her.

For a moment, she can't speak. Even her thoughts go wobbly around the edges.

She reaches for the railing to steady herself. Thunder leans on it beside her, close enough that their arms almost touch.

"This is..." Pearly tries again, but words fail her. "It's so..."

"I know."

For a few moments, they just stand there, taking in the majesty.

"So..." he says finally. "I take it we're celebrating?"

"Yes!" She pulls her gaze from the Womb, turns to him. "One last treat from Paris to mark the end of a successful mission." She hands him the bag. "And to thank you for being such a fabulous co-pilot."

He opens it, peeking inside. "Whew," he says, pulling out a croissant. "I'm really glad it's not a jelly doughnut. That would've been totally off-theme."

"Please," she says. "I had to stop myself from including a beret." She pauses, evaluating him. "Actually, no, I'm not going to stop myself." She reaches into the folds of her dress one last time, emerging with a scarlet red beret. He lets her place it on his head. "Ugh," she smiles. "You are seven shades of adorable."

"As are you, Miss Gates." He nods to her outfit. "It takes a special soul to pull off holographic cats on formalwear."

"It's true."

He tears off a piece of pastry and hands it to her. They eat in silence for a moment, watching the light shift below them. Crumbs stick to her cheeks. Thunder gently brushes one away with his thumb.

"Why are delicious things always so messy?" she says.

"I like it that way. Keeps you on your toes." He turns to her, cupping her face in his warm, flaky palms. "Maybe the better question is, why are messy things always so delicious?"

She starts to swoon, but then her brow furrows. "Do you think we're a mess?"

Thunder considers this. "I mean, yeah," he says. "But look." He gestures out toward the swirling cosmic cradle. "Creation's messy too. The best things usually are."

She smiles. For once, she doesn't feel like she has to defend herself—to prove anything. Not to the Higher-Ups. Not to Thunder. Not even to herself.

"Is this what peace is supposed to feel like?" she says.

"You know, I think it might be." He squeezes her hand. "Are you ready for that?"

She takes a breath, really looks at him. *Is she?* The dramatic highs and lows were addictive, for sure. The threat of a break-up always lingered, fueling intense emotions and erratic decisions. But Thunder isn't going anywhere. Neither is she. Maybe it's time to trade in the drama for something more substantive. To get curious about the deeper layers of relationship. "I'm not sure," she admits. "But I'm willing to give it a shot."

He laughs—oh god, that sexy baritone—and Pearly decides the universe could use a little more of that sound.

The world softens. Thunder leans in.

For once, Pearly doesn't overthink or cling or spiral. She just lets herself be loved.

Author's Note

Thank you for spending time with Pearly and friends. If *The Midnight Croissant* made you laugh, cry, or crave butter at inconvenient hours, I'd be so grateful if you'd consider leaving a review on Amazon, Goodreads, or wherever you talk about books.

Reviews help readers find stories like this one—and they truly mean the world to indie authors. Even a sentence or two makes a difference.

Acknowledgments

This book was inspired by a magical trip to Paris I took with my mother, Susan Lindgren. My grandmother always dreamed of taking us there, and while life never lined up for the three of us, Mom and I finally went in her honor in September 2025. Many of the settings in this story sprang directly from that adventure, and I'll be forever grateful for those memories. Thanks, Mom.

Josh Grapes is a phenomenal editor. We've worked together since 2018, and it just keeps getting better. Thanks also to John Crye; my writing group — Barbara Boone, Krista Carpenter, Mike Conboy, Ben Cooper, Sarah Griffin, Dave Melody, Rene Thomas, and Ronda Waley — my beta readers (Sarah Greene, Tsilah Burman, Flo Aliviado, Celia Bernstein); and my aroace sensitivity reader, Sophia Melina C.Y., for your invaluable feedback.

Thank you to my incredible ARC team and to all my Kickstarter backers. Your support means the world to me. Special shout-outs to Amy Gabrielle and Austin Rappazzo-Hansen.

Thank you to Lana Shybinska for designing my gorgeous cover, and to Thomas Queyja for producing my audiobook.

Thank you to the LGBTQIA community for your bravery, perseverance, and commitment to queer joy.

And finally, my sincere apologies to the French for any butchering of your beautiful language in my audiobook narration. Please accept my good intentions and my wholehearted admiration for your vowels.

About the Author

Bonnie Solomon is a novelist and screenwriter with a passion for crafting humorous, life-affirming stories in magical settings. As a queer writer, she is dedicated to authentic and aspirational LGBTQ+ representation. She lives in Los Angeles, where she divides her time between petting the cat, shaking up the dance floor, making ridiculously fancy lattes, and searching in vain for pastries as good as those in Paris.

bonniesolomon.com
Instagram: @bonnie.solomon